WHAT SHE SAW

DIANE SAXON

Boldwood

First published in Great Britain in 2020 by Boldwood Books Ltd.

Copyright © Diane Saxon, 2020

Cover Design by Head Design

Cover Photography: Shutterstock

A CIP catalogue record for this book is available from the British Library.

Paperback ISBN 978-1-83889-267-8

Large Print ISBN 978-1-83889-768-0

Ebook ISBN 978-1-83889-268-5

Kindle ISBN 978-1-83889-269-2

Audio CD ISBN 978-1-83889-265-4

MP3 CD ISBN 978-1-83889-765-9

Digital audio download ISBN 978-1-83889-266-1

Boldwood Books Ltd
23 Bowerdean Street
London SW6 3TN
www.boldwoodbooks.com

To my Aunty Letty, my dad's youngest sibling. A lady I aspire to be when I grow up.

1

Pain seared through her shoulder, nowhere near the burn in her chest that desperate despair clutched at.

Poppy cracked open her eyes, only to slam them shut again before he looked over at her.

Silhouetted against the background of the hall light, he stood in the entrance to her darkened room.

Daddy?

Horror gripped her throat, but she forced her muscles to relax, held her breath like she did in the swimming pool when she practised her free diving. The more she slowed her heartbeat, the longer she could hold her breath. Under controlled circumstances, she could hold it for two minutes. The world record was over four and a half, but she'd only started on their holiday in Cuba at Christmas. It was cool joining the local free divers. Proud of her achievement, she'd practised three times weekly at the Shrewsbury School for Boys swimming pool which the Girls' High School were allowed to use.

But these weren't controlled circumstances, and the only pool she was in was that of her own blood.

The furious hammer of her heart pulsed through the base of her neck, making it swell until her face threatened to burst.

She squinted through veiled lashes.

Daddy!

She stopped the breath from rushing from her lungs, parted her lips and released it in a silent sigh while she watched, terror holding her still where she lay on the rumpled bedcovers.

It was her fault. She'd persuaded Aiden to sneak in through the back door and up the stairs. If she hadn't, it would never have happened.

Daddy!

He must have known.

Rifle still in hand, he leaned over where Aiden's naked body lay crumpled on the floor, grabbed a fistful of his hair and yanked his head back to study the boy's beautiful features.

The ugly sneer on her daddy's face froze her blood. Never one to physically abuse his children, that face was the one he used to control them all with the threat of underlying evil and barely suppressed fury.

She'd learnt long ago not to open her mouth in his presence, never to challenge with her eyes or they'd all suffer the consequences. His gaze would turn to ice while his jaw flexed as he clamped his teeth together. Then there would be nothing to eat that night.

The delicate flicker of her mother's fingers, the quiver of her beautiful, soft lips, was a sure sign she'd read the situation before anyone else. Poppy had learnt well to read those signs as Daddy's mood changed on a whim.

Control.

He held it in a tight fist.

They all appreciated he worked long, hard hours to keep them in the manner they'd all become accustomed to, as he frequently reminded them. They appreciated even more those long, hard hours keeping him away for as long as possible.

The wet thud of Aiden's head as it slapped back onto the oak floorboards sent a sickened judder through her, but she held her nerve and remained still.

Pain radiated across her left breast, numbing her shoulder, while the slow pump of blood oozed from the bullet wound to trickle down her arm.

He'd shot her.

Daddy!

Unable to control the tremor, she tensed, her muscles seizing until they cramped.

Poppy closed her eyes as black clouds washed over her vision. She pulled in a long, slow breath, held it, pressing down on the panic threatening to surge upwards.

When she was ready, she opened them again to peer through the smallest crack in her vision and prayed he didn't check to see if she was alive. If he grabbed her long hair in the same way, she wasn't sure she'd be able to stop from screaming.

Could she play dead?

He placed the rifle on the floor, set his fists on his hips and breathed in through his nose as he stared down at Aiden's body. His nostrils whitened with the flare as though the dead boy had caused him a mild irritation.

As he raised his head, Poppy slid her eyes closed again and held everything still.

Play dead, Poppy. Play dead.

With his back to her, he moved through the open doorway into the hall and paused. His shoulders rotated and he bent at the waist, picking up a shotgun he'd leaned up against the wall and sent Poppy's heart into a frantic panic.

Oh god, there was more to come.

More killing.

Daddy!

2

Gordon Lawrence stared down the barrel of his shotgun, took aim and fired, blowing out the brains of his fourteen-year-old son so blood, grey matter and tiny shards of bone pebble-dashed the garish green patterned wallpaper behind the boy. Joshua had never liked the wallpaper in his bedroom in any case. At least he'd never have to bitch about it again.

Gordon curled his lip as he cruised his gaze over the blood, tissue and bone splatter.

Distasteful.

It was the messiest by far of the five members of his family. Maybe he should have stuck to using the Remington 700 bolt-action hunting rifle he'd used on his wife.

No matter now. It was done.

He thought his son would have put up more of a fight, hence the choice of shotgun. It gave a better spread. Instead, Joshua hadn't even heard him coming. Propped up in bed, his ears had been plugged with the overpriced Bluetooth EarPods. No doubt turned up to full volume to mask all other sounds in the house while he'd been absorbed by his online gaming.

It had been to Gordon's advantage.

He gave a shrug as he placed the shotgun on the floor by his feet and slipped the Taurus LBR revolver from the back of his trouser waistband to check it for ammunition. No need to attach a silencer as he had with the first two weapons. The quiet pop, pop was muted enough so the others hadn't been alerted. If they'd heard anything, they'd have assumed he was outside shooting rats. Nothing unusual there.

Each of his prized weapons had been selected with care and thought out to suit the demise of each member of his family.

His wife, Linda, had been the first to go. Disappointment etched across her fine features with a decided lack of surprise as she hugged the little chihuahua to her chest. Resigned. As though she'd expected it. She'd gone with the silent dignity and disapproval he'd come to expect from her.

Gordon hadn't cared enough about the dog to pull the trigger on her as she dashed off through the house, tiny little yelps accompanying the scurried rush down the stairs and the faint clatter as she hurtled through the cat flap. Little fucker might just save herself if the big bastard of a buzzard didn't get her.

Talisha and Geraldine, his eight-year old twins were next. Gordon had used his .204 Ruger, the one he reserved solely for fox shooting. Thankfully asleep, the entry wound barely grazed through their small heads and left little of note behind on their soft pillows. He hadn't wanted to hurt them, merely put them out of a misery that was to come without him there to protect them. That was the point. He *was* protecting them from a life that would otherwise be hell. It was for the best. For their own good. They belonged to him. This way, no one else would possess them.

His eldest daughter, Poppy, was the hardest for him to kill. Awareness and terror, probably not for the right reason, filled her eyes as he stepped into her bedroom. Who knew she'd sneaked her boyfriend in after the party had ended? The pair of them rolling naked on the bed.

On any other occasion, Gordon would have broken the boy's legs for him for daring to have sex with his precious daughter. Instead, too numbed to process any emotion, he dispatched them both with the same gun, a quick one-two.

Bam-bam.

Neat, precise, effortless.

Finished.

He'd cocked his head to one side. Narrowed his eyes. He'd seen the boy out the front door at ten p.m. Thought he'd gone home. His wife would have had a hissy fit if she'd known he'd sneaked back in. She'd have killed them herself if she'd known they were having sex, even if she had thought he was a nice lad. Witnessing that would have changed her mind.

With a mild curl of dissatisfaction, Gordon had reached down to clasp his hand around the skinny ankle of the youth to drag him from his daughter's bedroom.

The boy, whatever his name was, Gordon couldn't remember, he'd been unimportant. Allowed to attend the family gathering by Linda.

A quiet affair. Gordon had asked for nothing for his forty-fifth birthday. Instead, the black and gold balloons still floated above the chair backs where they'd been tied just hours earlier. A meal with his family. A late night for the young ones. An early one for him. Only he'd not gone to bed at the same time as Linda. He'd stayed downstairs with his two fingers of Balvenie Vintage Cask single malt whisky. Sipped it with the reverence it deserved. The decision already made. The plan laid down. His precious firearms already selected, cleaned, loaded.

Remorse. There was none. He'd never allow them, his family, to suffer the humiliation and rejection that was to come with the knowledge of what he'd done. What he'd been discovered to have done. He had no qualms about what he'd done, only regret that he was about to be caught.

The revelation that their advancement in society had been based not on his family's naïve belief of his business acumen but on an enterprise he'd steeped himself in to drag himself out of the gutter too many years ago to count. His strong, respectable reputation with a chain of estate agents bearing his name that he'd taken years to build, to establish as a front to the real money-spinner. An entire criminal organisation. One that had propped up the way of life his wife and children had taken for granted. A way of life that the estate agents could never have provided for alone. But he'd nurtured the reputation, worked long hours and turned up at the offices every day in his Savile Row suits and shirts. He'd treated his staff with respect and above-average salaries which garnered him the prestige he sought.

Solid. Congenial. Dependable.

Bitterness flashed hot and brief. He'd believed he was untouchable, but no one was. In the end, not every obstacle could be removed. Not every palm greased. Certainly not the chief crown prosecutor's, it appeared. Either that, or they hadn't found his price before he found the link. Even if he didn't know what he'd discovered yet. It was only a matter of time. He had all the files, he simply needed to pull the thread and wade through the paperwork.

Gordon clenched his jaw until white-hot needles of pain shot through his ear canal and he relaxed again. Resignation. There was nothing left. No other road to take.

In the deathly silence of the cool spring night, he turned his head and peered along the gloomy grey hallway of his stone built fifteenth-century hall. Home for the past six years. And during that short sprint of time, he'd enjoyed it, indulged his wife in her fantasies, bathed in the sycophantic admiration of the locals who'd previously looked down on a woman who'd been brought up in their village. They'd changed their mind about the poor little girl who'd grown up, moved out and made good. He'd seen to that. Determined no wife of his would ever be looked down on, he'd provided her with the means to rise above them. Facilitated her climb through the echelons of society.

Not through love.

He let out a delicate snort.

He'd never loved her. Never loved anyone. He witnessed it between his wife and children, but it was a foreign language to him. He didn't love them. He possessed them. They were his and therefore their rise through the ranks was a necessity.

Of course, the old money remained unconvinced, unmoved by brash new money, but he didn't give a fuck about them, provided his wife remained untouched by their malice.

Despite them all, he'd renovated his classic U-shaped brick-built Tudor hall, which stood in fifty acres of formal gardens and parkland. He'd greased the palms of those very same people who turned their noses up at his wife so that he could speed up the renovation processes of the Grade-I listed building. Where money had failed, he'd taken advantage of his knowledge and contacts to persuade those he couldn't buy in other ways.

It wasn't difficult. Everyone had a price whether it was money, security, safety of a loved one, pride, position. They could all be bought.

With a long, slow pull, Gordon filled his lungs with air and loaded the handgun for the last time. He hunkered down and paused for one brief, infinitesimal moment as blood thundered through his head to fill his ears with a dark, persistent pounding.

He reached out and sent a small lick of flame from his lighter, touching it to the thin trail of accelerant he'd laid. Irritation streaked through him as the tiny blue flame spluttered and almost died on the pure wool hallway runner, refusing to ignite until the weak, guttering flame hit the pool of accelerant on the wooden floor and leapt, zigzagging onto the antique furniture his wife had painstakingly chosen and he'd splashed fuel over. When it reached the restored, overstuffed chaise longue where the hallway opened into a wide square above the staircase, oxygen from the windows he'd cracked open wafted in to bellow the flames into a golden, flickering hue.

Fascinated, Gordon stared until his eyes stung and the dark smoke whorled around the hallway, fumes from the stuffing burning the soft tissue of his nose and throat. He yanked his burgundy, fine-knit cashmere jumper over the lower part of his face as he gave a last glance around his house.

Satisfied there was no more he could do, he raised his gun, and for the last time aimed and fired.

3

On silent, naked feet, Poppy gripped her trainers in one hand and crept from the bedroom, every step a screaming nightmare of agony. With the desperate need to remain silent, she didn't dare put her trainers on.

Each breath she took burnt the whole of the left side of her chest until she could only take small, hurried sips of air.

Her head reeled, pinpricks of light popping behind her eyes as she leaned against the door frame of her bedroom to catch her breath and listen.

She'd check on her mum, but it would be of no use. She'd have heard nothing. She never did once she'd consumed a bottle or two of red wine and a handful of sleeping pills. A regular occurrence, but with Daddy home and a party in hand, she'd excelled herself. Daddy was oblivious. He never seemed to notice. Maybe he didn't care.

Her mum thought Poppy didn't know, but of course she did. The amount of times Poppy had sneaked into her mum's bedroom when Daddy had been away, into her en suite because she'd run out of sanitary towels and needed to pinch some of her mum's. She'd seen the bottle of pills behind the mouthwash, knew how many her mum took. Knew how much her mum drank. She'd watched her earlier, weaving her way up the wide staircase, gripping onto the handrail as though it could save her life, not just steady her.

Poppy dipped her head, her world taking on a weird disconnection as she studied the dribble of blood which ran down the inside of her arm and dripped off the end of her thumb.

The bullet wasn't in her arm.

She knew where it was.

Wedged deep in her chest, just below her armpit. At the rate her breath was coming, it had pierced her lung. She'd heard about things like that, her and Aiden watched real life trauma on TV.

Her gaze stayed on the drip of blood. It would be justice if she died. After all, it was her fault. She'd as good as killed Aiden when she'd persuaded him to come back inside.

Her chest tightened and she hitched in another painful breath as tears leaked from her eyes.

She loved him.

The trail of blood came from the thin, soaked T-shirt she'd wadded up and jammed between her arm and her chest to try and stem the flow.

She squeezed her elbow tighter against her side and drew in another staggered breath as she clenched her teeth until they ground to stop the hysterical sob lodged at the back of her throat from escaping.

Silent. She had to stay silent in case he came back to check. Back to shoot her again. Finish the job he'd started.

She needed to move. Check on the others. Make sure the little ones hadn't been disturbed by all the crashing around. She'd drag Josh away from his gaming and ask him what they should do. He was good. He knew how to handle Daddy. When she wanted to challenge, Josh was the voice of reason.

She rubbed her forehead. This was different. Josh couldn't change things, but he'd help her. If they called the police, Daddy would go to jail and they'd blame her. There had to be another way.

Before she moved, she needed a moment to drag oxygen into her deflated lungs.

She had no idea where Daddy had dragged Aiden's body, but what she imagined was the muffled bump of her boyfriend's head bouncing along the hallway had stopped.

She'd managed to yank on a pair of fleecy pyjama bottoms without much effort but drawing a top over her head and getting her arm through the armhole had proved a different matter. After the struggle, she'd flopped back on the bed, breath soughing through her burning chest, wild spirals of light shooting behind her closed lids.

After a brief struggle, she'd managed to prop herself up to listen.

The house was silent.

The house was rarely silent. Even in the dead of night, there would be creaks and groans. It was as though it knew, as though it waited.

She swung her legs off the bed and with a grunt of pain, slipped to her feet. And there she was, head reeling and barely a memory of how she'd come to be propped against the doorframe.

Poppy pressed her hand to where she'd slipped her mobile phone into her pocket and stared unblinking down the length of the brightly lit hallway until her eyes stung. She concentrated on the end wall where it took a right-hand turn down another length of hallway to her brother's room. That's where he was. Where he'd taken Aiden, she was sure. But not so sure she didn't hesitate. What if he was in the twins' room next to hers, or Mum's?

A blink released a torrent of tears that washed down her cheeks and dripped off the end of her chin, but she quelled the desperate desire to sob, to run screaming into her mum's room. There would be no point.

She pushed away from the door jamb and took three tentative steps towards the area above the stairs where the landing widened into a large square with her mum's overstuffed antique chaise longue placed against the back wall so it overlooked the split staircase and galleried hall.

She drew in an anguished breath. It *was* her fault. If she hadn't persuaded Aiden to stay, her daddy would never have killed him.

Whether he'd meant to shoot her or not, she couldn't be sure. Maybe it was only Aiden he'd wanted to kill, but the deadened glaze over her daddy's eyes lent her no hope.

She skimmed her shoulder against the short stretch of wall between her room and the twins' just to give her balance and a sense of direction as her head whirled.

Reluctant to wake them, but conscious she needed to do something, check they were asleep before she went to Josh, she edged their door open slow enough so it didn't creak. Please don't let them be witness to Daddy's violence.

Exhausted with the effort, she leaned against the doorjamb as her energy drained from her as surely as her blood did. If only she had the strength.

A muffled thud had her whipping her head around to scan the hall.

Was Daddy coming back? Had he heard her?

Her breath stuttered in her throat, stuck there as the rhythmic thud, thud, thud of her heart filled her ears before she blew it out again in a violent rush.

She pushed away from her support to stumble into the room, and edged the door closed behind her before she took three faltering footsteps into the pale golden circle of light from the nightlamp the twins still insisted on having.

Poppy held her breath as she moved deeper inside the room. She reached out trembling fingers to touch Geraldine's soft cheek and froze.

Horror gripped her at the sight of a small neat hole in the centre of Geraldine's forehead as the thick trickle of damson red blood pooled in her closed eye sockets.

Rasping in a small breath, Poppy swung her head to look at Talisha. With almost perfect precision, the exact hole bled out, but this time left a trail of blood which dripped crimson onto her sister's pristine white broderie anglaise pillowcase.

Poppy sank to her knees by the side of Talisha's bed and pressed a hand hard against her mouth to stop the sobs from erupting.

Her stomach pitched and threatened to throw up the ribeye steak she'd been obliged to eat for the sake of keeping the peace with Daddy earlier that evening. While he was out of the house, she went pure vegetarian, but it had been his birthday, his meal choice. His insistence that it was a treat. But he knew she didn't like to eat meat. It was his little show of power, superior strength of mind.

She screwed her eyes shut until plumes of white light exploded behind her eyelids. She didn't want to open her eyes again. Didn't want to see, but she had no choice.

Swallowing the bile, she kept her eyes downcast as she opened them again so she didn't have to see her sweet little sisters.

Miss Tilly, Talisha's raggedy doll lay in a crumpled heap on the floor by the bedside. One of a pair their grandma had bought for the twins when they were born. Talisha had cherished hers, even more precious since grandma had died the previous year. Unlike her son, grandma had been warm and generous to a fault.

Poppy took hold of Miss Tilly and rocked as she hugged her, silent tears streaming down her cheeks. She didn't deserve to be alive. It was her fault. She'd killed her baby sisters through her thoughtless selfishness. All because of a boy.

Clutching the doll, she pushed up from the bed, the sharp stab of pain shoved its way between her ribs and her knees turned to water, but she forced herself to swivel around without looking again. She wrenched open the door, no longer caring whether she made a noise or not, and beat a quick exit, but blood and desperation drained from her to sap her energy.

Along the landing, Poppy stumbled to a halt. Hesitated. She leaned her left hand against the pristine white balustrade as she pressed the T-shirt hard against her wound, knowing it made a difference to staunch the flow. She'd taken her St Johns Ambulance lessons. She knew what to do. Her teeth gave an involuntary chatter. It wasn't the same as in class. That was controlled, calm. Her head juddered. It wasn't the same at all. The class instructor never mentioned how hard it would be in real life. With real blood and real dead people.

Exhaustion washed over her. She rocked on her heels as the weight of her head became too much for her to hold upright while wave after wave of blackness welled up to darken her vision.

The boom of a shotgun exploded from the direction of her brother's bedroom at the far end of the hallway. The house shook and Poppy reared back her head, the swift rush of adrenaline pumping through her system to lend energy to her flagging body.

With no further thought of checking on her mum, Poppy shoved away from the balustrade, leaving the bloodstained print of her hand. Terror spliced through her heart. Her fingers gave a spasmodic twitch, letting Miss Tilly drop to bounce down the stairs ahead of her as she threw herself after the soft doll.

Away from the sound. Away from the fear. Away from Daddy.

A chorus of pain rocked her body as her knees gave way and she careened down the stairs, rebounded off one side of the railings to bounce against the other. Agony tore through her as she jammed her hip against the rail, stabbed her elbow on the white wood. All the time panic clenched like a fist as her feet skimmed over the thick navy-blue-patterned stair runner, barely keeping her upright while she gripped her trainers in one hand.

White-hot pain shot through her chest as she reached the bottom step and skidded through the wooden hall. She heaved in small snatches of air.

Confused, she stared at the partially open front door offering a view of their brightly lit driveway. An invitation to run out. Straight into Daddy. He must be there, why else would the door be open?

She backed away from the light and glanced back up the broad stairway, frowning as her nostrils burned with the acrid scent of fuel. A thin plume of smoke wafted from the right side of the landing above, then a trail of yellow flame raced along the hall onto her mother's chaise longue and burst into a dynamo of fire.

Horror chased through her and, without hesitation, Poppy whipped around and raced along the hall to the kitchen that dominated almost the entire back of the house, overlooking the perfection of their landscaped gardens.

The security lights would be on there too, but it was a short sprint to the woods which curved around the rear of their property in a wide expansive sweep all the way to Much Wenlock.

Breath rasping with agony, Poppy dropped her trainers on the floor and slipped her feet into them before she wrenched open the back door and staggered out into the cool night air.

To escape.

To run as far as she could.

So he'd never find her.

So they wouldn't blame her.

4

Detective Sergeant Jenna Morgan flung herself upright, desperate to squeeze a lungful of air past the constriction in her throat and dispel the terror that held her firmly in its grasp.

She knocked the dead weight of an arm that had her pinned down from around her waist and blew out a gusty sigh.

'Jesus.' She cupped her hands over her face.

'It's okay. Sshh.' Adrian Hall, Chief Crown Prosecutor, who'd recently taken to sharing her bed when time and distance allowed, sat up beside her, hitching the covers up against the cool of the night.

Mortified, Jenna squeezed closed eyes that had sprung open. She'd been crying in her sleep.

'It was just a dream.' She swiped the heel of her hand across her face and scrubbed away the tears.

'Do you want to talk about it?' The soft smokiness of his sleep-filled voice soothed as he'd intended.

'No. It's okay, I was just...' Trapped. Darkness pressing down on her.

She sucked in a breath and held it until her lungs almost burst.

Their relationship still too new for her to trust enough. Since they'd met during her sister's abduction a few months earlier, matters of the romantic type had taken a back seat and only recently made any kind of advancement.

Gentle hands turned her, and Jenna pressed her face into the welcoming, naked skin of Adrian's neck and took the silent comfort he offered her, grateful he understood. She breathed in his calming warm scent as her heart rate stumbled back to normal. Despite Adrian only staying over a couple of times, there was no awkwardness, no need for words as she snuggled into him, no desire to pull away, but she wasn't yet ready to divulge her darkest fears to him.

The strident ring of her mobile phone almost shot her through the ceiling, her heart ratcheted up to full pelt as she dragged herself out of Adrian's arms, flipped over and grabbed the phone before the jarring noise alerted the damned Dalmatian. Her sister's dog. He'd be in there like a shot, leaping all over the damned bed, given half a chance.

'Jesus, that's loud,' Adrian's sleep-husky voice grumbled from behind her.

'It has to be when I'm on call otherwise I'd sleep straight through it.' The light stabbed her in the eye as she flicked the phone case open and punched the green answer button. 'DS Jenna Morgan.'

'Sergeant Morgan. Sorry to disturb you this evening. It's PC Ted Walker here.'

Surprised, Jenna glanced at the dim glow of her bedside clock. She'd barely been asleep an hour, she'd thought it was the middle of the night. Technically it was, as she'd been on earlies for the last week. Up at 5:00 a.m., work for 6:00 a.m. Bedtime became a skewed 9:00 p.m. She'd been later that night to accommodate the arrival of Adrian for dinner.

'No worries.' She shuffled herself upright in the bed and leaned back against her pillows, bringing her knees up to stop herself from sliding back down. If she did, she may just fall straight back to sleep. She'd only just dipped into that deep rejuvenating sleep when she'd been hauled back out of it by the dream. 'What have you got, Ted?'

'A fire, Sarge.'

Brain still blurred from sleep, Jenna reached up and scrubbed her hand through her short, choppy hair. 'A fire?'

'A bloody big one, Sarge. Out at Wenlock Edge, just past Farley. A place called Kimble Hall, Sarge. Looks like the whole bloody lot's gone up in flames.'

Her brain kicked into gear and shoved the fog away in an instant. 'Fire service?'

'Already there.'

'Ambulance?'

'In attendance.'

'Problems?'

'It's gone up like a tinder box.'

'Great. Witnesses?'

'None to speak of. The neighbour called it in. It's a fifty-acre property. Remote. By the time they saw anything, the whole house was ablaze.'

'Survivors?'

'Can't tell, Sarge. At this stage, the fire crews are still arriving, they're telling me they can't even get near the premises, the fire's burning too hot. They're already talking arson, but it's a really old house, it could just be an accident. We don't know if anyone is in residence. There's certainly no one here coming forward.'

'Jesus.' She slipped naked from the bed and headed to her small en suite, already wide awake and in work mode. 'I'll be there shortly. Can you text me the postcode?' She glanced over her shoulder and shot Adrian a regretful smile as he flopped back on the pillows, his eyes already closed.

'Can do, but honestly, just drive towards Much Wenlock, at Farley head for the orange glow lighting up the whole bloody sky, Sarge.'

'Right. Thanks. I'll be there shortly. See you soon.'

The text beeped through just as she finished peeing. She ran the tap until the water was warm enough to wash her hands and then splashed it over her face to rinse away the last remains of sleep. Sleep she'd just been deprived of for the foreseeable future.

As the cool night air stroked over her skin, Jenna shuddered and reached for her dressing gown to wrap it tight around herself, before she blinked at her reflection in the mirror.

With a long drawn-out groan, she grabbed the overpriced moisturiser her younger sister, Fliss, insisted she use now she was on the sharp rise to being thirty. She sneered at herself as she smoothed the heavy cream over her skin and refused to acknowledge any of the fine lines feathering out from her eyes, and the deeper ones bracketing her mouth.

Fliss was the reason she had them. Not that Jenna blamed her. Her sister had been a victim of circumstance. Kidnapped and held in a dank, dark cellar until she'd found the inner strength to haul herself out. She'd saved herself and filled Jenna with a deep sense of pride and admiration for her younger sister. But the taste of true fear had stayed with her to haunt her in her weak moments.

Memory of the dream shuddered through her with a mild sense of relief as the pieces of the dark puzzle fell into place. A reflection of her fear. Fear of what was to come. Not for herself, but for the safety and sanity of her own sister.

After Frank Bartwell had attended Kidderminster Magistrates Court and pleaded not guilty for the abduction of Fliss, he'd been committed to Stafford Crown Court and the case was finally due to start the following Tuesday.

No matter how hard Jenna pushed it to the back of her mind, the sinister evil of it still touched her and gnawed at her insides that Fliss would have to relive the ordeal of her kidnap. She'd have to face the man who had murdered his mother, wife and child. Allegedly in the eye of the law, but Jenna and Fliss both knew it was true. Horrific in itself, but the element that he'd almost killed Domino, Fliss's faithful Dalmatian, and kidnapped Fliss, coming after her a second time once she'd escaped, had made it personal. They'd both been there for the final confrontation when Frank, the trusted intel analyst at Malinsgate Police Station, had broken into Jenna's house with the sole intent of killing Fliss.

Fliss was in for a rough ride, but Jenna would be by her side every moment of every day in court.

Jenna let the buzz of the electric toothbrush lull her for the full two minutes it took for apparent ultimate cleanliness, then spat and rinsed.

She pulled open the door, and hesitated. Adrian no longer occupied her bed, he'd gone, leaving her bedside lamps on to cast a golden glow over the room. They'd not yet had the opportunity to become familiar with each other's personal routine or work schedules, although he had known what he was getting into with a police officer. Routine and schedules were two words she rarely used and there'd never be a time when it became familiar.

She ran her gaze over the smoothed-out duvet and plumped-up pillows with a twinge of disappointment. She appreciated his consideration in making the bed, but he could have stayed long enough to say goodbye.

With a twinge of regret, she yanked on her clothes. It would have been nice to have had one last kiss.

Jenna stole downstairs in her stockinged feet, so she didn't wake her sister and dog as she headed towards the white gleam of light Adrian had left on for her in the kitchen.

It took a split second longer for the inviting aroma of rich dark coffee to register and send her senses into a riot. She wondered if it was that or the sight of her half-naked Chief Crown Prosecutor standing barefoot in her kitchen that had a curl of warmth building in her stomach and the delight that he hadn't left without saying goodbye. He'd been taking care of her as he seemed to time and again. Subtle, understated.

As he turned with a quirky smile on his lips and a travel mug full of steaming coffee in his hand, her heart gave a little stumble. This man was the first ever to look after her. She'd always been the strong one. Her strength often the downfall of her relationships as the men had either crumbled or leaned on her too hard.

Her smile came quick and natural. 'Thanks.' It felt good. 'I thought you'd gone.'

'Not yet.'

She stroked her fingers across his as she accepted the mug from him, little ripples of pleasure making her wish she could stay.

The tremble of thunder had her gripping the mug in her right hand and whipping around so she could face the threat head on.

Domino hurtled into the kitchen. His cat-like paws skidded as he punched the kitchen door wider with his head and leapt from the hallway carpet onto the smooth, pale grey tiles, his claws tip-tapping as he fought to stay upright in his haste to get to her.

The full weight of a thirty-two kilogram Dalmatian smacked into the front of her knees, jarring her all the way through her body until her teeth cracked.

'Bloody hell, Domino. Get down.' One-handed was never the way to tackle an exuberant Dalmatian.

Unrepentant, the spotted dog twirled around in tight circles, stomping on Jenna's feet. His frantic tail whipped time after time against her legs.

'For the love of Jesus, Domino. Stop.'

As she reared her head back up to stop the dog cracking his skull into hers, her detective constable and sister's current boyfriend, Mason Ellis, sauntered into the kitchen, clearly comfortable, a weary smile on his sleep-puffed face.

The little jolt of surprise couldn't be helped. She had no idea her sister was sleeping with Mason yet. Not Fliss's fault. Jenna had made it clear to both Mason and Fliss that she wanted to know nothing about their relationship. Her initial thoughts being that she never wanted to have to take sides between her sister and her work partner.

She now realised, she did need to know. She needed to know who was walking around her house at night, who let Domino run wild when he should have been fast asleep on Fliss's bed and who the hell swiped her thick as treacle, black coffee from her hand without a twitch of remorse.

'That's mine.' She reached out to snatch it back.

'Not any more.' He took a deliberate swig and shot her a wicked grin. 'You want it back?'

She returned his grin with a cool stare. 'You're a child.' What was it they said about familiarity breeding contempt?

As he hunkered down and yanked the huge Dalmatian into a good strong one-armed cuddle, she knew she could always forgive him, for the care he'd shown for Domino when he'd been injured and the obvious love he had for Fliss. Not that love had been mentioned at this stage, but it was love. She knew. She could see it, even if they couldn't yet.

It could have been awkward, but Mason had feelings for her sister long before Fliss was aware. He'd never have made a move if Jenna had disapproved. The heartache he'd suffered when Fliss had disappeared had served to convince Jenna that he deserved a shot at happiness for both their sakes. Fliss deserved to be adored, and Mason adored her.

Of course, if he ever hurt Fliss, Jenna would rip his heart out and leave it bleeding on the ground. She'd made that quite clear.

The same surprise she'd felt at his presence flashed through Mason's eyes as they centred on Adrian who leaned, arms crossed over his chest with quiet casualness against the kitchen counter. 'Hey. Umm.' Mason took another slurp of the coffee and raised the cup in a salute. 'Do you want some?'

Adrian's lips quirked. 'A little late for me. Thanks.'

'Late? We're only just getting started.'

'Good luck with that. I'm just off home to a good night's sleep.'

'Nine-to-fivers,' Mason acknowledged. 'Bloody lucky.'

Still half asleep, Adrian raised his chin before turning his back to stick another pod in the Tassimo.

To distract Mason from his obvious attempt to wind Adrian up, Jenna nudged at him. 'I didn't know you were here.'

Mason ducked his head, his backside hit the floor as Domino swiped a long tongue over his ear and stomped on him. The dog's attention didn't even put a hitch in Mason's voice as he continued to rough him up. 'Fliss and I just got back from the cinema.'

With a grateful smile, Jenna took the second coffee Adrian handed to her and grabbed a swift sip. 'I just got called in.'

'Major fire.' Mason pushed himself up from the floor, held one hand up in a stop motion at the overexcited Domino. 'Wait.'

The command had Domino slapping his backside on the floor. He stretched his long elegant neck full length, chin up and sent an adoring gaze at Mason without even a twitch. Jenna wasn't sure which one of them she should kick. Not that she'd dream of kicking the dog. Mason, possibly... but the dog was never that obedient for her.

Instead, she ground her teeth and turned to Mason, hoping her expression wasn't as intent as Domino's. 'You've been called too?'

'Yep.' He took a long gulp of her coffee. 'I'll meet you at the station. I'll grab the keys for the vehicle when I get there.' He paused and narrowed his eyes at her. 'Who's driving?'

Jenna swiped her bag from the back of one of the kitchen chairs and swung it over her shoulder. 'Me. Always me, Mason.'

Mason scrubbed the top of Domino's head. 'Go back to your mum, lad.'

Jenna's jaw dropped as the spotted dog turned tail, trotted out of the door and thundered up the stairs back to Fliss. Used to Jenna's on-call schedule, she'd not rouse herself from a comfortable, warm bed. There was no reason. And she'd be having a bloody sleep-in the following morning.

'How the hell do you get him to do that?'

Mason gulped the rest of her coffee and slipped the empty travel mug into the sink. 'Personality, boss. Personality.' He raised a hand. 'Good to see you, Adrian.' As he swung on his heel and headed for the door, Jenna couldn't resist a quick glance at the offending travel mug he'd stuck in the sink. Her pet hate. No one should ever leave crockery in a sink. There would be a little re-alignment of his attitude next time he stepped foot in her house.

She chewed her bottom lip, torn between washing it up and putting it away, or slipping out of the door and leaving it for Fliss to deal with. She caught Adrian's gaze.

'I see your demon in there. I've got it.' He moved to the sink and swiped up the mug, bringing a fast grin to her face. The man was a minor miracle.

She stepped into his space and grabbed a quick kiss. 'Thank you. I'll see you later.'

'Possibly not. I need to be back in London on Monday morning for a few days, it depends what you end up working.'

'Oh.' Disappointment curdled her stomach, but until he'd finished with the major drugs case he was working, life would continue in this vein. That just had to be accepted.

As she turned to go, he snaked an arm around her waist and whipped her back around to face him. 'If you can dovetail something in later, let me know. I'll let myself out.' He grabbed another kiss and then released her, but not before he trailed his knuckles down her cheek and softened her heart.

'There's no need, you can stay.' Her voice came out in a breathless rush.

'No, it's okay. I'll get off now. Somehow it won't be the same without you in that bed.'

The warmth in her stomach spread to her chest as she backed out of the kitchen, a vague confusion rolling through her system. He made it simple.

Before she turned to go, she had to check. 'Make sure you lock the door behind you. It's important to Fliss.'

His small nod accompanied an understanding smile. 'Important to you too. I'll see you soon. I'll be back full-time once the courts call me for Fliss's case.'

'It could be weeks.'

His gaze held hers.

'It won't be weeks before I return. I'll call you later.'

Flustered, she ducked her head. 'Bye.'

She slipped out of the door and down the pathway with confusion uppermost. Her chest reeling between warm excitement and anxious anticipation. No one had ever treated her the way he did. There was respect and care. It was the care that all her previous relationships had lacked. Her boyfriends may have respected her, but she'd always been the stronger one, the one to reassure, to nurture, to care. Now it was mutual.

It left her strangely shaken.

She slipped into the car and glanced back at her house. It may take some getting used to, but it felt good to have him there.

5

He pulled off the road and bumped his Jeep Wrangler through deep ruts into the treeline before he cut the engine.

All the best laid plans could take a turn for the worse. He needed to know this one hadn't. The only way he could make sure was to check for himself.

He made his way through the thick forest of trees and kept the beam from the flashlight trained on the ground, aware anyone could see it. If they were looking. There was no reason for anyone to look.

Yet.

Satisfaction warmed his stomach as the glow of light flickered to reach gnarled fingers through the gaps in the trees.

He slowed his footsteps, aware of the precipice not far in front. The steep drop into the valley below.

Way above the fifteenth-century stone building, he stared down, satisfied the plan was initiated.

A rolling stone. There was no stopping it now.

He turned his head to the right to scan the long driveway. As yet, devoid of any traffic. It wouldn't be for long.

Movement caught his attention and he narrowed his eyes. Twin lights of a vehicle approached from the direction of Much Wenlock. Not following the road as he would have imagined, but surprising him by crashing across the fields in a direct line towards the old house.

As it tore through the sparse treeline and made for the middle of the long driveway, a number of upstairs windows blew out from the house in an explosion of ferocious golden flames and black smoke in amongst what he could only imagine a profusion of tiny shards of glass.

Hypnotised, his gaze lingered on the flames licking their way up the outside of the house, consuming the place as though it was a living, breathing being sent to scorch and destroy.

Destroy is what it needed to do.

Sirens sounded in the dead of the clear night. Stars, normally clearly visible without the light pollution towns and cities had, petered out, overpowered by the strength of the flames dancing to their own tune.

The car slewed to a halt and he squinted to get a better view as the two front doors were flung open. Black silhouettes, intermittently illuminated stumbled towards the house, hands held up in defence.

Interested, he took a step back, aware that he could be visible should someone choose to look up. He angled his head, the pulse in the base of his throat throbbing. Anticipation, excitement. Dicing with possibilities.

Blue lights flashed on their approach. Fire. Ambulance. Police.

He retreated. Curious, interested in the process. Aware of the possibilities of being noticed. He took one more step back. Hunkered down, his back against a tree to watch the light show.

6

Once they'd parked their cars at Malinsgate Police Station, Jenna took the keys Mason had grabbed from the duty desk and slid into the driver's seat of the police-issue vehicle. One of the older cars in the fleet, the interior held the vague reminiscence of sweat and pee, as though the vehicle had transported one too many drug addicts and drunks.

'Did it have to be this one?' She tried not to breathe in through her nose.

Mason shrugged and she suspected he hadn't even noticed the stench, or perhaps wasn't bothered by it.

Jenna slotted her travel mug into the plastic holder in the centre console as Mason made the car bounce when he flopped into the passenger seat. 'That's mine!' She stabbed her finger at the mug. 'Don't touch it, or you're dead meat.' With a deliberate hard glance at Mason to make sure he got the message, she turned again for a closer look at him. 'What the hell are you grinning at?'

He shrugged and reached for his seat belt, the long creases bracketing his mouth cut deep as he continued to grin.

Jenna pushed the button to fire the engine up but took it out of gear as she turned in her seat to stare at him. 'What?'

'I think you've gone soft on him, all for a dopey smile and a hot mug of coffee.'

Speechless for a moment, she narrowed her eyes at him. 'I've not gone soft, and you were the one who got the coffee.'

'Only because I took it from you. If we'd been at work, you'd have knocked my block off for that.'

'It was precisely because we weren't at work that I didn't.'

'You didn't want to frighten him off with a display of unprecedented violence.'

'It wouldn't have been unprecedented. It would have been justified. So would your burial in the shallow grave in my back garden. You stole my coffee.'

'That's a stiff accusation.'

'It's an accurate observation. And you were in my house. I was being congenial towards you. It was nothing to do with Adrian.' And yet it was everything. He was integrating into her world, being accepted by Mason.

'Interesting.' He fell silent and stared straight ahead as he waited for her to respond.

With emotions a little too tender and new for her to examine, Jenna turned and pulled her seat belt around her, put the car in gear and pulled away from the parking space to head for the exit.

She put her foot a little too hard on the accelerator and the car leapt to life, shooting into the mainstream of traffic as she took the ring road around Telford Town Centre. That in-between time of couples heading home after a date night of restaurant and cinema, but too early yet for the turning out of the clubs, the mid-flow of traffic hadn't reached its peak.

She sailed through green traffic lights at Hollinswood Interchange and took the fifth exit onto the A442 Queensway towards Ironbridge.

Jenna guided her vehicle between the other cars, negotiating the pimple roundabouts which were a recent addition to the area. The whole of Telford had been affected, slowed down, clogged up. At one time she remembered, she could get from her house to the retail park in under ten minutes. Now, with all the additional traffic lights and roundabouts and narrowing of lanes, and feeder lanes, she was lucky if she made it in twenty.

Progress. This is what they called progress.

Gone were the days, and not so long ago, when Telford was renowned for its roundabouts, traffic flowed freely, and one-way systems worked. It hadn't taken so very long from the advent of the first set of traffic lights on those roundabouts to manage to snarl up the traffic.

Unable to stop the yawn, Jenna reached out to turn the heating down and keep some fresh air flowing, then she pushed back in her seat. She glanced right and swooped the car around the round-about at the top of Jiggers Bank, the steep, undulating road that dived down into Ironbridge. The narrow road, opened in 1818, had serviced the Industrial Revolution but had crumbled into the deep valley below until the last few years when they'd shored it all up with gabion baskets filled with stone.

She opted to take the more direct route along the bypass, lifting her foot off the accelerator as the car swooped down the steep embankment. Instead of following the steady curve in the road that would take her onwards to Shrewsbury, Jenna touched her foot to the brake, changed down gear, indicated left and opted for the narrower road over the Buildwas bridge and headed towards Much Wenlock.

'Oh, dear God.'

Brilliant amber and gold scythed across the glass-clear night sky, dulling out the bright stars. Like a sunset, multicoloured hues dashed across the horizon, but unlike a sunset, the colours wavered like great flags, never still, interlacing with huge plumes of smoke, which could have been mistaken for clouds but for the vicious spiralling upwards into the ether.

'That's one hell of a fire,' Mason observed.

Jenna blew out a breath. 'We're still miles away. It must be enormous.'

'It'll take some putting out. Let's hope the fire service have enough resources on hand to deal with this. I don't think I've seen anything like it.'

Sparks licked into the night sky, pushing the illumination higher, and Jenna pressed her right foot a little heavier to the accelerator.

'They'll have to pull in everything they've got.' Not her problem, Jenna nevertheless considered the logistics of adequate cover from a county whose fire stations mainly had one tender in each location.

She followed the smooth flow of the road, hugging the bends as it took her past the sparse smattering of houses, meandering down past the old renovated pub on her left and then climbing back up again on its approach to Much Wenlock.

Hands soft on the steering wheel, Jenna peered up into the sky at the encroaching vast swathe of red, purpling at the edges as it dispersed into the night.

Distracted by the sight, her heart leapt in her chest as a dark shadow burst from the treeline in the hills above her to spring onto the road. Survival instinct had Jenna slamming her brakes on. Lit up in the swathe of white headlights from the police car, the fallow deer continued its dash in front of their bonnet almost skimming the paintwork and then dodged at the last minute. Its white spots glowed against the pale golden tan of its hide.

As Mason was almost thrown through the front windscreen, but for the immediate action of his seat belt, the inertia flung Jenna back in her own seat. Her head slammed against the headrest as her breath jammed in her chest. 'Shit.'

'Shit.' Mason rubbed his chest as he let out a deep grunt.

Oblivious of her near-death experience, the deer danced with grace and finesse into the embankment on the right-hand side and disappeared into the undergrowth.

Before Jenna had time to suck in the breath she desperately needed, a small fawn high-stepped across the road in front of the car, a new-born with legs still gangly and thin, unlike the beast who'd come before it.

The bright band of headlights coming from beyond the curves in the road from the opposite direction had Jenna's heart lodging in her throat. She slapped her hand on the hazard light button and hoped to hell the other driver saw her as a third deer trotted with unfounded casualness in front of the car, then a fourth, fifth and sixth. In a desperate bid to slow the oncoming driver down without further spooking the herd, Jenna flashed her headlights at the approaching car.

Almost too late, the driver slammed on its brakes. The advancing car kangaroo-hopped straight at them so Jenna gripped the steering wheel and braced herself. At the last moment, the car slewed into the middle of the road and jerked to a standstill. Orange hazard lights blazed within a split second of it coming to a halt, bright flashes illuminating the darkness.

Jenna released a slow breath as another three deer pranced across the road on spring-assisted legs. She clawed her short hair back from her face, gasped out a breath and sat in silence waiting for the next member of the herd to pop out of the trees while the pulse in the base of her neck stammered.

When nothing further emerged, Jenna depressed the clutch and shoved the car in first gear to let it crawl alongside the other vehicle which displayed the green 'P' sticker on its bonnet to indicate a newly qualified driver.

7

Jenna stabbed the button to wind down her window. She pulled her warrant card from where it was attached to her waistband on a bungee cord. She'd given up wearing it on a lanyard around her neck ever since Fliss had almost been strangled by an attacker with the dog lead she'd had looped around her neck. It was a lesson she'd determined not to ignore.

She peered through the dark at the other driver, who'd wound down their window. 'Hi. I'm DS Jenna Morgan and this is DC Mason Ellis. Everyone okay in there?'

Fear glazed the young driver's eyes as they almost popped out of her head while her lips trembled into a vacant smile. 'I wasn't going too fast. I was only going fifty.'

Jenna inclined her head and, with one eye on the burning sky, lowered her voice to soothe rather than terrify. After all, she'd been going fifty too and with all the experience in the world and an advanced grade one driving certificate, she'd almost taken the damned deer out. If she hadn't been distracted by the fire in the sky, it probably would have made no difference, wildlife was just that. Wild and unpredictable. At around forty-five kilograms and almost the height of the car, the first female had been no lightweight. Hitting an animal that size wouldn't have resulted in a small dint in the car but a complete wreck.

With a reassurance she didn't quite feel herself, she forced her lips to curve into a gentle smile. 'Fifty is the speed limit along here, and you stopped in good time, but just be careful along this road. The deer frequently bolt across and if you hit one at fifty, at best you'll kill a deer and write off your car, at worst you'll kill a deer and yourself.' She'd been so close herself, the shock of it still ran cold through her veins.

The wide eyes blinked, and the baby-faced girl jerked her head three times in acknowledgement, the smooth plumpness of her young cheeks wobbled while her mouth worked to say something, but no sound came from her lips.

Jenna glanced beyond the girl to the other two wide-eyed passengers and understood their inability to catch their breath. The tight band around her own chest still squeezed, but she had a job to do.

'Where are you off to?' The distinct scent of alcohol drifted from the over-warm interior of the other car and Jenna's heart sank as she narrowed her eyes to take in the occupants again before she centred her attention on the driver.

The young woman's eyes cleared in an instant and she sat bolt upright as awareness of the situation hit her. 'We're on our way home. I haven't been drinking. My friends have. We went for a quick one down at the local. But I didn't drink. I wouldn't. My mum would kill me. I've only just passed my test. Mum doesn't want us out late. She said she'd be awake until we got home. She'd kill me if she thought I was drink-driving.' Words spilled over themselves as she tried to get them out in some semblance of an order and Jenna's lips twitched with amusement.

'Like, she bloody would kill 'er. 'Er mum's like a dragon. Terrifies the frickin' life ou' of me. But Sophie hasn't been drinking. We did, like, but she's just passed her test and 'er mum would kill 'er. It's the first time, like, we've come out since she passed last week.' Jenna's brain fogged as the passenger leaned over and almost blew her head off. Vodka, with fumes like that, it had to be vodka.

'Have a good time, did we?' Jenna barely acknowledged their quick giggles and nudges as they chorused their approval. Concerned, she glanced at the road ahead and behind her, the kick of urgency to clear the route uppermost in her mind. She needed to get the kids off the road, but knowing what she knew, there was no way she could let them go. She glanced up at the burnished sky. PC Walker was at the site. It would have to wait. The more pressing matter was right in front of her. Her number one priority was to get the girls to a place of safety. Protect. Always protect.

Aware of Mason in the passenger seat finishing up his call for assistance she ducked her head back inside the car and cruised a searching gaze over him. 'You want to drive our car, or the one with the three potentially drunk women?'

He ducked his head, moving closer to Jenna so he could take a good long look in through the windows of the car at the three girls, their twittering voices raised in panicked whispers. The blink and slow pull of his breath told her everything she needed to know even before he spoke. 'This one.' He'd happily step into the path of a charging psychopath for her, but he'd rather not get involved with teenage girls.

'Wise decision.'

Aware she needed to get a move on in case any other traffic pulled up, Jenna turned back to the driver. 'Sophie, I can smell alcohol, so I'm obliged to get you breathalysed. I can't do it myself, so we've sent for a uniformed officer to come out. They won't be long, but we need to get off this road before any other vehicles come along. Hop out of the driver's seat and I'll drive your car just down to the pull-off where it's safe.'

Sophie's bottom lip quivered.

'Do you understand?' Jenna sent her a long, searching look as she checked her over for signs of inebriation. None that she could tell, but the moment she'd smelled the alcoholic fumes, she'd been under an obligation to call it in.

Sophie nodded.

With her hazards still flashing, Jenna left the engine running while she unclipped her seat belt and slipped out of the driver's door just as Mason flopped himself from the passenger seat into the driver's with long drawn-out grunts as he caught himself up on the central console.

'Bugger. Ahhh, bugger.'

Jenna ducked her head into the car. 'You should have walked around.'

He shot her a pained grin as he grabbed at his thigh and rubbed. 'Too easy. I like the bruises. Shows I've been working.'

'Shows you're an idiot.' She slammed the door and turned towards the other car as all three girls opened their doors. The tiny front-seat passenger tottered around the bonnet of the car, her own skewed logic dictating her direction, on heels high enough to scaffold The Wrekin. She weaved past Sophie, who strode in the opposite direction in sensible, flat shoes obviously specific for driving. Sophie leaped into the front passenger seat while the diminutive figure with an enormous bosom shimmied her way into the vacant back seat next to the shadowy image of the third passenger. All the time, their desperate dramatic twitter carried on the quiet night air.

Dear God! Save me from teenage girls.

Jenna heaved out a sigh and slipped into the driver's seat of the brand new, cute little Fiat Panda Pop in a bright tango red.

After a speedy check in both directions for oncoming traffic, she whipped the seat back to accommodate her long legs, adjusted the mirrors, strapped herself in and put the idling engine into first gear. She let it kangaroo-hop along for a moment before flooring the accelerator just to get a little poke out of it. With a full house, the small 1.2 litre engine would struggle with the weight and loading. But with a surprising whoosh, it kicked in and careered them along the road, within seconds reaching the 50 mph speed limit.

The fresh smell of new car was almost overpowered by the alcohol.

Impossible to tune out their voices, Jenna allowed them to free-range around her.

'Sophie, you should ring your mum. Let her know. She'll be out here quick as a flash.' Surprised at the enthusiasm of the girl in the back who so far Jenna hadn't heard from, she opened her mouth to reply, but the little one jumped in first.

'You have got to be frickin' kidding, Chanel, if Sophie's mum comes out, she'll be ripping tits and balls off every frickin' copper in sight.'

More amused than offended, Jenna slowed the car down.

Sophie turned in her seat to engage the others. 'Mum wouldn't do that. She'd be very respectful, Olivia, as should you be.'

Olivia snorted and collapsed back against the seat just as Jenna flung the car into a driveway on the left, circled it around and made her way back the way they'd come, knowing there was a good length of driveway further along the road at Farley where the old Rock House Inn nestled between two sweeping bends. No longer a public house, it nevertheless had good enough access for Jenna to pull in behind where Mason waited for them, leaving enough room for a response vehicle to come alongside.

'What the hell is that red bubble in the sky?' Chanel hitched herself forward to lean in the gap between the two front seats. 'Shit. That looks like something's on fire.' With a quick stab, she poked one long, acrylic nail into Jenna's shoulder. 'Shouldn't you call the fire brigade? There's a fucking fire over there. We could be in danger. Do you think we should move?' The drama queen stabbed her in the shoulder again. Jenna whipped around to face her and, with her patience starting to wear threadbare, she cast the girl a strained but reassuring smile.

'We don't need to move. We're in no danger. The fire isn't anywhere near us. I don't need to call the fire brigade. They're already there. We would be too if you and your...' She flicked her gaze down at the purple can of Shake Baby Shake vodka cocktail Chanel grasped to her chest and sighed. Four per cent. They would have had to have drunk a hell of a lot to get wasted. '...Alcohol consumption hadn't detained us.'

Not to be distracted, Chanel continued to gaze up out of the front windscreen. 'Where's it coming from?'

They'd know soon enough in the morning, there was no point trying to hide it now. 'Kimble Hall.'

'What?' Sophie whipped around in her seat, huge blue eyes almost bursting out of her head. 'Poppy Lawrence lives there.'

Dammit. Jenna's heart sank, perhaps she should have kept it to herself. 'Poppy Lawrence?'

'Yeah, she's a friend.' Chanel and Olivia both vied for the middle position on the back seat so they could squeeze themselves into the gap. The sweet smell of chemical colouring, sugar syrup and alcohol wafted into the front. 'She was supposed to be with us tonight, but she had some kind of family do she had to go to.'

'Okay. So, she wasn't allowed out?'

The girls exchanged uneasy glances as Sophie shook her head, lowered her voice. 'No.' She shrugged. 'What her dad says, goes.' She chewed on her bottom lip and Jenna gave her the time while the girl contemplated whether to say more. And there was more, there always would be with family dynamics. 'She's a bit scared of him.'

'Fuckin' A she is. He's terrifying. Some big-shot estate agent. My dad can't stand him. Says he a fuckin'...' Olivia nudged Chanel in the ribs. 'Well, he is. Poppy's brother, Joshua, is always in trouble at school cos his dad keeps telling him he's better than everyone else and he can have anything he wants. Poppy's not like that. She's nice, but her brother's turning out to be a right little git.'

Jenna made a mental note to check out the good Mr Lawrence when she got to the scene.

Bright headlights cut through the dark as the approaching car rounded the bend and flashed on its blues to strobe around, bouncing off the warm white walls of the old converted pub.

The squad car slowed down and pulled alongside them to effectively block them in.

Aware of time slipping by, Jenna needed to stop the constant jabbering, if only for her own sanity. If she could have slammed her hands against her ears and yelled for them to shut up, she quite happily would have. But she was a police officer. She needed to show professionalism.

She raised her voice, pitched it with authority. 'Right.' Jenna glanced around at them. 'Sophie, you'll need to take a breathalyser.'

Back to terrified, Sophie jerked a nod at Jenna.

'I don't think you have anything to worry about,' Jenna reassured her with a soft smile. She'd bet her badge the young woman hadn't been drinking, she was too proud of her newly acquired driving licence to be so stupid, and by the sound of her mother, she'd be jerked right back on those rails if she threatened to go off them. 'You other two, Olivia, Chanel...' Jenna turned in her seat and the blue lights illuminated their faces in quick flashes. 'You'll need to let the officer know you're old enough to drink.' At the quick intake of breath from Olivia, Jenna closed her eyes. Give her strength, someone else needed to deal with all this crap. 'Do yourselves a favour? Lose the fake IDs, tell the truth and take the punishment, because quite honestly the officer is just going to want to pack you off home to your mums.'

She unstrapped her seatbelt and let herself out of the door, hoping she knew the officers who had arrived.

As PC Donna McGuire stepped from the vehicle to greet her, Jenna couldn't help but grin. She couldn't have found herself a better officer to deal with these three, if she'd put in a personal request. Donna's experience, judgement and empathy were next to none.

'Hey, Donna.'

'Sarge.'

Mason stepped up alongside her as Jenna glanced at the young police officer with Donna. New to the force, Jenna recognised her but couldn't for the life of her pull the woman's name from her overtaxed brain.

As usual, Donna never hesitated to keep things smooth. 'This is Natalie Kempson. She's shadowing me until she gets her feet under her.'

'Natalie. Hi.' Aware of time slipping by, Jenna shot the newbie a fast smile and a perfunctory nod, anxious to get off. 'Donna,' she took the PC by the elbow, more than comfortable with their familiarity, and stepped her away from the little Fiat Panda Pop. 'Look, we had a little issue with deer leaping out in front of us. Nothing happened, nobody got hurt, we all just pulled to a standstill. When they wound down the window, I smelled alcohol so couldn't let it go.'

Jenna's lips twitched as Donna grimaced. 'Great.'

'Yeah, I know. I don't think the driver, Sophie, has been drinking and the other two are hardly on the hardcore stuff. Bloody four per cent vodka cocktail, smells far worse than it is, I think, because of the bloody chemical flavourings. Anyway, could you breathalyse the driver and send them on their way if she's negative. Take their details and just zap them over for me to pick up later?'

'Sure, no problem.' Donna fished in her pocket for her notepad and pen. 'Do I need to put the fear of God into them, or is it softly-softly?'

This time Jenna grinned. 'Definitely the soft approach. I think they're nice girls.' She lowered her voice. 'I just wish they'd stop twittering like overexcited brainless birds.'

Donna let out a soft snort. 'That's teenage girls for you.'

'I don't for one moment think they're brainless.' Jenna let out a soft shudder.

'I know. Their mouths just don't stop.'

Jenna cast a quick glance back at them. 'Yeah.' She drew Donna a step further away. 'Turns out they're friends with the girl that lives at Kimble Hall.' She jerked her head in the general direction of the lit-up sky.

'The house fire?' Donna sucked air in through her teeth. 'We've just come from there. It doesn't look good.'

Mason edged in closer, effectively cutting off the girls behind with his broad shoulders.

Even so, Jenna lowered her voice so the girls in the car couldn't catch what she said. 'Tell them nothing.'

Donna's thick black hair fell forward in a curtain and the blue lights bounced off it as she shook her head, throwing a soft blue satin halo around her head.

'Do me a favour, Donna?'

Donna lifted her head, her liquid eyes gleamed in the myriad of illumination. 'Yeah.'

'Presuming young Sophie blows a negative, which I suspect she will, hang around to make sure they get off home. They're all a little overexcited.' At Donna's nod, Jenna leaned in. 'And make sure our little drama queen, Chanel, doesn't get a hare-brained idea to shoot off and check on the fire situation. We don't need any rubberneckers at the scene.'

'Right, Sarge.'

Jenna patted Donna's shoulder, knowing from her own experience with the woman how gentle and empathetic she would be. There was no one better at assessing a situation than PC McGuire.

Jenna turned away, strode back to the Fiat Panda and leaned in through the front window. She gave them a moment for the excited twitter to fall into a breathless silence. 'Good to meet you, ladies, I'm leaving you in the competent care of PCs McGuire and Kempson.' Jenna ran her gaze over Sophie. 'Drive carefully and keep safe. Goodnight.'

The girls chorused their goodbyes with varying degrees of enthusiasm as Jenna made her way back to the unmarked vehicle and slid into the driver's seat.

Mason gave an exaggerated shudder as she pulled the car back onto the road. 'Gah, teenage girls. To be avoided at all costs.'

'Yeah, I'd like to think we could avoid them, but I've a horrible feeling we're going to be meeting up with them in the not too distant future.'

Her feeling of disquiet grew as she brought Mason up to date on the way to the scene.

8

SUNDAY 19 APRIL 0155 HOURS

Jenna stepped from the car and slammed the door at the same time as Mason climbed from the passenger side to join her.

The cool spring night breeze whipped away in a blaze of fury as the wind changed direction and heat blasted through in a whorl of energy to suck the air from her lungs and knock her back a step.

'Well, fuck!'

She scrubbed fingers through her thick, choppy hair and snorted at Mason's predictable response. She took a moment to adjust her senses to the full impact of the fire.

It had been some years since she'd been to a bonfire, but the scent of the burning house evoked memories of freezing temperatures and fireworks.

Jenna tipped her head back and gazed up at a sky ablaze with colour and deep, dark clouds of smoke. She'd never seen a bonfire of such epic proportions nor experienced such power as the inferno syphoned the oxygen from the atmosphere.

'This is bad. Very bad.'

Jenna scanned the area, pleased to note PC Walker had it in hand. Vehicles she needed to check had been logged were dumped outside of the double cordon the fire service had set up. Outer and inner with tighter restrictions the closer to the incident.

With a silent nod to Mason, they made their way through the outer line and held still in front of the inner cordon as the heat seared through. Shoulder to shoulder, they stood in the pool of amber light to watch as the inferno spat golden sparks into the sky, accompanied by a cacophony of cracks, pops and small explosions, while Mason spoke into Airwaves, the Force radio system, to obtain an update on the vital information they'd need.

Flames shot from windows devoid of glass where it had already exploded outward. Fire licked up the outside of the old stone building and danced like a live being to hold Jenna enthralled.

A giant of a man kitted out in the ugly beige fire service PPE strode with purpose from the far side of the inner cordon into her eyeline to break the hypnotic pull the burning building had on her.

He swiped the mask from his face, removed his headgear and scrubbed the fine sheen of sweat from his chin with the back of his hand.

'Hey.'

Jenna held her badge up high so he could squint at it in the liquid light of the flames. 'DS Jenna Morgan, this is DC Mason Ellis.'

'Charlie Cartwright, I'm the watch manager.'

Jenna's gaze darted down to the oblong sign on his chest to confirm his position. She reached out a hand to have it enveloped in his powerful grip.

He jerked his chin in the direction of a circle of firemen at the far side of the inner cordon. 'Phil Hutchinson, the incident commander, is over there.' Masks on with the burnished orange flicker of flames reflected to obscure their eyes, in deep discussion, they paid no attention to Jenna and Mason's arrival. It was of no consequence, the watch manager was as capable of updating her at this stage as the incident commander.

Mason stepped forward and the two men exchanged handshakes. 'Hey, Charlie. The information we have from Control is the Lawrence family are on the council register as living here. Mr and Mrs, together with four children under the age of eighteen. No specifics yet, but we'll get that information shortly.'

'So, possibly six people?' Grim, Charlie's lips tightened. 'What are the chances they're not home?'

Jenna dipped hands into her pockets. 'Doubtful. We just met some friends of Poppy Lawrence. They said she had a family party she had to go to. Maybe they went out for the evening, but even so, wouldn't you think they'd be back by now with kids?' She shrugged. What the hell did she know about kids? 'Has anyone checked the garage?' She glanced around. 'The drive for cars?'

'Yeah.' Charlie indicated a huge barn to the left of the main house. Nestled amongst several outbuildings, it was being doused in water from the tenders. 'Several cars inside I'm told, eight or nine. Looks like he may have been a collector. Can't tell straight off if any of them are the "family" car.'

'Is the outbuilding on fire too?' Steam rose from all around, but she couldn't see any flames.

'No, they're damping it down, purely precautionary at this stage to make sure no stray sparks send it up in a ball of flames. Everything is really dry.'

'Okay.'

She made a mental note to get the registration numbers checked once they had access to the outbuilding.

'What else have you got, Charlie?'

With a shake of his head, he glanced over his shoulder. 'It's not good. We received a 999 call at 2335,' he checked his watch. 'The nearest neighbours, a Mr and Mrs Crawford, live over that rise.' He jerked his head to indicate the direction. 'They'd gone to bed, fast asleep when their smoke alarm alerted them. Elderly couple.' He raised his head and scanned the area, his eyes crinkling at the edges as he narrowed them, looking for the couple. 'They're over there when you're ready to speak with them.'

'How come *their* smoke alarm went off if they live that far away?'

Charlie shrugged his broad shoulders. 'The wind's strong, all it would take was a sudden change of direction, which has happened several times now, and the smoke probably got blown into their open window. Trapped inside, it would activate their smoke alarm. It's not unusual for that to happen.'

Jenna nodded. It made sense. 'So, what about now?'

Face rippled in shadow as the fire raged on behind him creating a barrier of a roaring, gushing waterfall, she had to lean in as Charlie shook his head. 'By the time we arrived, the place was already an inferno. You know, it's out in the middle of nowhere, we don't know what time it started, but we do know that once it got going, it was only a short sprint from the start to this.'

'How long did it take you to get here?' She glanced at the time on her phone. Just past 2:00 a.m.

'After the call? The first tender arrived in under eight minutes from Wenlock, that was mine, I took control of the scene. We've sectorised the incident. Four sectors. Second tender arrived in nineteen minutes from Tweedale, third and fourth took almost twenty-two minutes from Bridgnorth. Because of the scale of the fire, the size of the property, the amount of barns and outbuildings, we requested another two tenders, but they're finishing up at a house fire the other side of Telford. ETA another twelve minutes. It's only the main house on fire, but with the wind changing direction, we've got to keep the outbuildings dampened down so they don't catch a spark. Mostly wooden with roofs, they'd soon go up.'

'Can you tell if anyone was still inside?'

Charlie manoeuvred himself to stand at her side so he could indicate the house beyond. 'We can't be sure. By the time we arrived the place was too far gone for me to risk my crews. Anyone in there...' He shook his head. 'The place is compromised, with the age of the building. It's stone, but the structure inside could be anything. We conducted a risk assessment. Once at this stage, house fires tend to burn at around a thousand degrees.' At her blank look, he expanded. 'Five times the temperature of an oven you'd cook your Sunday roast in.'

'Surely that's hot enough to cremate?' Not wanting to dwell too long on the effect it would have on anyone in there, Jenna fixed her gaze on Charlie.

'No, 1400 to 1800 degrees for cremation, and don't forget that when cremation takes place it's under controlled circumstances.' He used his hands to squeeze down the size of the imagined area. 'Confined in a small area. It takes two and half hours to cremate a body.'

'With nothing left but ashes.'

'No. That's a fallacy. Even then there will be a skeleton. They put it all into a grinder and...' the hands he demonstrated closed into fists, 'crush it.'

Rocked by the horror of it, Jenna sucked in a breath. Fire, ambulance and police never held their punches in their descriptions. Fact was fact. Between them, their sense of humour could be ribald at times, even when the occasion didn't call for it. It was a defence mechanism. They dealt with death, and what some may consider worse. There was no cover-up of gory details, no hiding from the stark truth despite the macabre element.

Charlie tucked his helmet under his elbow and swiped at his forehead with the back of his other hand. 'If I thought for one moment that there was anyone in there alive, I would have sent a crew in straight away. There isn't. It's not possible for anyone to have survived in there.'

Jenna squinted against the bright glaze of light flickering beyond Charlie, expecting to see the paramedics attending to victims of the fire, but apart from the crew with the elderly lady, Mrs Crawford, the other two teams were stood watching the blaze.

In amongst them all, her solid PC Walker had a handle on it. He raised a hand to acknowledge her as he pressed the people who'd come to observe back beyond the cordons. Relatively few were there at that time of the morning, such was the remoteness of Kimble Hall. Stood in its own fifty acre grounds, it was secluded, but surrounded by even more arable fields, it was isolated.

The sense of loss pressed heavy on her chest and she glanced up at Mason's tight features as the realisation that there were no survivors hit them both.

'When are we expecting NILO?' NILO, the National Inter-Agency Liaison Officer, was the tactical advisor responsible for liaison between the separate forces to keep everyone informed in a major incident. The incident was major so far because of the ferocity of the fire.

'On his way. Roger Ayman. He's based in Worcester. They're trying to contact him now. In the meantime, I can tell you anything you need to know, but there's relatively little that I can say at the moment, except that's a shit-hot fire and no one will be going near it until the morning. We'll pour water on it from the outside. Keep an eye on that oil tank over there.' Charlie indicated with a broad sweep of his arm. 'We're keeping water on it to make sure it doesn't combust. And, as I said, dousing the outbuildings and barns so they don't catch light. Other than that, there's no more we can do at present than put the fire out. My crews won't be going in there until we have it completely under control.'

'Suspicious circumstances, or accident?' The age of the property indicated it could simply have ignited and gone up like an inferno without much encouragement.

'Can't tell at this stage. If you can locate the residents, that would be good. Otherwise it doesn't look promising.'

A cool breeze sneaked under the blaze of fury to stroke across Jenna's fiery skin in a promise of relief only to be whipped away by another gust of heat.

She fell back a step and puffed out a breath before it scorched her lungs. 'We'll go and question the neighbours. If you need us, we'll be over there.'

Across the stretch of land, she caught Ted Walker's gaze and raised her right hand, circling her thumb and forefinger into the *okay* sign. He raised his thumb in acknowledgement and she pointed in the direction of the ambulance she was about to make her way to.

More than capable of setting up the scene, Ted Walker would shout if he needed her.

Mason followed her through the thronging mass of new arrivals as the two remaining tenders pulled in, making a total of six. Almost unheard of in a rural location where only one tender resided at each of the stations, manned primarily by reserves.

Jenna jiggled her shoulders to stretch out the cricks that had set in as she stared up at the old manor house. Not visible from the road, she'd never seen it before, had never needed to be there. As far as she was concerned, she'd never heard any rumours, seen any reports of trouble out there.

An outlying house, with a quiet family.

9

Mason and Jenna turned their backs on the building and made their way towards the ambulance, where two paramedics tended to an elderly lady. Dressed in a quilted full-length dressing gown of faded pink, she perched on the edge of the flip-down seat in the ambulance. Her blue-veined hand gripped onto the bed rail, her wizened little face almost obscured by an oxygen mask.

'Hi,' Jenna showed her badge. 'I'm DS Jenna Morgan, and this is DC Mason Ellis.' She tossed a friendly smile at the short, round-faced female paramedic whose cheeks glowed an unnatural red in the white light of the interior of the ambulance. 'Is everything okay?'

The paramedic shot them an easy smile. 'Sandy. I'm Sandy. This is Mrs Crawford. Mr Crawford is just outside. He was concerned Mrs Crawford was feeling a little faint, so we gave her some oxygen to assist her breathing.' She raised her voice. 'Didn't we, Mrs Crawford?' At the old lady's owl-like blink, Sandy raised her voice another notch. 'We've given you oxygen Mrs Crawford. To help with your breathing.'

Mrs Crawford gave one long slow blink to make Jenna wonder whether she appreciated Sandy almost shouting.

Jenna lowered her voice to a discreet level, just above the roar and crackle of the fire. 'Is it okay to speak with her?'

'Sure. She didn't want to lie down.' Sandy turned to pat Mrs Crawford on the knee and raised her voice to accommodate the lady's ability to hear above the sound of the ambulance engine and the fire. 'You're good aren't you, Mrs Crawford? Just a bit breathless there, but you're okay now, aren't you, my darling?'

Mrs Crawford patted her chest and squeezed out a weak smile as she nodded.

Sandy turned to Jenna. 'What a darling. Heart as strong as an ox. She's eighty-nine, she's going to live another bloody thirty years with a heart like that.'

Jenna glanced at Mason. Lips twitching, he dipped his hands into his pockets and looked at his feet as he kicked at the dirt.

Jenna gave a quick survey. She'd stick with Mrs Crawford and let Mason deal with the older man lurking at the side of the ambulance, a sneaky cigarette, lit end turned inwards to the palm of his hand. He shot guilty little glances over in his wife's direction. His thin shoulders hunched over, less as a defence than a sign of age, Jenna suspected. Before his wife caught sight of him, he turned his back on them and a stream of smoke floated above his head and then was whipped away by an errant gust of wind. As though his wife wasn't astute enough to notice he was smoking.

'Okay. Thank you, Sandy. Mason, would you like to speak with Mr Crawford? See what you can get from him.'

Mason grunted out an agreement and ambled over to speak with the gentleman who hovered a few paces away.

Jenna climbed into the ambulance, edging past the attentive Sandy, and hunkered down, so she came face to face with the other woman. In the bright, unforgiving lights of the ambulance, Mrs

Crawford's pale, parchment skin stretched translucent across her cheekbones.

'Mrs Crawford?' Jenna reached out with a light touch to the older lady's elbow.

Washed-out grey eyes turned their sadness on her. 'He wasn't a very nice man, but I wouldn't wish this on him.' Her voice, muffled by the oxygen mask, croaked out.

'Who wasn't nice, Mrs Crawford?'

Confusion stole into the woman's eyes as though Jenna should know exactly what she meant. She plucked at the mask and pulled it from her mouth to speak around it. 'Why him. Gordon Lawrence, of course.'

'Gordon Lawrence.' Jenna slipped her notebook and pen from her top pocket and scratched down the man's name. Not that she'd forget it. She tapped her pen on the page, interested to note that the second person to comment on Gordon Lawrence had the same opinion as the first, Olivia, and was similarly quick to express it. 'You know him?'

Mrs Crawford stretched a tight smile. 'Not well. He didn't allow that.' She glanced over Jenna's shoulder at the fire raging on and slipped the oxygen mask further down onto her chin so she could speak unrestricted. 'Shouldn't speak ill of him. I wouldn't wish this on anyone.'

A frisson of awareness sneaked through Jenna's system and she shuffled closer, her curiosity piqued at the old lady's words, a reiteration of Olivia's earlier assessment. 'You said he's not nice? In what way was he not nice, Mrs Crawford?'

'Ethel, you can call me Ethel. I prefer it. Him out there will be called Mr Crawford, never known to anyone else as anything other than Mr Crawford.' Her lips twitched. 'Even me. Mr Crawford, or Father. Once the children came along, I only ever called him Father. Like he was the lord of the house.' Laughter cracked out of her and she pressed a pristine white handkerchief to her lips.

Jenna waited. Gave her a moment to recover herself but found she didn't need to prompt Ethel. The woman was a talker. It happened. Some people simply went with nerves or adrenaline and ran with it. Some wanted to vent, and some were simply lonely. As a police officer, it proved highly useful when they came across a talker.

'But this man. He wasn't nice. Gordon. He said to call him Gordon, but he was the devil.'

Jenna blinked, but remained quiet. Interesting that of the people she'd met so far in a short space of time, he wasn't well liked. She needed to revisit the girls. There was more. Definitely more.

'He's a show-off. Egotistical. Thought he could come along and invade our community just because his wife originated here. Doesn't mean you belong. She's a quiet thing. He thinks he can throw his money around and buy people's respect. It worked with some.' She half closed one eye and pinned Jenna with her sharp look. 'Respect isn't bought in my book, it's earned. Others aren't always so discerning. They believe along with money comes a God-given right to demand anything without question.' She paused while she scrubbed the end of her little bobble of a nose with her handkerchief. 'Not everyone saw it.'

In for the long haul, Jenna slithered herself up onto the edge of the stretcher bed and made herself comfortable. If she'd stayed where she was, her legs would be dead from the knee downward in no time at all. And this was not going to be a short interview.

She peered out the back of the ambulance a few paces away to catch sight of Mason. Hands plunged deep into his pockets, his head bounced up and down like a nodding dog as Mr Crawford, lit cigarette dangling from his mouth, appeared to be as verbose as his wife.

As she turned her attention back to Ethel, the old lady was off with barely a spare second to drag in a breath between sentences. The oxygen appeared to have revived her.

'Him and his family, they moved in a few years back. Six, I think. Kids seemed okay, settled in. Wife is nice enough. I don't remember her from a child. Very beautiful. Poor soul, having to put up with him and his shenanigans day in, day out.'

Before Ethel could move on, Jenna snatched her opportunity. 'Shenanigans?' Was the man having an affair?

'Ugh.' Ethel shook her head and sucked in her cheeks, so the flaccid skin sank inwards, forming wrinkled craters to make her face skeletal. 'Shooting. Shooting. All the time, the man was obsessed with shooting.'

As unobtrusively as possible, Jenna jotted down notes, taking care to keep eye contact with the old lady as much as possible. Gordon Lawrence. Did he have a firearms certificate? Something to check on. 'What did he shoot, Ethel?'

Her breath crackled in the back of her throat as she wheezed out a bitter laugh. 'Anything that damned well moved, I would imagine.'

'Did you ever see him shooting anything?'

'No, but I heard. The sound would carry over to our house when the wind was in our direction. Some days it was as if he was in our own back garden.'

The man obviously liked his guns. Ordinarily, it wouldn't be an issue in Shropshire. So many farmers and country dwellers had gun licences but they used their firearms for shooting foxes that encroached on their land, or birds that threatened their chickens. What he did sounded like target practice.

She looked back up at Ethel. 'How often did he shoot things?'

'Daily.'

Surprised at the quick comeback, Jenna scratched the side of her nose with the end of her pen. 'Did you ever report him?'

'Whatever for?'

'Disturbance of the peace.'

Ethel shrugged. 'Would there have been any point? Everyone shoots around here, it was more a matter of how much he shot. The frequency, the length of time.'

'Do you know if he was allowed to keep guns?' It wouldn't take her very long to establish if he was a registered keeper of firearms, a quick call, but that was for later. The priority now was to find out what had happened to the family. Were they in the house? Had they gone elsewhere for the evening? Until she knew, her hands were tied. They needed cold, hard facts. In the meantime, gathering information on the family didn't harm. With her police officer's instinct, Jenna knew that the best knowledge gathered was often when it appeared you were having a casual chat. A little nudge and a myriad of information spilled out.

'Oh, he was allowed. He boasted about his gun collection loud and often, when he wasn't firing it, that was.' Ethel jiggled about on the narrow cot bed, getting into her subject matter. 'Obnoxious man, made those poor children fire the guns too, I believe.'

This did not sound good. The more she heard, the more uncomfortable Jenna became. It may only be one old lady blowing off steam because she didn't appreciate the disturbance from her neighbour, but no police officer worth their salt ignored that little itch that told them something wasn't quite right.

Jenna tilted her head to one side. She didn't have the data on the children yet, but she would and it would be another line to follow if the children were under the age of fifteen. Under that, legally they weren't allowed to handle a firearm, even under supervision, let alone shoot one. Why the hell would anyone allow a child to shoot a gun? 'Did you see the children firing the guns?'

'No.'

Damn. She'd come to investigate a fire, a possible arson, not a whole host of firearms offences, but she'd still pick at it. 'How did you know, Ethel? What made you think the children fired guns too?'

'Because my great-grandchildren, Emma and Joseph told me. They come over for cake and tea every Thursday afternoon.' Warm pride softened her voice. 'Emma's in Rainbows with the twins. Oh, I forget their names, but sweet little ones.' She tapped her wrinkled forehead as though she could persuade the names from her mind. 'They sometimes come over to join Emma and Joseph. My Joseph is thirteen, he said the older lad, ooh, he's a bit older than Joseph, wasn't keen on shooting and the girls have to watch.' Her eyes brightened. 'Talisha and Geraldine. Nice girls.' She raised the oxygen mask to her face and sucked in a couple of lungfuls before she continued. 'Joseph said they didn't like to see the rats' guts splattered up the stable yard. The squirrels were even worse. Said it gave them earache and made their chests burn from the inside.' Her eyes turned cool. 'Joseph seemed to think it would be good to have a go. But there's no way he's allowed over there. Irresponsible if you ask me.'

Discomfort stirred in the pit of Jenna's stomach. She wasn't there to investigate the inappropriate use of firearms by a potentially dead man, but her ethics, training and natural curiosity all got the better of her. Nosiness was one of the most important attributes to have as a police officer. It may only be gossip they listened to, but it was often the gossip, if you cared to listen, that had a ring of truth about it.

'Did you see much of the family?'

'Not really.'

'How old are the twins?'

'Our Emma is...' she screwed up her face. 'Oh, my memory isn't what it used to be.' Ethel didn't appear to have anything wrong with her memory. 'Emma is eight, so the twins would be around that age. They were in the same year at school. Not that they go to the same school. They're at that posh, private school in Shrewsbury. You know. Ummm. Prestfelde.'

'Isn't there another child?'

Ethel frowned. 'Yes. The eldest girl goes to Shrewsbury Girls' High. Quiet. Sweet. She comes to collect the twins sometimes. Her mum'll stay in the car if she brings her, or sometimes on a good day, she walks across the fields. I've seen her with some older girls occasionally in Much Wenlock. Nice little group. Sophie and Olivia something or other. They go to the Girls' school too.'

Circling around, little connections, Jenna wrote Sophie and Olivia's names down. She'd definitely be going back to them for some more information.

'You say older girls. How old is the daughter, Poppy, isn't it?'

'Poppy. That's right. She must be sixteen. I know Sophie is a bit older, just passed her driving test, so I heard. Parents bought her a brand new little car.' Ethel's mouth twisted with disapproval. 'We used to have to earn anything we had. These days, it seems they're just given things. It doesn't give them any respect, these children. No respect for property or value for money, I'm sure.'

Jenna's spine creaked as she straightened the curve of it and jotted down a couple more notes. She needed to get Ethel back on track, but before she could draw breath, the old lady rattled on.

'Of course, I expect he...' she jerked her chin in the direction of the burning house. '...will buy his children bigger and better cars. Just to show he can.'

The picture Jenna was building of Mr Lawrence wasn't a favourable one. More important was whether the family were alive or not. None of the information Ethel was imparting was of partic-ular relevance currently, but it could be.

Jenna tapped the nib of her pen on the notebook.

Ethel wasn't going anywhere. They knew where she lived. Jenna could always come back to her if the need arose, but right now, she had the basics and she needed to get along, find out more. Ethel was a great source of information, but the immediate requirement was to establish if there were any survivors.

Jenna raised her head and scanned the area, narrowing her eyes against the burnished orange glow that only made the outer edges of the night even darker. Not many onlookers; it was too far out of most people's way to bother. Despite the radiance in the sky, it was late. People were in bed. Most people. Except...

Jenna closed her eyes and breathed in deep. When she opened them again, Kim Stafford, local reporter and bane of her life was still there, his back to her, but unmistakable, nonetheless, with his shaggy, dishevelled look. His thin, rounded shoulders gave him the appearance of a much shorter man in his long, loose mac. His thinning hair plastered to his head. If she wanted to stereotype him, she'd classify him as a flasher. Pathetic and snivelling.

Instead, she chose to ignore him. After all, he was outside the cordon, doing his job. Reporting. Shame it would be thin on facts and heavy on speculation. Just as it had been during her sister's kidnap ordeal. He'd accused the police of pulling out all the stops simply because Fliss was related to an officer. Never further from the truth, the stops were pulled out because Fliss was a missing person and there was the naked body of a dead woman at the scene of her disappearance.

Sure the lowlife would kick off the rumours again once Frank Bartwell's court case began, Jenna's fingers itched to get a hold of him and give him a good shake.

Kim hated Jenna, ever since they were in school and she humiliated him in front of everyone by bloodying his nose. He'd never forgiven her. She'd never cared until recently when his problem with her nudged at her work as he tossed lies and exaggerations about cases into the public eye.

No good would come of him turning up tonight. There'd be something unsavoury reported, some dig at the police. Especially if he knew she was there.

He glanced over his shoulder, his gaze met hers before it skittered away.

Oh yes. He knew she was there.

Jenna didn't have time for Kim Stafford. She had a job to do. As long as he stayed where he was supposed to and didn't sidle through the outer cordon, all would be fine.

Not that Kim Stafford had ever done as he was supposed to. He spent far too much time skimming the legal boundaries to get what he considered a story. Including the careless and ruthless use of a police source who he dropped like a hot coal when the finger of suspicion was pointed.

She'd have a quick word with Ted Walker before she left. Make sure he was aware of the lurking reporter. Knowing Ted, he already would be, but it didn't harm to make sure.

Jenna turned her attention back to the old lady. The cool flutter of night air teased through the ambulance where five minutes before the heat of the blaze had surrounded them. The wind had changed direction to whip away the bonfire smell and smoke.

Ethel hunched over, shoulders rounded in on herself and a fine tremor in her hands.

'Ethel, you must be cold.' Jenna reached out and took both of Ethel's icy hands in her own while she caught Sandy's astute eye.

The paramedic turned, all bustle and movement, to slip a light blanket over Ethel's legs. 'We're just going to warm you up, Ethel. Looks as though you trotted out in your nightwear, haven't you, my darling?'

Ethel's straight lips wobbled up into a smile. 'We wanted to make sure no one was hurt.' She flashed the house a wary glance. 'Nobody's come out.' Her jaw clenched. 'It got cold so quickly then.' She shuddered again as Sandy wrapped a honeycomb blanket around her shoulders and squatted by her side.

'Hold on a minute, my love, we'll get you seen to.' Sandy tossed Jenna a quick smile. 'A touch of shock setting in, I think.' She took Ethel's hands in her own and gave them a gentle rub. 'You were nice and toasty a few minutes ago. It doesn't take long for hypothermia to set in when you get a shock.' She gave Ethel's hand a last quick pat and came to her feet.

Sandy bounded down the steps out of the ambulance, lowering her voice as she took hold of the other paramedic's arm and led him away. When she returned, she swung the doors to the ambulance closed behind her and made her way to the electronic panel. She punched a couple of buttons and hot air flowed through to warm the cabin instantaneously.

Ethel huddled into the blankets and waited while Sandy carried out more checks. Her movements quick and efficient.

'It's so easy at your age, Ethel, to get cold.' Ethel's fingers jerked against Jenna's hands as Sandy continued. 'Even in this milder weather, you need to wrap up before you come out at night.' As Ethel opened her mouth, Sandy added, 'It only takes a matter of a few minutes when you're not very mobile for hypothermia to set in.' The fingers jerked again and then curled into a tight ball of gnarled bones.

Oblivious, Sandy moved away to rummage through the medical equipment. As she produced the blood pressure cuff, Ethel moved her head close to Jenna's, her lips almost grazing her ear, so she whispered her annoyance. 'That woman can't half talk and she's repeating herself. Does she think I'm stupid?'

Jenna rubbed the old lady's hands. Evidently, she didn't want to acknowledge her age or any vulnerabilities that accompanied it.

Jenna leaned back to allow Sandy to do her job, but she needed a couple more things from Ethel first.

'When was the last time you saw your neighbours, Ethel?'

With barely a pause before Jenna had finished her question, Ethel was off. 'I haven't seen them all winter. Heard them plenty. The acoustics carry sound across from their place to ours. Just like it carried the smoke over tonight.'

'Tell me about that.'

'They had a party. Oh my God, I prayed it would just stop. It seemed to go on forever. Loud banging music. Voices.'

Jenna resisted the temptation to look at her watch. If she'd gone to a party, they'd probably still be going strong. 'What time did it finish?'

'I don't know. About 11:00 p.m., I think. Far too late for those little ones. I lay in bed wide awake, listening to the voices and music. Then it went quiet. There was a long silence.' Ethel rolled her lips in on themselves, the wrinkles deepening as she did. 'I thought, thank God for that. I must have drifted off.' She screwed up her tiny face and her thinning skin covered her eyes in soft folds. 'And then there were gunshots.'

Jenna couldn't stop the fast blinks and only hoped Ethel didn't pick up on the shock that rippled over her skin. 'Gunshots? At that time of night?'

'Yes. I said, didn't I?'

She'd said he was always shooting. She hadn't said she'd heard shots earlier that evening. 'Didn't you report it?'

'Report it?' This time Ethel leaned forward to pat Jenna's hand. 'Oh, my dear, it never occurred to me. He did it every weekend. Friday, Saturday, for the past five years at least.'

'At night?'

'Especially at night.' Ethel's right eyebrow flicked up. 'That's when the rats come out.'

Didn't she just know it. Rats not only of the animal kingdom, but the human variety too. Darkness was always a friend to the rats of the world. And, like Ethel, Jenna smelled a rat. It may be something. It may be nothing. Accidents happened, fires started, but Jenna wasn't a coincidence kind of person. She lived by cold, hard facts.

A party.

Gunshots.

A fire.

Jenna blew out a breath. 'How long after the gunshots would you estimate it took before you could smell the smoke?'

'I didn't smell it. Not at first. I haven't a very good sense of smell these days, not like it used to be. When I was a girl, I could have told you what direction the scent of apple blossom came from, and from what variety of tree. These days, I wouldn't know if my dog pooped unless I stood in it.'

Jenna ducked her head so Ethel didn't see the smile. She didn't need any more encouragement than a captive audience to rattle on in the wrong direction. In an attempt to pull her back to the subject matter, Jenna placed her hand on Ethel's knee and felt the warmth seeping back into her. 'Ethel, how did you become aware of the fire?'

'Our fire alarm went off.'

'Okay.' That verified what the watch manager had said.

'The nice fireman out there said it often happens. That's how people realise there's a fire. The wind changed direction and the smoke came through our open window. I always sleep with the window open. I swear I never stopped getting hot flushes since the day I turned fifty-six.' She drew in a long breath of oxygen before removing the mask again, her lungs remarkable for a woman of her age. 'I almost peed myself when that thing went off. I was up out of bed with my dressing gown around me and my boots on my feet before Mr Crawford had stopped snoring.'

This time Jenna allowed herself a laugh. She wouldn't have put it past Ethel to have left her husband in bed.

'I'd have left him there, if it wasn't for the dreadful noise from that fire alarm.' She pulled her little handkerchief from her sleeve and swiped it across her eyes first and then her nose and Jenna felt the woman's sadness despite her apparent bravado. Ethel's watery gaze met hers and her voice sank to a hoarse whisper. 'I didn't see any of the family. Do you think they're all still in there?'

Jenna still hadn't managed to haul an answer from Ethel to give them a timeline from when the shots were heard to when the fire started. It may be relevant, it may have absolutely no connection. Jenna's gut instinct convinced her otherwise. 'I'm afraid I don't know yet, Ethel. Did you fall asleep after you heard the shots?'

Ethel sniffed. 'No. I don't think I did.'

'Okay.'

Jenna raised her head and caught Sandy's concerned gaze. 'I think Ethel needs to go home to bed now. We can have another chat in the morning, but it's late and she's cold and tired.'

'Agreed.' Sandy nodded her head. 'Ethel, would you like to get on the bed, I'll make you nice and comfortable and we'll take you home.'

Ethel reared her head up, her faded eyes sparking with life. 'Mr Crawford won't like that. He won't want me going off in the ambulance without him, and he won't want to leave his car behind.'

'Oh, I...' Alarm filled Sandy's eyes.

'Ethel, one of my officers will drive Mr Crawford home in his car.'

A loud snort exploded from Ethel. 'He won't let anyone else drive that wreck of a car.'

Jenna said nothing as she came to her feet to allow Sandy to manoeuvre Ethel onto the bed. The crunch and grind of her own knees made her wonder who was the eldest as Ethel hopped up onto the bed with apparent ease.

'Ethel. Thank you very much for speaking with me. If you don't mind, I'll call around tomorrow morning to have another chat.'

'That's fine, my dear, but don't come too early. Mr Crawford likes his sleep on a Sunday before we go to church.'

'I'll bear that in mind.' Although Jenna knew a sleep-in for a retired farmer would mean he'd be up at seven instead of five.

Sunday – they were already there, and Jenna would be lucky if she managed to go home and get her head down for a few hours before she needed to get back on it again.

She waited as Sandy pushed open the door to let her out of the ambulance and glanced over her shoulder as Ethel turned on her side and tucked the blanket under her chin, her weary gaze meeting Jenna's. 'I hope those children are okay. I hope they get them out.'

'Me too, Ethel, me too.'

She knew there was no chance. If they'd managed to get out before the fire took hold, she'd have known, but there was no one.

As she stepped from the ambulance, Jenna gazed over at the inferno lighting up the sky. From Ethel's information, Jenna now knew that the family party had been at the house and Gordon Lawrence had been firing his gun just before the fire. The fire crew hadn't brought anyone out. If the family had been in there, they were already long dead. Her job was to establish whether it was an accident, or a deliberate act.

10

Jenna drew in a breath and looked around to locate Mr Crawford and Mason. As she approached them, Mr Crawford turned, one painful step at a time on legs bowed with age and crippling arthritis.

'Mr Crawford.' She stepped closer and held up her badge. 'I'm DS Morgan.'

''Ow do?'

She smiled at the twang of old Dawley in his voice. One of the original villages of the new town, it stoically refused to be pulled into modern times. 'I'm fine, Mr Crawford. I've been speaking with your wife.'

'Ah, Ethel. I'll need to get her 'om, she's not as young as she were.'

Jenna's lips twitched as Mr Crawford shuffled to transfer his weight from one hip to another. 'That's fine, Mr Crawford. The paramedics are taking her home now in the ambulance.'

'She day need an ambulance.' His wrinkled forehead dipped low over intense blue eyes that hadn't lost any of their colour with age. 'I'm capable of taking my own wife 'om.'

He was the type of man, Jenna sensed, that wouldn't appreciate a young woman reaching out with a comforting touch. Instead, she drew her shoulders back. 'I'm afraid the paramedics would like to keep an eye on her a little longer. They were concerned about her breathing earlier and her temperature just took a bit of a drop.'

'Aye well, silly owd girl came running out in her nightclothes.' He indicated with a quick flick of his hands his own attire. Decked out in brown corduroy trousers, boots and a thick jacket over what Jenna assumed would be layers of clothes, perfectly ironed by his wife. With slow, stiff movements, he turned his head and squinted at the ambulance, its blue lights chasing shadows across the deep wrinkles in his face. 'I'd better follow her 'om, she'll need me to look after her. Gee 'er a cup of tea. Hers had a bit of a shock, I think. Hers not used to being woken in the dead of night.'

Without further preamble, he turned to hobble towards his car.

Worried about his fragility and age, Jenna made a quick decision. 'Mr Crawford.' Jenna raised her voice to catch his attention again. 'I'd like DC Ellis to drive you home if you don't mind.'

Mr Crawford continued his uneven gait and flicked his hand in the air to dismiss her. 'I've come in me own car. I can make me own way 'om.'

'It would be better if—'

'If you have anything further to say,' the old man scuttled fast enough to take Jenna by surprise, his voice fading as he neared his wreck of a car, 'I suggest you follow in your own car.' He jerked to a stop and spun around to face her, his neck and shoulders making the turn together in one rigid motion. 'Unless you need a lift.'

'No, I—'

Without a pause, he yanked open his car door, slipped inside and fired up an engine that rattled loud enough to be heard above the crackle of the fire. Before Jenna gathered herself, Mr Crawford was off.

Undecided, Jenna hesitated, torn between her duty to ensure the old man was safe and staying at the scene.

'Bloody hell.' Jenna scoured the perimeter of the cordon, patting her pockets for her car keys. 'Is there anyone else to question?'

'No one.' Mason yawned as he scrubbed a hand over his chin making it rasp against the stubble. 'I had a quick word with PC Walker. He's noted the details of any onlookers. There aren't that many. Most people have probably slept through it. The ones who are here have been questioned, but no one knows anything. Nothing urgent. No eyewitnesses. Any further questions will keep until later this morning.'

Jenna nodded her agreement.

Mason jerked upright and shook the tiredness away, 'Jesus, is that a classic?'

Jenna scrubbed the flop of hair back from her face. 'I don't think it's considered a classic, not with that much rust on it.' She really hadn't a clue.

'Isn't it the age that defines whether it's a classic, not necessarily the state it's in? Someone would do it up, I'm sure.' His unexpected enthusiasm did nothing to reassure her.

She took another glance at the rickety old car. 'Bet my badge it's not insured or MOT'd.'

As the Volvo rattled off along the dirt track and then took a sharp left over farmland, Jenna heaved out a long groan.

'Great.' Decision made, Jenna jerked her head towards the police vehicle. 'Quick. Jump in.'

Mason's wicked chuckle filled the car as Jenna strapped herself in.

'Right, let's get after Mr Crawford. Make sure he gets home safely.' She glanced over as the ambulance pulled away behind the ancient Volvo.

'Really, do we need to?'

'He's a bit unsteady. At this time of night, I couldn't forgive myself if he didn't make it home.' Jenna took one hand off the steering wheel to run it through her hair, almost tempted to tug it out. 'Please tell me the ambulance isn't going to follow him, that would mean we have to because, bloody hell, I didn't get their address.' She shot Mason a quick glance before concentrating on the two vehicles ahead. 'Did you?'

'No, Sarge, I assumed you...'

'Shit.' She blew out a breath 'Ted Walker will have it.' She'd bet her life on it.

As the ambulance continued towards the main road, Jenna contemplated which vehicle to follow. She made a snap decision. 'I think it's got to be him, because if we lose him and something happens, how the hell would we know?'

'I agree. Besides, it could be a long way around by road.'

'But legal.'

'I don't think we'd be doing anything illegal by pursuing him across farmland.'

'Not us, you dopey sod. If we need an excuse, I'll think of one. But, dear God, if I don't follow him and he disappears, we'll have to call out Air Unit One.'

Mason's mouth dropped open. 'You're kidding me, right?'

Only half kidding, she veered off the track to follow the dim tail-lights of the vehicle ahead. A slight hitch of concern tightening her throat. The last time she'd called out Air Unit One, it had been for the disappearance of her own sister.

With a light shudder, Jenna pressed her foot to the accelerator to speed up and catch Mr Crawford before he disappeared. Their vehicle bumped and banged over the uneven ground enough to rattle the teeth in her head.

'Maybe his Volvo isn't so old, it's just lived a hard life.' Mason's voice jiggled unevenly in rhythm with the car movement, little grunts emitting from his lips as he clung on to the grab handle above the door.

Jenna barked out a laugh. 'Did you see the registration number? It was made in 1985. 1985! Before I was born!'

Mason cast her a sly sideways look. 'Not that long before.' His teeth clacked together as she hit another pothole. 'Mind, but it did look rough.'

Jenna jerked her head in his direction. 'What are you implying?' She squinted at him in the pitch black to see if she could detect his sarcasm. The merest twitch of his lips made her think he'd had another poke at their age difference. Only a few months, but he liked to rub it in, have a little dig.

The breath whooshed from her as she hit a deep rut in the field. Mason's arm jerked out to slap on the plastic fascia and the loud grunt that accompanied it filled the car.

She huffed out a breathless laugh. 'Serves you right.'

The steering wheel jerked from her hands as they hit another pothole and she raised her foot from the accelerator to allow the car to slow down, comfortable she still had the old Volvo in her sights.

'Call Control and let them know we've left the manor house and are... hmm... pursuing Mr Crawford. Obviously, not in so many words.'

'Do we want to inform them yet when we don't even know where we're going?'

'Good point. Let's keep it to ourselves. Of course, I'm probably in the mire anyway because this vehicle is not going to escape unscathed from this.'

'Who would have known the territory would be so rough?'

Jenna sighed. 'We should have. One look at Mr Crawford and we should have known.'

'Yeah, feisty little bugger he is. Your typical old Dawley boy.'

Jenna's teeth jarred. 'What did he have to say about the fire?'

'It was short. It was sweet. He didn't like Gordon Lawrence. Thought he was an arrogant git, but he wouldn't wish harm on him and hoped the family had gone out for the night. He seriously doubted it.'

'Why?'

'He said Ethel couldn't stop whining about the noise from the party. Loud music. He's deaf as a post, though, so he heard nothing.'

'Did he mention how he noticed the fire?'

'Yeah, he was fast asleep when Ethel woke him. Says she has a screech like a vixen. Almost gave him a heart attack. She told him the house was on fire and to "get out, get out!" She flung on her housecoat...' he peered sideways at Jenna '...dressing gown, I assume he meant. He got himself dressed. Checked the house over and realised the smoke – which he said he can't smell since he kept pigs for the past sixty-four years – wasn't coming from their house. He couldn't smell it, but he could see it. Jesus, thank God he's got his eyesight, because all his other senses are fucked.' Mason's laughter hiccupped out of him as they hit another pothole. 'Mrs Crawford panicked and rushed outside. When they saw the fire on the horizon, Mr Crawford called it in. Fire, police, ambulance. Said he hadn't a clue who needed to know so he'd requested them all.'

'Well, he got it right. They needed everything.'

Mason shot out a hand to steady himself as Jenna flung the car over a rise, straight into a deep dip. Breathless, he took a moment before he spoke again.

'He was annoyed with himself. He reckoned they'd probably wasted time searching their own property before they realised. When he saw the direction it was coming from, he thought initially it might be a barn fire. They jumped in the car and drove over and then they realised it was the house. They were there before the fire tenders arrived. Just. It had already taken a good hold on the place.

Mr Crawford said he didn't even consider going in, the windows were already blown on the first floor. Ground floor had black smoke pouring out of it. He said if anyone was in there, it was too late.'

Jenna tightened her fingers on the steering wheel. 'That poor family.' Her chest tightened.

Mason grunted. 'Poor kids.'

She blew out a breath, blocked the dark thoughts that could do more harm than good if they were allowed to embed themselves. The self-preservation of the emergency services involved skills to block, laugh and move on. She wasn't yet ready for the last two, but she could block. For now.

The high beam from her headlights cut a swathe across the field as they took another rise before it dropped into a deep valley where a long rambling farmhouse made of Wenlock Limestone nestled. Outbuildings, like afterthoughts, scrambled outwards in all directions.

Ahead of them, the dull grey Volvo edged its way in between rickety old wooden gates and then shuddered to a halt, the whole car rattling as though it were about to shake apart, before it breathed a last breath and came to its final resting place.

Jenna pulled her vehicle over to park it alongside the dilapidated wall, leaving enough room for the ambulance to pull in as close to the farmhouse as possible.

Jenna stepped from the car at the same time as Mason. The loud screech of the Volvo door as it opened disturbed the still of the night, interjected by Mr Crawford's groans of pain as he hoisted himself out of the car and leaned against the open door while he squinted at them.

'We'd better get inside. I need to put the kettle on for Ethel. The owd girl will need a hot-water bottle.' He looked up, sad regret etched across his face and Jenna followed his gaze up to the orange glow beyond the horizon. 'It's a sad night, whichever way you see it.'

Her chest tightened. Sad indeed. For the loss of a house, a home and very likely a family. The tragedy of it knotted her stomach.

With a shake of his head, Mr Crawford pushed away from the car door and slammed it shut as he made his way up the broken pathway to the front door of his farmhouse. Without pause, he turned the doorknob and walked straight through the unlocked door.

Mason rubbed the back of his neck with his hand and sent her a crooked smile. 'He thinks the world of her.'

'Evidently.' Her opinion of Mr Crawford had taken an upward turn. 'I don't think we need anything further here tonight. Do you?' At the shake of Mason's head, Jenna stepped inside the old house. 'We'll just make sure the ambulance turns up and then go back.'

She turned right from the hallway into the kitchen, where old-fashioned lights cast a warm buttery glow. She took a quick look around the place to assess. Hoarders they may be, with piles of magazines and books, but the kitchen was clean. Not so much as a plate on the side. The old brass taps shone as though they'd been buffed to perfection.

Mr Crawford had his back to her and the sound of water spraying into the kettle filled the room for a long moment. He picked up a dishcloth and, in a completely natural move he'd prac-tised for years, he swiped the drips from the countertop and ran the cloth along the taps before he wrung it out with gnarled old hands and placed it back where he found it.

Capable, he probably ironed his own shirts. Typical of the old boys from the original villages formed long before the advent of Telford fifty years previously. Well established but still considered a new town.

Mr Crawford circled around with a stiff-legged motion, a twinge of pain slashing across his wizened features. 'Can I make you a cuppa?'

Tempted, Jenna ran her tongue across her teeth while she considered the invitation. 'No thank you, Mr Crawford, DC Ellis and I are just about to get off. Thank you so much for your assistance. If you think of anything further, please contact either one of us.' She reached out and placed a card with her contact information on the huge oak dining table, scrubbed to a pale whiteness.

He glanced at the card but left it where it was and reached instead into a cupboard for fine bone china teacups and a matching teapot. As he selected a canister of tea leaves, his face wrinkled up into a grin. 'The owd missus likes her tea made the proper way. I wouldn't want to disappoint her with anything less if hers had a shock. Her wouldn't like to think of those kids harmed in any way.' He narrowed his eyes as his gaze landed on hers. 'He war'nt a nice man, but her wouldn't wish bad on 'im.' He turned to stare out of the window at the approach of the ambulance, watched it swing around and reverse up to the gate, blue lights flashing in circles. 'It's a tragic thing, but her'll be fine. Once we know what happened.' He took a hold of the full kettle and, with a shaky hand, poured the boiling water onto the tea leaves in the teapot to scald them. 'You'll let us know, won't you? When you find out.'

'We will, Mr Crawford. We may need to come and see you and Mrs Crawford again. If that's okay?'

'Yes, it's a nasty business. Whatever happened. Nasty.' He squinted up at her. 'Ethel heard him shooting his guns again, not long before the fire alarm went off. Did she mention?'

Jenna inclined her head, interested to hear his viewpoint. 'She did.'

The furrows in his brow deepened. 'I hope he didn't do anything bad up there. I never did trust him.'

With a sense of disquiet, Jenna reached out and touched his elbow. Perhaps he was the type to take comfort from a young police officer. 'We'll look into it. I promise. All angles. Take care, Mr Crawford. We'll be in contact.'

Heading back outside, she stepped into the cool night air and a sky on fire as the paramedics opened the rear doors to the ambulance.

'Ethel,' Jenna raised her hand to wave goodbye as Ethel sat up and swung her slippered feet onto the ambulance floor. 'We're going to get off, but we'll see you again when we've all had a sleep.'

The lines of strain around Ethel's mouth deepened. 'Those poor babies.'

'We don't know anything yet, Ethel.' Jenna conjured up a weak smile for the sake of the old woman. 'Mr Crawford has a cup of tea made for you.'

Sandy looped her hand under Ethel's arm as the old lady made her way to the steps and raised her chin in acknowledgement. 'Ethel insists she can walk her way up the path to her own home.'

Ethel's rusty laughter jiggled as she took one cautious step at a time. 'Can't have Mr Crawford thinking there's something wrong with me. He'll only worry.'

Warmth at the affection the couple showed for each other spread through Jenna's chest and moved her concern along, so it became secondary. This time when she smiled, it came from the heart. 'Bye, now.'

As she slipped inside the car and fastened her seat belt, Jenna blew out a breath.

'She's probably right, you know. Poor babies. Poor everyone. It sounds as though they were in the house.'

Mason stretched a wide yawn, letting out a loud groan. 'Yep. What a shit night.' He shot her a narrow-eyed stare. 'Lawrence doesn't exactly come across as an exemplary character. Bit trigger-happy. You don't think he...?'

'I don't think anything yet.' Nothing she was willing to voice.

She nudged the start button and put the car in gear.

'Are we off home now?' His voice hopeful, Mason gave her a pleading smile.

Jenna checked the time on the dashboard. She'd love to go home. 'Sorry, Mason, we need to check that we've covered everything first. We'll drop back to the site, check on Ted Walker. It's not his area, officially, but I'm assuming he was the closest when the shout came up.' The location was equidistant between Ted's patch of Ironbridge and the area of Much Wenlock.

Mason slipped down in his seat and wrapped his arms around his middle in a petulant shrug. 'Just as long as you follow the road back. I'm not sure my spine can take any more if you try and cut across the fields.'

Jenna pulled off the dirt track and onto the main road. 'I'd never find my way back.'

'Yeah. We'd probably die out there in the wilderness.'

Jenna snorted out a laugh.

11

Poppy scrubbed shaky hands over her sweat-filmed face as she collapsed into the thick, dirty straw in the old barn, sending up a cloud of dust.

Forthefuckoffucksake!

She sucked in breath after breath of filthy air and puffed it out through her nostrils.

Stupid, stupid, stupid of her. She'd taken a diversion out of the woodland once she considered herself far enough away from the house not to be seen. It had proved too hard to push her way through the undergrowth, but she'd been halfway across the farmer's fields before she'd thought to turn her phone off.

Forthefuckoffucksake!

She should have known better, reacted faster, but she'd been too panic-stricken to think straight.

She had bloody Find-a-Friend on her phone.

Mum liked to know where she was. A safety net, she insisted. Daddy kept track of her – she'd had no say in that matter as he paid the bill. The twins thought it was fun to know where she was, they got a thrill out of checking up on her. She never minded. If they needed her it was okay. They were her babies too, she'd virtually raised them herself while Mum was too comatose to care.

Her heart gave a painful hitch as a mewling sob broke free. They'd never need her again.

She never allowed her younger brother to track her. That was just weird. But he was dead too. She'd heard the boom of her dad's shotgun.

The hot scald of tears tracked down her face as her heart contracted.

Aside from direct family, Olivia and Sophie were connected to Find-a-Friend, although she'd never trusted Chanel. Chanel was a bitch, always vying for the position of top dog. A drama queen, always ready to diss someone else to get ahead.

Poppy allowed her head to sink into the sharp prickle of straw while she clutched at the side of her chest, exerting a firm pressure to get the bleeding to stop.

Pain sent a rhythmic, pulsing throb to radiate outwards from the wound.

It was too dirty in the barn for her to risk a look and too dark without the light from her phone to see in any case. Another thing she didn't dare risk. To switch it on, to have a look, even for a moment, would be madness.

She did need to look though. To check for infection, bleeding, evidence of a lung wound.

She wasn't squeamish. She wanted to be a vet. She'd had her hands inside a cow's heart, her sensitive fingertips delicately investigating the heart strings while the other girls stood by pulling faces.

'*Eeeewww, Poppy, how could you?*'

She could. She'd spent her work experience at a vet's practice and loved every moment of it.

Another snivel escaped her as she pushed aside her memories.

Once she could move, she'd inspect it. If she could wash her hands, she'd have a good poke. It would hurt like crazy, but she needed to know how bad it was.

An airy, light-headed disassociation swept over her. For the first time since Daddy shot her, she had a chance to think about more than just escape.

She calmed her breathing.

The police would be looking for her. It was her fault. They wouldn't listen. They'd arrest her and she'd spend the rest of her life in prison.

Tears leaked from her eyes to roll down her temples into her matted hair.

She sucked in her breath.

Relax.

It was always better if you could relax.

She blew out a long, controlled breath. There was no rattle to her breathing. Her chest remained tight, but the pain was external, and she wasn't coughing up blood. Surely, she'd cough up blood if the bullet had pierced her lung?

She blew out another breath, her limbs going to liquid as exhaustion insisted on pressing down.

If it had been a lung shot, she'd have been dead by now.

She was safe. The old, black, dilapidated barn was a safe haven. No one could find her here. No one apart from Aiden knew she came here. And he was dead.

Daddy shot him.

Daddy shot everyone and then he set the house on fire.

She closed her eyes and fell. Down, down into the dark abyss.

12

Blue flashing lights competed with amber and gold from the raging fire as Jenna pulled the car up in front of the outer cordon and climbed out, leaving Mason to follow as he dragged his feet in a childish protest at not being allowed home. She was tired too, but for her own peace of mind, she needed to ensure that all the ends were tied up. For tonight at least. Because until they could establish the facts, there wasn't a whole lot more they could do.

Ted Walker raised his head, lines of weariness etched deep into his face as he huddled with a small group of uniformed officers.

Mason jerked his chin at the group as Jenna and he approached. 'Donna McGuire's back with Natalie Kempson.'

Relieved, Jenna smiled at the other women. The density of Donna's black hair bounced the bright lights around her head while the glow of the fire reflected in the liquid brown of her eyes.

'Ted, Donna,' Jenna stretched her smile further to include the new recruit, 'Natalie. How's it going?'

Natalie snapped to attention, eyes bright and intelligent. 'Good, Sarge. PC Walker was giving us a debrief as you arrived.'

'Excellent. Then PC Walker can continue.' She turned her

attention to Ted Walker and gave him a moment to take his notepad from his pocket.

'The cordons are all set up, Sarge. We have a register for anyone coming in and out of the area. SOCO have arrived and they're setting up in sector two.'

She peered over to where tarpaulins were being laid out and a large tent erected to shield the public from seeing anything. Her heart quickened as she gazed at the site where the bodies would be removed to once they'd located them.

'So far, there are no witnesses, other than Mr and Mrs Crawford who called it in.' Ted pointed the end of his pen at her, smiled. 'I saw you talking to them, but I have their details. Address, et cetera.'

At her hum of approval, he continued. 'I kept our favourite reporter away from Mr and Mrs Crawford, shuffled him over there while we had the paramedics look at Mrs Crawford. I didn't want Stafford taking advantage of anyone in a weak moment.' He inclined his head to indicate Kim Stafford in a small group with two others. '*Express and Star* photographer and a freelancer. I've segregated them. Don't need them sneaking under the cordon to get a closer look.'

'Indeed, we don't.' The man stuck around like a bad smell. The last thing she needed was Kim Stafford shooting one of his inaccurate reports out.

Mason grumbled in her ear. 'If you want me to go over and sort him...'

'No. It's okay, Ted has it all in hand.' Aware Mason would love to give Kim a good, hard punch for the trouble he'd caused when Fliss had disappeared, Jenna preferred to defuse the situation and not allow the reporter to take any more time, energy and resources than he already did.

With a twitch of his lips – Jenna suspected because most of the

PCs had a desire to take the local reporter into a corner and give him a good hiding – Ted nodded. 'I have. I've marked off tyre marks and put down markers of a couple of things for SOCO to look at. Nothing of any relevance at this stage, apart from one hell of a lot of empty shells from a shotgun over there.' He raised his arm to indicate an area on the far right of the property bordered by a wide stretch of fields. 'Looks like a target practice area. Difficult to tell because I can't get too close, but I'll get SOCO to check it out once it gets lighter.'

It gelled with what they'd already heard about Gordon Lawrence. The slide of discomfort deepened.

Mason looked up. 'It won't be long now before the sun comes up.'

Jenna sent him a sharp look to check if he was bemoaning his lack of sleep, but there was no hint as he gazed up at the night sky and a wave of sadness crossed his features.

With a collective sigh, the group paused, the weight of the atmosphere pressing down.

Not wishing to dwell on the matter until they had cold, hard facts in front of them, Jenna turned to PC Walker. 'Are you happy to continue as scene guard?'

Ted's face scrunched up. 'I should have been off at 2:00 a.m., Sarge. I've already worked over.'

Jenna shrugged. It was the way of things, she couldn't expect him to work through after a long shift. As she turned to Donna, the other officer shook her head too. 'We're off back to the station, Sarge. Off at 6:00 a.m. Got a lot of writing up before we go.'

Jenna nodded her understanding. Nobody particularly liked scene guard duty. Most boring job invented, but PC Walker had a handle on it.

'Can you give me another few minutes, Ted, while I get someone set up?'

'Sure. No problem. It'll take me that long to do handover notes.' He flipped his notebook closed and headed back towards SOCO.

Jenna turned to Donna and Natalie. 'I take it from the speed at which you've got back here, Sophie blew a negative.'

Natalie nodded while Donna patted her pocket, then flipped out her notebook. 'Yeah, she did. Nice girls.'

'Chatty.' Natalie's eyes glazed over and Jenna snorted.

'Enthusiastic. Good to know they were okay.' Jenna glanced over at the burning building and then back again. 'I'm going to have to question them all. We need to build up a profile. So far, I'm not all that keen on what I've heard about Mr Lawrence.'

13

Charlie Cartwright hovered on the far side of the inner cordon, but when he caught sight of Jenna, he made his way over, one large hand cupping his chest as though he was about to have a heart attack. A blast of heat whipped ahead of the wind, bringing with it fiery sparks and the scent of woodsmoke.

With a backdrop of burnished orange and the blackened shell of the house, Charlie moved closer. The hand holding his heart wriggled with a life of its own.

'Hey, Charlie, what's going on?' Jenna nodded her head at the hand on his broad chest. 'Are you okay?' They had a second ambulance on standby, but there was nothing about Charlie that indicated he was unwell apart from the fist clutched to his heart.

As his hand unclenched and moved again, a sheepish grin spread across his face and he ducked his head to peer down the front of his partially open jacket. Two tiny tufts of fur popped out from behind the zip followed by two chocolate-drop button eyes bulging with terror.

Mason leaned in, horror streaking over his features. 'Dear God, what the hell is it?'

Jenna smiled as she reached out a tentative hand to touch the fine chestnut hair on the miniscule dog's face. Its cold, wet nose quivered as the dog buried it in her hand to snuffle at the scent of her. 'Where did she come from? How come you've got her?'

Charlie grinned and shot Mason a quick wink. 'Babe magnet.' He jerked his head in the direction of the building. 'One of the lads found her under the oil tank. He almost booted her.' He raised his hand to scratch the top of her head. 'Poor baby. She was about to become toast, instead she was a drowned rat where we soaked the area down to keep it from combusting.'

Mason's lip curled. 'She looks like a rat.'

Charlie covered her head with one large hand. 'Don't let her hear you say that. She's a sensitive Sally. Poor bugger. I don't know how she survived.'

The dog's entire body trembled as her ears flickered back with uncertainty. Anxiety filled her bulbous eyes until they almost popped from her head and Jenna's heart melted. She reached out and dipped both hands into the top of Charlie's jacket to draw the little pooch out. Jenna snuggled her into her much thicker, warmer and more inviting coat while she felt rather than heard the dog's anxious whimpers, her tremors vibrating through to Jenna's heart.

'How come you ended up with her?'

'Because I'm the soft shit on the watch.' He shrugged. 'Other than that, I'm the one not actually hosing down the fire.'

Jenna stared up at the raging inferno as the dog snuggled in. 'Do we have an update?'

Charlie shifted to stand shoulder to shoulder with Jenna, snaking his hand around to scratch the top of the dog's head again and offer her some comfort, proving his words that he was a soft shit. 'Our further two tenders arrived a while back. NILO are coming from Worcester. He's on his way. Be here in another half hour.'

'Good.' It meant any information gleaned would be shared between all the forces involved; police, fire, ambulance. In the meantime, it was a case of Mason and her waiting for a building to cool down before SOCO could enter and tell them what the hell went on. 'Is there anything we can do while we wait?'

Charlie shook his head and pointed to the flames still licking out of the top-storey windows. 'Nothing anyone can do. We have the fire contained. We've managed to keep it to within the main house, the outbuilding on the left caught a few sparks, but we've controlled that, and we've got the hoses on the oil tank keeping the temperature down. With the ferocity of temperatures in there and the spread of it, we won't have this out for a good few hours. Hard to predict exactly how long.'

'If there was anyone in there...?'

He puffed out his cheeks as he shook his head. 'They didn't stand a chance.'

'Okay. We're going to get off in a minute. Get some sleep before we're needed again. PC Walker has everything under control by the look of things, but I'm about to relieve him and leave you a scene guard who will keep an eye on things until SOCO can gain entry into the building. Until then, we'll know nothing.'

'You take advantage of the opportunity to sleep. It may not come around too quickly again if this proves to be as big a job as we think. Me, I'm here for another two hours, then we'll have another crew relieve us. It's been a long night.' Eyes bleak, they met hers. 'This is a hard one.'

He reached out and cupped the top of the little dog's head in the palm of his hand, taking comfort from the living.

All jobs were challenging, but some hit home harder than others, especially those where children were involved..

Jenna's fingers bumped Charlie's as she dipped her hand into the front of her jacket to smooth the dog's fluffy ears. 'What do you want me to do with this one?'

Charlie held out both hands and wiggled his fingers in an invitation for her to hand the chihuahua back.

Jenna fished inside her coat and lifted the dog out. The tiny body quivered all over with powerful shudders enough to shake its tiny frame apart. The dog's pitiful whimpers grabbed her heart and squeezed. She nestled it back in and shook her head at Charlie. 'Ah, poor baby. She's too scared.'

His lips kicked up in a wry smile. 'We couldn't get hold of the dog warden. He's not picking up. You want to take care of her?'

She flicked a quick glance at Mason to catch the eye-roll. It didn't matter, a little princess like this needed cosseting in the bosom of a loved one, not putting in a holding cell until someone claimed her. Her gaze met Charlie's spry one. She'd been conned. Definitely. It wouldn't have mattered. She wasn't about to let the little sweetheart go.

Jenna gave the dog's head a gentle scratch as she snuggled back in, the shudders coming in little waves. 'See you tomorrow, Charlie.'

'Yeah, see you tomorrow, Jenna.'

Weary, Jenna dragged her feet as she made her way through the outer cordon. She scanned the area for a uniformed police officer to assign as scene guard. Her heart sank as she spotted PC Lee Gardner. 'Shit.' Her breath puffed out on a sigh. 'Why does it have to be him?' She'd been obliged to put in a complaint against him a few months previously when she'd suspected him of passing on information to Kim Stafford. Despite internal investigations, nothing had come of her complaint. No evidence had been produced. The only accusation he had faced was from Detective Inspector Taylor for insubordination. He held a grudge and she preferred not to deal with him. On this occasion she didn't have a choice in the matter.

Mason shoulder bumped her. 'Oh great. Of all the uniforms, we have to get the wassock.'

She hesitated to join the officer as he stood alone with his back to them looking out over the messy scattering of vehicles that had pulled up. Hands on hips, he surveyed the scene as though he owned it, but he hadn't made a move to contain it.

Mason leaned in close and lowered his voice. 'I didn't know he was back.'

Jenna let out a disgusted snort. 'Yeah. I heard he took a couple of weeks' holiday after his disciplinary hearing and then tagged some sick leave on, citing stress. He only bloody had his wrists slapped. Disciplined.' She rubbed her hands together to chase the chill away, then slipped one back into the top of her jacket to calm the dog as her panic escalated as soon as Jenna had removed her hand. 'His insubordination is registered on his record, but back to duty. I don't think internal enquiries took the incident as seriously as we did. They certainly claimed they couldn't find any proof that he'd leaked information to our local friendly journalist.'

'What about the family connection?'

'No proof he actually contacted his brother-in-law and told him anything.'

'Wanker.'

She barked out a laugh and, with no other obvious choice in the matter as the other PCs in the vicinity all appeared to be occupied, she headed towards Lee Gardner.

'PC Gardner.'

The slow turn and flat look he raked over her told her he'd been aware of her presence at least since they arrived back from the Crawfords' house. She'd not even noticed him.

'PC Gardner,' she repeated before he could turn away and pretend not to have heard her. His attitude didn't bode well for the future, but it wasn't her concern. He wasn't one of hers and normally she'd not need to deal with him.

On this occasion, she needed him to carry out his job and for that to happen, she had to not only remain the commanding officer, but also, it appeared, the adult. She summoned up a smile, but from his response, she suspected it looked as tight as it felt. 'I need to appoint a scene guard.'

'And...?' If he could have got away with folding his arms over his chest, she was convinced he would have. For the time being, though, it appeared he was only on the cusp of his next foray into insubordination.

Jenna lowered her chin and gave him her mother's look. It had always worked for her on Fliss. It was a command. Eyes flat and a superior lift of the left eyebrow. It got Mason every time, not to mention DC Ryan Downey. Whether PC Gardner would be influenced was yet to be seen. 'You'll be delighted to hear I've elected you, PC Gardner.' She gave him a chance. Waited a beat. 'Would you mind complying, or would you prefer me to go via your inspector?'

He cricked his head to one side, a jerky move. 'You might want to find someone else, I'm only on until 10.00 a.m.'

'Excellent, that gives us a good few hours.' With a decisive clap of her hands, Jenna took a step back and then pressed her hand against the top of the dog's head to stop it leaping out of the top of her jacket in fright. 'I'll arrange to have someone take over by then.' She raised a hand in salute and took another step back, then another as the man continued his hard stare in response to her own.

As she reversed into Mason, he leaned in. 'Please don't prostate yourself on the floor, it's embarrassing enough as it is, Sarge.'

Jenna whipped around to face him but didn't have the control to shoot him her mother's look. PC Gardner had managed to rattle her again. Instead, she drew in a breath and sailed past Mason to the police vehicle.

Mason followed. 'I wish they'd send him to another division. Honest to God, every time I see him, I want to punch him.'

'You want to punch most people.' As they approached the car, Jenna shoulder-bumped Mason. 'You drive, I'm otherwise occupied.' She stroked the top of the tiny dog's silky head and peered down into the top of her coat as it quivered in response to her attention. Poor thing.

Still seething, Mason grabbed the door handle and yanked it open harder than necessary. He was in the car, buckled up, before Jenna had rounded the bonnet.

As she slipped inside, she cast him a sideways glance. 'It's best to ignore him.'

'You didn't. You made a beeline for him.'

'I'm his senior officer. I needed to make sure I appointed someone as scene guard.'

'You could have chosen someone else.'

'No. He was the only one free.'

'Bollocks.'

He stabbed his index finger onto the start button and the engine roared to life with a little more pressure than necessary on the accelerator.

'It isn't bollocks.'

'You rub each other up the wrong way. End of story.'

'He's a cocky...'

'Twat.'

As Mason broke the tension, Jenna's laughter hooted out as he steered the car along the single track.

A fine drizzle settled on the windscreen as Mason turned onto the main road back towards Ironbridge and the windscreen wipers took a lazy swipe across the screen to streak it in grease.

Jenna sucked air in through her teeth as the beam of light from the headlights picked out the wet settling on the tarmac road. Hopeful, she cupped her hands around the dog's face and spoke directly to her, rather than Mason. 'This could be good. It may help put out the fire.'

'Unless the roof gives way, then any forensic evidence will be washed away.'

'Let's hope that won't happen. We need SOCO in there as soon as feasible to find out what the hell went on. Was it an accident? Was it deliberate? Where the hell are the family?'

Mason let out a robust yawn and flexed his shoulders against the seatback. 'Nothing we can do now.'

'You're right. We'll slip into the station, debrief what we have so far.' She checked the time. Already almost 5:05 a.m. She slipped her fingers under the dog's chin and gave her a gentle scratch until the dog's muscles went to liquid and she closed her eyes and fell asleep in the snug nest Jenna had made for her in the front of her coat.

Jenna scanned the horizon as she settled back and relaxed as the miles flew past, no longer a solid black blanket interspersed with tiny pinpricks of white, but a hazy bluish grey curtain, heavy with rain giving a slow lift from the bottom to tease her with the promise of dawn breaking and the sun rising on a day she could only hope would get better.

She checked the time again. 'Right. With the full shift we worked yesterday and another one almost over, let's work until midday. That's twelve hours straight again. I'll do a handover, then we'll get ourselves off home, get our heads down and start fresh tomorrow at 6:00 a.m. How does that sound to you?' She glanced over at Mason, hands relaxed on the steering wheel, gazing straight ahead on the long and winding road, his snit with Lee Gardner already forgotten.

'It was supposed to be our day off. I promised Fliss Sunday

lunch out at The Woodbridge. I booked it for 1:00 p.m. We'd planned to walk Domino beforehand and take him in with us.'

'Nice. Make sure he doesn't snatch your beef off your plate.' Mason was definitely a beef guy.

He tucked his chin down, his bottom lip poking out. 'I'll be bloody bad company and too knackered to move.'

'Change the time. They serve all day, don't they?'

He tilted his head to squint at her. 'They do, but they're popular.' He turned into Malinsgate police station car park and reversed the car into a space. He killed the engine, flipped open his phone and tapped with some urgency at his screen. He slumped back. 'They have a 5:30 p.m. slot.'

'Great, take it. Fliss will understand, she's used to my schedule constantly changing and you may not get much of a chance once the court case starts.' The lucky guy, to have a girlfriend already accustomed to police hours.

Jenna considered her own situation and pulled out her phone to make a quick online reservation at Clays of Broseley, surprised she'd managed to grab a slot at 7:00 p.m., for what must have been a cancellation. As far as dovetailing was concerned, she'd give it a go.

She shot Adrian a brief invitation.

A fast slide of delight warmed her at his immediate response. She smoothed her fingers over his message. Not sloppy, not romantic. Just thoughtful and welcome.

'Right then. We have a plan.' She'd learnt over the last couple of cases how important it was to have a plan. To take care of her own health and well-being to enable her to work her most effective. 'Take your downtime while you can. There'll be more than enough to keep us busy once the fire service and SOCO get into that house.' She let the silence hang for several minutes before she spoke again. 'This is going to be messy, Mason.'

She raised her gaze to meet his grim one.

14

Mesmerised, he melted into the shadows of the tall pine trees that formed the boundary to Kimble Hall and avoided the swathe of headlights flooding from the vehicle as it passed by his viewpoint.

The corners of his mouth twitched up into a bitter smile as he surveyed the whole scene, lit up before him to highlight every last detail.

Interesting. The house had erupted into an inferno that the fire service had been unable to contain. Wind conditions whipped up to perfection. Luck and good planning were both on his side.

He leaned his shoulder against the nearest tree while he scanned the area below him, noting the position of the police officers, the fire crew, the observers.

When the old couple had turned up, he'd had a moment to wonder if they could ruin things. But it hadn't made a difference. It was too late, the fire too intense.

He turned his head to watch the taillights of the retreating car disappear around the bend and squinted into the distance as the pale hues lightened the rain filled sky.

Time to go. He shouldn't have stayed as long, but the temptation had been too much.

Satisfied, he pushed away from the tree, turned his back and walked away.

A successful night's work.

15

Boom!

Poppy jerked upright, the breath jamming somewhere between her chest and throat as heat flooded her face. She slapped a hand to her ribs as she gasped in air, desperate to breathe as red-hot pokers seared through her. The echo of shotgun reverberated around her head and made her question whether it was real or imagined.

She flopped back onto the straw, her heart hammering so hard she thought it might burst from her chest. A nightmare. It was just a nightmare.

She closed her eyes and tried to level off her breathing only it wasn't *just* a nightmare, it was her living nightmare.

Fire burned over a side so stiff she thought her skin would split in two if she moved. But she had to move. There was no choice unless she lay there and died. And she wasn't willing to die.

Pained grunts fluttered from her dried lips as she pushed herself, one-handed, back into a sitting position as beads of sweat popped out across her forehead and upper lip.

Bright sunlight streamed through the narrow gaps between the wooden slatted barn door to cast an eerie light all around as dust bunnies danced on the air. The irony of the beauty of it didn't escape her. The most romantic setting, soft sunlight and dust bunnies. She gazed around while she tried to shake off the wild spinning of her head.

A shudder wracked her body. The injury wasn't the only reason she was stiff. The chill of the night air may have worn off, but the barn was a bitterly cold draughty hole.

Her teeth rattled in her head and she scooted to the edge of the bales of straw she'd laid on, not even bothering to pluck strands of it from her hair. Her knees creaked as she edged onto the barn floor and stepped over the abandoned wooden feeding trough, letting out little grunts for each step she took.

Poppy crept stiff-legged to the double barn doors and cracked them open an inch to peep out. The furthest outbuilding from Sunnyside Farm, Poppy was fairly confident no one would stumble on her. Old man Crawford had long since stopped coming out so far. Only when his sons visited did he venture further, his old springer spaniel, Bess, by his side. The twins loved to play in the old ramshackle barn when Mr Crawford's great-grandchildren came to visit after they'd finished school each Thursday. In the same year as Talisha and Geraldine, they went to the local comprehensive. They all ran wild for a couple of hours, just happy to see each other, until Poppy was sent to collect the twins and bring them back home.

She leaned against a wooden post by the barn doors and screwed her eyes shut to rid herself of a memory that could serve to destroy her if she thought too hard about it.

Ready to move, she bumped the doors wider and stepped out into the early-morning sunshine, absorbing the heat on her face as she sidled around the edge of the barn to squint down at the farmhouse, which looked like an abandoned scrap yard.

The heap of a car that belonged to Mr Crawford was missing

and Poppy sighed, relief making her weak. So weak, she could barely put one foot in front of another.

It was Sunday. Without switching on her phone, she had no idea what time, but they were most likely at church. Much Wenlock church every Sunday was their habit. Ethel told her, it was a social affair. Then they'd go to one of their sons' houses for Sunday lunch. Poppy loved Ethel. She put a stop to that thought mid-flow too. But if they were at church, it meant it was later than she thought. She cast a quick look up at the bright, clear sky with the sun already high, as though that could give her a hint.

Feet dragging, she forced herself onwards, her gaze focused on the khaki green cracked and peeling front door she'd never really noticed before. Compared to the perfection of Kimble Hall's double opening front door, the Crawfords' door gave the impression of a house lived in and loved.

It would be unlocked. She'd never known them to lock it. Though why they would believe they were safe just because they lived in the country, she had no idea. No one was safe. No matter where you lived. No matter who you lived with. She'd learnt in the harshest way possible never to trust. Death was only a step away.

16

Ethel's cupboards overflowed with every kind of food imaginable. Like her husband, she was a hoarder. Used to her great-grandchildren visiting, she made sure there was a plethora of fun food to choose from.

Poppy didn't want food. Her stomach lurched and her gag reflex leapt in to grab at her throat.

She opened each cupboard to check inside until she came across the one she needed. The one with medical supplies. Too many to contemplate. Poppy stared at the masses of accumulated boxes of plasters, paracetamol, ibuprofen, bandages, sterile wipes, antibacterial wash.

Light-headed, she rolled back on her heels and blinked to focus on the contents of the cupboard. There was so much there and so neat and tidy. Would Ethel notice if she took some?

Poppy's stomach clenched. Stealing wasn't something she was familiar with. She'd never taken anything that belonged to someone else before. Never had the compulsion to.

She reached out a hand, then hesitated, her insides turning to jelly as she tried to imagine what Ethel would say if she thought Poppy had stolen from her. Would her face be wreathed with disapproval? Would she understand?

Desperation overrode guilt until Poppy glanced around and snatched a carrier bag from a pile of them stuffed into a box. She raised herself up on her toes so she could reach to the back of the cupboard. If she didn't dislodge the items at the front, Ethel would never know. A worm of worry wriggled, but she didn't have any choice.

Into the bag, she threw a box of paracetamol, ibuprofen, a small bottle of neat Dettol – that was going to sting – bandages and cotton wool. As little as she could take so it was less likely to be noticed.

She swiped the back of her hand across her forehead and stared at the sweat coating her skin. The tremble in her fingers rattled the bag she held.

She darted a quick glance out of the window. She could never be too sure if they would come back or not. They'd taken Bess with them, but that didn't mean to say they couldn't return.

With one more reach into the cupboard, Poppy drew out a small packet of steristrips and dumped them in the bag before she closed the cupboard door and turned to face the kitchen again.

Her stomach contracted once more. She may not feel up to eating, but if she didn't, she was just as likely to die of starvation as blood loss. And didn't Mum always say she needed a cup of hot tea and a biscuit whenever she gave blood? It restored her energy, just as wine restored her good humour.

As Poppy scanned the kitchen, her pulse tripped a beat. Ethel may be old, but her great-grandkids kept her up with the times and the sight of an iPhone charging lead neatly coiled and plugged into the wall beside the kettle gave Poppy's chest a little squeeze of excitement.

Barely any battery left, Poppy plugged in her own phone and

propped it up against the splashback tiles next to the sink. As the screen burst into life, she snatched it up, breath coming in fast gasps. Her fingers shook as she pressed her thumb against the power button desperate for it to switch off before any of her profile downloaded.

Heat seared up her neck and suffused her face as she placed it back with trembling fingers and melted against the counter while her heart rate returned to normal.

She touched the side of the kettle with tentative fingers. Still hot, but not too hot. She looked from the plastic bag to the bench and back again. It would be far more hygienic to tend to her wound here. Her pulse throbbed as her breath quickened. Dare she?

What if they returned?

She squinted out of the kitchen window.

She could do it. If she was quick.

She dumped the bag on the bench and gingerly raised her arm to slide it from her hoodie sweatshirt. Each move sent lightning bolts of pain stabbing deep into her side. She bit down on her lip as she let out little mewling whimpers.

'Forthefuckoffucksake!'

Air whistled through her teeth as she clenched them together and she whipped her head around. Where the hell had the T-shirt gone?

She took two steps back and peered into the passageway that led to the front door. The blood-stained rag lay in a small heap on the floor.

Heart pounding, Poppy darted forward and snatched it up. If she'd missed that and someone had seen it, they would have known.

Ethel was lovely, but she was an upstanding citizen. If she knew she was harbouring a criminal, she'd have the police around.

Poppy grabbed another plastic bag, shoved the bloodied T-shirt into it and then rolled it into a ball. She'd think about what to do with it once she'd cleaned herself up.

She picked up the paracetamol, popped two into her hand and then two of the ibuprofen. She should eat before she took them, but she didn't have time. She grabbed the little water glass on the windowsill and filled it with water, throwing the tablets into her mouth and gulping everything down, surprised at how thirsty she was. Twice more she refilled the small glass before she rinsed it, dried it and placed it back where she'd found it.

The sink looked clean enough, Mr Crawford was always wiping around it when the great-grandchildren and twins were there. Poppy contemplated it for a moment before she opened another cupboard. The one she already knew Ethel kept her mixing bowl in. She poured the hot water from the kettle in and leaned against the bench, each move sapping the strength from her.

With her hoodie half off, Poppy slipped it one-handed over her head and let it drop to the floor, the bloodstains on the pink material turning brown. She sucked in a breath. The wad of cotton wool on the bench wasn't about to go anywhere near cleaning up the amount of dried blood skimming over her flesh.

In the utter silence, she dropped her head down so she could cup it in both hands, the burn worth the movement. Dry-eyed, she waited for the weakness to pass.

Naked to the waist, the cool chill of air had her shuddering and looking up again. At least here, she could see through the window, all the way along the driveway.

Poppy slid open a drawer, took out one of Ethel's neatly ironed tea towels and dipped it into the water. She made quick work of rubbing the dried-on blood from the lower half of her side, but the rub and stretch of it had black shadows threatening to overwhelm her. She drew in long pulls of breath and rested, her hipbones pressing hard against the cupboards while she dipped and swiped again, this time down the length of her arm.

She skimmed the tea towel over her left breast and smeared the blood, every move she made with her arm left her gasping for breath, but she flexed her fingers, then rinsed the thin cotton tea towel in the bowl, watching as her blood bloomed in pink clouds across the water. She squeezed it out, threw the water into the sink and refilled the bowl with the last two inches of boiled water from the kettle. She sloshed in some of the Dettol, ripped off a piece of cotton wool and dipped it in as she prepared herself to look for the first time at the gunshot wound.

She sucked in a breath.

Her skin pebbled up and tightened with goose bumps.

Poppy glanced at the kettle and snatched it up, filled it again one-handed and switched it on. A cup of tea. That's what her mum would say, after giving blood. And Poppy had given a whole stream of blood.

She shot a quick glance out of the window and squinted as she looked at the furthest point she could see. Held her breath. Waited. No one coming. No one knew. Yet.

They might think she was dead with the rest of them.

Maybe she'd have to remain dead.

When she had time, she'd think about it, but the most important thing was to clean herself and dress the wound.

She dipped her hand into the cooling water and squeezed the cotton wool with fingers shaking so hard she could barely hold onto it.

Technically, she knew what to do. Mum had always let her see to the twins when they skinned their hands and knees, not through a lack of care, because her mum adored them all, but because she knew Poppy had a passion to look after her baby sisters.

She held her breath and poked her tongue out of the side of her mouth as she raised her left arm and twisted to expose the tender flesh at the underside of her budding breast. They'd grown bigger lately, probably because she'd gone on the pill when she knew Aiden and she were about to have sex. Or maybe because she was having sex. She didn't know. Didn't care. She'd never have sex again. She'd never have Aiden again.

She drew in a breath and pushed Aiden from her mind. If she allowed herself to think of him, she'd be destroyed. She needed every resource she had just to carry on.

Surprised not to see her flesh gaping open, she inspected the entry wound. The flesh around it charred and singed like a black halo, feathering outwards in a scattered speckle of dust. But it wasn't dust. Dust would wash off. Burned skin wouldn't.

Another quiet sob squeezed from her tight throat as she placed the cotton wool against the wound and almost passed out.

Forthefuckoffucksake!

She screwed her face up, breath soughing through her teeth. But she kept the wad of cotton wool pressed against the bullet wound. Fresh blood oozed out as she took the pressure off and removed the cotton wool.

Sure there was a lump there, Poppy stuck her index finger into the top of the Dettol and tipped it up, soaking her finger in the antibacterial liquid before she put the bottle back on the bench.

With short, laboured breaths, she touched her naked finger against the wound. Not as big as she thought. And only an entry point. Which meant the bullet was in there.

She closed her eyes and worked her finger inside the wound, following the direction of the hole towards her back. The small slide of a groan slipped from her lips as her finger encountered a hard lump. She held still, her head spinning in wild revolutions as she gave her finger another delicate wiggle.

She sucked in a breath.

It was the bullet.

It was right there.

It hadn't gone into her lung, it hadn't pierced her heart. It had skimmed through layers of skin and sinew and wedged solidly into her rib.

She withdrew her bloodied finger and stared as crimson pumped a lazy stream to trickle down her side again. She plucked another piece of cotton wool and this time soaked it in pure Dettol before she pressed it against the wound.

Pure fire ripped through her and in the silent house, no one could hear her scream. Knees like water, she propped herself by her elbows against the bench and clenched her teeth until she was sure they'd break. Still she kept the pressure on until her the screams faded to desperate whimpers.

She pushed the weakness back as she searched the horizon with a gaze darkened at the edges.

She wasn't about to die. But she was going to need help. The bullet needed to come out. For now, it was enough for her to stop the bleeding, dress the wound and get the hell out of the Crawfords' farmhouse.

Every movement drained her as she puffed out and reached for the steristrips.

Forthefuckoffucksake!

With fingers that trembled so hard, the steristrip twined around them until she crumpled them up and threw them on the bench. Tears rolled down her cheeks as she hauled in a hard breath. She could do it. She had to do it.

She took one more steristrip, held onto her breath and stuck it across her wound to pull it closed. She grabbed one of the adhesive dressings, peeled off the backing and pressed it firmly in place, realising that the constant buzzing in her ears was her own rasping breath.

Finished, she leaned weak against the sink, her body cooling by the minute so tremors ran through her body. She recognised it as shock, but the knowledge didn't help as her fingers shook so hard she could barely push the items back into the plastic bag.

She needed to warm up. She needed clothes that weren't covered in blood.

Ethel was far too small for her to borrow her clothes.

Mr Crawford wasn't though.

Poppy peered out the window for another quick check, then pushed herself away from the bench, forcing each step to the back of the kitchen, where a small oak doorway led to what the twins called the servants stairway.

She gripped the thin wooden rail running along the wall to haul herself up step by step and sank to her knees when she reached the top.

With no idea which room to go into, she took the nearest and crawled on hands and knees inside.

She pushed back on her haunches and chose an enormous dresser. She dragged out three drawers, almost too heavy for her to pull, before she found what she was after.

None of them looked like the clothes Mr Crawford would wear and Poppy wondered if they belonged to one of the sons. She didn't care. She hauled on a short-sleeved T-shirt that hung loose from the shoulders almost to her thighs. She grabbed another one. Long-sleeved, it fell past the tips of her fingers once she'd got it on, but that was probably for the best.

She yanked open another drawer and grabbed out two enormous sweatshirts. They definitely belonged to the sons. Ethel had evidently never disposed of them. Possibly kept them for when the boys came over to help out on the farm.

Poppy jerked the sweatshirt over her head, thankful it wasn't tight as each move tugged at her injury. Her teeth rattled as she jammed the second sweatshirt under her good arm and made for the stairs.

Panic sliced through her as she headed down them, shouldering through the door at the bottom anxious to grab another quick check out the window.

Still no sign of them coming back, Poppy whipped a carrier bag out of the cardboard box, flung open Ethel's food cupboard door and reached in. She'd need to eat to give her the strength back that had sapped away in the last hour or so.

Careful to take from the back, she selected ring-pull tins. Baked beans, pineapple chunks, ravioli and a packet of Uncle Ben's rice. She bent to look at the lower shelves and drew out a packet of Jammie Dodgers and a bar of chocolate and rammed them all into the bag.

Poppy stared at the kettle. No chance of a cup of tea now, but she opened another cupboard and took out three cans of Coke. A poor substitute for her mum's cure-all, but it would have to do.

Would Ethel notice if cutlery went missing? Poppy slid open a drawer and took out a fork and spoon. She tilted her head to one side, then slipped one of the small, pointed-end steak knives from the drawer and pushed it into the carrier bag with the rest of her loot.

With another furtive peek out of the window, her heart almost exploded from her chest as Mr Crawford's rusty old car turned into the track and stuttered towards the farmhouse.

Wild panic shot adrenaline racing through her veins. Poppy scooped up her bloodied hoodie, stuffed it into the bag with the rolled-up T-shirt and clenched the bags to her chest as she whipped a frenetic gaze around the kitchen to make sure everything was in place.

With one last glance out the window, she shot out of the front door. She crouched low, to dip down below the level of the stone wall surrounding the front of the farmhouse. With a quick glance behind her, she slipped through the gap into the field and away.

17

Forthefuckoffucksake!

Poppy reared her head up. Heart pounding, she skidded to a halt.

Her phone!

She'd forgotten her fucking phone.

She dumped the bags on the ground and shot back to peer over the stone garden wall which normally came to chest height on her. Pain seared through her side as though it was being ripped apart and she pressed a hand against the dressing, each gasping breath burning her chest. Open-mouthed she sucked in air and pushed aside the darkness that threatened. She had no time for that. She needed to be strong.

The old car was still a way down the track, spluttering and coughing as it approached. She could only hope Ethel and Mr Crawford's eyesight was as shit as it should be at their age. Knowing her luck, Ethel would have better sight than a shitehawk.

Heart lodged in her throat, Poppy ducked down, pushing aside the pain and exhaustion as sheer panic shot through to lend her strength.

Red-hot pokers stabbed her chest as she crouched, each breath soughing out. She grabbed the handle of the old front door and shoved it open a crack. She dashed through the narrow opening, slammed it behind her as quick as she could and raced into the kitchen, all the time hunkered down below the level of the countertops.

She popped up and snatched her phone off the bench, wrenching out the charging lead. With fingers that shook hard, she barely managed to roll it back into the neat coil she'd found it in.

In a heartbeat, she bobbed her head up and stared at the approaching car. She'd never make it before they saw her.

Head exploding with the force of the pulse pounding through her system, Poppy turned and threw herself along the passageway leading to the back of the house. She'd never been through the house, only ever entering the kitchen.

She darted into a huge old conservatory and skidded to a halt. She grabbed the handle of the glass door and shoved.

As it flew open, she dashed through and slammed it behind her and then circled around to grab the bags she'd left on the ground just as the bump and grind of the car spluttered to a halt at the garden gate.

Without a second thought, Poppy darted for the far side of the garden and lobbed herself over the wall.

She landed full stretch out on the soft carpet of grass. Agony rocketing through her ribs as she belly-crawled for as long as she could before she pushed to her feet and ran.

Ran for safety.

Ran for the black barn.

18

It was a shithole.

He hadn't visited for months and in those few months, they'd managed to destroy it.

He'd left it to his underlings. His downline, the men who worked for him, believing them capable of looking after this side of the business while he sweat himself into a grave trying to dodge legal proceedings which threatened to bring him down.

Disappointment etched itself into his being as he conducted a slow check of the place, one room at a time.

He'd bought the premises seven years previously. An investment for his future. Security. A bolthole. Set up for him to run to under exactly these circumstances. Only it was no longer set up. The neat, precise operation he'd had running like a well-oiled machine had collapsed in on itself, as though the extra pressure he'd applied during its expansion had imploded.

He circled around. Disgust coating the back of his tongue. People he'd believed reliable had let him down. They'd virtually abandoned what once had run sleek and systematic.

It was his fault. He should have kept a closer eye on the finer operations of the organisation. Instead, he'd assumed because the money was rolling in, it was all in hand. He hadn't expected it to be a palace, but this. This level of neglect churned his stomach with a deadly fury.

His deep, even breathing through clenched teeth was the only sound in the empty room.

Anger gathered pace to tighten his chest. Anger at his right-hand man, but more so at himself. It wasn't as though he'd had to travel far. He should have checked earlier, ensured the place was fit for his purpose. He'd been busy, distracted. Frantic in his effort to pull strings that still remained unpulled. He'd had to move fast. Faster than he'd imagined. He'd had no alternative, been given no choice. He'd relied on others to do work he should have kept a closer eye on.

He studied the dilapidated room in the ex-RAF aerodrome with its high, domed ceiling, narrow windows twenty foot above floor height. A deliberate choice at the time of purchase with the sole purpose of making sure no one could see in.

With the clear blue sky he knew was beyond, barely a glimmer of light made its way through the filth and the bird shit smeared over the windows. That wasn't the issue though.

Yellowed paint peeled in great swathes from the walls, leaving behind dull grey, powdery concrete which shed onto the floors in layer upon layer of dust. Dust he'd made sure had been cleared every week so their product wasn't contaminated. That's how you kept a good reputation. How you built your empire. His had crumbled along with the dust.

He'd left the two abandoned aeroplanes outside, keeping up the pretence of an airfield undergoing renovation. Provided no one came close enough to inspect the premises. And it had worked. After the first year he'd bought the place, he'd never had anyone inspect the premises again. He paid his council tax and business rates, water, electricity. No need for heating. The low-lives that worked for him could throw on another layer of clothing.

With the business running smoothly, he'd recently allowed his junior to keep the operation going as the money flooded in. He'd never thought anything other than it was as efficient as when he last checked. His time had been taken trying to break into the bigger game, not the small fry he currently dealt with.

His footsteps echoed across the huge empty room as annoyance swept through him, tightening his jaw. For God's sake, he should have checked. The operation could have been ten times the size. Ten times the income. That's what he'd been aiming for all these months, believing what he'd handed over control of was running fine. If only he'd dropped by. Seven months he'd let roll by in the belief that it was all under control.

Anger boiled in the pit of his stomach, churning up acid to bubble in his chest.

He circled around 360 degrees. All this empty, unused space could have been utilised to perfection. That had been his ambition. Ambition that had made him blind while he pursued his dream.

He had only himself to blame, of course. He'd rested on his laurels and by sheer dint of that had allowed the people who worked for him to rest on theirs. They'd ruined it.

Twenty-four hours ago, it hadn't mattered. He'd not cared enough.

Things had changed. So rapidly he barely had time to take it all in.

He slipped through from one doorway into a long musky-scented corridor with dingy mustard walls and discarded the idea that he could take up residence in the place as it was. He'd whip it into shape though in no time at all. The smaller rooms could soon be converted into living accommodation for him. A bed, a bathroom, a kitchen.

He sneered as he bumped through to the next enormous room. One that had been set up properly, with several rows of tables outfitted with highly sophisticated equipment he'd recently purchased which had replaced over two dozen people. A reduction of workforce and risk. Equipment worth a small mountain of cocaine for which it had been purchased to cut with an accuracy no human hand could compete with.

He stopped just inside the doorway with fury building into a thick, dark oil. A two-million-pound operation and no one there to oversee it.

As an intruder, he should have been shot dead the moment he walked through the front hangar doors of the building. As the fucking owner, the least he'd expect is to be challenged, greeted, acknowledged. Instead, there wasn't even a sign of a security guard, never mind the eight he believed were working around the clock. The place was deserted. Where the hell were the workers? It should be a buzz of activity, not a mortuary.

He glanced at the time on his Omega watch. The Constellation Co-Axial Master Chronometer his wife had paid the better part of twenty-five grand for on his birthday. As it was his credit card she'd used for the purchase, he couldn't have been happier. With them all dead, nobody would be paying the bill.

He twisted his lips in a bitter smile and dropped his arm back down to his side. She'd never earned a penny of her own in her life, but she magnanimously splashed out all his money on gifts apparently from her. Irony. He'd bought the fucking over-priced watch himself.

Only 5:30 p.m., time enough for work to be done.

He fisted his hands and rested them on his hips, pressing down on the rage threatening to explode. A twenty-four-hour, £900,000-a-week-turnover business was his dream. Hardly one he'd see at this rate.

He circled around again. And froze at the slow creek of a door. If none of his men were apparent, just who the hell was sneaking around his building, his business?

He tilted his head to catch the soft shuffle of shoes heading his way along the corridor and palmed one of the small handguns he'd tucked in his pocket. If he'd known what he'd come across, he'd have brought more firepower from the boot of his car. Foolishly, he hadn't imagined he'd need it. Another mistake he'd be sure not to repeat in the future. Now he had one again. He narrowed his eyes.

He snorted out a laugh. Someone was about to get a hell of a fright. He was back from the dead. Lazarus they could call him.

Phil Hart's eyes shot wide as he appeared in the doorway, fear lurking in their watery depths. His voice stuttered out from between stiff lips. 'I wasn't expecting you.'

'Evidently, Phil.' He allowed a slow easy smile to spread across his face, raised his eyebrows and let the smile slide away. 'Is that why you sent everybody home?'

The scarlet flush over the man's pale skin confirmed his suspicions and he took satisfaction at the panic that flashed through Phil's eyes while he passed his gun from one hand to the other, as efficient using either left or right when firing a weapon. He held the Taurus LBR revolver with casual deadliness, gratified at the dread it seemed to evoke in the other man.

'I'd not heard from you. For over a week. Last time we spoke—'

'Last time we spoke,' he cut in, 'I told you I needed to keep my head down, Phil, that the heat had turned up.' He quirked one side of his mouth up in a crooked grin. He certainly had turned the heat up. Full on blaze.

Phil, the one he'd put his trust in, his right-hand man, gave a weak, pathetic shrug. 'I thought this was all over.'

Vicious annoyance slapped through him. When had he ever given the impression it was over? He'd thought it himself for a short time, but he'd never revealed his thoughts to Phil. 'What the hell made you believe that?'

The muted scuff of a footstep had him swinging his gun to point at a second man who stepped through the wide doorway.

This one didn't show the same fear, his cool disdain undisturbed by the gun aimed at his heart. His air of arrogance a refreshing relief but also a warning that he could be an adversary in the game.

With no idea who he was, he studied the other man with cautious interest.

With the smooth coffee-coloured skin of mixed heritage, the stranger had inherited disconcertingly pale eyes. They glowed an unnatural green as his gaze flickered over to where yesterday's delivery of blocks of cocaine hydrochloride powder were stacked across four pallets. Half would remain in the pure form, half would be processed into crack using the baking and talcum powder which was neatly stacked further along the room. The organisation of products with a street value in excess of £200,000 was a tribute to Phil's abilities. Unfortunately, his panicked actions to shut up shop when the pressure was on were not.

Where had the pressure come from? Another operation? A drugs lord trying to muscle in on his success?

This new man wasn't one of his, the one with balls of steel, the one he didn't recognise, but from the slick, expensive dress sense and attitude, he believed he was somebody. Perhaps he was, or wanted to be, but he was in for a surprise if he thought he was going to be handed a fully functioning operation as easy as that. Perhaps he needed to witness just who the boss was.

With a deliberate turn of his head, he ignored the stranger, his mind sharp and clear as he addressed Phil. 'I suggest you get your arse into gear and get my people back up and running within the next hour.'

'But—'

He cut him off before Phil had barely opened his mouth. 'There are no buts. If you wish to...' He handed the gun back again to his right hand, raised his arm and took easy aim directly at the other man's forehead. He sighed out an exaggerated breath. '...Live.' This time he stretched a smile, flat and sharp, as he dipped his left hand into his pocket. With ease, he flicked the safety off his Walther 9mm PPK ambidextrous semi-auto pistol and withdrew it.

Guns were his passion, the desire to use every one of his collection a driving force he obsessed about night and day.

Lightweight, the 9mm fitted neatly into the palm of his hand. With no time to take an accurate aim, he raised his arm and shot one-handed. The bullet hit the stranger dead centre of his nose with a slight upward trajectory to blow blood, bone and grey matter out of the back of his head and splatter them into the narrow corridor and up the walls behind.

Surprise stayed etched on the stranger's face long after he was dead, and his body slumped to the floor once the message reached it that it no longer had a brain.

Horror froze Phil in place with his hands raised, palms outward, with not so much as a breath moving.

Dark satisfaction winged its way through Gordon Lawrence. Aside from money, the one thing guaranteed to get the job done was fear.

'I should kill you too.' He pursed his lips as he considered his options with ice-cold detachment. He trained both guns on Phil with steady hands. He should kill Phil for selling him out to the stranger with barely a moment to mourn his supposed demise. With the swiftness of Phil's move, he'd already put the wheels in motion for the takeover, that much was evident.

A takeover that would never happen.

He ran his tongue over his teeth as he considered the advantage of dispatching Phil.

The man could potentially be worth more alive than dead. He'd run the place into the ground, but he knew everything, everyone. It was the route of least effort to use Phil again to get it back on board. Keep the man in place, let him prove himself. Until his usefulness was spent, and dependent on his response.

With a long, even breath he kept his voice a low gravelly threat. 'Like I said, do your job, Phil. Get everyone back to work with immediate effect.'

Phil raised his hand and pinched the top of his nose as he closed his eyes. 'I'm not sure I can get them back. Not immediately.' He opened his eyes, his gaze searching for compassion.

He wasn't about to get any. 'Then I might as well shoot you now.'

Dread filled the other man's eyes. A man who feared him was far more useful than a man who thought him a fool.

'It may take me a little while, but I'll do it.'

Amused at the tremor in Phil's voice, Gordon let a satisfied smile spread over his face.

Cowardly little shit. Once he had everything running smooth again, Phil would be the next to die. Not one minute too soon. 'Excellent. *Your* priority is to get *my* security back in here.'

'Yes, sir.'

He circled his gun around for effect. 'From now on, I'll be living here. Get someone reliable in to make the offices liveable.'

'Yes, sir.'

'And, in the meantime,' a sneer curled Gordon Lawrence's lip, 'You can clear up that mess.' With a flick of his gun, he indicated the crumpled body in the doorway and laughed as Phil almost genuflected, his breath puffing out in panic-stricken bursts.

'Yes, sir.'

19

Amazed at what effect a long, hot bath to rid herself of the over-powering scent of the fire that clung to her could have, Jenna let out a sigh. It had helped to slip into freshly laundered bedding, courtesy of Fliss, who'd taken pity on her having to work her day off. The five-hour nap had gone a long way to restoring her too. She'd still need an early night to prepare her for the long days she imagined ahead of her, starting tomorrow. But tomorrow would keep.

Surprisingly refreshed, Jenna stared at her reflection in the bathroom mirror while she smoothed on her moisturiser.

Her lips curved upward. Even if it did nothing, it gave her a sense that she was making an effort. She squirted a tiny amount of foundation on the tips of her fingers and applied a thin layer. Barely worth the effort, but it gave her skin a flawless finish, just as advertised.

With a quick flick of a brush, Jenna applied a little bronzer to her cheekbones, then leaned into the mirror as she swept a mascara wand over eyelashes that were already thick and black, lengthening them so her eyes darkened and sparkled with life.

She glanced over her shoulder into her bedroom. Her heart

gave a hitch at the sight of the little dog curled in a tight ball on her bed. Poor little thing.

Fleur, it said on the minute name tag, barely even visible under the plethora of diamantes encrusted on the collar. They'd almost requested forensics to decipher it, but Donna took a photograph on her iPhone and expanded it until they could read the name.

Jenna finished rinsing her hands and then towelled them dry.

Donna couldn't be persuaded to hang onto Fleur until they could locate a family member. *Skinned rabbit*, she'd called her. Jenna tried to convince herself she'd had no choice in the matter, but she could have called the dog warden, or left her with the front counter. Instead, the little dog had melted her heart and she'd brought her home. It wasn't unusual for an officer to take in a stray while they waited for the owners to contact the station. It was less stressful. Fleur would not have suited kennels and it would not have suited Jenna to let the sweetheart go.

Jenna made her way into the bedroom and lowered herself gently onto the bed so she didn't disturb Fleur.

Domino had been decidedly unimpressed with their visitor. After a sniff all over, he'd looked at Jenna as though she'd lost her mind. *Skinned rabbit* may also have been his opinion.

For her own comfort and pleasure, she ran the back of her fingers down the curved length of Fleur's back and the dog rolled over to expose her furless fawn belly. Softer than silk. As the dog cracked open one eye to gaze up at her, Jenna's heart clenched with sympathy and she made up her mind. Fleur was not a dog to be left alone. She'd accompany Adrian and Jenna to dinner.

20

SUNDAY 19 APRIL 2015 HOURS

The painful clench of her stomach woke her, the burn almost as bad as the fire in her side.

Tongue stuck to the roof of her mouth, Poppy raised her head and squinted into the dimming light inside the barn.

The contents of the carrier bags lay strewn across the floor from where she'd staggered in earlier and dropped onto the bales of straw just before she blacked out.

She flopped her right arm out, her knuckles grazing against a can of Coke. She needed it. Needed energy, even though her stomach still rebelled.

Poppy grasped the can and propped herself up on her right elbow, whimpering all the time as she popped the lid.

The fizz almost choked her as she guzzled it down. Sugar and energy her most pressing need.

She flopped back onto the straw, gasping for breath. No idea what time it was, she blinked in the murkiness of the barn. Pale shafts of golden light still filtered through. The last dregs of daylight. It still had to be Sunday. She surely can't have passed out for more than a few hours.

Letting out a grunt, she pushed up again and stared around at the scattered tins. Beans would have to do. Better than ravioli. As she looked at the tin, her stomach rebelled. She wasn't the biggest fan in the first place, but the thought of cold, slimy pasta sliding its way down her throat made her throat clench. She hadn't been thinking straight when she snatched it out of the cupboard, the main priority had been not to take more than one of anything so Ethel wouldn't notice.

She reached out and groaned, as her fingers skimmed the tin so it rolled further away.

Frustrated with the pain and the effort, she sat up and leaned over with one hand clutching her side as though it could keep the throbbing pain at bay. Nothing but sleep did that, and even that was fitful.

Light-headed she suspected more from hunger than pain, she forced herself to grasp the tin and shook it. Peeling back the ring pull, she reached for the spoon and scooped out the beans into her mouth. More ravenous than she'd realised, she shovelled it in, gulping it down as though it was her last meal. She should have grabbed some bread, but Ethel would have known and then the police would be all over the place.

She pushed more into her mouth, barely chewing as she swallowed it down. It may well be her last meal.

Poppy scraped the tin clean and then looked around, her stomach still protesting its need for sustenance. After all, she'd not eaten since the night before.

As she reached for the pineapple, her side burnt. She looked around for the packets of paracetamol and ibuprofen. Her mum had made her promise never to take them more often than it stated on the packet, even if she had wracking period pains.

No period could compete with the pain she was in and she

didn't give a flying fuck how long ago she'd last taken the painkillers. She needed them and she needed them now.

She flipped them into her hand. Two white tablets, the ones she always had difficulty swallowing as they tended to stick to the back of her tongue, and the coated ibuprofen which slid down easily. She rarely took them. Mum said they thinned the blood and made you bleed more when you were having a period. It was probably a pile of crap, and she didn't care.

Poppy sat cross-legged, popped the lid on the pineapple, threw the tablets into her mouth and washed them down with the pineapple juice. She scooped the cubes of refreshing pineapple into her mouth until every one of them was gone.

Annoyed with herself for not bringing more food, she let the empty tin roll from her fingers and lay back in the straw to stare at the wide, rounded roof of the old Dutch barn. A miniature version, Mr Crawford had told the twins. Miniature it may be, but it was big enough to hide in amongst the bales of hay and straw.

Unused for years, the dust puffed up in plumes every time she moved.

Relieved she'd cleaned her wound in the kitchen, Poppy heaved a sigh as her eyelids drifted shut.

She touched her fingers to her phone and considered switching it on. Who was there to ring? Who could she ever trust with her darkest secret?

She needed to think.

She needed to make decisions.

But, right now, she needed to sleep.

21

'Hey, triple shot. To take out?' He knew her so well. It was the same guy she saw every day at the same time. She preferred an early start to the day. He was always there. Solid, reliable. Much to her delight, he remembered her order before she could ask.

Shaun, his name badge declared.

'Hi. Yeah, that's good.' Voice still smoky with early morning lack of use, Jenna responded to the young barista's welcoming grin with one of her own instead of the raw-eyed stare she really wanted to give him.

She'd had a good run at sleep but hadn't yet shaken off the tiredness. Shift work got at her that way. It was the lack of routine.

She kicked up the sides of her mouth and sent him her best effort.

His dark eyes danced as he punched her order into the till and leaned closer, all flirt and mischief. 'Can I get you anything else?' He jiggled his eyebrows at her and coaxed another grin from her. She took comfort in it, and a little pleasure in the harmless flirtation that passed between them. She'd never consider it serious, nor did he. A man ten years her junior, interested and cheeky enough. It usually got her day off to a good start.

Jenna raised her left hand and passed over the tuna melt panini. 'Just this please.'

'Toasted?'

'Please.' It may not be everyone's ideal breakfast, but it was exactly what she wanted.

'No problem.' The quick wink wrinkled one side of his perfectly straight nose. If she had been ten years younger, she may have fallen for his fake flirtation, but she knew better. He thought he was a ladykiller, she didn't suffer from the illusion that he had a thing for older women. He was a barista, it was his job to be friendly.

Jenna tapped her phone against the reader. Apple Pay made everything too easy. Easy to spend. Easy to keep track.

She smiled as the short message from Adrian slid in from the top of the screen. A bunch of roses emoji and a kiss.

Poor Adrian. Second day on the trot she'd pushed him out of her bed and through the front door with barely time to pause. It was his decision to stay and risk the early train to London instead of catching it the previous night.

She ducked her head to hide her smile. From her point of view, it had been worth it. He did things to her heart, not least of all when he'd tucked Fleur in close as they drifted off to sleep.

From his farewell kiss and follow up message, he didn't have an issue with her shift pattern either. He'd taken it in his long, lazy stride as they left the house together, with her heading for the police station and him bound for the train station and London.

Jenna shuffled along the counter to make room for the big guy crowding her personal space and wait for her order just as her phone vibrated. She glanced down at the screen again.

I see you in there, get me one.

Jenna whipped her head back up to glance in the mirror behind the counter and search for Mason's reflection in the car park.

From the corner of her eye, she caught the exchange, the fast sleight of hand as her lovely young barista handed over a wodge of small packets in exchange for a roll of money to the broad-shouldered man next to her.

Disbelief crowded her mind and she gave a long, slow blink.

Shit! She couldn't unsee what she'd just seen. Nor as a police officer could she ignore it. As if she didn't have enough on her plate.

Aware of time pressing, she drew in a breath and considered her options. She had a major incident to deal with. Debrief at 6:00 a.m. That gave her a brief window of opportunity to deal with something she simply could not ignore but had limited time and resources to handle.

With controlled stillness, Jenna gave a casual slide of her gaze upwards past the mirror, where she spotted the reassuring reflection of Mason's car, and then onto the price list above. She leaned into the counter and narrowed her eyes to further study the board, determined not to give herself away.

Her heart thundered in her ears, blocking out the sound of the coffee machine, grinding away to create an overwhelming background noise to drive all thoughts from her head. The pulse in the base of her throat pounded as heat rose up her neck to flood her face.

Mind racing, Jenna clamped down on the instinct to whip out her warrant card and arrest both of them on the spot. She had no doubt the moment Mason realised there was an incident in progress, she'd have the necessary backup, but that wasn't the issue. From the brief flash of packets and oversize roll of money, this wasn't just an exchange for personal use. There'd been a lot of white stuff in those little packets and too much money for the barista's smaller hands to handle, which was probably the cause of the quick fumble.

Young, good-looking barista wasn't merely a two-bit pusher, he was up a few rungs higher on the supplier ladder. And the big guy. Unless he was laying down his supply for the next three months, it wasn't just for personal use.

She drew in a breath and dropped her gaze back down to her phone as though it had only just buzzed. No one took notice of what anyone else did on their own phones.

When she raised her head again, she caught the barista's gaze and shot him a bright, sparkling smile careful not to overdo it.

'Sorry,' she waggled her phone at Shaun, almost cringing as she hauled back on the overt obviousness and could only hope that neither of the men thought anything of it, other than she was an attention-seeker. 'I've just been asked to grab another coffee for one of my colleagues.' She stretched a wide smile for the benefit of both of them and turned to the big guy beside her as the queue beyond him grew. 'Sorry. Do you mind me butting back in?'

With an insolent shrug, the guy grunted in her ear and tucked his hands deep into his jacket pocket without a hint that he suspected anything.

In the grudging silence, she gave a quick assessment of the man before she turned back to the barista, who flashed his perfect white teeth in a brilliant grin. 'What else can I get you?'

'I'll have a grande latte.' She squinted up at the board. It was probably what Mason was drinking at the moment, he quite liked the fancy shit, even though he pretended not to. She had no pretence. Straight up, strong, black, caffeinated, maybe some brown sugar, maybe not. Kept her heart rhythm regular, she swore.

Jenna scooted along and grabbed her triple shot, raising it in a toast to the sweet, young barista, who shot her a quick wink before he turned to the next customer in line. His multitasking the true sign of excellent training.

Sweet.

Hell.

Who could tell these days? Sweet had gone out of the window.

She flashed her Apple Pay across the screen once more and hoped he wasn't also scamming the pay reader. That would really screw up her day.

The bell on the grill oven dinged and the handsome barista handed over her panini so she could tuck it under her elbow. She hung on for the grande latte, resisting the temptation to tap her foot, and then scooped up the two coffee cups, one in each hand.

As she turned to leave, she tossed another smile over her shoulder. 'Cheers, Shaun.'

Jenna kept her muscles loose as she bumped open the door with her hip and wandered out into the car park as though she had all the time in the world. With a deliberate turn, she strode away from Mason to her own car. She stretched out to place one of the takeout cups on the roof while she pressed the key fob to unlock the car and opened the door. With her back to Mason, Jenna grabbed the cup, slid inside the car and placed both in the cup holders, tossing the paper bag with the hot panini on the passenger seat.

Fleur raised her head from where she was curled in a tight circle on Jenna's favourite fluffy grey scarf in the passenger footwell and twitched her black, shiny nose at the smell wafting her way.

'You've had yours.' Jenna leaned down to stroke her fingers over the tips of Fleur's ears, the only downy part of her virtually naked little frame.

As though she understood, Fleur lowered her head and closed her eyes. They'd probably overfed her anyhow. Jenna had no idea how much to give such a diminutive creature. They'd had to soak

Domino's food in warm water and mash it up so Fleur could pick at it while Domino hovered above, too polite to snaffle it from her, but too interested to move more than six inches away.

Jenna straightened and flicked a look up at her rear-view mirror just as the big guy pushed open the door to The Coffee Shack, balancing four takeout cups in a cardboard tray.

'Shit.' That wasn't going to make it easy. Four.

Her radio crackled to life and shot her heart rate into overdrive.

'What do you want, boss?' Mason's calm tones smoothed over Airwaves as she snatched the radio from the middle console, adjusted the driver mirror so she could watch the big guy and hunkered down in her seat.

'Big guy just coming out of The Coffee Shack. Six-two, black Caribbean I would say, built like a brick shithouse.' Smile like a shark. Unlike the barista, the hardened eyes of a long-time scrapper.

'Got him.'

'He's just obtained a considerable number of little packets with white powder from our local, friendly barista. More than I'd consider reasonable for own use.'

'In front of you?' Disbelief tinged his voice.

'They thought I'd turned away. I only just caught the action out of the corner of my bloody eye when you sent your text. I couldn't believe their bloody cheek.'

'Did no one else see?'

She shook her head, even though Mason couldn't see her. 'There were a couple of people at the tables, but no one else in the queue at the time.'

'Okay.'

'It filled up within minutes after that. Way too many people around for me to do anything. And anyway, I wanted to think things through. We have a bloody major incident to deal with. This is the last thing I needed bowling over the top of it.' She scraped the hair back from her forehead, clinging on to it in frustration.

'Right, Sarge.' He grounded her, always did. Gave her the respect for the authority she held and empowered her to use it. 'What's the order of the day?'

She narrowed her eyes as the big guy paused, all wide smiles and flashing eyes while he flirted with a pretty young woman proving he did know how to be nice. What an arse.

Mason left her in no doubt that whatever she requested, he was her backup. As reliable as the rising sun, Jenna knew he'd never let her down. Their partnership ran smooth, with barely a hitch in its stride, even since he'd started dating her sister. It could have changed their relationship, but it hadn't.

Brain in gear, Jenna hit the talk-through button again. 'We need to make an arrest of big guy without alerting the barista.' Without taking her attention from the big guy in case he passed anything to the woman, she paused while she thought it through, balancing the risk of losing a damned good arrest, or holding out for the bigger fish. 'I want to leave Shaun in place for the Drug Squad, because he obviously has a far higher-reaching contact somewhere along the way.'

'Gotcha.'

'Big guy has four cups of coffee. We need to know who the other three are for before we grab him. Is he pushing to them, or is he simply buying coffee to take to friends?' She had her doubts. You didn't buy that much cocaine and hang on to it while you innocently doled out cups of coffee.

'Agreed.'

Mason made it easy. If he was uncomfortable with her plan, he was straight enough to say so without preamble. She'd be left in no doubt.

She continued to scan the reflection in her car mirror as she thought out loud. 'There are only two of us. Four of them.'

Mason and she had badges, what did those four have?

'Three. Ryan just happened by. He was about to slip into The Coffee Shack without informing us of his whereabouts.' Mason lowered his voice to a gruff London accent. 'I fingered his collar, Sarge, and now the boy will, through his own machinations, not have that nice, tasty zinger of a latte he was about to order without having the decency to ask his colleagues if they'd like to participate in this daily ritual.'

A lick of guilt slid in sideways. She'd not asked the others. She'd done a sneaky drive-by. But Ryan was the youngest and newest member of the team. It was his duty to run around after them, not the other way around. She comforted herself with that thought.

DC Ryan Downey, still relatively new to the team, had been through harrowing times on a previous case where the finger of suspicion had jabbed at him. He still had a long way to go. Not that Jenna wasn't confident in his ability and certainly his honesty and enthusiasm, and despite everything he'd been through none of that had been tarnished.

Ryan's voice grumbled over Airwaves from where, she assumed, he sat in his own car. She'd not spotted him when she walked out, but then she hadn't been looking for him. 'I don't see why you find it funny. Yours will be bloody cold by the time you get it anyway.'

Jenna snorted as a hot wash of relief flooded through her. She had her team. They stood a fighting chance if the big guy decided to protest. Despite his size, Mason and Ryan could take him.

Her mind whirled as she tossed together a quick risk assessment in her head. As a police officer, it was her duty to arrest the law-breakers. As an investigator, it was her obligation to follow the upline to its source.

She swivelled around to sweep her gaze over The Coffee Shack door, knowing Mason had his eye on the big guy.

'Okay. Here's what we'll do. We know who the barista is. Shaun.'

'Shaun, the barista,' Mason repeated. 'Helpful, but we could do with a little more than a first name.'

'Shit. Shaun? Yeah.' Ryan stumbled over his words. 'Shaun Cunningham.'

Jenna snapped a grin in the mirror. That's her boy. A natural. Always managed to pull something out of the hat.

Disappointment laced Ryan's words. 'He's sound, he is. Or at least I thought he was.' Ryan sucked in a breath. 'He knows what I do.'

For clarification, Jenna spoke into the radio. 'He knows you're a police officer?'

'Yes, Sarge. I speak with him most days.'

So did Jenna, but she'd never mentioned what she did for a living, nor had she snagged his last name. He'd never asked her profession, and she made it a policy not to tell people she barely knew. Judgement could be a funny thing. They'd either ask you to arrest someone for them or spit in your face.

She leaned back in her seat, made herself comfortable while she watched the big guy wrestle with the tray of cups as he opened his car door. 'Did he see you?'

'No, Mason grabbed me before I even reached the door.'

'Okay.' She blew out a breath before putting them in the picture. 'Shaun will be back to his job where he works every day. We'll see him again tomorrow and the next day and he'll never suspect that we know anything.'

'He'd never have risked the quick switcheroo in front of you if he'd had any clue who you were.'

'Provided he doesn't get wind of a problem with his downline because we have no idea how often big guy comes in to visit Shaun, the barista.'

'Okay.'

'So, I'll ask the Duty Inspector to contact the Drug Squad. They can do what the hell they like with him then.'

As the big guy slid into his red BMW X4, Jenna stabbed the start button on her own car and reversed up ready to follow.

'You don't want to stop him here, Sarge?' Excitement reverberated through Ryan's voice.

'We'd definitely run the risk of Shaun seeing. No, we'll tail him. Did you see if there was anyone else in the car with him?'

'Not that I can see.' Mason pulled his car out of its parking space and nudged it forward, ready to turn left onto the one-way system around Telford town centre.

'Nor me. Also, I'm curious as to who he's about to meet up with.'

Jenna had no idea where Ryan was in his little Suzuki Swift, but he wasn't far if he could call... There he was, just edging out of the drive-through on the right.

'Mason, fall in behind the big guy. Ryan, you follow at a distance, if you need to swap and change do that.'

'Received.'

'Received.'

'Right.' Decision made, she rolled her car forward to follow the others at a discreet distance. 'There are three others he's going to meet. It could be we make a pretty hefty arrest if they're all pushers. What's the betting he won't have bought the end-game contacts coffee.'

'So, it could be more pushers.'

'Yep, just further down the food chain. Let me contact Control.'

Jenna changed channel on Airwaves. 'Control, this is Juliet Alpha 77, who is the DI on today?'

Silence behind the static filled the car as she pushed it into fourth gear and took off, keeping her distance as they approached the first roundabout and Mason slipped into the inside lane to go all the way around. Ryan followed, leaving Jenna to bring up the rear.

'Juliet Alpha 77. DI Taylor's on duty this morning.'

'Excellent. Can you put me through?' A wave of relief swept over her. She had backup, support she could rely on with a man who lived and breathed the job. His knowledge was second to none and his dedication unquestionable.

'Jenna? What's going on?' His gruff tones over Airwaves only sought to reassure. With an open line, both Mason and Ryan were privy to the conversation.

'DI Taylor, sir. We have a situation. I was in The Coffee Shack—'

An indelicate snort came over the air before his voice laced with sarcasm came back at her. 'No doubt you were.'

'Yes, sir. I was collecting myself and DC Ellis some coffee when I witnessed what I believe to be an exchange of Class A drugs in a quantity that concerned me considerably.'

'Right.' His brevity assured her he was listening.

'I'm aware I have the major fire incident to deal with, but I can't ignore this.'

'Relax, Sergeant Morgan, we have everything in hand here for the time being. So far, there's very little progress with the major incident that you need to concern yourself over. Debrief has been re-scheduled for 10:00 a.m.' The crackle of the radio filled the air before DI Taylor cut back in. 'What do you need, Sergeant?'

'The Drug Squad, sir. They need to set up obs on the barista, Shaun, who I've left *in situ* at the moment as he's already passed the drugs on, although obviously I have no idea if he has more.' She checked in her rear-view mirror and manoeuvred across the lanes. 'The current situation is we're tailing a red BMW Series 4, registration number...'

As she paused, Mason filled in the gap. 'Bravo Yankee six-nine Sierra Mike Romeo.'

She blew out a breath, hoping the distance he kept wouldn't arouse the man's suspicions. 'The driver took the drugs. Big guy. Black Caribbean. Six-four.' She remembered the bump of his shoulder against hers, the tops of his arms wider than her thighs. No fat, pure muscle. 'Eighteen stone. Aged...' she blinked to bring the man back into her mind. 'Twenty-three to twenty-six.' Smooth, glossy skin. 'Definitely no older.'

'Okay, Sergeant Morgan.' There was a pause with a vague tapping of keys in the background. 'Car registered to one Lamonte Junior.'

'Is that his official name, or is he a younger version?'

'Official name, Jenna.' Her lips kicked up in a smile at the dryness of Taylor's voice, evidently unamused at her little quip.

Ryan's soft snort had her narrowing her eyes as she concentrated on keeping her distance. 'Ironic. Doesn't Lamonte mean something like man of law?'

'How would you know that?' Jenna grimaced at the radio as though it were Ryan himself.

'One of the instructors at the gym is called Lamonte. Specialising in the weights section. Funny guy, always telling us its Lamonte's Law when he instructs us.'

'Right.'

Ryan filed away information like a memory drive. Always useful when you needed to sift through data. His quick, lively mind forever willing to share.

Interesting, but irrelevant; she needed to get them back on track with limited time. Big Lamonte couldn't be travelling far.

'He was carrying four coffees which makes me assume he's about to meet up with three other people. I don't think it's a knitting club, sir.'

The little snort of laughter burst through the static. 'Can you hold back till I get my ducks in line?'

'No, sir. If I do, I suspect I'm going to miss out on a four-way drugs pass. I need to be on it right now. As I said, I have DC Ellis and DC Downey with me. We'll be fine, but backup would be appreciated as soon as...'

There was a second's pause as Jenna followed the others at a distance onto the retail car park. 'Leave it with me, Sergeant, and I'll get it sorted. Keep me informed.'

Lamonte pulled his BMW up in front of Rude Health, the new gym on the retail park, a mere four and a half minutes' drive from The Coffee Shack. Handy.

Mason bypassed him and made his way to park in front of one of the cheap stores, far enough away for him not to raise any suspicion. Ryan pulled up short in front of Sainsbury's, slipping his car in between two others on the lot. It was quiet at that time of the morning, but Sainsbury's opened early and had a healthy stream of customers.

Jenna cruised her own car several spaces away, positioning herself beyond a small white Kia Picanto. She cracked open the passenger window an inch to keep the air circulating for Fleur and hoped the little dog didn't freeze. Her body had a permanent tremble.

As Lamonte unfolded himself from the seat and emerged balancing the tray of four coffees in one hand, Jenna's radio exploded into life almost popping her heart out through her throat.

'Shit. Sorry, Sarge.' Ryan's voice stumbled a little before he continued. 'I know him. It's not a coincidence, he is the bloody instructor from the gym.'

'You're only just telling us now?' Incredulity laced Mason's voice.

Ryan's voice wound up to a higher pitch, just short of squeak. 'I didn't see him come out of The Coffee Shack. He was already in his car when I realised we were on a case.'

'It's okay.' She kept her voice even, they needed to move, but the information Jenna required from Ryan was more pressing. 'Tell me about him. Make it quick, Ryan.'

'He's one of the instructors at Rude Health. That's the one I registered with about six weeks ago now. He's been spotting me on the weights.' Ryan let out a groan. 'He knows I'm a police officer.'

Shocked, she couldn't help herself. 'Do you tell everyone what you do for a living?'

'Well. Yeah. I'm proud to serve.'

Sometimes discretion was the better part of valour. Call her cynical, but he'd learn. Not everyone thought the police were wonderful. Not everyone wanted to be your friend once they found out what you did for a living.

'Jesus.'

Jenna ignored Mason as her mind whirled through a quick realignment of the possibilities. 'Right, Mason, you and I will go in. Me first. I want to see if he's passing over more than just coffee to these other three. Mason, you just tail me until something happens. If he doesn't pass the drugs, I want to know where he stashes them.'

'Right.' Mason agreed.

'Ryan,' she instructed, 'two minutes and I want you to follow up the rear. Keep the exit closed off in case anybody bolts.'

'Sarge.'

'And for the love of Jesus, don't let him see you.'

'Yes, Sarge.'

Jenna glanced into the footwell and pointed a finger at Fleur. 'You. You can stay where you are.' The little dog's bulging eyes gave a slow blink as she lowered her head onto her front paws as though she understood every word.

Jenna nudged open her door and slipped from the car. Not

looking back as she slammed the door, she depressed the key fob to lock it.

She lengthened her stride to catch up with Lamonte and arrived at the entrance to the gym, slipping inside before the automatic doors fully closed.

Adrenaline spiked through to make her heartbeat speed up. Not through fear or anxiety, but a kick of energetic excitement. This was the job. This was what she loved.

She glanced at the small lift in the left corner of the confined, sterile entrance and caught her reflection in the brushed steel doors. She tilted her head to catch the sound of Lamonte's footsteps tapping up the L-shaped stairwell above her. Big, he may be, but he could move.

Careful to keep on her toes, she took the stairs two at a time. The trick was to keep far enough behind so he didn't notice her, but not so far that she'd lose him before he reached his targets so she could witness the drug swap before she made a move.

She bumped open the door at the top of the stairs and moved fast into a hallway. She kept him in sight as he rounded a corner to enter the main reception area.

Breath coming in quick snatches of excitement, she put on a spurt and slipped through the automatic doors at the end of the short run of hallway. She followed him as he grunted at the receptionist, all belligerent arrogance and rolling shoulders.

Evidently unimpressed with his attitude, the receptionist raised her hand to tuck a thick swathe of gunmetal hair behind her ear and pursed her lips, so a fine spray of wrinkles feathered out from her mouth. As her gaze clashed with Jenna's, her eyebrows twitched skywards, and she broke into a genuine smile.

Jenna raised one hand to display her badge and tapped her forefinger against her mouth to indicate for the lady to keep quiet as she sailed on past, keeping just ten paces behind Lamonte.

She could rely on Mason to brief the woman and take her details for when they needed to question her. If there was one thing Jenna had learnt in her career, it was don't piss off the receptionist. They were the door-openers of life and they knew everything.

Muscles bunched, ready for any eventuality, Jenna welcomed the dash of anticipation coursing through her veins. It had been a while since she'd tailed someone.

Lamonte's arrogance was such that he never even thought to turn around and check if anyone was behind him. If he did, would he even recognise her? Had he 'seen' her in The Coffee Shack, or had she remained invisible to him?

She stepped through the next set of sliding doors as Lamonte approached a group of three people all wearing the gold and navy uniform of the gym. Jenna veered off and headed straight for the water cooler on her right. She flipped a plastic cup from the dispenser and touched her finger to the button for ambient water as she gave the room a quick scan.

The dedicated and the devoted focused on their workouts, without so much as raising their heads to check out who else might arrive. EarPods in, gazes firmly fixed on the screens with the early-morning news. There was little chance they'd take much notice of her.

The cool of the air conditioning sent a quick shiver down Jenna's spine. Damn, but she could have done with that coffee she'd left in her car. The caffeine shot to her blood was just what she needed.

As she kept her head bowed, Jenna surveyed the four people.

Young female, bright blonde ponytail high on her head. The whippy end reached the bottom of her shoulder blades. Petite, around five-foot two, verging on skinny with her hipbones clearly visible through her expensive Lycra leggings. Muscles stringing out over sharp bones. Lips plumped, eyebrows drawn on. Fake tan, but the nails were natural and her own. Probably wasn't allowed to wear fake ones when helping with spotting. Rip one of those suckers off and she'd soon know about it.

With a wide smile exposing bright white teeth, the young woman reached with both hands for the coffee Lamonte passed to her and cradled it between her bony fingers. Long, heavy eyelashes flirted over smoky grey eyes. If an exchange had occurred, they were damned slick. Too slick.

Lamonte passed another cup to a short, square guy. Five-nine. Dark hair, neat beard cut in so he resembled a garden gnome, with his head squatting on broad over-blown shoulders, which gave the appearance he had no neck. His short forehead permanently wrinkled, dipped thick eyebrows over piggy eyes. Possibly blue. Mid-thirties. Neanderthal man. He wrapped one stubby-fingered hand around his cup and took a long hard swig of the coffee, his throat working as he glugged down the fluid.

The third guy leaned in. He slipped his fingers under the tray and took it, together with the last remaining cup. Perfect white teeth flashed against flawless coffee-coloured skin. Smooth, handsome, his brown eyes danced with intelligence. Not enough to distract Jenna from Lamonte's sleight of hand. Although barely noticeable, she'd been looking for it as he slipped it under the tray in the pass-over.

Confident without glancing behind to check that she was in Mason's sights, Jenna took the eight long strides to reach the foursome just as the handsome man slipped one fisted hand deep into his trouser pocket.

Jenna held her badge in her left hand and raised it as she approached, fully aware that the first thirty seconds of reaction from the group would dictate the way the situation went.

'Morning guys, I'm Detective Sergeant Jenna Morgan from Malinsgate Police Station, and this,' she indicated behind her as

Mason drew up, 'is Detective Constable Mason Ellis.' She trailed her gaze around the group and kept a fixed friendly smile in place while she evaluated them.

Lamonte's already hard gaze went flat as he clenched his jaw. Directly opposite her, Garden Gnome returned her assessment with cool, squinty eyes. Definitely blue. The young blonde's knees buckled before she took a hold of herself and her coffee sloshed through the little sippy hole in the top. Shame. Jenna had hoped it had only been Lamonte and the handsome one involved, but from the guilt sliding across all four of their faces, they all played a part.

'I have reasonable suspicion to believe you are in possession of a controlled substance and I'll be detaining you all for the purposes of conducting a drugs search.'

The blonde's jaw dropped, and her sleek black eyebrows shot up into her hairline. 'Not me.' She took a step away. 'Not drugs. No way have I got anything to do with drugs. My dad would kill me.' Her desperate protest held a spark of truth, but Jenna already had her plan of action. It wouldn't do blondie any harm to be questioned. She'd soon be out if it was established she had nothing to do with it.

Cold fury slid through Lamonte's narrowed eyes. 'What makes you think anyone here has drugs?' His jaw flexed as he stretched himself to full height. Tall and imposing. Meant to intimidate, but Jenna stretched her lips into a patient smile, confident she had a handle on the situation. 'I witnessed you passing something over.'

He made one negative shake of the head, superior and overconfident. 'I think you'll find the only things I've passed over were their coffees.' His lips twisted as he ran a critical gaze over her, and recognition slipped into his eyes. 'Which, as you know, because you were stood beside me, I've just bought at The Coffee Shack.' It was good he'd confirmed that piece of information voluntarily, then there would be no question of it along the line when she testified in court.

He took a breath and a lopsided grin slid across his face, but the hard-eyed stare never slipped. 'The only other thing you might have seen was me handing over sugar. You're going to look fucking stupid when all you come up with is a dozen little packets of white sugar.'

The zap of doubt fizzed through Jenna's head to make her question herself. If it had only been the exchange in the gym she'd witnessed, he may have thrown her conviction to the wind, but the scene in The Coffee Shack flashed into her mind and shot confidence back through her veins. Sugar came in little white paper packs from The Coffee Shack, not packaged in tiny see-through zip lock bags.

She kept her smile easy. 'You won't have a problem then if we conduct a search, will you? Then we can escort you to Malinsgate Police Station, should the need arise.'

On high alert, Jenna's muscles twitched. Now was the moment of reaction. Would it run like a handbook exercise, or go to hell in a handbasket?

Aware of Mason as he stepped to her side, Jenna kept her attention on Lamonte and handsome boy.

The little blonde was no threat, she'd already frozen with shock. Her perfect lips still forming a silent 'oh'.

Garden Gnome was the one who broke from the opposite side of the wide circle, a classic ploy Jenna expected, although for the size and build of the man his speed was impressive. It was a ruse, a diversionary tactic. The one without the drugs made a break for it and in those first twenty seconds with all attention on the breaker, the evidence would disappear, and they'd have no case.

Adrenaline spiked through, but Jenna held her ground without taking her gaze off Lamonte as Garden Gnome rushed her, a mere eight paces away. She shot her right hand out towards the group, not quite sure where Ryan had positioned himself. 'Don't move!'

Blondie squeaked and leapt back, still in Jenna's eyeline.

Barely an inch away from her, Garden Gnome hit the ground, the mezzanine floor shuddered under his weight and vibrated through the soles of her feet as Mason delivered his classic straight-armed punch. He dropped the man to the floor before Garden Gnome had the chance for his meaty fists to connect with Jenna.

A spume of frothy coffee burst upwards from the takeout cup which Garden Gnome dropped as he hit the ground. Jenna's lips twisted, but she never so much as flinched as it splattered down the front of her smart, black work trousers and across the top of her neat, leather ankle boots, her attention purely focused on Lamonte and the other male.

Handsome boy dropped the tray, whipped around as his coffee hit the floor, but before he could take more than a step, Ryan had the man's arm up behind his back. Considerably lighter-framed than the other man, Ryan held the upper hand on training, technique and the element of surprise as he lowered him to his knees on the floor with a certain gentility and slipped on a pair of wrist restraints. A beautiful textbook manoeuvre. The boy was coming on.

Jenna parked the small sliver of admiration for her young officer's development until later when she'd allow herself to gloat a little. Not least because a deep, guttural growl resonated from behind her, making the hairs on the back of her neck stand on end. If there was one sound that would make her freeze her arse to the spot, it was that of Blue, a highly trained police search and drugs dog. He may not be one of their attack dogs, but that didn't mean to say he didn't have long, sharp teeth he'd willingly sink into human flesh should the need arise, and the command be given.

Without taking her gaze from Lamonte, Jenna held still as Blue moved past her, sniffed Lamonte from the ankles, all the way up the length of his legs, and ended up with his nose in the man's crotch. Lamonte might have attitude, but he never twitched a muscle, didn't so much as breathe as fear whipped through his eyes. She had to admire the dog's style. There wasn't a man on earth who would do anything different when his tackle was quite clearly at risk.

Without a verbal command, the Belgian Malinois dipped his head and started digging at Lamonte's feet.

Jenna recognised the aggressive alert sign for drugs and relief swarmed through her. She was right, she'd not made a mistake. Jesus Christ, she'd had no doubt, but she'd never have lived it down if little baggies of sugar were the only thing that exchanged hands.

Affirmation from Blue made her heart sing.

The solid, square form of Sergeant Chris Bennett stepped into her peripheral vision. 'I heard your call. I was just grabbing my breakfast from Sainsbury's.' He cast a cool, calm gaze over the scene and ran his tongue over his teeth. 'Blue says we have drugs.'

Jenna grinned. Blue had never been known to be wrong.

'Come, boy.' The dog shot to Chris's side, whipping his backside around so he sat to attention, bang up against his handler's left leg. Blue lifted his right paw and waited for his reward, which was quick in coming and then slid his gaze back to Lamonte to keep him frozen to the spot.

With all the eyes she needed on her suspects, Jenna stepped back to survey her scene and take in Garden Gnome on the floor. Mason seemed forever to step into the fray to take someone out on her behalf. She kept her voice low as she moved closer to him. 'Did you hit him because I'm a female?'

'I hit him because you're human. He was bloody close. I thought he was going to have you around the neck. It would have been messy. You were in the line of fire, and he's a big bastard.' He slanted her a look. 'I'm a bigger bastard and there's no way I'll stand by and watch you, or anyone for that matter, get hurt.' He stared down at the inert body at his feet and clucked his tongue. 'All it took was one punch from me. If I'd let him get to you, I have total faith that you would have got him – eventually. But you'd still be scrambling around on the floor right now, and that's too painful to watch. Call it ego, call it sexism. It's neither. It's preservation. Of you, me and a whole lot of time we don't have.' Mason hunkered down next to the body and gave the man a prod. 'I may have exerted a little more force than I thought.' He sucked air in through his teeth with over-exaggerated regret.

As his head came up to look at Jenna, the man on the floor sprang to life, wrapped a beefy arm around Mason's throat and dragged him down across his barrel chest.

Mason's eyes went wide and he coughed out a surprised splutter as the man's muscular forearm tightened around his throat to send his face an unhealthy puce.

Without a moment's hesitation, Jenna placed her booted heel directly across the other man's throat, exerting enough pressure to cut off his oxygen supply. She rubbed her fingers across her lips and met the man's panicked gaze while she applied a little more pressure.

He dropped his arm from around Mason's neck, his own eyes bulging, his face purpled.

'Come on, Mason, stop scrambling around on the floor and get up.'

Mason thrashed around on his back for a moment longer, then rolled off the other man, flipped over onto his hands and knees, and staggered to his feet as he sucked in rasping mouthfuls of air. He shot Blue an accusing stare and then whipped his gaze up to Sergeant Bennett. 'It would have been good if he could have helped.'

Without so much as a twitch, Blue remained where he was, gaze firmly fixed on his own suspect.

Chris Bennett glanced down at the dog by his side and then back up again. 'Could have. Didn't need to. Wouldn't want him biting the wrong arse now, would we?'

Without taking her gaze from the man under her foot, Jenna's lips twitched. 'You're under arrest for assaulting a police officer.'

That should take care of him while they conducted further investigations. She seriously doubted he had drugs on him, but that would all come out once they conducted their initial search.

22

Jenna touched her hand to Mason's arm and drew him away from the uniforms they'd just handed over to so they could take their four suspects to Malinsgate Station. 'Not bad for a morning's work.' She grinned, the excitement of the arrest still pumping through her veins.

'The day hasn't officially started and we've made the best arrests of the week.' He nudged her almost taking her off her feet.

'The week has only just begun.'

'No one's going to do better than this.' His lips quirked up in a smile as he rubbed his knuckles.

'Yeah, but we're not dealing with it. I'll hand the legwork over. We're going to need to know what's going on with the major incident.' She snapped him a sharp grin. 'Keeping the balls in the air, Mason.'

'Chuck me a few if you need to.'

'You'll be having a few thrown your way. There's going to be plenty to do. In the meantime,' she nodded to the suspects as they were being searched by uniform. 'We'll let them cool their heels down at the station.'

'Right.'

She cruised her gaze over the young blonde. 'Tanya Boulding. Thoughts?' She turned to Ryan, knowing he was desperate to answer.

'Young, impressionable... innocent. I see her all the time. She's a nice girl.'

Pale skin turned ashen. Inclined to go with her DC's impressions, convinced the girl had nothing to do with drugs, Jenna unclipped her radio from her belt.

As Mason opened his mouth to speak, Jenna raised her forefinger to halt him while she depressed the button on the Airwaves radio and patched herself through to the person she wanted. 'DC Salter.'

'Sarge. I hear you have a little activity going on. Would you like me and Wainwright to be a part of it?'

'I certainly would.'

'Tell me what you want, Sarge. There's nothing much going on here until we get an update from NILO for the fire. It's been postponed again until later this afternoon, I'm told, as the fire service are still unable to enter the building.'

Satisfied there was nothing further she could do on that case until she had an update, Jenna consoled herself with the fact that she could see this one through without breaking her stride.

Before that, she did want something from Salter and Wainwright.

'Uniform are escorting four suspects back to the station.' She glanced over just as Tanya turned a delicate shade of green and looked like she might just puke. If she were the uniform, she'd be wise to take a step back. She glanced down at her own coffee-splattered trousers and grimaced. Perhaps she wouldn't.

Jenna turned her back and put a few more steps between herself and the general activity in the room. She spoke into

Airwaves again. 'They have a young girl, Tanya Boulding. Would you see what you can do to get her processed in a speedy manner? She's young, frightened, and in my opinion most likely innocent.' She'd been in the job long enough to get a sense of a situation and this was one young woman Jenna believed was harmless. Willing to take another opinion, Jenna was content to hand the responsibility over to the indubitably reliable team of Salter and Wainwright. 'See what you think when you question her. I don't think she has any knowledge, but I'll leave her with you. We'll catch up later.'

'Sure, I'll make my way down once I've had my coffee. That should give them enough time to process her.'

Finished with DC Salter, Jenna jerked her head in the direction of the exit for both Ryan and Mason to follow. She raised her hand to attract Chris's attention. She would need the services of Blue for what she was about to do.

'You and Blue fancy a trip out, Chris?'

With a mild grin, Chris gave the top of his Belgian Malinois' head an affectionate scrub. 'Aye, Blue will be looking forward to biting another arse or two. Won't you, lad?'

Flanked by the three officers and the dog, Jenna made her way along the corridor and past the receptionist, who appeared to have developed a permanent state of surprise as a uniformed officer took out a notebook and leaned on the reception counter to write.

'What we doing, Sarge?'

Jenna slipped her radio from where it bumped against her hip. 'I need to have a word with Control, Mason. I think we can search Lamonte's premises under a Section 18. I think this one's got a lot more to do with drug pushing than just that little bundle.' In reality, it had been a hefty bundle they'd extracted from him, all neatly bagged and in the safe hands of one of the uniforms. The bags in handsome boy's pockets had been extracted but looked only enough for personal use.

'What are you going to do about Shaun?'

'His involvement's the next step up. We don't have time to conduct that kind of operation. We'd be stepping on Drug Squad's toes.'

Ryan's shoulders jiggled as he slouched in an effortless sulk. 'We're going to hand off a great bust.'

'No, we're going to let someone else do the long job, Ryan. We couldn't ignore what went on this morning, but Shaun is much more complex. They'll do obs on him for a while, arrest him and possibly turn him so they can infiltrate the bigger ring. That's what they do. That's their speciality, we'll stick to ours.'

Mason shoulder-bumped Ryan. 'We pursue our bird in the hand and leave the one in the bush to the Drug Squad. The majority of those packets were still on Lamonte, he only handed over enough for personal use, so we need to follow the little trail of white powder back to his place. He who hesitates is lost. Remember, continuity. I'd guess there was a street value exceeding a few thousand pounds if it were genuine.'

Chris nodded. 'Blue says it was.'

'Who are we to question his expertise?' Jenna reached out a hand to touch the dog's head and withdrew it quickly as his ears flicked backwards. Perhaps she wouldn't. She lengthened her stride and took the stairs without pause. 'Let's go and see if Lamonte's got any evidence at his home address.'

Ryan's loose-legged stride kept up with hers. 'He was a bit pissed off to see me there.'

She shrugged. 'He knew you were a police officer. He's the one taking the risk, Ryan.'

'I thought he was a mate.' There were undertones of sulk in Ryan's voice.

A ripple of pity stole over her. 'Unfortunately, mates in this business aren't always genuine.' She didn't want her cynicism to rub off on him. Not just yet. 'I don't have many friends outside of the job, but those I do are die-hards.' She wasn't sure she had any friends outside of the job, but she didn't want to sound pitiful. She'd think of someone.

Nobody came instantly to mind. Apart from one. Adrian. That relationship was too fresh yet to class him as a die-hard.

Fliss was her best friend, and if you could count a dog as a friend, she'd never find a human as faithful as Domino. Then there was Mason. He was more like a brother.

She grabbed her radio again and puffed out as she reached the bottom of the stairs. 'Juliet Alpha 77 to Control. This is DS Jenna Morgan, could you put me through to DI Taylor?'

Already on stand-by, it took a brief moment for DI Taylor to respond.

'DS Morgan.'

'Sir, I'm taking DC Ellis and DC Downey to conduct a Section 18 on 33 Doseley Way, Mountside, the residence of Lamonte Junior.' She raised her hand to acknowledge Chris and Blue as they headed towards the back exit of the building where the dog handlers' van would be parked up. 'We also have Sergeant Bennett and Blue in our company.'

'In connection with the arrests, I assume?'

'Yes, sir. Uniform are on their way back to the station with four suspects and a whole pack of evidence we've obtained.'

'Reasonable suspicion?'

She nodded. 'Yes, sir.'

'Go ahead, Sergeant.'

Once again, she replied, 'Yes, sir.'

'Let me know if you need SOCO when you get there.'

As they swept towards their respective cars, Jenna barked out her instructions. 'Mason, Ryan, meet me back at the station, we'll drop off our own cars and pick up a police-issue vehicle instead of pitching up in three cars. Mason, you grab the keys when you get there. Meet us out front.'

'Yes, Sarge.' He came to a halt and turned back. 'Do you want me to drive?'

Jenna slanted him a look, quirking her lips. 'Yeah, okay, Mason, you can drive.'

She slipped into her own car, trying not to laugh at the stunned disbelief that flashed over his face. She rarely allowed him to drive, preferring to be in the driving seat herself, but on occasion it amused her to take him by surprise.

Fleur raised her head, her little whippy tail gave a gentle wag and she dropped her chin back onto her paws.

Jenna studied her. Poor little girl. She reached down and smoothed one hand over Fleur's head. 'What are we going to do with you, my lovely?'

She straightened up and in the close confines of her car, the waft of strong coffee beans greeted her. As she mulled over her little dog predicament, Jenna picked the takeout cup from the console holder and took a tentative sip. Tepid it may be, but the strong, smooth tones of liquid pleasure slid over her tongue and down her throat with no effort.

As Mason shot off in front of her, she popped the cup back in the holder and followed at a more sedate pace, with Ryan bringing up the rear behind her in his little Suzuki Swift, close enough to make her twitchy. She touched her brakes at the first roundabout and hoped to hell he was paying attention and didn't ram into the back of her.

On the straight, she snatched up her cup again and took a good, long swig. Cold, black coffee wasn't so bad. It may be in her mind, but the effects of the caffeine had an instant reaction and her mood took a quick upward swing.

She glanced in her mirror and held her breath as she drove in through the police station car park only sighing out her relief as Ryan veered off to race down the first aisle as she continued along the thoroughfare to the further end of the car park.

She unbuckled herself and finished the last of her coffee before she snatched the second disposable cup from the cup holder. With the milk content, Mason's coffee was even cooler than hers. Her stomach gave a little hitch as she imagined the cold swirl of curdled milk.

With a quick glance around to check she had everything she needed, she wrinkled her nose as she swiped her bag from the passenger seat, stuffed the now cold panini in the top so she could grab it later and nuke it in the microwave at work. She scooped a scarf-wrapped sleepy Fleur into her arms, and juggled the two cups. She gave the door a shove open with her elbow and then closed it with a hard nudge of her hip and strode towards the front entrance of the station.

Mason drew the police vehicle alongside just as she threw her empty cup in the green metal waste bin at the edge of the public footpath.

She raised his cup and waggled it at him as he wound down the passenger window. 'Do you want this, or should I chuck it? It's stone cold.'

He screwed up his face. 'Nah, I don't want it. It'll be rank now.'

'I'll have it.' Ryan swiped it from her raised hand as he swooped past, a wide grin on his face.

'Ah!' With that one sharp word, she stopped him before he had a chance to slug down the coffee. 'You don't really need to come. Mason and I can handle this.' Jenna tightened her grip on Fleur ready to hand the dog over for Ryan to take care of.

'No problem.' He flashed her a cheeky grin. 'I want to, really it's great experience.'

Before she could suggest he might go into the station and

complete paperwork, he yanked open the car door and was already in the back seat, not even trying to take her position in the front passenger seat. She suspected he knew that would be one step too far. Shotgun was her privilege. She'd already established that with him on previous occasions.

She may be his senior officer, but there was a boyish persuasiveness about Ryan that had her giving in. Resigned to putting up with him, she leaned down and spoke to both of them through the open window. 'Give me a minute.'

She turned her back and trotted over the moat bridge to the station's automatic doors where she paused to let them swish open. She turned right and stepped up to the front counter where she grinned as she saw the ever respectable Tim Harper. A quiet man, close to retirement, he simply goggled at her as she thrust the little chihuahua into his arms and gave her a little chin scratch, resisting the temptation to make coochy noises, which would only spoil her reputation of tough.

'This is Fleur. Fleur needs to be looked after while she waits for someone to claim her. Keep a hold of her, would you, Tim? Just until I come back.' She knew he'd pass her on to one of his female colleagues as soon as he could. From the way he held her, it looked like he thought he had a ticking time bomb.

Jenna back-stepped towards the doors, hearing them swish open behind her. 'She'll probably need to pee soon.'

She turned just as his mouth opened and closed like a landed fish and hot-footed it over the little bridge with a slide of guilt. Fleur would be fine. She'd been fed. She'd be safe.

Jenna slipped into the front seat and strapped her seat belt on, she tapped the postcode she had for Lamonte's address into the satnav and leaned back to clear her mind while Mason navigated his way into the early-morning traffic. There was no rush. They needed to check out the location. If they found anything incriminating, they could hand it over to SOCO and continue with the case from the previous evening.

She took out her phone and tapped the WhatsApp icon. A million one-line messages from Fliss as was her habit. She typed a few words, zapped send, typed a few more. A lengthy monologue she'd have been better off sending in one missive. She started with the first message.

Domino with Lena.

Lena was the dogwalker Fliss had engaged. As a teacher, Fliss needed to get into school early on Monday mornings to set up for the week. The other times were relatively flexible so they could work his care between them. He'd fully recovered from his trauma when they'd almost lost him to a madman, but he needed attention and he needed exercise. Lena had been taking him out for the last several weeks. Jenna wasn't sure it had made such a difference to his attitude. It didn't seem to matter how much exercise he had, he still leapt around with boundless energy, never happier than when he was on a mission. A mischief mission.

She scrolled further down her messages. Most of them from Fliss were one-way exchanges, quick reminders.

Get milk.

Jenna sighed. Fliss liked her little emojis. There followed a stream of them. Wine, a plate of pasta. Damn, but she wasn't going to have time for a shop. They'd bloody well starve, especially if they didn't have any pasta, the quick fix in their lives.

She punched in a brief message. Fliss would understand. She'd grab them something on her way home or slip into the local Co-op when she walked Domino. Her sister knew what shifts could be like. Eight hours or sixteen. You never could tell.

The next message brought a smile to her face. Adrian. Quick, perfunctory, perfect.

On the train. Have a great day. Speak later.

And they would.

She sent a quick reply and clicked off the phone so she could think.

If they found nothing at Lamonte's, it would be a quick paper exercise. All in a day's work, juggling a dozen or more cases at the same time. She might simply hand it over to Ryan and let him close it off, assured that he would never miss a trick.

In the meantime, using Section 18 of the Police and Criminal Evidence Act 1984, which covered the police for entry and search after an arrest, they could conduct a thorough inspection of Lamonte Junior's house. She wrapped her fingers around the single front door key he'd handed over with reluctance, but it was better than them having to break the door down. He'd seen the wisdom of that in the end.

He hadn't had the opportunity to contact anybody to give them the heads-up or dash in and remove any evidence. He'd not made any attempt to use his phone. They'd taken him far too quickly by surprise. Nor had he been able to dispose of all the cocaine he had.

Jenna flipped the passenger sun visor down and peered at Ryan's reflection in the mirror. Credit where credit was due.

'That was a good arrest, Ryan. Smooth.' She moved her attention away as he flushed up, happy to give him the praise and let him preen for a while. His development was coming along. She cast a sideways glance at Mason. 'You too. Although do you think you can try to refrain from hitting people?'

'It wasn't a hit, it was a block.'

'With your fist.'

'There is that, but I was left with no choice.'

'There's always a choice.'

'I have no regrets. My only regret was the bloody awful waste of coffee all over the floor. I could have had one of those. My fix for the day.' His mouth pulled down at the edges in a classic Mason sulk. 'Now I'm going to have to wait till we get back to the station.'

'I did buy you one.'

'It was bloody cold. Nothing worse.'

Jenna flicked her gaze up to meet Ryan's in the mirror. His cheeks dimpled as he raised the cardboard cup in a salute and took a gulp of the cold liquid.

Jenna took pity on her partner – after all, she could barely function without caffeine. 'We'll call and get you one on the way back if you want.'

Easily consoled, Mason grinned.

'I'll have one.' Ryan piped up from the back seat and made her grin. If there was one thing Ryan brought to the party it was his boyish enthusiasm and exuberance.

They pulled up outside the address and before Mason could get out the car, Jenna reached out to stop him.

'Hold on a moment. Let's just look at what we're taking on.'

23

MONDAY 20 APRIL 0730 HOURS

Jenna scanned the outside facade of the building. Typical new town Telford build. Red brick, red roofing tiles, lifeless. Windows flat. Built in the 1970s to accommodate the influx of people from the surrounding areas. The overspill of Birmingham and Wolverhampton. Rabbit hutches that served the purpose of a utilitarian house with none of the attractiveness of the current new builds.

Jenna squinted as she studied each of the flat unattractive windows, checking for any movement behind curtains that hung limp and lifeless as though they'd been dragged back in haste that morning.

A movement out of the corner of her eye caught her attention and Jenna turned her head to watch the approach of a handsome Dalmatian high-stepping along the street towards them on the end of a jaunty red lead.

Three additional dogs by his side failed to catch her attention so fully. Dalmatians had that effect. Once you had one, you would always immediately have your attention drawn by the sheer beauty of the breed, the elegance, the powerful presence.

With a small jolt of recognition, Jenna gawped for a split second longer, a frisson of electricity flowed through her and stopped the breath in her chest.

She lowered herself down her seat and tugged at Mason's jacket sleeve. 'Shit, shit.'

Mason's eyes widened before he hunched his shoulders and slipped down in his seat, his knees giving a hard knock against the steering wheel as he scrunched himself into the smallest space he could.

'Fuck! It's Domino.'

His brows pulled low as he peered over the steering wheel, his neck stretching as he took a quick peek at the fast approach of the woman and four dogs.

'It's bloody Lena, the dog walker. What the hell is she doing all the way over here?'

Confused, Jenna ran a quick hand through her hair as she considered her options. With suspicion dominating, Jenna met Mason's bewildered gaze.

'Don't let her see us.'

Aware of Ryan's silence in the back of the car, Jenna glanced through the gap between the two front seats to see Ryan stretched out, coffee still in hand.

Jenna peeked out of the front window again as the dog walker paused while the big black Labrador squatted. Lena fished a bag out of her pocket and hunkered down to perform a very efficient one-handed scoop of the poop. As the woman looked down at the bag while she tied the handles in a knot, Jenna raised her radio to her lips.

'Chris, where are you?' From where they'd parked, she couldn't see the dog van.

'Just stopped around the corner from you, by the field. I thought the boy might want a quick run and a pee before I brought him in. Clear his nasal passages and keep him on point.'

'Good. Could you stay there? I have a bit of a strange situation. Domino's here with his dog walker. I don't want to spook her if she sees the dog van.'

'Your new dog walker? What's she doing here? It's a long way off your patch.'

'It certainly is. That's what I'm hoping to find out. I'll let you know when I have something interesting to tell you. In the meantime, let Blue have his run.'

'No problem, I'll join you when he's done. I'm in the unmarked van today.'

'Great.'

Jenna turned the volume down on Airwaves, so instead of the harsh crackle it was a low buzz while she considered her options. She could get out of the car and approach Lena, but everything about the situation screamed at her not to. She stayed low and frowned as the group of canines headed towards their vehicle again.

Jenna blew out a breath. 'I don't know why, but I have a bad feeling about this.'

'Me too. What the hell is she doing here? She must have driven. Why would you walk dogs in an entirely different part of Telford?'

'Maybe she got her schedule mixed up and had to juggle things.' Ryan shuffled forward to poke his head in between the seats. 'Perhaps she had an emergency to cover, someone else let the team down. One of the other walkers has gone sick.'

'Maybe.' Jenna agreed. 'Doesn't sit right though.' She lowered her voice to a whisper as though the woman could hear every word she uttered. 'Would you recognise her car if you saw it?'

Mason raised his head again and searched the street. 'Yep. There it is.'

24

'Ryan, can you see? Have a look out.'

Ryan shuffled around in the back seat, nudging his bony knees into the back of Jenna's chair hard enough to have her oofing out a lungful of air.

'Watch where she's going.' Jenna kept her voice to a low hiss. Instinct had her slipping lower in her seat and hitching up the collar of her jacket in case the woman happened to glance over as she passed by.

'What's she doing, Ryan?'

The pressure on her kidneys was miraculously relieved as Ryan shot back up behind her.

He scooted over to the other side of the car for a better view while Jenna kept low. 'She's crossed the road, and she's... Oh, shit.'

Tempted to leap up, Jenna held still. 'What? What?' She wriggled around to look through the gap between the front seats at Ryan. 'What's she doing?'

Ryan turned his head to meet her gaze, confusion streaking through his eyes. 'She's going down the pathway to number 33.'

'You're shitting me.' Jenna shot upright and twisted around. Unable to believe it, she squinted out of the rear window.

Lena Alexander strode along the path with a determined, jaunty bounce to her stride and four prancing dogs by her side. Her long ponytail swung in a synchronised pendulum with the wagging dog tails.

As the woman approached the house, she dipped her hand into a small dog treat pouch strapped to her hip, took out a key and slotted it in the lock. Before she pushed open the door, she glanced both ways as though she was checking if anybody was watching and Jenna ducked down again.

The quick kick of adrenaline from the cold coffee had her heart thrumming in her chest as her mind whirled with unanswered questions.

Questions that she feared she wasn't going to like the answers to.

As Lena slipped inside with the four dogs on their leads, Jenna, Mason and Ryan bobbed back up in their seats, with Mason rubbing at his abused knees.

'What the fuck is she doing?'

Mouth open, Jenna stared at Mason while she shook her head. 'She's supposed to be walking Domino local to our house, not all the way over here.' As a thought occurred to her, she stabbed her finger in the direction of the garish blue door Lena had taken the dogs through. 'We're paying her for exclusive one-on-one walks, she's not supposed to be walking him with other dogs. She must be making a bloody fortune out of all of us. Cheeky mare. And now she's taken Fliss's dog into a drug pusher's house. What the hell is going on?'

Mason stared over his shoulder and then turned back to Jenna. 'Maybe she made a mistake with her schedule, mucked up. Let's give her the benefit of the doubt and see if she's picking up another dog or dropping off one of the other three. It could just be coincidence.'

Doubt circled in her mind. 'No, something isn't right.' She tapped her fingers against her lips as she studied the door.

Ryan shuffled forward and pushed his face between the two front seats. 'What's her connection with Lamonte Junior? Is she just his dog walker?'

'I don't know, but I suspect we're about to find out. Who knew we'd be investigating the secret life of a dog walker?'

Jenna twisted the rear-view mirror and trained it so she could keep a visual on the house behind her.

Mason snorted as he turned around to face forward, crossed his arms over his wide chest and relaxed back in his seat. 'Let me know when there's movement, kiddo.'

Ryan huffed out a breath and flung himself back to look out of the rear window, making the car rock under his bouncing weight.

Jenna patted her pockets and fished out a tissue. She gave her nose a quick blow while she stared at the entrance to the house. Lena had been in there what felt to her an interminable length of time, but was possibly only a matter of minutes.

Mason turned his head to meet her gaze. 'What do you want to do? Should we go in?'

At the white flash of movement in the mirror, Jenna changed its angle to watch as Chris Bennett pulled the dog handler car alongside the kerb twenty-five metres behind them.

'No, no, I don't think so.' She flicked her gaze back up to the mirror. 'I'm going to have a word with Chris, see what he has to say.' She flashed Mason a smile. 'Back in a moment.'

She slipped from the car and shot down the road to the white unmarked dog van. Her heart raced as she kept a close eye on the front door of the house, willing it not to open, because if Lena came out and spotted her, she was either going to look very stupid, or she was going to have to act fast.

Breathless, she wrenched open the passenger door of the dog van and jumped in.

A quiet whine came from the back of the van and she turned her head to give Blue a quick smile. Not that a smile from her would make any difference.

Chris's weathered face screwed up, deepening the lines around his mouth as she bounced around to face forward again.

She slipped down in the seat. Covert operation it had now become, and excitement coursed through her veins. This was the very reason she'd become a police officer. The tension and exhilaration. The sheer exuberance of being on a job. Her second that day and she still hadn't come down from the high of the first.

They were just rolling in.

'So, what the hell has Domino got himself involved in?'

Jenna snorted out a laugh and wriggled in her seat so she could see the front door of number 33 past the solid form of Chris and through his side window. She shook her head. 'I don't know what the hell is going on.'

Chris reached over and patted her hand, but the little chugs of laughter rattled his chest. 'If you ask me, it looks like your dog might be pushing drugs.'

'What do you mean pushing drugs?' A zap of confusion hit her. In all the scenarios she'd run through her mind, a drug-pushing Domino had not filtered through.

Chris nodded at the front door. 'Give her another five minutes. When she comes out, we'll have a look what's on those dogs' collars.'

Ashamed at her naiveté, Jenna gawped at him. 'They do something to the dog collars?'

'Yeah. Little baggy rolls that most normal people attach to the dog's collar, so they carry their poop pouches themselves. Well, this is a different kind of shit. Yeah?' He nodded and a bitter grin flitted across his face. 'Fill one of those with a little bit of white stuff. You've got yourself a transporter.'

Chris settled back in his seat, so Jenna had a better view of the closed front door. The little flutter of her heart turned to a hammer.

'Okay, let me think. I wasn't expecting this. We were supposed to go in, inspect the place, gather bloody evidence. Not run a whole operation.'

She glanced at him and despite his laughter, she knew she could rely on him without question. The same rank as her, he was by far the more experienced officer, but he'd let her take the lead in this case. With the knowledge he was behind her all the way, Jenna's heart steadied. This was a job, like any other job. It may involve her sister's dog, but that didn't detract from the fact that something was going down, and she needed to decide based on the facts she currently had to hand.

She could pull back and hand it over to the Drug Squad. But by the time they were in place, Lena, the dogs and the evidence would most likely have disappeared.

'Right. Assuming Lena is about to come out of that house with dog drug-couriers, I'm going to leave you and Mason to wait for her to clear the place and then conduct a search of the house for drugs.'

Serious now, Chris nodded his agreement.

'Ryan and I will follow Lena. We'll watch where she makes her drops.'

'Well, don't be too hasty. Let's just check first if there's something on their collars once they come out the door.'

As the time ticked away, Jenna deferred to Chris's experience and wisdom. It didn't make her any less fidgety, though. 'What she's doing in there?'

Relaxed, Chris smiled at her. 'She could be finding the drugs. Loading them on the collars.'

'I think she's cutting them herself.' Jenna slapped the heel of her hand against her forehead. 'How the hell did I let this get past me, Chris?'

Chris chuckled. 'She could be dropping off his dog, after an innocent dog walk, having a cup of coffee. She'll come out soon. She has four dogs to walk.'

Jenna glanced at the time on her phone. 'She better do, I swear we pay her for a two-hour walk, which means she has about forty-five minutes left. It's not much of a walk, stuck inside someone else's house while she has a bloody cup of tea, or whatever.'

'You mean the *whatever* being loading up your dog's collar with drugs so he can push them for her?' Chris's humour rumbled out of him in a deep laugh.

'I wouldn't care but she knows I'm a police officer.'

'That's a bloody slap in the face then. Brazen bugger.'

About to reply, Jenna scooted down in her seat so she could peer over Chris's shoulder as Lena slipped out of the front door with the four dogs walking to perfection. Two on the left, two on the right. The sweet little shih-tzu trotted with her mouth open as she gasped for breath, trying to keep up with the others.

Jenna sank lower in her seat again as Lena walked the four dogs towards the car. If she saw Chris, it wasn't such an issue. A man in his car. But if she recognised Jenna, the game would be up.

Chris pointed, keeping his voice low. 'Can you see them?'

Jenna stretched her neck so her eyes were just above the level of the bottom of the window.

On each of the dogs' collars hung a small barrel-shaped holder which could be mistaken for poop bag holders. Genuine shock rippled through Jenna despite the suspicion. Until the moment she saw them, she'd held out hope that the young woman was purely carrying out her job.

'Oh God, I'd hoped it wasn't true.'

'Looks like her resumé didn't cover all her activities.'

'She came so highly recommended by one of the other teachers at Fliss's school.' Jenna glanced at the shih-tzu. 'I'm pretty convinced that's the teacher's dog as well. I've met her over at Dale End Park a few times and I think that's little Lily. I can't remember her mum's name, but I bet she doesn't have a clue what's going on.'

Chris's body vibrated with laughter as she leaned against his shoulder to get a better look. 'I bet she doesn't know poor little Fifi's being walked to death to deliver drugs.'

'I hope to God she doesn't – and it's Lily, not Fifi. I'm pretty sure she wouldn't have recommended Fliss use the dog walker if she'd been aware or involved. She knows I'm a police officer. But obviously questions will have to be asked. We'll need to interview the owners as the dogs can't speak for themselves.'

Jenna held her breath as Lena crossed over the road and walked past on Jenna's side of the car. Jenna hunched her shoulders and turned so her back was towards the side window. As Lena walked past with Domino and the other three dogs, an amused grunt came out of Chris's mouth.

'What happened?' Jenna swivelled around.

'Nothing.' He grinned. 'But take a look at that.'

Jenna watched the rear view of Lena and the dogs as they marched along the street. Domino no longer walked to heel but looked backwards at Chris's car.

Chris pointed at the Dalmatian. 'He knows you're here.'

'No.' Jenna wriggled upright. 'He surely can't know.'

Domino stopped and pulled Lena up short as he refused to go any further. Impatient, Lena jerked the lead, but Domino leaned into it, dragging back towards the dog van, his nose in the air.

'Shit. You're right. He knows I'm here. How can he?'

Chris jiggled his shoulders. 'They're not stupid. He can smell you. Your scent will be all the way from your vehicle to mine and he's had no problem picking it up. Good lad.' Chris's voice vibrated with admiration.

'I hope she doesn't look back.'

'She won't. She's got her hands full, look.' The plump black Labrador yanked in the opposite direction and almost took Lena off her feet. Irritation streaked across the woman's face as she gave a good hard snap at Domino's lead. Reluctant to leave, he continued to send quick glances behind him as he followed her, with Lena giving short, sharp tugs on the lead every couple of steps until they were almost out of sight at the end of the long road.

'You know if I wasn't on a stake out, I'd get out and poke her in the eye for that. I'd say it's abuse. Would you?'

Chris narrowed his eyes not taking his gaze from the subject. 'It's not abuse, it's just a little snap on the lead to get his attention. He's certainly not in the least worried about it. His tail was whipping like crazy.'

Unconvinced, Jenna huffed out her irritation. She'd still poke her in the eye. Domino was a sensitive soul. He wouldn't like being treated like that.

Jenna rubbed her hands over her face. 'I'm starting to sound like my sister. He's a dog, for crying out loud.'

'Aye,' Chris tossed her a quick look, 'the most precious things in our lives.'

With her fingers around the door handle, Jenna cast Chris a last look. 'Okay, I've got to leave you to it. If you and Mason enter the house, call SOCO in anyway. We've seen enough to know there'll be evidence in there.'

Jenna fished in her pocket and handed over the house key while the words rushed from her mouth in her haste to get out of the car and back to her own. 'Here's the key, I'll send Mason to meet up with you. Ryan and I will follow Lena and see where she's taking the dogs. I assume she walks them here and then piles them all back in the car to drive them home again.' She huffed out a breath. 'I'll call for backup. Keep me informed.'

Jenna slipped from the car and raced around the bonnet as fast as she could in case Lena looked back as Domino stopped dead at the end of the street. His high-pitched whine reached her as she yanked open the door to the police vehicle and dived inside.

'Ryan, you're with me. Mason, get out.' As surprised whipped through his eyes, she nudged him. 'You're with Chris, he's got the front door key. You can both do the search.'

Mason leapt from the car and slammed the door behind him while Jenna flopped over the centre console into the driver's seat and fired up the car, cringing as she over-revved the engine in her excitement.

Mason swivelled around as he dipped his hands into his jacket pocket, made an over-exaggerated flinch and headed off towards the dog vehicle.

'I can drive.' Ryan volunteered from the back seat.

She stared over her shoulder at him. She'd seen his driving before. Wild, erratic. She let out a derogatory snort. 'You need to go on a police driving course first.'

'I've already been on one.'

'That's even more worrying.' Jenna put the car in gear and slid smoothly away from the kerb. 'I'll take it this time, Ryan, thank you.'

She cruised the car along the road just as Lena and the dogs disappeared around the bend at a fast stride, dragging the little shih-tzu along behind her as Domino, who now pranced back by her side again, cast a quick longing look backwards.

If Lena let him off the lead now, Jenna would bet her life he'd come sprinting back into view. The dog never forgot a single thing. Too intelligent for his own good and quite often Fliss and Jenna's too.

As Jenna nudged the car around the bend, Lena came back into sight and crossed the road ahead of them. Jenna let the engine idle as she hovered at the kerb, far enough back so Lena wouldn't notice.

Starting to recognise Lena's body language, Jenna paid close attention as Lena cast a quick glance over each shoulder. 'Here she goes.'

'How do you know?' Ryan bobbed his head between the two front seats to peer out of the front window, his head close to Jenna's.

She pointed. 'Watch.'

Lena walked down the pathway to another small two-bedroom house with red roof tiles on the front facia. Smart white venetian blinds covered the windows, kept closed so no one could see inside.

Jenna picked up the radio, pressed the button and spoke into Airwaves. 'Juliet Alpha 77 to Control.'

'Control, go ahead.'

Jenna narrowed her eyes to keep a focus on Lena as the woman did another head turn and then knocked on the shiny, white high-gloss door.

'I'm at number 82 Doseley Way, Mountside with DC Downey in pursuit of a suspect while DS Bennett and DC Ellis are carrying out the warrant on number 33 Doseley Way. I could do with some uniform backup to help me out please. We're going to need to arrest several suspects and possibly perform more searches for suspicion of drugs on the premises in several houses, by the look of it. Number unknown at present. No blues and twos, silent approach.'

As Jenna gave half her attention to Control, the front door of the small house swung open and Lena lengthened the leads to allow the dogs to greet the woman who stepped into the weak morning sunlight.

With a jolt of recognition, Jenna jerked forward, resting her arms on the steering wheel.

A young emaciated woman, straggly, dull brown hair down past her shoulders, deep-set eyes bruised and red-rimmed, reached out to touch the dogs with a casual lack of interest.

Jenna cast a quick sideways glance at Ryan and lifted her forefinger to point at the woman on the doorstep. 'That's Marie West. Do you recognise her?'

Ryan leaned forward for a better look and shook his head. 'No. I don't think I've come across her before.'

'She's well known for her habit.' Jenna huffed out a disgusted sigh. 'I didn't know she'd moved to a new house. She must be going up in the world.' She tapped her fingers on the steering wheel as they watched. 'She used to live in an old squat in Randlay.'

The radio crackled to life.

'Juliet Alpha 77, this is Sierra Romeo 36. We've pulled up three hundred yards behind you. What can we do to assist?'

Thinking on her feet to formulate her plan, Jenna pushed herself upright without taking her gaze from the suspects. 'Sierra Romeo 36, you take 82 Doseley Way once our dog walker moves out of sight. There's a known user there, Marie West.'

'Yep, I know her well.' The response was fast and unhesitating.

'Did you know she'd moved to a new house?'

'No, but we do now.'

'You'll have to be quick in there. She's going to have that little white powder up her nose before you can count to twenty.'

'We've got a handle on it, Sarge.'

Satisfied that they knew what they needed to do, Jenna placed the radio on the centre console without once taking her attention from the smooth exchange that went on as Marie hunkered down to give the large brindle greyhound a fussy greeting.

As Marie came to her feet, she stepped her skinny frame back into the house and closed the door with barely a second glance at the dogs. Lena reached over, gave the greyhound a quick ruffle around the neck with her right hand and slipped the dog a treat. Domino, full attention on the treat, sat with neck stretched up and left paw raised. Lena smiled, slipped her hand under his chin and offered him a treat before giving the remaining two their share. It was her saving grace that she evidently did love dogs.

Lena turned with all four of them and made her way back down the pathway casting quick, furtive glances up and down the street before she turned her back on Jenna's car and continued along in the same direction as previously. The greyhound bumped shoulder to shoulder with Domino, minus its little baggy on the collar.

Ryan chewed his lip as Domino looked over his shoulder again. 'She might think she's checking, but she's not too observant, is she? Hasn't she recognised this as the same car that she already passed further down the street?'

Jenna turned the engine back on and nudged the car at a snail's pace further along the street, ensuring she kept a good distance. Lena may not be the most observant person, but once she did spot them, the game would be over, and Jenna was curious about the destination of the remaining three little baggies. Was she about to discover more known addicts who'd moved into this tight little community?

'Good for us she doesn't'.

With a hint of admiration in his voice, Ryan flung himself back in his seat. 'God, I've never seen anything like it. I didn't know dogs pushed drugs.' Ryan's whole body jittered with excitement as his caffeine fix chose now to kick in, Jenna suspected.

'Neither did I. What a bloody cheek, she's getting paid full whack for walking dogs that she's actually using to aid and abet her.'

'A bit risky, I'd say, to use a police officer's dog for the job.' Ryan chuckled. 'She must have known.'

'She did, cheeky mare. Fliss made all the arrangements. Lena comes while we're at work, so I rarely see her. She walks Domino. As far as we knew, everything was fine. She sent photos, images of them, each time she walked him. Bloody hell, she's a wily one.' She shook her head. 'I wouldn't classify this as an energising walk. Yes, she's strutting along with them all, but we thought Domino was getting a good off-lead run. I wonder if she takes him elsewhere after the drug drop-off.'

'She probably wouldn't have enough time.'

Jenna ran her hand through her hair while they watched and waited. 'I wonder if I can charge her with fraud too.' She spoke her thoughts out loud.

'When can we pick her up, Sarge?'

'Not yet. Hold your horses, Ryan. We want the full picture.'

She put the car back in gear and crawled it along the kerb until Lena arrived at her next destination.

Jenna reached for her radio. 'Juliet Alpha 77 to Control, put me through to DI Taylor.'

The connection was instantaneous.

'DS Morgan, what's your update?'

'Sir, I need another team to do a search at number 295 Doseley Way.'

'They're already on their way, Jenna.'

'Don't let them approach too quickly because our suspect is in transit with the drugs.'

'Acknowledged.'

As the next door opened, a young man bounced barefoot from his doorway, his arms and legs jerked and twitched in the small myoclonus spasms of someone who had already taken too much cocaine.

Domino wrenched back on his lead and then surged forward, his neck stretched out, his lips pulled back in a snarl. The deep unmistakable Dalmatian bark echoed around the house-lined street as Lena hauled back on his lead.

Jenna gripped the door handle ready to surge out of the car.

The man bolted back into his house whipping his hands away from the imminent threat of being bitten.

Jenna hesitated as Lena held tight to Domino's lead. She knew exactly how to handle a big, defensive dog. Defensive only since his encounter with Frank Bartwell, who had almost killed him and attacked Fliss twice.

Jenna trusted his instinct one hundred per cent as she recognised the young drug addict just inside the doorway. Domino sensed a bad person when he met one and he was right.

'Joel Hopkins.'

'Domino doesn't like him.'

'I don't like him. Nasty little toad. Been in and out of youth custody since he was sixteen, and more recently just finished a two-year stretch in Lowdham Grange Prison.'

'He doesn't look much older than nineteen or twenty.'

'He's thirty-two. He's so emaciated, it makes him look like a boy.' She cast Ryan a quick glance, conscious that she might insult him with her next words. 'All skinny neck and gangly arms and legs.'

Nothing on Ryan's face indicated he'd taken insult. Quite comfortable with his own long-limbed gaucheness, he was probably oblivious to the youthful vibes he exuded. 'What was he in for?'

Jenna appreciated his insatiable curiosity and willingness to learn. 'Aggravated burglary to feed his addiction. He used a twelve-inch screwdriver to threaten an old man.'

The enthusiasm dropped from his face as his eyes turned into cold, pure copper. 'Should have been in longer.'

'They let him out early and look where that's got him.' She nodded at the man as his limbs twitched and jerked. 'Obviously been hitting it too hard.'

Lena gained control of Domino. A little ripple of pride ran through Jenna. An obedient dog, once the threat had backed away and he saw his job was done, he sat by the woman's left leg. He may be obedient, but he remained alert.

Ryan jiggled forward in his seat. 'What's Lena telling Joel?'

From the hand signals Lena made, Jenna assumed, 'I think she's had to switch dogs. It looks like she's telling him to take the baggie from the black Labrador.'

'Hmm. Possibly. They must both be carrying the same dose.'

'I'm not sure Lena cares. She doesn't look happy. In fact, she looks progressively more uncomfortable.'

With a slow, cautious move, the man went down on his haunches and called the black Labrador to him, gave him a wary little fuss and then stood abruptly dipping his hand into his pocket.

Jenna tipped her head to one side. 'And there it goes.'

'Not so smooth.'

'Not a dog lover, obviously.'

Joel reached out and touched the girl's hand in what Jenna assumed was him passing the money, as Lena shook her head and flung her clenched fist in the direction of the Labrador. Joel rolled his shoulders in an insolent shrug. Lena's lips tightened and as Joel shut the door, she made her way down the pathway, doing her quick check once more.

Surprised she still hadn't noticed them, Jenna held her breath and waited until Lena was almost out of sight again before she put the car back in gear to catch up with her. She crawled the car along, letting Lena stay just on the horizon before moving on. As she came back into sight, Lena dipped down to take a narrow path to another front door, with her fast one-two head turn, which appeared to achieve nothing.

This house, unlike the others, had a bright, vibrant, red front door, with curtains sashed across the windows in big blousy colours and flowers spilling over bright and gregarious. Flowers in colours that should have clashed but, as with nature, simply looked beautiful together.

Instead of Lena knocking, this time she withdrew a key from her little hip pouch and opened the door to disappear inside with the four dogs.

Jenna tapped the steering wheel. 'What's she doing?'

She never had an expectation of Ryan answering her question. It was rhetorical.

She watched for a moment longer while her mind juggled with the possibilities. 'I think she's dropping off one of the dogs. This is what she does for us. She has a house key. She picks up the dog, takes him for a walk. She drops off the dog, gives him some water, makes sure he's settled down.' She glanced at Ryan, his intent gaze centred on the red door. 'I wonder how many other dogs have been inside my house.' Jenna let the annoyance circle around. Fliss was being cheated out of her money. Domino was being used to push drugs.

The bright red door swung open and Lena stepped out with Domino, the black Labrador and the shih-tzu. As Jenna suspected, the handsome brindle greyhound had been left behind having carried out his duties.

'Okay, we're gonna have to conduct a search on this house too. I suspect the owner here is like Fliss and me and literally doesn't know about the drugs. We know the greyhound no longer had drugs on him, so get on the radio, Ryan, and ask for a team to contact the owner of that address. Get them home in order for us to conduct the search. Taking a considered judgement on this, I'd bet they're not involved.' She took a sideways look at Ryan. 'Get on to DI Taylor and let's have it checked out anyway.'

He lifted the radio and pressed the button, speaking into it as it came to life, his voice a background noise as Jenna blocked him out while she concentrated on their next move. She put the car in gear and followed Lena again at a safe distance.

Lena got a good trot on with the remaining three dogs. Even though the little shih-tzu struggled to keep up, its tail wagged and its tongue lolled out while they continued for a further ten minutes before Lena slowed down and turned to dip through the walkway between two link detached houses and disappeared from view.

With a small whip of excitement, Jenna pressed her foot on the accelerator to speed up in case she lost the woman on the other side of the linked houses. She drew up and peered through the walkway just as Lena carried out her quick glance left, right, then left again. This time, her head took a slow turn and she stared straight at the car, her mouth dropping open in a silent 'oh'.

'Shit. She's spotted us.' Adrenaline kicked in to set Jenna's pulse hammering through her throat as she froze, both hands gripping the steering wheel.

Lena narrowed her eyes for a brief moment before she turned her back while Jenna held her breath.

'It's okay. I don't think so.'

As Ryan finished his last word, Lena took another two steps and the dead giveaway was in the glance she flicked over her shoulder before she dropped all three leads and raced off with the dogs scattering from around her in the wild belief that it was a new form of exercise. A game.

Jenna rammed the car into first gear and flung it through the walkway, almost scraping the mirrors against the narrow brick walls. She took an immediate right and headed towards the entrance of a cul-de-sac. She hit third gear just as the little shih-tzu changed direction and decided to prance towards them.

Jenna slammed her foot on the brake hard enough to make the car rock.

'Ryan. Go. Go. Go.'

Ryan flung himself out of the car, slamming the rear passenger door as he raced after Lena.

Jenna threw open her own door, leapt out of the seat and whistled. Domino's head shot up and his tail went out straight as he screeched to a full stop and then whipped around to face her. Delighted, he bounded towards her, the other two dogs following in their determination to join in the new game. Jenna wrenched open the rear door and as the dogs raced to her, she flung her arm wide to indicate the car.

'In!' she raised her voice to a sharp command.

As she expected, Domino bounded straight into the back of the car. His huge, muscular body spinning around in tight circles on the back seat, absolute delight in every twitch of his muscles to have accidentally found Jenna on his daily walk.

Jenna reached out and gave his broad head a quick scrub. 'Good lad, good lad.'

As she turned, the fat black Labrador eased his way onto the back seat with a little more delicacy and, with no regard for the Dalmatian, shoved his way across and let out a loud huff of dog breath as he collapsed in a happy heap on the seat.

With nothing to do but see to the small dog, Jenna wasted no time in hoisting the shih-tzu in beside them. She took a split second to touch each animal's head before she slammed the door, hitting the lock button as she grabbed her radio from her belt and spoke into it whilst she raced down the street and around the bend in pursuit of Ryan and Lena.

25

Arms and legs pumping, Jenna pushed herself until her breath heaved in her throat as the pair in front of her came back into sight, both of them running like international marathon champions. She kicked up her heels and stretched her long legs into a full-pelt run, picking up speed as she raced downhill, the gap never seeming to close.

Ryan's voice shouted a third time. 'Police! Stop!'

He was wasting his breath, he just needed to grab her. When you had a runner, you just needed to get the job done.

Jenna willed him on because hell, he was almost a decade younger than her, he should be fitter and faster.

Within touching distance, he reached out and grabbed at Lena's shoulder. He yanked her off her feet and she tumbled backwards into his arms.

Relieved, Jenna slowed her pace, her lungs burned with the effort. She'd not run as hard in years. She wasn't a short-sprint runner, more of a solid march all day without stopping kind of girl. This would kill her. The burn in her calves already making itself known.

Ahead of her, Ryan's voice, pitched low and breathless, could barely be heard, but Jenna assumed he read Lena her rights as he held on to her shoulder, his chest heaving.

Still some way down the street, Jenna sensed the moment he made his mistake.

He let go of his suspect to pat his duty belt and as he reached for the speed cuffs, Lena whirled.

Face contorted in a wild snarl, she lunged at Ryan, lashing out with feet and fists.

'Jesus.' Jenna's reflexes kicked back in and she broke into another run as Lena leapt at Ryan and slammed him to the floor, long fingers like claws reaching for his scalp. His yowl echoed along the street as Lena clutched his hair with both hands and jerked his head upwards.

Jenna's heart hammered like a wild bird as Lena let out a high-pitched scream and moved to smash his head into the pavement. With ice running through her veins, Jenna stormed through to grab Lena around the waist. She hoisted her high and wrenched her off Ryan. Surprise rippled through her at the weight of the smaller woman as Jenna used it to her advantage and slammed Lena face down on the floor. Using her own weight she dropped, punching her knees straight into Lena's shoulder blades, she leaned her whole weight into her, pinning her where she lay.

Lena's breath shot out in a loud grunt. Jenna grabbed the back of her head before Lena had the chance to buck. She pressed her cheek hard against the tarmac road and never afforded her a second chance as she whacked on a pair of speed cuffs one-handed.

The blue lights and two tones warned of the approach of the backup vehicles.

Jenna edged slowly off the woman, not trusting her to behave as she came to her feet and dragged Lena up after her. There was one thing she'd learnt early on in her career: if you had a fighter, don't ever give them the opportunity to kick off once you had them controlled. The only one to get injured would be the officer. She'd seen too many taken out like that. Trust was not an option, especially when dealing with drug related crime.

She drew in a breath through her nose to slow down the hard puffs wheezing out, making her sound like she smoked fifty a day.

Before her backup team reached her, Jenna gave Lena a light shove towards them. Lena stumbled and Jenna made another grab for her, linked her arm through Lena's and marched her over to the waiting uniforms.

Fury burned from eyes that met hers before doubt filled them and Lena's forehead crinkled. Her mouth dropped open and recognition flooded her features.

'Yeah. Me.' Jenna shot her a tight grin. 'Recognise me? I'm the one whose dog you chose to push drugs for you.' Technically, Fliss's dog, but she wasn't about to split hairs.

'I—'

Before Lena could speak, Jenna raised her forefinger to her lips. 'Sshh.' As the woman stuttered to a halt, Jenna dropped her hand and guided Lena forward. 'Lena Alexander, I'm arresting you on suspicion of possession and supply of class A drugs and assaulting a police officer. You do not have to say anything, but it may harm your defence if you do not mention when questioned something which you later rely on in court. Anything you do say may be given in evidence.' She handed her over to the safekeeping of PC Liz Oliver, her freckled face well known amongst the officers, having been in the job for more than twenty-five years. 'This is PC Oliver, she'll be escorting you to Malinsgate Police Station where you will be interviewed.' She smiled at the PC as she handed Lena over. 'Watch her, she's not all sweetness and light.'

Seasoned as she was, Liz grinned, her cheeks plumping out like a hamster. 'I can see that for myself.' She nodded in Ryan's direction

as she took possession of Lena and manoeuvred her into the back
seat of the police vehicle, hand on the top of her head to protect it
from the door frame. She shut the door on her and turned to look
at Ryan again. 'Is he okay?'

Satisfied now her prisoner was contained, Jenna turned around,
her breathing still fast and shallow. Not in the least worried about
Liz, she knew the other woman would never pass judgement on
how out of shape Jenna was.

On the ground, Ryan gingerly touched his scalp where Lena
had wrenched his hair out by the roots. His hand came away with a
handful of the pale, sandy hair as horror streaked over his face.

'Oh, I think so. He should never have let go. He had her pinned.
Perfect arrest.'

Liz crossed her arms over her chest and snorted as she leaned
her backside against the car door. 'We all learn by our mistakes. I've
caught a few myself.'

Jenna nodded. She'd been on the painful end of a couple of
errors too. 'It's a lesson. He won't let his guard down again once he
believes he's got a situation under control.'

It was never under control until the suspect was cuffed and
adequately restrained, whatever form that may take.

Liz's lips kicked up into a sympathetic smile. 'Some come along
like lambs, others like lions.'

'Yeah.' Jenna brushed her hands down her black trousers,
flicking off the dust. From the hammering they'd had that day,
they'd probably end up in the bin failing a good boil wash. 'It was
Ryan's day to have the lion.'

With her pulse rate returning to normal, Jenna squinted down
at him. She needed to get on. She'd never imagined the short
search warrant job was going to morph into a major incident. She
still had one of those waiting for her back at the station. Still
keeping all the balls in the air. It wasn't unusual to be busy, but in

the last forty-eight hours she'd managed to squeeze in an entire week's worth of work and still had more than double that to go with the fire investigation. Confident DI Taylor had his hand to the tiller and would let her know the moment anything kicked off there, at least she could concentrate on this case.

'Anything more you need me for, Sarge, or should I get this one back to the station?'

'No, we're fine. Thank you, Liz, you get off and I'll see you there soon. As you heard, I've read her her rights.' It never harmed to have a witness to that when some suspects would claim they weren't read their rights and get off on a technicality. 'Book her in with the duty sergeant and she can stay in the cells until I get back. DC Downey and I will interview her. Until then, it won't harm her to cool her heels.'

Jenna flicked a look at the time on her phone, surprised at how fast the day had sped by. Almost ten o'clock. They really did need to get back to the station, get the paperwork sorted, interviews done all before the debrief on the fire. Lamonte Junior would have his turn, too. Balls in the air. That was one she'd let Mason and Ryan catch.

Satisfied everything was wrapped up as best it could be, Jenna made her way over to Ryan as he placed his hands on the floor and pushed to his knees while his chest heaved, and he dragged in lung-fuls of air.

Her own breath still coming in heavy puffs, Jenna bent at the hip. She really needed more exercise. She was out of shape. She needed to do something about it. A brisk walk with Domino every day hardly prepared her for the hundred-yard dash. She drew in a long breath. Perhaps she'd take up jogging. Domino was going to need more exercise for the foreseeable future. She might as well make use of it. She doubted they'd be employing another dog walker in a hurry.

Jenna rested her hands on her knees as she brought her face level with Ryan's. 'You okay?' She leaned forward and touched his elbow. His shins would probably show the results of the hard kicks Lena had administered to him for some time to come.

'Yeah, yeah just a little winded.' He thumbed his hand in the direction of the departing police vehicle. 'I didn't expect her to run so fast.'

Amusement rippled out on a chuckle. 'You didn't expect her to fight so hard.'

'She caught me.'

As she straightened, he came to his feet.

'I saw. Your shins took a good bashing.'

His face, already pink, flushed a deep crimson to light up his ears. 'Not just my shins.' He let out an embarrassed cough. 'She got my family jewels too.'

'Oh.' Jenna quashed the desire to laugh at his diplomatic way of expressing himself. Mason would have said 'bollocks' and she'd never have given it a second thought. 'Is that what made you breathless? I thought it was the run. I was pretty impressed with your speed. You were good.'

He narrowed his eyes as his mouth quirked up at one side. 'I've been training with Carla. I can't have her put me to shame. She's due to run the London Marathon this year. She's at the peak of her fitness.' His obvious pride in his new girlfriend warmed Jenna's heart, but he didn't need to see it softening.

'Jeez, Ryan with all that and the gym, you could be Superman.' He'd certainly put in plenty of effort since he'd started dating the woman of his dreams. A red-haired, honey-eyed nurse who he'd met through an online dating app. Fit, intelligent and feisty, Ryan had plenty to keep him on his toes.

Ryan peered at her from under his eyebrows, suspicion lurked in his gaze. 'What are you trying to say about me? Do you think I look like Clark Kent?'

There was something about Ryan that squeezed at Jenna's heart and made her want to scrub the top of his head like she did with Domino. He brought out a maternal instinct in her that was less a reflection of their ages and more of his appealing innocence and lack of maturity.

'No, Ryan, I was thinking more of your superpowers rather than your looks.'

As he preened at the sly stroke of his ego, Jenna glanced at her phone again. Time was running away with them and there were only so many hours in a day. A police officer might use more of them than most in carrying out their duty, but she couldn't squeeze any more than twenty-four hours out of one. It looked like she needed all twenty-four of them today.

'We've got to go. Those dogs have been in my car for long enough. I know it's not that hot, but there are three of them in there and I never had a chance to leave a window open. I didn't think about it when I saw you hotfooting it after Lena.'

She took off, her stride lengthening to eat up the distance between her and the car without actually breaking into a run, her heart still thrummed at a steady pace.

'All right. Let's see what we have here.'

As she approached the car, one sweet little face peered at her and the very tips of the shih-tzu's ears twitched behind the fine layer of dog spit and steam from the back seat. Big brown eyes and ears to attention.

She couldn't help but smile at the third dog. 'Bloody typical.'

Domino perched on the front seat like Little Lord Fauntleroy. He stared with superiority straight at her, as though he hadn't a care in the world and his expectation was that she would arrive to transport him home, as was his due.

Jenna unlocked the car and slipped into the driver's seat, taking a moment to greet all three dogs as their tails wagged in unison and bashed at the sides of the police vehicle as they stomped their paws over the seats in a flurry of dog hair and spit. She scrubbed the heads and ears of each one of them before she turned to strap the seat belt around her. She clipped it in and punched the ignition as Ryan opened the passenger door. Jenna blasted the demister at full pelt to clear the steamy windows and then glanced over to see what the delay was with Ryan getting in.

He stood frozen at the open doorway while Domino stared straight ahead.

'Oh, for God's sake, tell him to move, Ryan. We've taken long enough here.'

Ryan stepped back and bobbed down so his face came into view beyond Domino. 'I could always get in the back seat.'

Domino swivelled his head to stare at Jenna as though the battle he'd fought for dominance of the front seat had been won.

'Don't be silly, Domino won't harm you.' She reached out to pat the dog's neck.

Doubt wriggled over Ryan's face. 'That's all very well for you to say, but you're not the one with the teeth.'

Jenna chuckled. 'Stop messing about, Ryan, and just get in, we need to get back to the station.'

He reached his hand into the car and with a cautious move, touched Domino's neck and then whipped it away again as Domino rumbled out a low-pitched warning.

Jenna smiled. 'He's all right. He won't touch you. He's a big softie really, you can shove him over. You know he just talks.'

'Your dog's a drug pusher. I'm not going to trust him.'

She snorted.

He reached in and tentatively took hold of Domino's lead.

Out of patience, Jenna gave Domino a quick shove. 'Out,' she commanded as Ryan tugged at the lead.

As though it was his own idea, Domino made an elegant bounce out of the car and trotted to the back door as Ryan opened it for him.

The car rocked as Domino leapt in the back seat. Ryan slammed the door and made a dash for the front, leaping into the seat just as Domino squeezed his way in between the two front seats and landed on his lap.

Ryan wrapped his arms around the dog's neck as Domino raked his tongue from his chin to his ear and then repeated the action, adding a soft rumble of contentment that vibrated through his chest.

Ryan let out a chuckle of amusement, having never been subjected to such close attention from Domino. 'Christ, has he never been trained?'

Jenna grinned. Domino was perfectly well trained. He did everything he was told. Until he didn't want to. But enough was enough and she needed to move.

'Domino, get in the back.' Jenna put on her voice of command and the dog instantly leapt into the back seat to join the other two.

Ryan threw her a grateful glance. 'Better drive carefully. None of them are strapped in.'

Jenna turned to glance at the furry friends on the back seat, the little shih-tzu looking at odds between the two huge dogs.

Ryan was right. Domino normally sat in the boot of her car with a small black dog guard across the back seats, so he didn't leap over. She couldn't do that with the police vehicle. 'Do you want to tether them?'

'Will they sit with a seat belt around them?' Ryan squinted at her.

'I don't know.' She shrugged. How was she supposed to know? She wasn't the damned oracle.

'Perhaps we should have called the dog handler.'

'Chris is occupied at the moment. I don't think we've got anybody else on shift today. We'd have to call them out of area and that means waiting.' She turned to check on the animals again. 'We'll just go steady.' She put the car into gear and set off at a sedate pace. 'I thought I might take Domino back home, drop him off there first, but then I just realised SOCO are going to have to check him over. We're going to have to take all three of them back to the station. It could take bloody hours if we can't get hold of SOCO. I bet they're all tied up with the fire.' She slid a sly glance at her passenger of the human variety, hoping he might take the hint to contact his dad, Chief Forensics Officer, Jim Downey.

Head down and self-absorbed, Ryan tapped at the screen on his phone.

Ryan needed more than a hint, he needed a good hard shove. Dispensing with subtleties, Jenna got to the point. 'Is your dad about?'

Without raising his head, Ryan continued to tap. 'He's probably tied up on the fire.'

That's what she'd said. He wasn't listening. Evidently whatever was on Ryan's phone was more interesting than what she had to say. She made loud tutting noises to grab his attention.

He jiggled his shoulders in a self-conscious shrug. 'He's not going to be able to drop everything for a five-minute job. I don't like to ask.'

Jenna chewed her lip as she glanced over her shoulder and pulled out into the overtaking lane, cruising at a steady fifty-five miles an hour. Decision made, she reached forward, scooped up her radio and offered it to Ryan. 'Give the station a shout. Ask who is about.'

Ryan raised the radio to his mouth and depressed the button. 'Juliet Alpha 77 to Control.' Static crackled in the background to join the gentle whine from the little shih-tzu.

Jenny glanced at the back seat. 'I hope she doesn't get car sick.'

Ryan opened his mouth to answer, but the radio kicked back in. 'Control, go ahead.'

'Control, could you check if there's anyone from SOCO available to carry out drugs forensics on three dogs we're bringing into the station?'

A long stream of static filled the pause on the other end of the line. 'Juliet Alpha 77, please confirm you wish SOCO to check three *dogs.*'

Ryan chuckled as he glanced at his watch. 'Confirmed, Control. We've picked up three *drug-pushing dogs.*' He clicked off the speak button and snorted out a laugh.

Jenna stared at him. Who was this person in the car with her? It appeared young Ryan had found his place in the team, his effervescence spilling out.

After a moment, he sobered and spoke into Airwaves again, only to take her by surprise. 'One of them belongs to DS Morgan.' This time his laughter pushed out to fill the car.

Jenna shook her head as she pulled the car out onto the main ring road towards Malinsgate Station. 'Thanks, Ryan. You big kid. I'll never live this down.' Every last person in the station would take pleasure out of ribbing her about it. There had to be a bright side. 'At least he got his walk.'

Ryan's laughter came harder as he shook his head. 'I'd love to see your sister's face when you tell her Domino has been making his own living. Bad boy.' He tossed over his shoulder at the dogs on the back seat. 'He's moved over to the dark side.'

Domino's ears flicked back in complete understanding.

Jenna joined in Ryan's laughter and let it roll off her, happy with the momentary distraction. It was an eon ago they started work and yet they hadn't managed to get into the station so far. Some days went like that. 'Who would have known the day would go this way?'

Ryan turned to face her, and Domino stuck his snout between the two front seats to snag a quick kiss with him. With another hoot of laughter, Ryan reared his head back out of the way of the errant dog tongue.

'I fucking love my job.' A happy grin settled across his face as the laughter died out. 'I fucking love it. There's never two days the same.'

She couldn't agree more. Nothing ever remained the same. Some days floated past on paperwork and politics, others on domestics and theft. Very rarely did they catch a big case. She suspected the fire was about to become one of their biggest.

Although... she snapped out a grin of her own. Who would have suspected she'd rumble an entire drugs ring, including the drug-pushing dogs when she picked up her coffee that morning? Kudos to the team for jumping on board so quick. Task Force couldn't have done any better. But they'd be picking the up-line drugs ring up if they could through young Shaun.

Jenna glanced in the rear-view mirror at the two large dogs posed to perfection on the back seat, staring out of the side windows as though it was their right to ride in a police vehicle, and assumed Lily was somewhere on the back seat between them.

Her gaze flickered down to her handbag wedged on its side against Ryan's leg in the passenger footwell, the contents spilling out. Resigned to the loss of her lunch, Jenna sighed as she raised her gaze again to the pure innocence of the panini-loving Dalmatian on the back seat.

Airwaves sprang back to life and the deep tones of Morris King, the communications operator, flowed over them. The best voice in the station, deep and sexy with the melodic undertones of Wales filtered through. Used to his five foot five square frame and bald head, his appearance still managed to disappoint every time Jenna saw him, but she could listen to his voice forever.

'You're in luck, DC Downey. Jim Downey's just walked in the station for his refs break. He says to tell DS Morgan he'll take your three dogs and raise you a few dead bodies at the scene of the fire.'

The smile wiped from Ryan's face. He fell silent. No evidence left of his humour.

A wave of sadness brought her exhilaration crashing to the floor as she pressed down on the accelerator, every minute of those twenty-four hours she had at her disposal needed to count.

26

MONDAY 20 APRIL 1050 HOURS

Jenna leaned in through the back door to pick up the leads of the three dogs. They bounded out of the car and Domino high-stepped his way proudly by her side in through the station's front doors, where Jim Downey stood, hands in pockets, waiting for them to arrive.

No one could do quizzical better than Jim Downey as he raised one eyebrow in Roger Moore style and peered at them from over the top of his half-moon glasses. 'You want to brief me?'

Jenna held on to the overexcited dogs and flicked a hand to indicate for Ryan to brief his dad.

'Yeah, we were doing a search as a follow-up to a drugs bust we carried out this morning.'

'A drugs bust.' His voice turned droll as Jim centred his attention on his son. 'You do know we're not in America, don't you?'

Jenna dipped her head to hide her smile. She loved Jim Downey. His response to his son wasn't exclusive. He spoke to all the overexcited, inexperienced officers with the same casual disdain. She didn't know an officer who didn't respect the man professionally and like him personally.

Jim nodded at the dogs as Domino pushed forward to greet him. With a light grunt, Jim drew in a breath and reached down to push the intrusive nose from where Domino had wedged it in Jim's crotch.

'I thought you said you were bringing in dogs for drug forensic testing.' His brow creased as he looked back up at them. 'So, what's Domino doing here?' Jim dropped onto his haunches and gave the Dalmatian a good scrub all over his shoulders until the dog fell on the floor and rolled onto his back to expose his pale pink belly. 'Hey, boy, you're looking good. Better than the last time I saw you.' He swiped his long, nimble fingers along Domino's side in a quick inspection of the raised scar that ran the length of it.

As Ryan waited, Jenna elbowed him in the ribs and took over. They were fast running out of time. 'Long story short, we went to carry out a Section 18 in response to an arrest we made and discovered Domino with his dog walker outside of the house we were about to search.' She used the quick efficient language Jim liked and understood. 'They entered the premises, coming out a short time later with little bags on their collars. They then proceeded along the street to visit various neighbours, coming away with nothing on their collars. The little dog still has one. Lily, I think she's called. And so does Domino.' A little ripple of pride ran through her as she remembered his response. 'He refused to give his up.'

Jim Downey patted Domino's ribs until the sound vibrated like a drum and the dog rolled in delirium while the little shih-tzu and Labrador watched on.

'Good lad.' With the pride injected in Jim's voice, Domino preened.

Jim took his hand away, pushed to his feet and stood, hands on hips, staring down at the reposed dog. 'So, Domino.' Jim Downey's mouth twitched and the resemblance to his son struck Jenna in that moment of understated humour. 'From victim to drug pusher, lad. It didn't take you long.'

Jim dipped his fingers inside his pocket and drew out two pairs of blue nitrile gloves, snapping them onto his hands in layers. It was his efficient way of working. He'd carry out the first part of his job, strip off one layer of gloves and then continue.

All business, he clapped his hands to draw the attention of dogs and humans. 'Right. Let's have you in interview room three.'

Jim led the way, with Jenna and Ryan following and all three dogs in tow, wagging their tails like it was a great adventure.

Jenna closed the door behind them, surprised to see forensic plastic sheets already spread on the floor, taped down, prepped and ready to go.

Jenna offered Domino's lead to Jim. 'You can go first, sonny boy.'

Domino trotted forward, sat to attention and waited with one front paw raised in a begging manner to shame her.

'I never taught him that.'

Jim's lips tipped into a smile as he took the lead Jenna offered, dipped his hand into his pocket and offered a dog treat while he unclipped the little baggie roll from Domino's collar. He peered inside and then tipped the contents onto his hand. A small, neat bag containing a white powder. 'Looks promising, but we'll get it tested.' He placed it inside an evidence bag.

As he labelled it up, Jenna's stomach gave a howl which echoed in the confines of the small interview room. She put her hand to her stomach with the stark realisation she'd not eaten all day and she had roughly twenty-two minutes before she was due in the debrief.

She scrubbed her fingers over her face and then shot Domino an accusing look. 'You ate my panini.' His ears flicked back. It may have been her tone of voice, but she suspected the dog knew exactly what she was talking about.

'You had a panini?' Ryan's mouth dropped open as his stomach echoed hers. 'I never saw a panini.'

'No. Well you wouldn't. It was on the back seat of my car and when we swapped to the police vehicle, I dropped it in the top of my handbag. I never had time to eat it.'

Ryan pointed at Domino. 'What makes you think he did?'

Jenna stared at the dog from beneath dipped eyebrows. 'Because there was no evidence left. He'll have eaten everything, cardboard wrapper included.'

Jim raised his head and gave her one brief nod. 'Off you go, the pair of you. I don't need you here. It won't take me long and then I'll join you upstairs for the debrief on the fire. Latest I heard, they'd pushed it back simply because we had nothing earlier.'

Jenna pushed her hands inside her trouser pockets. 'But you said on Airwaves we do now.'

Jim squatted again and took a gentle hold of the black Labrador. He flipped the name tag over and glanced up at her. 'We do. The fire service have gained limited access, but they've confirmed there are bodies in there. We don't have a firm count yet. Hopefully there'll be more information shortly.' He reached out a gloved hand to scratch Lily's head. 'These kids will be fine. They can go in the yard for a while when I've finished. Leave them with me and I'll get someone to contact the owners to come and collect them.' As he finished speaking, the door cracked open and two of Jim's new recruits slipped inside the interview room, kitted out in their full personal protection equipment.

Jim looked up. 'Should I call Fliss to collect Domino when I've finished with him?'

Jenna grazed a glance over to the Dalmatian as she chewed on her lip. 'No. I'd rather you didn't. I need refs at some point, I'll whip him out and home.' Her gaze met Jim's as a thin thread of worry tugged at her. 'I'd prefer to explain it to her face to face rather than

worry her with a phone call. She'll think there's something wrong.'
She sent him a smile as understanding flickered through his eyes.

Content that he had everything in hand, Jenna slipped out of
the door, followed by Ryan, her sigh of relief jamming in her throat
as she came face to face with the most feared of all their comms
operators.

'Does this belong to you?'

Della Prince's hard stare rooted Jenna to the spot. Keeper of the
car keys, Della took her position with a seriousness unrivalled by
anyone else and instilled fear into the hearts of every officer. About
the only person who could actually make Mason quail with fright.
With her bleached-blonde hair in two-inch spikes all over her head
and kohl-black-rimmed eyes, Della was a warrior who Jenna had
nothing but respect for. No car keys ever went astray on Della's
watch.

Not normally the subject of confrontations with Della, Jenna
stumbled over her words. 'Well, no. Not really.'

With one large, square hand, Della reached out and thrust the
little chihuahua at Jenna's chest so she had no choice but to snatch
Fleur from Della's hand and snuggle her in tight.

Della's ice-blue eyes froze her to the spot. 'You owe me fifty-five
quid.'

Jenna reared back her head. 'Fifty-five quid?'

'Give or take a penny or two. Consider yourself lucky I haven't
added mileage.'

'What the hell for?' She could feel the screech in her voice
threatening to take over.

Della's painted on eyebrows shot up to her hairline. 'Because if
you abandon an animal to the care of front desk, without so much
as a bite for the poor soul to eat...'

'But...'

Della shot her hand out, palm forwards and halted Jenna's

protest midstream. 'If you do that, someone is going to have to go out in their own lunch hour to find it something to eat.'

Jenna dropped her head down to stare at Fleur, and then looked back up at Della, her eyes narrowing. 'It cost fifty-five quid for food? For this?' She pointed at Fleur. 'What the hell did you buy her? Caviar?'

Della crossed her arms over her ample bosom. 'Of course not. Do I look stupid?'

Jenna clamped her teeth together and let Della continue her rampage.

'You can't expect to leave a little one in this kind of weather without a decent coat...'

Jenna glanced out of the automatic glass doors. It wasn't that bad.

'... and she needed a lead. A water bowl. A dinner bowl. Oh yeah, and a bed.'

Jenna huffed out a gusty breath. 'She's not mine.'

'Evidently.' Della held out a hand.

Jenna almost choked. 'I don't have fifty-five quid on me. Who would?'

At the soft clearing of a throat, Jenna spun around as she adjusted Fleur into a more comfortable position. 'Ryan.' His eyes shot wide. 'Give Della fifty-five quid.'

'But...'

She strode off towards the stairwell leaving Ryan to fumble in his back pocket for his wallet. 'Thanks, Della. Oh, and Ryan? Don't forget to pick up all the stuff you're paying for.'

Team already assembled, the room buzzed with excited undercurrents as Jenna stepped inside, half-consumed meatball baguette in one hand, large black fully caffeinated coffee in the other. She was never going to sleep tonight, but with the energy she'd used so far, this would barely touch the sides.

The quick dash out of the station for food had not been via The Coffee Shack. On the pretence of giving in to the whining PC Downey, Jenna had left Fleur in her brand new fluorescent pink bed under his desk. She'd picked them both up a half-decent lunch and cash to pay him back for the purchases Della had made. There was fifty-five quid she'd never see again once someone laid claim to the pretty little pooch.

Jenna nudged her backside onto a desk next to where Donna perched and, with a smile, gave her a gentle elbow in the ribs. She'd not had the chance to speak with her since the night of the fire and would catch up as soon as the briefing finished.

DI Taylor let out a cough to grab their attention. The room fell silent and Jenna afforded herself a moment to take stock of the team they'd assembled. Her heart sank. With so many in the room, it was a big job.

Not only had the DI called in their normal team of herself and DCs Ellis, Downey, Salter and Wainwright, but the room was packed with PCs, intel, admin, the management team all vying for a chair to sit on or a wall to lean against. The only person she didn't recognise was the one at the head of the room who leaned forward and spoke to DI Taylor in tones too low to hear from where she was.

Jenna took advantage of the brief distraction to take another bite of her baguette. The outlook didn't look too hopeful for her next meal.

She drew in a long breath through her nose. The day had already been interminable, but it looked as though it may go on forevermore at this rate.

'Thank you. Thank you.' DI Taylor raised his hand and cruised his gaze around the room until every movement ceased. 'As you are all aware, we had a major incident on Saturday night. At 2240 hours, fire, police and ambulance were called to a fire at...' he squinted down at his notes, his thin grey hair barely covered the bald spot on his crown that gleamed in the electric lighting, '...Kimble Hall. The call was made by concerned neighbours, Mr and Mrs Crawford. No witnesses have come forward. Currently the family remain missing.'

He sucked air in through his teeth as he circled his gaze around the room. 'Due to the nature of the fire and its ferocity, whereby six tenders were required, we have been unable to get SOCO on site. However, in the last couple of hours, the fire service, after conducting a risk assessment, have been able to enter the building in their PPE with breathing apparatus. The site is not yet suitable for entry by any other personnel.'

Eyes bleak, he continued, 'What they have found inside, are bodies. None of which have been identified and these are by no means the only ones on the premises. The search has only just commenced.'

Jenna's chest tightened. The news wasn't unexpected, but having verification still sent a shaft of desperate pity for the whole family.

DI Taylor waited to allow the quick whispers to circulate the room, then gave out a small cough to pull them back into order. 'Further information does put a sinister spin on matters.'

Jenna's heart thrummed and then paused as she held her breath.

'According to Roger Ayman,' Taylor indicated the man stood to his right, 'our National Inter-Agency Liaison Officer, there is immediate evidence that a number of firearms have been discharged and abandoned several times on the premises. Through the site mapping they're carrying out, it appears so far, one firearm has been laid next to each of the bodies.'

The pulse in Jenna's throat hammered harder. Was that symbolic? A different gun for each one of them?

Ryan shot his hand into the air. 'Sir, were the firearms discharged before the fire was set?'

DI Taylor nodded to acknowledge Ryan. 'At this stage, we are cognisant of the fact the fire service has carried out its duty to protect human life to the best of their ability and having arrived on scene when the blaze was already well under way, DC Downey, we don't yet know, nor do we wish to surmise, what has taken place. The most important aspect currently is the protection of evidence, which the fire service again is deeply involved in until SOCO can get their team in there.' DI Taylor turned his head. 'DC Wainwright, you have a question?'

Slow to the point of almost painful, as was his way, Wainwright took his time before the question came out. 'Aye, sir. Do we know at this stage what the body count is?'

Again, DI Taylor nodded and then motioned with his hand at the NILO.

Roger Ayman stepped forward. 'As DI Taylor said, a complete search of the entire premises has been impossible due to safety issues. We can confirm so far we've discovered five bodies.'

Ryan's hand shot up and a collective groan came from the room. 'Sir, how many members of the family did you say are missing?'

She didn't care about the groan, young Ryan always hit the nail on the head and his enthusiastic participation propelled what could be a long drawn-out process along at a rapid rate of knots.

Her conversations with both the group of girls she'd stopped, and Mr and Mrs Crawford circled in her mind and a sick sense of what might have happened nagged at her.

Jenna's gaze met Taylor's across the room and the thought was already there in his steady, experienced look.

He squared his shoulders and stepped forward. 'There are six members of the family registered as living at that address. Mother and father, Linda and Gordon, and the children, Poppy – sixteen, Joshua – fourteen, and twins Talisha and Geraldine – aged eight.' He held up a hand. 'We cannot, until we have forensic evidence of the identity of those victims of the fire, assume that they are all family members.' His voice deepened with command to hold onto the team. 'Our duty now is protection of evidence and essentially protection and respect of any potential relatives and consideration of their needs and requirement of privacy.' DI Taylor held his hand out towards the police media representative, Jasmine Tate. 'Press announcement should be kept to bare details at present. You know the form. A fire at a residence in Farley. As yet the cause is unknown.' He circled his hand in the air. 'We would ask you respect the family's privacy at this stage, et cetera, et cetera.'

Jasmine inclined her head and made a quick note on her notepad. New to the position, Jasmine's first forays into journalism had proven her an excellent judge of diplomacy and tact. Exactly the requirements the Force had for their media, unlike newspaper journalists who would dig deep and in the case of some, dirty. Jasmine's job was to deal in cold, hard facts ensuring the need to protect individuals against the public's desire for information.

Jenna caught DI Taylor's eye and he nodded for her to go ahead. 'On the way to attending the fire, DC Mason and I almost took out a herd of deer along the Wenlock road.' She paused to allow the hoots of laughter to roll around the room, nodding her head to acknowledge police humour. 'Coming from the Wenlock direction, we came across three young women who also stopped to allow the deer to cross the road. Sophie Maxwell, Chanel Gosling and Olivia Brown. The eldest, Sophie, just turned seventeen. Chanel and Olivia only sixteen. On talking with them, I could smell alcohol, so I had to arrange for them to be detained and for the driver to be tested.' She held her hands out, palm up and shrugged. 'Nice girls, but once I felt they were compromised, I had no choice.' She turned to pat Donna on the knee. 'PC Donna McGuire and...' she scanned the room to acknowledge the other officer, conjuring up a name she seemed to have difficulty grasping, '... PC Natalie Kempson tested the driver at the scene.'

Donna drew a breath and Jenna nodded for her to continue. 'As Sergeant Morgan suspected, the driver blew a negative.' She let out a low humorous chuckle. 'She was too scared of her mum to even begin to think of drinking.'

Jenna took up where she'd previously left off. 'During my conversation with the girls, it transpired that they knew Poppy Lawrence.'

Donna tapped her pen on the notebook in front of her. 'The girls were really put out. Poppy was supposed to have been with them that night, but apparently her father insisted she attend his birthday party. According to the girls, Poppy was peeved because she knew it would be a washout and they'd all end up going to bed early and she'd miss out on her trip with the girls.'

Jenna swivelled to look at Donna, confident that she could trust her steady officer with this. 'Could I ask you and Natalie to pick up on this and interview all three girls, individually and at their home addresses?' At Donna's nod, Jenna continued, 'There was mention of Gordon Lawrence being not a very nice character.'

Donna nodded. 'Yeah, they implied Poppy was too scared to say no to him.'

'I didn't think much of it at the time, but later in the evening when DC Ellis and I spoke with Mr and Mrs Crawford, we gained the same impression.' Jenna turned her back on Donna to search the other side of the room. 'Which brings me on to Mr and Mrs Crawford.' She held out one hand towards the two officers in the corner. 'DC Salter and Wainwright, could I ask you to follow up with them? They had some very interesting information regarding Gordon Lawrence and his penchant for what sounded like inappropriate use of his firearms. The quantity, variety and frequency of use is a little suspect.'

The buzz around the room made her pause. She didn't need the team to formulate ideas, even though they were planted in her own head.

She held one hand up and raised her voice. 'Let's not get ahead of ourselves. Salter and Wainwright will be collating facts and *no* assumptions should be made. We need to put together a robust background on the entire family.' She turned to the team of three intel officers. 'Any chance you can check on a shotgun and firearms certificate issued to Gordon Lawrence? Furthermore, we need to find out who else attended the party. Who were the guests? We need information, timelines. What happened?' She scanned the room to ensure they were all on board, paying attention.

She caught PC Gardner's sullen stare.

Paused. He gave her a little hitch in her stride and a whip of annoyance.

She moved on.

'Why did the party finish early? Was it early for them? Was it a domestic? Did they have a fight and all go to bed early? Or have the Lawrence family been the subject of a targeted crime. A break-in gone wrong? A planned target?'

Whatever it was, they could make no assumptions at this point. But the sneaking suspicion had already taken root and Jenna had difficulty pushing it away.

Satisfied she'd allocated her best people to deal with key areas, Jenna zoned out as DI Taylor assigned further tasks to each of the team members.

Six family members at home for a party. What had happened for it to end the way it did?

She took in DI Taylor's confirmation that the intel officers had initiated an investigation into the family's finances. Always a good baseline to start an investigation.

DI Taylor addressed the duty management team, grabbing her attention at the mention of her name. 'At the scene, DS Morgan assigned scene guards. I assume you have the continuation of that plan in hand?' At Rob Fenwick's nod, DI Taylor drew in a deep breath to expand his broad chest. 'And finally,' he tapped the papers he'd rolled up while he spoke against the palm of his hand, 'I cannot stress enough. Remember – T.I.E.! Trace. Identify. Eliminate.'

As the shuffle of movement started, DI Taylor held up a restraining hand.

'Before we go. There's more.' He shot Jenna a wide grin. 'Congratulations to DS Morgan, DS Bennett, DCs Ellis, Downey and Blue on a swift and successful operation on their way into work this morning.'

The vertical creases down each side of DI Taylor's cheeks deepened and Jenna almost groaned out loud.

'It turns out DS Morgan has a drug-pushing dog, but, more to the point, our officers took quite a downline of pushers and users this morning without pausing for breath. Currently, DS Bennett and DC Ellis are continuing the search of three houses on the Mountside estate after arrests were made this morning at the gym. We have our hands full in custody. You may recognise some of the names: Lamonte Junior, Lena Alexander, Marie West and Joel Hopkins.' A collective groan rumbled around the room at the mention of the last two names. 'I've allocated officers who are already questioning our suspects. Most importantly,' DI Taylor eyeballed everyone in the room from underneath a furrowed brow, 'there is one Shaun Cunningham, barista extraordinaire at The Coffee Shack. He is not to be approached or touched. Drug Squad have requested we leave him in place for them to conduct further investigations without arousing suspicion. They may well use him to get further up the chain of command.'

DI Taylor plopped his notepad on the nearest desk and clapped his hands together, sharp enough so every head in the room shot up. 'We have a lot on our plates. Let's get to it, team!'

28

MONDAY 20 APRIL 1215 HOURS

Poppy unfurled from the ball she'd tucked herself into to keep warm. With the second oversized man's sweatshirt on, hitched down past her knees, she'd managed to generate enough heat to sleep, waking only once when she needed to pee. She'd sidled over to the furthest corner and used a small amount of cotton wool to wipe with.

She popped more painkillers and washed them down with a few swigs of Coke. aware of how little she had left.

On her right side, she gave a tentative stretch. Sonofabitch! Her side burned.

She propped herself up on her right elbow to have a look around. On first entry into the barn, no one would be able to see her lying down. She'd positioned herself further back in the hollow of loose straw behind a short stack of bales. Laying her right arm on top of them she rested her chin on her arm. Her stomach moaned a protest and had her reaching out for the food bag she'd placed nearby.

Ravioli was her only real choice. She opened the lid and stared at the contents. Her throat closed at the thought of cold snot-like slime sliding down her throat. It was bad enough hot.

She scooped a couple of squares onto her spoon and shovelled them into her mouth. Three chews and she swallowed. Gagged.

Her stomach clenched and her side burnt.

She repeated the action. Scoop, shovel, chew, swallow. Gag!

She needed her strength. There was no point dying now when she'd survived so much.

Scoop, shovel, chew, swallow.

If she stared at the shafts of sunlight coming through the barn doors, it became easier.

Scoop, shovel, chew, swallow.

With no concept of time, Poppy rolled her options around inside a head which had started to clear.

She needed a plan. Every plan she conceived was pivotal to one essential thing.

The time.

She tapped the spoon on the empty tin and then threw them both into the plastic carrier bag. She reached out and picked up the Ted Baker iPhone case smeared with dried-on blood. Dare she risk switching it on?

Daddy.

There was no doubt in her mind he was still out there. The heavy blanket of evil thickened the air until she could barely breath.

She drew in a shaky breath as she rubbed the brown flaky blood from the phone case with her forefinger in light, rhythmic motions to soothe herself.

If he looked, he'd locate her. And he would look. She knew her own daddy. Manipulative. Obsessive. She'd never even tried to disable the find-a-friend function once he'd set it up. He'd never have allowed her to before.

He'd broken his hold over her but not his connection.

The only way to do it would be to switch the phone on. She'd need to be quick.

She flipped the cover open and stared at the shiny, black screen. She touched the tip of her finger to it. What if she was quick? What if she switched it on, checked the time, switched it off again?

Would it work? Would he know?

Poppy pressed and held the on button for a moment and gazed mesmerised as the screen flashed the white apple and started to load. Her heart thrummed in her chest to make it ache until the breath she held threatened to burst out of her.

The screen loaded and she couldn't contain the tremor as she held her forefinger on the recognition button.

A rude buzz came from the phone and she tried again. Then a third time, but it wouldn't allow her access. Please. A desperate sob burst from her lips as her fingers shook. *Please.*

Panic tightened the muscles around her throat as her breath rasped in and out. *Please, please, please.*

She touched her fingertips against the button again and the phone vibrated in her hand refusing her access again.

Her eyelids fluttered down, then sprang wide. She sucked in a breath, tapped in the code manually and the screen blinked to life.

Monday.

12:25 p.m.

White-hot panic raged through her and she stabbed her finger on the power button, switching the phone back off again, praying Daddy didn't just happen to glance at his phone and see her location.

If he did, she was as good as dead.

She whipped her head around, eyes narrowing as she scoured the huge barn before she made a move to gather up all the evidence of her presence, panic slicing through her heart.

She needed a safe place. Somewhere daddy wouldn't instantly see her.

She traced her gaze up a tall stack of straw.

If she could get up there, it may give her a chance.

A chance against daddy when he came for her.

29

Gordon Lawrence leaned forward. He dangled his hands between his knees, his head lowered.

That had to be the worst night's sleep in the history of his life.

The small cot in the aerodrome offices made for a lumpy resting place.

He'd barely snatched a wink, and when he had, it had been plagued with ugly flashes of scenes he didn't want to see.

The plan all along, since its inception the week before, had been to take his own life once he'd despatched his family. Cemented in his mind, he'd not been side-tracked from the statement he'd make to the world. Death didn't bother him.

Up until the very last minute, he'd not wavered.

His daughter was the one responsible. Poppy.

As he'd shot her and then the nameless boy, a flash of inspiration hit him.

With no time to think it through, he'd acted.

It was all about the body count. And fate had found him an extra one.

30

Jenna's stomach growled with hunger. With Fleur tucked safely under her arm, she slipped in through the front door in the vain hope that she wouldn't be accosted by the huge spotty dog who she'd sneaked home only three hours earlier.

The warm waft of savoury food hit her stomach and her salivary glands danced with joy. Knees weak, she almost sank to the floor with relief.

Today, it appeared, was one of the days Fliss had decided to cook something other than junk food, which probably meant that they were going to be joined by Mason, despite the fact that he hadn't mentioned anything. Not that they'd had much time to mention anything personal between the two of them, nor did Jenna encourage it. During the hectic day, they'd had a lot on their respective plates. He'd been at Mountside dealing with the drug scenes for most of the day and they'd had a quick debrief before they went their separate ways again.

She nudged the front door closed, holding onto the deadlock to deaden the sound of the loud click. But when she turned around, Domino's fat, black, wet nose was already by her ear as he planted his paws on her shoulders and gave her the greeting she already expected, and God forbid anyone else should know, but she loved his greetings.

She wrapped her arms around his shoulders and cuddled him in for a few precious moments, taking comfort from the adoration he bestowed on her while a squished Fleur snuffled into his neck, squeaks of delight coming from her.

Jenna lowered him to the ground and let him trot ahead of her into the kitchen. She'd known more frenetic greetings from him, which went to prove her secret theory that the Dalmatian suffered from separation anxiety. Long before he was beaten, he'd shown signs of anxiety, but since then, he hated to be alone.

Fliss turned from her place at the sink as Jenna made her way along the short hallway into the kitchen, her eyes lighting up at the sight of the little one Jenna plopped on the floor to be stepped on by Domino.

'I take it no one has claimed her?'

'Not yet.' Jenna huffed out a breath.

'Well,' Fliss's voice took on a sweet gentleness Jenna knew the children at school would respond to as her sister bent down to greet Fleur with a scratch to her head. 'You're most welcome to stay until Aunty Jenna finds your mummy.'

With doubts they ever would, Jenna held her tongue. The day had been long enough without regurgitating all of the facts to her sister. She needed a little break herself.

Fliss straightened and turned her back. When she turned around again, she had a glass of red wine in her hand and a grin on her face as she offered it to Jenna. 'I've made pudding.'

So pleased with herself, Jenna plastered on a stiff smile for the benefit of her younger sister, but her stomach cramped in protest.

Pudding! She hoped to God there was more than pudding.

Quite honestly, she could eat a scabby horse, never mind a

damned pudding. She could have sworn the aroma that had assailed her nostrils when she came through the front door had been a meaty, savoury scent. She had reason to doubt her sense of smell. Perhaps she needed to get it checked out.

She kept her grin as she accepted the glass of wine from Fliss whose eyes danced with pleasure, before turning away to open the oven. The blast of heat that rolled out reminded Jenna of the conversation with Charlie Cartwright on how hot a thousand degrees would feel. Five times hotter than the heat of that oven.

From the safety of a few paces away, Jenna squinted into the oven to try and imagine the ferocity of anything hotter. She'd had a small taste of it the other evening. From a safe distance, it had been ferocious.

The loud growl of her stomach drew Fliss's attention and she turned from where she peered into the oven.

'I made a rice pudding.' The pride in her voice reverberated around Jenna's poor, empty stomach. 'Just like Mum used to when we were little.' She slipped on a pair of oven gloves, reached into the oven and pulled out a stoneware casserole dish. The dark sugar-bronzed skin promised a delicious offering, but Jenna's stomach still howled its protest. Fliss placed the dish on a cast-iron trivet by the side of the oven. 'Comfort food.' She dragged the gloves from her hands, placed them on the counter and smoothed them down before she grabbed a dishcloth from the sink, held it under the water until steam rose and then washed the counters clean.

With a jolt, Jenna shoved aside her own weak thoughts of savoury food and paid her younger sister instant attention as she scanned her soft features and clear sea-green eyes, finding nothing of concern there. 'Comfort? Do you need comfort food?' Perhaps something had happened at work. Or worse, between Mason and Fliss.

Fliss's laughter bounced around the small kitchen. 'No. Not at all.' Relief flooded through and Jenna found herself relaxing against the kitchen counter. 'It turned cooler this afternoon.'

Jenna hadn't noticed. She'd been too embroiled in a first-stage interview with Lena, who had already lawyered up before Jenna had got there. The woman then proceeded to cry in a long drawn-out, dramatic waste of everyone's time for the following two and a half hours.

Mentally and emotionally drained, Jenna made the decision to have Lena seen by the duty doctor and then settled down in the cell overnight until either the effects of the cocaine that she'd so liberally taken had worn off, or she made a decision to put the performance to one side and answer Jenna's queries so they could all get on with their lives.

Eight in the morning was time enough for Jenna to reconvene. Although Lena's solicitor appeared less than enthusiastic at the early start and suggested 10 a.m. As it didn't suit Jenna, she rejected it. Her day would be well underway by then, and with so many incidents to deal with, she simply didn't have the time to waste on a solicitor's personal preference for breakfast time.

Jenna raised the glass of red wine to her lips and took a sip, determined not to criticise the divine rice pudding. She gazed around the kitchen in awe. Immaculate, wiped down, gleaming. So her sister had spare time enough on her hands to clean but not a sign of any other food on the hob.

Jenna glanced down at her work clothes. She could get changed, but if she went upstairs and so much as caught sight of her bed, she'd be asleep in no time.

Her stomach grumbled out its vocal protest.

She could always fling on a pan of pasta.

Fliss slipped the oven gloves on her hands again and turned her back on Jenna, as she slid a small roasting tin out of the oven and put it on the side, followed by a casserole dish. She lifted the lid from the casserole dish. The steam billowed out carrying the savoury scent of something divine enough to hit Jenna's taste buds and almost brought her to her knees.

'Oh my gosh. What have you cooked?'

With a bright smile, Fliss hooked up a serving spoon and popped it in the casserole dish.

'Are we expecting someone else?' Jenna asked. She hoped not. Space and quiet was what she needed. And comfort food.

'No, no, I think it's just the two of us tonight. Mason sent me a message to say he was off to the gym with Ryan. Some sort of boy bonding thing going on.'

Jenna had a vague recollection that it had been mentioned earlier in the day, but it had passed by in the fanaticism of their work. They'd wanted to return to the gym, check it out. Mason's main reason was to ascertain just how fit young Ryan had become. Jenna suspected he was in for a bit of a surprise. And she couldn't be arsed with the slide of testosterone kicking in.

'Right. There's a lot for two.' She'd manage at a push.

Fliss sent her a bashful smile. 'He said he might drop by later. Just slip in. So, I'll leave enough for him and pop it in the oven to keep warm.'

'So, this...' Amusement laced her words as Jenna circled her hand above her head. '...All this food isn't just for my benefit?'

'No.' Fliss did a self-conscious jiggle of her shoulders as she picked up her glass of wine and took a sip as her face pinkened. 'It's for my benefit. I wanted to do it. It makes me feel good.'

The warmth in Jenna's chest spread. Fliss was doing things for herself these days. Food was often hit and miss as she was a junk-food addict to the extreme, but when she decided to cook or bake it was because she was in a good place. A place of days gone by when their mum was alive and being in the kitchen was a social event. It brought with it a sense of relief and delight that she'd become so independent.

Things could have gone quite the other way. After her kidnap, Fliss could quite easily have become a recluse. Almost did, but to Jenna's surprise and relief, Fliss had turned herself around. More energetic, more vibrant, more determined to live her life than ever before. The advent of Mason in her life had also driven that determination forward. She'd never admit it to him, she'd rather threaten to bury him if he disappointed her sister, but she loved him. Bastard that he was.

Fliss reached into the drawer in front of her, pulled out two sets of cutlery and handed them over to Jenna. Like clockwork, they interacted so free and easy together with unspoken communication. Jenna reached into the cupboard for three plates, assuming Fliss would prepare one for Mason.

'We were talking about nutrition today at school.'

'Oh yeah?'

'Yes. So, the children were talking, and I'm shocked at how many don't eat at home, or have such poor food when they return and the only meal they have during the day is the one that they get at lunchtime. And some of them are so young, they don't know what they're doing because the meals are almost self-service. They have no idea that the three chicken nuggets and six chips on their plate is no nutrition at all and it's not enough to sustain them throughout the day.'

Fliss's cheeks flushed with passion enough to make Jenna wonder if her sister's attitude towards junk food was about to take a complete U-turn and they would be health-food fanatics in no time at all. Jenna smiled. It suited her.

Fliss grabbed a spoon and scooped chicken casserole onto the three white plates. Bright, vibrant colours spilled across them with chicken, tomatoes, sweetcorn and red peppers in one dish.

She waggled the serving spoon at Jenna. 'They need so much more.' She took a slotted spoon and flipped roast vegetables – parsnips, potatoes and carrots – from the roasting tin.

Jenna's stomach gave in and shouted out another loud grumble, but this time in excitement as she drew out a chair at the dining room table. A mouth-watering waft of steam came up from the plate Fliss placed in front of her as she took her own seat at the small kitchen table.

Within a millisecond, Domino came to rest his chin on Jenna's thigh and Fleur sang in high-pitched tones until Jenna scooped her up and let her circle around on her lap until she flopped down oblivious to the large black nose she pushed up against. Jenna automatically placed her hand on the top of Domino's head and smiled up at her sister. 'Thanks.'

Fliss served her own dish of food up and the spare plate for Mason, slipping his back into the oven out of temptation's way of the Dalmatian. She took her seat opposite Jenna and waved her hand over their plates. 'This, this is what they don't get. And then I thought *how can you criticise? You're really bad at nutrition*. We eat such crap.'

Exactly what Jenna had tried to tell her sister for the entire length of time they'd lived together. Jenna raised an eyebrow and kept her expression mellow. 'I know.' When it was her turn to cook, it was a different matter. She always tried to serve them nutritious meals with interesting ingredients. She loved the spiciness of Indian cookery, the deep richness of Italian food.

Jenna picked up her knife and fork and barely had to cut into the chicken as it fell apart. She scooped a mouthful of it up and took a bite. This was so much more like their mum's good old-fashioned traditional satisfying British food.

The only thing missing that their mum might have added was dumplings. And the only addition to the casserole was the mange tout that Fliss had stirred through at the last minute so they still had a bite to them. But then Mum wouldn't have even known what mange tout was.

'So, what are you going to do about it?' Jenna knew Fliss would have already started to devise a plan.

'Something. Definitely something. I'm going to see if we can introduce a better system than trestle tables. Do something that makes their experience less of a chore and more of an opportunity to interact. Mix up the age groups.' She snapped out a sharp smile. 'It's not fully formulated yet, but I'll involve the PTA, knock around with some ideas and see what we can do to improve matters.'

Fliss chewed on her own mouthful of food and then poked her fork towards Jenna. 'So, did you have a good day at work today?'

Jenna knew her time to speak was coming. She laid down her fork and picked up her wine, took a sip and let the flavour mingle with the savoury casserole. 'This is delicious. Thank you.' A divine pleasure. She leaned back in her chair, lowered her glass and smiled at Fliss. 'I had an... interesting day.'

'Oh, okay.' Turning the subject Jenna was about to bring up on its head, Fliss interrupted her. 'Do you think Domino is so much calmer today?'

Jenna almost snorted her wine out of her nose, but Fliss never even noticed in her enthusiasm.

'I think it's starting to make a difference having a dog walker when we need one.'

Jenna clamped down on hysterical laughter and gulped to rid herself of the wine stuck at the back of her throat. She let out a delicate cough as she hid a smile behind the glass. She took another sip to soothe her throat.

'Is this the first time you've noticed the difference?'

'It is. I thought it wasn't going to work. He still seemed so energetic after she'd taken him out that I've been supplementing it by running him out as soon as I get home as well, just to calm his energy levels down.'

Jenna's lips twitched and she rolled them in on themselves to stop the laugher bursting out. 'That's not surprising.'

With overexaggerated casualness she placed her glass on the table and picked up her fork again. She popped a little more food in her mouth and chewed.

'What do you mean?' Fliss's smooth brow wrinkled.

'I mean, I don't think Domino has been properly walked by Lena.' She trapped Fliss's gaze across the table and cocked her head to one side in a little tease her sister was soon to acknowledge.

Fliss's confusion grew. 'I don't understand. If he's not been getting a proper walk, why is he so content tonight?'

Jenna dropped her chin down to stare at the semi-comatose dog, contentment in every line of his body as he pressed the heavy weight of it onto her thigh.

Her sister flicked a hand over the table at her dog. 'I thought he was so much more relaxed.'

'Well, he certainly is, because if nothing else he's had mental stimulation today.' Jenna pointed her finger at her sister. 'You would not believe what has gone on. Do you want to know?' She narrowed her eyes at her sister as Fliss placed her fork down by the side of her plate with a sharp snap and swiped up the wine again.

She didn't know whether to laugh or... Oh, what the hell? She laughed.

She scratched the top of Domino's head and he moaned his contentment. 'Did you know Domino is a drug pusher in his spare time?'

Fliss's mouth dropped open, jaw slack. 'What?'

'Yes, Domino spent the better part of today at the police station with me. After which I took him for an extra walk in my precious refs time to make up for the fact that he probably hadn't been very far on his trek with your dog walker. The lovely Lena. Together with the three other dogs that he was with.'

Fliss jerked upright.

'It's supposed to be a one to one. I'm bloody well paying her for that. What the hell?' Was she more concerned that her dog had been used to push drugs, or that she'd been overpaying for a non-exclusive service?

'Well,' Jenna grinned, warming to the subject and her sister's shock. 'I wouldn't pay her this time because he's been earning her more than enough money.'

Eyes wide, Fliss gawped at her. 'What the hell?'

Jenna chuckled, thrilled by her sister's response. 'Your dog walker comes highly recommended.' She whipped her hand in a circular motion and pointed her finger. 'And your friend who made that recommendation is currently being questioned about her contacts.' Jenna raised her hand to stop Fliss from exploding. 'Oh no, she's not involved.'

Fliss still managed to splutter out her disbelief. 'I don't believe Lena would do that. Surely not.'

Jenna raised her brows. 'No, I didn't believe it either.' She gave a quick shrug, irritated with herself for her oversight. 'And I'm a police officer, you'd think I'd have picked up on something.' She poked her forefinger against her chest. 'Just as you and I had no idea, neither did your friend. She told Mason that Lena had come from a recommendation via her husband's work, so she doesn't even know Lena personally. I'm not even sure where the original recommendation came from, but obviously that's what we'll investigate. However,' Jenna leaned forward and pointed a finger at Fliss again, 'we're going to have to make alternative arrangements for Domino for the time being, until we find somebody that we can actually trust. And, honest to goodness, next time, I'm going to do a security check on them. Because I had no idea, *none*, that this woman would use other dogs, who she's been making a fine living from, to push drugs.'

Fliss met her gaze straight on. 'How the hell do dogs push drugs?'

Jenna's stomach gave another protesting growl. She picked up her knife and fork and started to eat again. She chewed and swallowed. 'Oh, let me explain.' The thrill of it tickled her. 'She picked up the dogs from each of the houses. When we saw her, she had a shih-tzu, a black Labrador, a greyhound and a Dalmatian. Why she didn't use something less obvious than that combination, I don't know. Four black Labradors would have been more advisable. Anyway, because she had a Dalmatian, I *spotted* her immediately. It took me a split second to realise it was Domino.'

She paused to give one silky ear an affectionate rub. 'She then took them in her car to what we believe is a house she shares with her boyfriend, a drug pusher. She attached drugs to the dogs' collars, and then trotted around her neighbourhood on the pretence of walking the dogs. Well, technically, they were walking, but not in the fashion all the owners imagined. Why would any of us even think to double-check a dog and a dog's collar?'

Jenna continued to scoop small forkfuls of food into her mouth as she carried on. 'I've never come across it before but Chris Bennett the dog handler had. We're going to be doing *spot* checks.' She gurgled at her own joke as she traced the black markings on Domino's head.

'So, she went door to door. And when the people open the doors, they greet the dogs. Slip the drugs away. Pop the money back onto the collar in a little pouch attached there.'

'A pouch?' A flash of confusion crossed Fliss's face. 'He's never had a pouch when he gets home.'

'Of course not, she would have removed that when she was in the car before driving Domino back home.' She snickered. 'The only walk Domino had was a house-to-house visit. He wasn't having long, indulgent runs in fields as we'd been led to believe.'

'But she sent me a picture each day.'

'Yes, she probably just stopped somewhere, let him off the lead for five minutes and took a quick snapshot. But I said he didn't seem any different. He still seemed full of energy, as though he hadn't even had a walk. You pay for two hours, twice a week. And it made no difference. Two hours was a hell of a long time for her to have been dropping off drugs, I can tell you, although you have to factor in the dog pick up from various locations. We'll be tracking all that down. Unfortunately, we didn't manage to get the whole pattern, but she's in for questioning and we won't be letting her go anytime soon.'

'Well, he's obviously quite settled tonight.' Fliss peered over the top of the small table at him and his ears flickered in acknowledgement. Fleur let out a contented grumble and kicked him in the snout.

'He certainly is.' Jenna scratched the top of his head and his eyes blinked and then closed again. 'He was a good boy. Good boy,' she lowered her voice to an affectionate growl. He wagged his tail and pleasure filled his half-closed eyes. 'He spent a little time with Jim Downey being forensically checked and some of the time in the courtyard while I put my paperwork in order. He was with two other dogs and had the time of his life. And then, before I dropped him home, I took him for a walk. Let him stretch his legs out. All in all. That's why I never got much to eat today. A baguette sometime earlier, which barely touched the sides. Especially after I had to run.'

'You ran?' Disbelief echoed through Fliss's voice.

'Don't be funny. I can run. If I need to.' Damned if she'd confess she could barely bloody well keep up. That was for her to know and Fliss to find out...

'If something's chasing you.' Her sister knew her too well.

Jenna scraped her plate clean and leaned back. 'I was doing the chasing.'

Fliss continued eating. 'Good job I made you some decent food then.'

'It certainly is.' Appreciation flowed from her voice. She took a quick look at the oven. 'Are you sure Mason will want all of that?' She pushed a little pathetic into her voice. 'He'd never know.'

Fliss pointed her knife at her. 'You leave his dinner alone.' She laughed as she laid her cutlery across her empty plate. 'Your face earlier when I said I made rice pudding. It was priceless. Worth hanging on to see your response when you thought that was the only thing in the oven.'

Jenna stared at her sister across the table and said nothing. Waves of contentment warmed her heart. It was good to see Fliss happy.

'Would you like some?'

Jenna's stomach gave a little hip hip hooray and she abandoned the thought of swiping Mason's dinner in preference for the sweet fix she was about to have.

With a gentle nudge, Jenna pushed Domino's face from her lap, scooped up Fleur and came to her feet, popping the little dog back down on the padded seating of the chair.

She gathered their crockery and cutlery and made short work of putting them in the dishwasher as Fliss served up their rice pudding.

They took their seats again and Fleur barely roused as Jenna shuffled her onto her lap and stared at her sister. 'So, are we to expect this kind of meal from now on?'

Fliss snorted and poured a little fresh cream from its carton onto the steaming rice pudding. She raised her spoon and paused before putting any food into her mouth, a thoughtful expression on her face. 'Don't get too used to it. I know I'll revert to my old ways, but for the next couple of days you're probably in luck.'

Jenna could do nothing but admire her sister's honesty and hope her cooking stint lasted a little longer than a few days. But she'd appreciate every one of them, just as she appreciated Fliss.

She finished off her pudding, picking up every last morsel until the plate was almost wiped clean, then settled back in her chair, her stomach a gentle bulge.

Fliss pushed her own plate away and met Jenna's gaze. 'You sound as though you had fun today.'

Jenna sobered. It hadn't been fun, it had been damned long. A hard slog of a day with a small window of excitement that had pumped adrenaline through the department to lend them a boost of energy.

Jenna's lips tightened as Fliss slipped a hand over hers, her eyes darkening with concern. 'I know you don't like to burden me with the hard stuff, but I know about the fire you were called to the other night. I assume it's the same one I heard on the news today.'

Jenna sighed. She turned her hand over so her fingers linked with her sisters. 'It's a tough one.'

'Tough. There's an understatement. That poor family. I looked in *The Shropshire Star*. It sounds horrendous.'

It was a diluted version. And Fliss was right. Jenna didn't need to burden her with the details. *The Shropshire Star*'s version would suffice. Confirmation that bodies had been discovered at the fire-ravaged home of Shropshire estate agent Gordon Lawrence.

'It says there's been no identification of the bodies.'

'No. Nothing formal.'

'But the whole family are missing.'

'Yes.'

Fliss squeezed her fingers. 'It's them, isn't it?'

Jenna nodded. 'It appears so.'

'That poor family. Those poor children. I can't imagine being trapped.' Fliss's nightmare was to be trapped. Worsened by her kidnap.

'They may not have been.' She almost bit her tongue to stop the words that tumbled out.

Fliss tilted her head to one side, a frown sending a vertical crease between her eyebrows. 'What do you mean?'

Jenna slid her fingers from under Fliss's hand and raised her glass to take a sip of wine. 'The latest is that they've found five bodies.'

'They said it was arson in the press release. Some awful person setting fire to their house.'

Jenna met her sister's gaze. 'Yeah, but we found used guns.'

Fliss sucked in a breath and slapped her hand over her mouth as her eyes went wide. 'Oh dear God. They were murdered? Deliberately?'

Jenna inclined her head, regret circling in her stomach that she'd told her sister, but at least it was closer to the truth than her sister would read from an anti-establishment journalist.

'Who would do that? Was it a break-in?' Her sister fired the questions at her without waiting for a reply.

Jenna shook her head. 'It's only a suspicion, but we think Gordon Lawrence did it.'

Fliss's face froze into a mask, her lips barely moved as she stared at Jenna. 'The father? He killed his family?'

'Yes. Quite possibly.'

'Who in their right mind would do that?'

Jenna pulled in a long breath through her nose. 'That's just the point. No one in their right mind would. But we have six people missing and only five bodies accounted for. They haven't finished the search yet, but I think someone escaped the fire. With a combination of gossip and evidence, the finger points to the dad.'

Jenna pushed back from the table, sliding Fleur off her knee again, she picked up the two bowls, needing to change the subject. It had been on her mind all day while she dealt with the drugs case. She'd finished off the day with the debrief and she'd likely be dealing with it for the foreseeable future.

She placed her hand on Domino's head as he stared lovestruck as though she was his favourite person in the world just because he'd found her today and enjoyed an unexpected walk. 'Has he been fed yet?'

'Yes, of course he has. But there's nothing like cupboard love is there?'

His eyes filled with adoration.

'Drug pusher.'

Fliss snorted out a laugh. 'Oh my God. Just wait until I tell—'

'No.' Jenna held up her hand. 'You can't tell anybody, Fliss. I shouldn't have told you as much. Some of the information is okay for you to know, mainly because your dog has been trotting up and down the neighbourhoods pushing drugs.'

'More?' Fliss raised the bottle.

Jenna shook her head and placed her hand over the top of her glass. If she had another drop, she'd be asleep across the table. One glass was plenty on a work night. She'd probably only get six hours sleep before she had to be back at the station again.

'Obviously I need a statement from you about how you came to use Lena to walk Domino, but I'll get Ryan to do that. You mustn't say anything to anyone.' Jenna stressed. 'This could be a bigger operation than we anticipated when it kicked off this morning. So, keep it to yourself.'

Flustered, Fliss drained her glass and came to her feet to clear the dishes, stacking one on top of the other before she took them to the dishwasher. 'Yes, of course, of course. It's so funny really.' Fliss glanced sideways at her, her teeth pulling at her bottom lip, her eyes sparkling with mischief. 'How much was he carrying?'

It took a moment for Jenna to process the question. 'Domino? Jim Downey has got to double-check yet, but from experience, he was talking two grams. Around £85.00 a gram.'

'Wow, so how much does one person take?'

'You're a little too interested in this subject.'

'Knowledge is power.'

'It is, but not if you use it the wrong way.'

Fliss finished stacking the dishwasher and pushed the door to as Jenna dipped her hands in near boiling water to give the wine glasses a thorough wash. 'Do I look like I'm about to deal in drugs?'

Jenna regarded her sister with a professional eye. 'You look like a teacher.'

Fliss flashed her a grin. 'Why thank you. That was always my intention.'

Which circled Jenna nicely around in the right direction. 'Have you had any word about the promotion?' She grabbed a towel and dried her hands.

Fliss let out a delicate snort. 'I think from September I'll be taking over head of infants by the look of it.'

'Fliss that's great news. It really is and you do deserve it.'

Her sister preened just a little and Jenna's heart warmed at the thought that this precious woman had started to heal. 'I do. Actually, I'm good at my job.'

Jenna checked her over, relieved at how far Fliss had come since the kidnap. There would still be dark times. Times when Fliss slipped back into that dreadful cellar with its rising waters each time they heard the Ironbridge flood warnings. It triggered a gut-wrenching response. Not only in Fliss but Jenna too. Step by step they dealt with it, confronted it and moved on, stronger and better each time.

She reached out and cupped her sister's cheek and then pulled her into her arms for a silent hug, rocking her in unspoken understanding.

For now, she could be content that her sister's pale green eyes sparkled and the flush on her smooth cheeks made her skin glow, and the relaxed smile on her face washed away the tensions of the day.

31

A fine sheen of sweat slicked over Mason's skin as his feet slapped against the shiny rubber of the running machine.

Knees like jelly and breath heaving so his tongue turned to dust in a mouth devoid of saliva, he drove on, determined to keep going even though his heart might explode in his chest. His arms pumped as he fought to keep up with the loose-limbed youngster beside him. Ryan's gangly limbs seemed to have found a comfortable rhythm, enough to gain Mason's reluctant admiration.

Not sure if he could keep up the pace for much longer, Mason swiped the back of his hand across his forehead, mortified at the drip, drip, drip of sweat falling onto the electronic device in front of him

If only he'd taken Ryan's advice and attempted a run on the flat to begin with, but, no, he thought he was smart enough, strong enough, to take on Ryan in an uphill race.

Two and a half miles in and he was shocked. His muscles turned to liquid and he prayed to God Ryan would stop before Mason humiliated himself and collapsed in a heap on the running machine as his legs turned to overdone spaghetti.

Heat travelled up his neck to burn across his cheeks.

They'd already spent forty-five minutes going through the paces in the weight room. He hadn't been so bad at that. His upper-body strength was good. He had weights in his garage, together with a punchbag he used to blow off steam. He'd taken a casual interest in boxing, enjoyed the skill, the rhythm, the control.

But this, this was a piss-take.

Unfortunately, he wasn't as young as he used to be. And he hadn't kept up an exercise regime. He couldn't have everything and he was too busy with work and socialising.

Pride shot to hell, with the sound of his breathing turned to a strained rasp, Mason reached out and stabbed the incline button until he was once again on a flat. His fingers shook as he punched the console in front of him, so the machine slowed to a walk and eventually, just as he'd started to believe his life was no longer worth living, the treadmill wound down to a stop.

Tempted to collapse onto the railings and just breathe for a moment, he shot another glance at Ryan whose attention was thankfully absorbed by the huge television screen in front of him with music blasting from his Bluetooth EarPods so loud Mason could hear it above his own laboured breathing. The boy was going to burst his eardrums.

Mason sagged, his whole middle turned to mush.

Ryan wouldn't even notice if he had a cardiac arrest. He'd probably keep on running while Mason writhed around on the floor. Dying.

Mason pushed away from the machine and walked, weak-legged, over to the paper towel dispenser, ripped off several pieces, wiped down his dripping face, shoulders, arms, skimmed them over the length of his florid legs.

His stomach gave a painful hitch and he remembered he'd barely had anything to eat that day. Christ, he didn't even know why he'd come to the gym, except it had seemed like a fucking bonding exercise with Ryan. Or if he'd admit it, a little testosterone trial. One he'd failed badly.

He slipped his phone from his pocket, tapped the screen to open his WhatsApp and stared at a photograph. No words necessary, there was a clear invitation for him to go around for a hot meal and an even hotter girlfriend.

Without hesitation, his stomach took control and sent a surge of desperately required adrenaline to fight its way to the surface and instil enough energy in him to move his steadily stiffening limbs in the right direction.

He lobbed the paper towels into the bin and whipped some more from the roll to wipe drops of sweat from the running machine.

Mason tapped Ryan on the shoulder. Without a pause in his stride, Ryan turned his head to look at him and Mason raised a hand and pointed in the direction of the changing room to indicate that he was off.

Ryan gave him the thumbs up and continued. Damned youngster, not even a hitch in his deep, even breathing. Yet Mason's was still laboured as he gasped for oxygen.

Didn't Ryan have a life? The nurse he was dating was probably working and the kid just wanted to exercise after a hard mental and emotional day. The realisation hit him. He wasn't the kind to kick his arse into gear after a gruelling day. It may suit others, but he'd far rather sit back with a bottle of Stella snuggled on the sofa with Fliss.

He dragged his feet through the locker room to the showers, stripped and stepped under the stream of tepid water despite it being turned up to the hottest temperature. It didn't matter, a grateful groan still surged from his chest as his muscles protested and tightened up instead of relaxing.

Perhaps he could have a bath once he got to Jenna's house. He was still treading carefully in his relationship with Fliss. Not wishing to spook her, he took it at her pace. The wait for her commitment would be worth it in the end, but she still had so much to deal with and putting pressure on their relationship wouldn't gain him anything.

He could wait.

She was worth waiting for and he'd be there for her in the coming months once the trial started for Frank Bartwell. Admiration for Fliss's strength swelled in his chest, but she'd still need support.

He pumped the dispenser and dumped a handful of shampoo and body wash on his head. Where the shower had failed to revive him, the sharp citric aromas hit his senses to give him a well needed kick-start.

Scrubbing at his scalp, he let his mind drift on the possibilities of what tomorrow might bring because they needed a break. Both in the amount of work they had on their spinning plates and in the investigations, which were stuck on stalemate until they got the forensics back. They could all make assumptions. Gordon Lawrence had most likely murdered his family, set fire to Kimble Hall and then offed himself. Selfish bastard. All the forensic evidence in the world could be presented, but no one ever knew what went on in the mind of a disturbed being.

He swiped his hands down his hair and let the water slough from him.

By the time they'd left work, the body count was still off. Someone from that family survived. They just needed to find out who. And why.

Mason stepped from the pathetic shower and grabbed a fluffy blue towel from the peg outside the cubicle. Set to automatic, the shower turned itself off as he scrubbed at his revived skin, surprised at how the physical workout could offset the mental and emotional turmoil of the day.

No matter how tired, the exercise had done him good.

Late it may be, but that was shifts for you. No given time to eat, sleep or have sex. Not necessarily in that order.

He was ready for all three.

32

Deep overwhelming sadness weighed heavily on Jenna as she sank down onto the bed and laid her head on the cool of her pillow next to Fleur who'd already bagged her place. A whole family wiped out. She had her opinion, but she'd wait for the forensics. The proof.

She reached out a hand to touch the satin downiness of Domino's head as he climbed up after her and laid on the bed by her face with no respect for personal space and the little dog he almost lay on.

How did he always understand? Empathy oozed from him as he grumbled low in his chest and closed his eyes to offer her the comfort she needed as the exhaustion of two sixteen-hour days caught up with her and allowed dark emotions to sneak under her guard. Emotions she'd only experienced since her sister was taken, flinging her into the middle of a nightmare. Despite all her experience and knowledge as a police officer, once her heart opened to the reality of true distress, it was difficult not to apply it to other situations.

She curled her fingers deep into Domino's thick ruff and kneaded his neck, aware he was only with her for the brief time

Fliss was in the shower, then he'd be off, deserting Jenna for his one true love. It didn't matter to her. She'd take her comfort when she could from him. Just as she'd taken the welcome distraction of Fliss's amazing food and wonderful company and for a full hour they'd shared bad news and good, enough to lift her spirits.

And for now she had Fleur's company. The sweet little dog with sadness swirling in her eyes.

Adrian's messages had curled a warmth in the pit of her stomach too to sustain her while she had a quick shower before exhaustion took her completely. They were nothing, but something. They'd not progressed to the intense stage, things were still light and tentative, but he had a way of wording messages that warmed her heart. A tendency to always ask about her first. His hours were almost as long as hers while he worked a major case. He understood her shifts, appreciated she needed to get on with the job, eat, sleep. Some days were like that and he didn't press if she wasn't available.

Once the darkness closed in though, she was left with her own thoughts.

Her breath hitched in her throat and her chest burnt with the emotions she'd stifled for the past few hours, ones she'd felt the need to skim over in Fliss's presence. Fliss didn't need more pressure than she already had with the court case looming.

Domino moved his head to tuck his cold wet nose behind her ear and snuffle there, sending soft shivers along her spine. He wasn't supposed to be on the bed. She'd told Fliss off numerous times for allowing him in her bedroom before. But so much had changed between before and after Fliss's kidnap. So many things Jenna had considered important were no longer.

She reached out a hand to smooth it over Fleur's soft rounded belly.

What would happen with the before and after for the Lawrence family?

A quiet sob snagged at the back of her throat. Some days were hard.

Arson. The fire service had confirmed an accelerant had been used. As the scene had cooled down SOCO, led by Senior Forensic Scientist Jim Downey, had been allowed in. Jim had emailed initial photographs. Of blackened, gnarled husks, curled in on themselves as the heat of the fire had scorched through, rendering their fat content to liquid so it dripped away onto whatever surface each of the bodies had lain on. It had twisted the limbs into unrecognisable shapes. Two of them so small. Despite having it instilled that they should never jump to conclusions, the obvious conclusion was that they were the youngest of the Lawrences. Twin girls. Talisha and Geraldine. They had names. They were real. They were children who Gordon Lawrence had quite possibly murdered and then set alight.

Revulsion stopped Jenna from closing her eyes, the vision too vivid to push from her mind.

Those poor children. The poor wife.

What of the husband? No evidence, but a deep concern that he'd murdered his wife and children. Had he committed suicide elsewhere? Had he made a run for it? She couldn't dismiss it from her mind. From the initial mapping of the building, it appeared one figure, removed from the others, not in a room, but the hallway, had a shotgun by their side, the wooden stock burnt away, but the high alloy steel of the barrel had remained untouched by the fierce heat.

They'd had a case not too dissimilar ten years previously. A man had wiped out his entire family including the estate's animals and taken his own life.

What insanity would drive anyone to commit such heinous

crimes? What pain had they suffered that compelled them to murder their own children, their offspring?

She didn't truly understand the depth of despair and agony that would cause a person to take their own life. It was such a desperate cry. It happened with so many people unable to come out of the darkness. But to take others with them, each one of them deeply loved, was beyond Jenna's comprehension.

She sighed. It took time to piece together the puzzle and still they shouldn't jump to conclusions. They may find him dead in another location. No relatives had yet come forward. Had mum gone for a weekend away with the girls? Run to a friend because she'd had a domestic? What about the children? Had any of them gone to stay over with a friend? No one had come forward yet. They had no linking evidence.

Domino stirred and came to his feet. Unsteady on the deep, soft bedding, he threatened to fall on her. As though undecided, his empathetic dark gaze met hers for a moment, he touched his nose to hers and then reluctantly stepped off the bed. He turned at the door and then trotted down the hallway in the direction of Fliss's bedroom just as she came out of the bathroom. His instinct tied to her.

Exhausted, Jenna reached out a hand to rest it on Fleur. The poor little girl. No family of her own any more. Her eyes fluttered closed and darkness came to take Jenna down, down into a sleep beyond dreams.

33

The last of the Uncle Ben's rice stuck in dry bits at the back of her tongue until she swished it down with Coke, swilling it around her mouth to get rid of the small grains wedged between her gums and lips.

Poppy sat propped up against one of the bales of straw, her knees drawn upwards. She had no idea how long she'd slept again. Scaling the wall of straw had whipped every lick of energy from her as fire streaked over her side, but she'd created a hidey hole at the top of it.

The light outside hadn't faded, but it had changed to the warm glow of a night lit by a full moon.

She was about to spend another night in the barn, with no plan, no idea of what to do next.

She bit into the last of the Jammie Dodgers and chewed. She had one small bar of chocolate left and no more Coke. She still had a full strip of paracetamol and one of ibuprofen, but without some kind of fluid she could hardly dry swallow. With little memory of how much Mr and Mrs Crawford left the house, she could not rely on sneaking back in again for food.

Her side throbbed. She hadn't looked since she slapped the dressing on it, reluctant to get any dust near it in case it became infected. With a bullet still in there, it probably would become infected.

She slipped her hand underneath her loose clothes and touched her flesh, working her way closer to the wound with tentative fingers.

Heat spread across her skin like a furnace the closer she came to the injury, but the flesh didn't feel any more swollen than before. She'd been naked when Daddy shot her, so no material or debris would have punched through with the bullet.

Could she risk switching her phone back on?

Poppy picked it up and turned it over in her hand.

Irritation sparked life back into her. She was a coward. She needed to do something. Make a move. She couldn't hide out there for the rest of her life. Her life wouldn't last much longer if she didn't do something.

Her whole body gave an involuntary spasm as annoyance fired up her muscles. She let out a yelp as the pain slashed through her. She grit her teeth determined not to be distracted from her mission and stabbed her finger to the on button. She chewed her lip as she waited for the screen to load without a clear idea of exactly what she was about to do.

With a delicate touch of her forefinger to WhatsApp, Poppy stared at the list of regular contacts. She ran her tongue over dry lips and hesitated before she selected the girls' group at school.

The trickle of horror turned into a flood as she scrolled through the messages back and forth between Sophie, Olivia and Chanel. Her friends. Girls she loved and they loved her. The desperate outpouring of their grief proved that.

Her chest ached as she read their comments.

Dead.

In their minds, she was dead. And they were destroyed by the death of her. The power of their grief turned her muscles to water.

She covered her mouth with one hand as the screen in front of her shook with the strength of her muffled sobs. Unable to believe she had more tears inside of her, Poppy took her hand from her mouth and stared at the back of her wet hand.

Her family were dead. Even Mum.

Tears dripped from Poppy's chin onto the screen and welled again in her eyes to blur the words. Words of love, of pity, of desperate sorrow. Even Chanel's outpouring of heartache seemed genuine.

Limbs too heavy with grief to move, Poppy scrubbed the cuff of her sweatshirt across her face, swiping away the tears so she could see to type.

34

MONDAY 20 APRIL 2350 HOURS

In the dark silence of the compact little office, fury built inside him until his body vibrated as he read to the end of the press release in *The Shropshire Star* one of the workers had left behind.

With the business at the forefront of his mind, he'd carried out brief checks throughout the day. A fire. A country house. Bodies. Missing persons.

Nothing concrete, nothing solid.

Good. The longer it took the police, the more time he had to prepare for his unexpected future. But they were moving far faster than he'd anticipated. The fire service had got in there sooner than imagined, opening up the possibilities of identification. Once that happened, he was fucked.

He slapped the paper down on the cot and stared at photographs of his family in the press release, re-reading it again.

Five bodies have been discovered at the country home of the Lawrence family after fire ravaged the fifteenth-century hall.

Detectives confirmed the bodies remained unidentified, but that Mr Gordon Lawrence, his wife Linda and their four children

Poppy, Joshua, Geraldine and Talisha were still being treated as missing. No leads had revealed next of kin as yet.

The remains of the bodies will be examined by the Coroner to establish the cause of death.

DI Taylor stated that he could not confirm the age or gender of the bodies at present, but DNA and dental records would be used as all lines of enquiry were followed.

No longer able to contain the black fury, he surged to his feet. Five bodies!

Five.

With the boyfriend, there should have been six. That had been the whole point all along. The extra body should have bought him time.

So who the fuck had escaped?

He paced the small room and tugged his hair until his scalp stung while he played back in his mind each step of Saturday night with detached mercilessness.

His son was definitely dead. No one could have survived that amount of blood and grey matter sprayed over the walls.

Impassive, he thought the process through.

The twins both took a central hit to their brains. He'd killed them outright. No fear. No pain.

His wife, Linda, had died. He'd checked her pulse with detached disinterest. She'd never meant anything to him. Nobody ever had. He didn't understand the need for emotions but was intelligent enough to understand others did. He could emulate it. When the need arose.

He'd blown the boy's face off before he'd set fire to the house with the vague concept that if there were no teeth left, they couldn't be identified and if the fire burnt long and hard enough, the police would struggle with DNA.

He narrowed his eyes. Played back each scene in his mind.

That left Poppy.

Gordon snatched up his phone and wrenched the charging cable from the bottom.

Poppy!

His heart kicked up a beat. He'd not gone back to check on her. In the red mist of his fury, his mind had whirred to a halt as an alternative to his original plan had opened up.

An extra body.

Only there was no extra body. Not now.

He pressed his thumb against the button on his phone and swiped sideways to find the WhatsApp icon. He tapped his finger on his daughter's name and found the confirmation he needed at the top of the screen.

Last seen today at 2303

35

Gritty-eyed from a poor night's sleep and a tough hour in the interview room with Lena and her solicitor, Jenna looked up as the door cracked open. Surprise and delight chased each other as Adrian poked his face around the door and then nudged it open with his shoulder, holding on to the two large takeout cups of coffee in his hands.

'Good morning.'

'Adrian.' A spontaneous smile spread across her face as her heart gave a gentle flutter. 'I wasn't expecting you. I thought you were supposed to be in London.' She came to her feet, attention centred on the coffee ready to take one of the cups from him. Ambrosia, she knew it would be. Her gaze tracked upwards.

'I was.'

Her smile whipped away at the strain evident on his face and gave her a moment's pause as to the reason he was there. Ice froze her heart and her spine stiffened, instinctive pride kicking in as the warmth in her voice turned cool. 'Come in, make yourself at home.'

His serious gaze crashed into hers as he stepped into the room and kicked the door shut with his foot. 'Thanks.'

He reached out to offer the coffee to her, accompanied by a tense smile.

As the breath jammed in her chest, she made a quick assessment of him. 'What's the matter? Is there something wrong?' A tremor of uncertainty ran through her as she accepted the cup, the heat burning straight through the skin on the palm of her hand to make her wonder how he'd carried it. She placed it on the desk in front of her to replace the white plastic cup of watery station coffee she'd been obliged to grab on her way back from interview. She took her seat again, not taking her attention from him. She'd come to learn bad news was best delivered fast. She coped. She always did.

He raised his free hand to rub his fingers across his chin. 'There is... yes, there is something wrong.' He took a long slow breath while he centred himself before he spoke again. 'This fire, the one you were called out to.'

With a jolt of surprise, Jenna blinked at him, confused by the direction he'd taken. For some reason, she'd thought he was there to discuss something personal. Their relationship. Her past record with relationships hadn't work out too well, so her little flutter of insecurity wasn't unjustified. Work matters had not even crossed her mind as he'd come through the doorway.

Oblivious of her reaction, Adrian pulled out the chair opposite and slipped onto it as he placed his own takeout cup in front of him on her desk. He cupped both hands around it and leaned in. 'Gordon Lawrence. His home is out at Farley. I've just heard it was his place that went up in flames. Do you have any news on it?' Strain tightened his mouth to give his jaw a hard line and the implication he knew something about the case screamed at her, but she gave him a moment while she took the time to consider what information she should divulge to him if he knew the potential victim.

She slipped the lid from her coffee and blew the steam from the top while she watched the black liquid ripple outwards with the pebble-in-the-pond effect.

Was Adrian about to lob a bloody great brick into this pond?

Coffee too hot to drink, Jenna pushed back in her seat to give herself the chance to study him and consider the ripples he could cause.

'As of right now, there's very little news because the fire service and SOCO have only begun preliminary investigations, having not been able to get into the building until yesterday.' She blew out a breath. 'The fire was so hot. The Watch Manager explained it was over a thousand degrees, that's five times the temperature of your oven when you're roasting potatoes.' At his flat stare, she jiggled the scenario in her own mind. 'Pizza. Five times the heat. Like when you open the oven door to peep in at your Yorkshire puddings and poom! You're hit by a wall of heat that singes your eyebrows and melts your mascara, making your eyelashes stick together so you can't open your eyes.'

Expression still serious, his mouth nonetheless twitched up at the edges. 'Can't say I've ever had either of those issues.'

'Well, from your face, I was starting to wonder whether you even use an oven.'

His eyebrows took a slow ride up to crinkle his brow. 'I can cook.'

'Really?' He'd fed her, even brought fresh, hot food around, but he hadn't cooked it himself, it had been take-out food.

'Yep. I'm a damned good cook, if I say so myself. I just can't recall sticking my face so close to a hot, open oven that I've managed to singe my eyebrows. Never applied mascara, not really interested in trying it, especially if that's the result you get.'

She reached for her coffee and risked a sip. Still hot, but no longer so hot that it would scald her tongue. She shot him a grim look, squinting at him through the wisps of steam. 'So, Adrian, back to the fire, how do you know Gordon Lawrence?'

'I don't know him personally, but I certainly know of him and I think we have a problem.' He stroked his fingers across his chin. 'Possibly a significant one. This guy, Gordon Lawrence, he's amongst a group of people we've been investigating in relation to one of my major cases I'm prosecuting on based in London. I'd just started to dig deep into his connection. So far, I haven't found anything, but I just need to find the right thread to pull.'

Sufficiently interested, Jenna leaned her elbows on her desk and cupped her chin in her hands as she squinted at him. 'Major case in relation to...?'

'Drugs.'

Surprise rippled over her senses. 'Oh great.' Now she'd have the Drug Squad all over her patch and she'd never get to the bottom of the reason for the fire. It threatened to turn into a circus. She'd already passed over her barista to them. 'So, what are we talking? From initial findings, they believe it's arson, but we have no idea yet the whys and wherefores, we've been left holding our arses in our hands, if the truth be told, and I need answers.' She'd wanted them when she'd arrived at the station two hours earlier, but nothing further had come to light. Forensics took time. No one had stepped forward to claim next of kin despite the press release.

'Don't we all?'

She tapped the screen on her phone and glanced at the time, an idea formulating in the back of her mind. Early yet. 'We're not due a debrief for another couple of hours.'

'The Drug Squad are going to be all over this shortly.'

Damn. Just as she thought. She already had them nudging their way in on her other case. She'd enough balls in the air. She needed to keep them all there and the only way to do that was with information. Currently, she didn't have enough.

'The Drug Squad are going to have to wait their turn. As I said, the fire service has only just let forensics into the house. It's been too much of a hot spot to investigate. We're hoping for another update from NILO in the next couple of hours. Hopefully, SOCO have something more to give us, but the scene is still causing them problems with the heat.'

She considered how much she should tell him. Maybe not her theory, but the facts were all there if he cared to ask anyone he knew in the station for them. He only needed to go to Chief Superintendent Gregg. Since Adrian's involvement with Fliss's disappearance, it appeared Gregg and Adrian had become best buddies. Almost. There was always a line between officers and prosecutors. There needed to be for when matters went to court. And Adrian would possibly be taking this matter to court at some point in the future.

'We have five bodies *in situ* at present.' That was common knowledge, it had been in the press release.

Adrian inclined his head, dark eyes intense as she continued.

'Obviously, we need to verify the identities, but as of today they still couldn't do it. As it is a family of six, that makes us short one body.' She tapped the desk with her forefinger. 'That is an assumption at present as a full inspection of the scene is still taking place. The sixth body could be under the rubble. There was a family party, everyone, it appears, went to bed early. As all the bodies have been located from the first floor where the bedrooms are, in the east wing of the building some of the floors have collapsed inwards, so forensics will verify that at a later stage. But, and again an assumption, we think they'd all gone to bed as they were in different parts of the building.' Jenna blew out a breath and wrapped fingers turned to ice around her cup. 'SOCO sent photos of the bodies.' She dropped her hands back down to the desk and squinted at him. 'Last night.'

'Ah.' He made a slow inspection of her and inclined his head again. 'You should have called. I was back home. Available.'

Her smile came with ease at his understanding as she raised her cup and took another drink. 'I'll remember that in future. I just assumed you'd be asleep after a long day.'

'I'm always available for you, Sergeant.' His smile gave her a reassurance she hadn't realised she needed.

'They tried to lift one of the bodies last night but it was so hot it melted the plastic body bag and fell back through onto the floor.'

Adrian's mouth twisted. 'Unpleasant.' Again, his eyes made a quick tour of her face. She recognised the look, she did it to Fliss. He was checking her, making sure she was okay.

He had nothing to worry about, she'd survive. She'd survived worse. Nothing about this case was personal. Desperately sad, but not personal.

She gave a shrug. 'So, we have nothing to go on yet.'

Her mild impatience gathered speed, she tapped a rhythm out on her desk with her fingers as she continued to stare at Adrian. She wanted information as much as he did. If not more so. She raised her cup, surprised to see she was almost halfway through as time ticked away.

With her mind kicking into overdrive, Jenna pushed away from her desk and came to her feet in one fluid motion. 'Let's not wait for NILO to come and debrief us.' She caught his gaze in hers. 'Let's go down there and take a look for ourselves. See what information we can glean from it. It's my case, my investigation, my decision.'

Adrian's lips morphed into a satisfied smile as he rose to his feet and jammed the lid back onto his coffee. It was all the answer she needed as she strode around the desk and swung open the door, speaking over her shoulder to Adrian as she went.

'We'll pick up Mason on the way through the office.' She considered the amount of work it might entail, the information they might be able to extract once they were on site. 'It won't do Ryan any harm to come with us and see what's going on, either. It's good experience for him.'

Her mind whirled through who else would be involved.

She could only hope PC Gardner was not the scene guard at the site this morning. She'd seen his name on the rota but couldn't pull from her memory the exact times he would be there. Eight hourly shifts, offered on overtime, had been arranged so each PC on the rota would have the opportunity to keep up with their other duties, and it ensured none of them became bored. Of course, he'd jump at it. He wouldn't have voluntarily offered. There'd have to be something in it for him. It was the type of character he was.

Scene guard wasn't the most inspiring of duties. Tedious, it entailed keeping a log, ensuring the public stayed outside the cordon and registering everyone who entered or exited the cordons and where they went within the area. Preservation of the integrity of the scene was paramount, as was continuity of evidence. The job sounded important, but the truth of the matter was, it was eight hours of boredom, with feet that ached from standing continually. Although he deserved the tediousness of it, Jenna couldn't imagine anything more miserable than encountering Lee Gardner every day with his face twisted with misery.

With a philosophical shrug, Jenna moved on. The fact was Lee Gardner would be at the scene some time during the day. When that was would ironically clash with when she arrived. It seemed to be her fate.

Cradling her coffee in one hand, Jenna took another sip as she passed Mason's desk. Attuned so well to her, he raised his head and, as his astute gaze caught hers, she jerked her head in the direction of the door. 'Mason, you're with me.'

With measured movements, he rose from his chair, stiff-legged, and Jenna held her tongue as she cruised on past. Perhaps the gym had been a mistake. He wasn't as young as he used to be.

Ryan leapt from his chair in the corner and dashed towards her across the office, like an excitable puppy, eyes dancing with enthusiasm and hope.

She shot him a smile and a quick wink. 'Ryan, with me.'

She took the back way down through Malinsgate police station, as the boys exchanged the grunted pleasantries only men understood. Her flat-heeled shoes slapped out a rhythm which echoed in the stairwell as she swept down, with the other three following close behind.

Ahead of them, she leaned in through the front desk window, grabbed a set of keys for one of the police-issue vehicles and held up a pen to show she was about to sign for it before Della Prince's ice blue eyes could pierce her with a deadly stare.

Jenna whipped around from the window to come close up against Adrian, whose breath puffed out across her ear. 'We don't need to take a police vehicle, we can go in mine.'

Jenna grinned, tipping her head back so she could look him in the eye as she raised the car keys and jiggled them in his face, the same as she had the first time he'd tried to persuade her to let him use his vehicle. Then the jury had still been out on her opinion of him. Now, her response was tongue in cheek. 'Nice try. You know the rules, Adrian, we're not getting in your car. We're not insured. We're on duty.'

He shrugged his shoulders. His lips twitched up at the sides. 'It was worth a try. It's better than the heap of metal you're about to drive.'

As his vehicle was a Range Rover Autobiography LR-SDV8, almost any other car would seem like a heap to him.

Privileged, Mason had called him when they'd first met. He'd called him worse and revised his opinion in a short space of time.

She ran her gaze over Adrian and bestowed him with a sweet smile. Privileged he may be, but he'd never flaunted it, never abused it and the pleasant surprise was that since their first meeting, Mason and Adrian had formed a strong bond of mutual like and respect.

Adrian followed her out of the door to the accompanying rumbling laughter from Mason. She suspected Ryan may be amused, but he kept it to himself. Unlike Mason, Ryan was a little in awe of Adrian, both his rank and demeanour.

Jenna jolted to a sudden halt at the kerb as a police vehicle swept past them a touch too fast, swung in a wide circle around the car park and pulled forwards into the last available space.

Irritation swirled at the ignorance of the driver to have disregarded the pedestrians waiting to cross and even more so, her pet hate, they'd pulled the car in forwards so that it needed to be reversed out. Sheer common sense and etiquette dictated that all police vehicles were reversed into the spaces so that once a shout went up, they could be despatched without delay in the most efficient possible manner.

Jenna pressed the fob to unlock the doors of her assigned car but couldn't ignore the annoyance at the ignorance of the other driver swirling in the pit of her stomach. 'Just give me a minute.' She left the others to make themselves comfortable while she strode over to the police vehicle.

As the uniformed officer climbed from the vehicle, the breath stopped in her throat.

Shit!

Too late to backtrack, she conjured up a weak smile. Of all the people, she couldn't imagine why fate would fling this one in her path yet again. 'PC Gardner. How are things going?'

The flutter in her chest increased as he slammed the door

closed and turned to skim his insolent gaze from the top of her head to the tip of her toes.

'Jenna.'

She reared her head back, her eyes shooting wide. 'Sergeant Morgan, or Sarge will do. Thank you.'

The cocky grin told her he knew he'd managed to rattle her. Tempted to raise her hand and run her fingers through her hair with frustration, she chose instead to curl it into a tight ball at her side, squeezing hard enough to break bones.

'I don't know if you're aware, but we reverse the police vehicles into the spots.'

'Why?' His chin went up.

She tilted her head to one side but resisted the temptation to huff out a breath. 'Convenience and speed. It means we can get out quicker if we have a shout.'

'But I needed to get in quick. I have something I need to do as a matter of urgency. So, I'll hope you'll excuse me' His eyes filled with contempt.

'It's not an emergency, though, and there's a difference, PC Gardner.'

'Well, *DS* Morgan, I'd consider that the next person's problem.'

As he made a move to pass her, Jenna side-stepped into his path, and narrowed her eyes, but stopped her hand before she poked him in the chest. He'd only have her up on assault charges, the petty little shit. 'PC Gardner, I'd appreciate it if you got back into the car and turned it around so as not to inconvenience or delay the next person called out on an emergency.'

His dark gaze clashed with hers as he remained motionless, neither pushing past, nor retreating, his jaw a hard line.

'Sarge, do you have a problem?' Mason's calm tones almost whispered in her ear.

She opened her mouth to reply as PC Gardner pushed out his bottom lip while his eyes turned sullen and arrogant.

'No problem here. PC Gardner was about to move the car to make it more convenient for the next person.'

'I wondered which wanker had parked it in forwards so the next person to get a shout has to reverse it out while all the rest of them are already on their way to the job.' Mason stepped forward to stand shoulder to shoulder with her and leaned in to flash a shark-like grin at PC Gardner. 'Don't want to be a wanker, do we?'

Faced with another male, dominant, fit and challenging, PC Gardner backed down.

'I was about to reposition it.'

'Excellent!' Mason's voice roared out. 'Get it moved then.' Mason's fingers encircled her elbow to draw her away. 'We've got a job, Sarge. An emergency, so to speak. I'm pleased to say the last person to park the vehicle reversed it in. Clever little bugger. It must have been me.' He tugged at her arm and Jenna backed off while the heat in PC Gardner's eyes flared.

As they made it back to their police vehicle, Jenna resisted the temptation to glance over her shoulder. 'Do you think he'll re-park it?'

'Hell, no.'

She dug her fingertips into her brow, and then grabbed the door handle of the car, swung it open and slumped into the seat.

'Ignore him.' Mason shot her a fast grin as he plopped into the seat beside her and made the car rock. 'He's a wanker.'

'So you say. But he's more than that. He's a loose cannon.'

'Yeah. A dangerous wanker.'

'He has no respect for rank and he's quite blatantly sexist. You shouldn't have had to step in, Mason.' The heat in her face blazed as her anger grew. 'He'll get his comeuppance and it's going to be sooner rather than later.'

From the silence in the back of the car, neither men wanted to interfere in her conflict with PC Lee Gardner. It was best they kept out. It was about to turn ugly.

With a shake of her head, Jenna yanked her seat belt around her, hit the start button, slammed the vehicle into first gear and shot forwards out of the parking space in a bid to make up for lost time dealing with the arrogant tosser that was PC Gardner.

She powered the vehicle out of the car park at a speed more conducive to a fast-response vehicle on an emergency.

Adrian slapped his hands on the back of her seat as he slipped across the black leather seats in the rear of the car to crunch into Ryan. His low grunt only topped by Ryan's desperate whimper as he was slammed into the side of the rear door.

Keen to get there before NILO packed up and made their own way back to the station, Jenna kept her foot firm on the accelerator. She wanted to see them *in situ*, have a look around the site to experience the scene herself, not just have information thrown at her in a clinical, washed fashion.

She hit the Queensway dual carriageway and pressed down harder to take them over the speed limit. Speed always satisfied her. Steadied her. Gave her those precious few minutes of concentration to purge herself of her annoyance.

Pretty straightforward route, all the way along the Queensway to the end, over the roundabout with a cast-iron mineshaft. She throttled back as she navigated the new roundabout which accommodated the addition of the stretch of road to the overpopulated new houses with their single-drive homes, double-car families.

She slipped past the next roundabout, bypassing the narrow curving road that was Jiggers Bank, which would have taken her to Ironbridge. She followed the wide sweeping curve along Buildwas Road and turned left over the small bridge to take the winding bends to Farley and Kimble Hall.

As they bumped along the track, she scanned the scene in daylight. More organised than the night of the incident, the scene guard had evidently planned the parking. She squinted around through the thin tendrils of smoke still wisping skywards to disappear into the ether. It was all that was left of the fire.

She drew the car up next to one of the tenders.

All four of them stepped out of the vehicle at the same time, but it was Jenna who spotted Charlie Cartwright and made straight for him.

'Hey, Charlie, back on again?' His shifts had probably been as long as hers. She offered her hand for a quick, firm shake.

'Jenna. Yeah, I'm due off in about an hour. 'What about you? Did anyone claim the little dog?'

'No. Not yet.' At the twitch of Adrian's lips, she expanded. 'She's at my house with my sister's Dalmatian.' Jenna gave a self-conscious shrug. They were going to know just how soft she was. 'She took over sleeping rights of his bed.'

Charlie's face creased into a wide smile. 'Let's hope he doesn't eat her by the time you get back.'

It had never occurred to her. The thought circled in her mind. 'Nah, he wouldn't.' He gaze caught Adrian's warm one again as he twitched his eyebrows at her.

Charlie's gaze drifted across and Jenna held out her hand palm upwards as she introduced them. 'You met DC Mason Ellis the other night. This is DC Ryan Downey.' She circled her hand around to include Adrian. 'And this is Adrian Hall, Chief Crown Prosecutor.'

Charlie's eyebrows flicked up, but he said nothing, just held his hand out to each of them in turn.

He rubbed a finger over his top lip. 'We're just about finished here. There's no chance anything else is going to set alight again. We're doing a tidy-up job. Until this morning, everything was still hot, but we have a handle on it. I've sent the other tenders away. There's no need for them.' He kicked his boot into the ash-layered dirt and placed his hands on his hips while he squinted up at the stone building blackened with the fire. Grey smoke curled in ringlets up to the clear blue sky. His face showed the strain of the past two days and his voice dropped low. 'It was a bad one.'

They'd all felt it. The heavy weight of heartache pressed down on Jenna's chest making it difficult to breathe. The updates the previous day from the safe distance of Malinsgate police station had hit her hard, but there was no comparison to being back on scene. The taste, the smell, the black cloud of despair. The dark oppressiveness begged her attention as she skimmed her gaze over the vast burnt-out building. Thick, black soot layered every surface and ash hung heavy on the air, so her nostrils burnt with the scent of it. Piles of dampened-down rubble steamed in protest. She'd attended housefires before but never on such a vast scale, nor had she witnessed a ferocity that compared to this one.

She skimmed her gaze over the area. Quiet and calm in contrast to the last time she'd been there. An eerie cloud dampened the sound. Fire officers wandered, kicking over piles of wood to ensure every last flame had been smothered. A group of people stood at the farthest point, in front of the burnt-out shell of the house, backs to them. Instead of PPE one of them wore the simple high visibility jacket over the top of his suit.

'Is that the NILO?'

Charlie tossed a look over his shoulder. 'Yeah. Roger Ayman. We're about to have another update with him.'

As the man turned, she recognised him from the day before. Windswept and not so slick looking. Face strained.

'Oh yeah. Excellent.' She nodded. Out of respect, Jenna asked the question, but she was about to anyhow. 'Can we come over and join you?'

'Sure.' Charlie cast a quick look at the other three who stood like sentinels on either side of her. 'Come on over.'

As they approached, Roger Ayman turned, clipboard in hand, dark grey eyes serious.

Jenna offered her hand. 'Hi, I'm DS Jenna Morgan. This is DC Mason Ellis, DC Ryan Downey. I was at your debrief yesterday. This is Chief Crown Prosecutor Adrian Hall.'

Again, a quick flicker of surprise crossed Ayman's face as he introduced himself and Jenna considered that having the Chief Crown Prosecutor along wasn't considered normal. It didn't deter her or detract from the situation. She was there to find information and Adrian tucked his hands into his jacket pocket and let her take the lead.

She smiled at Ayman and got straight to the point. She no longer had time to twiddle her thumbs while she waited for information. 'Roger, Adrian's come to us today with information that may be linked to the fire. I appreciate we've needed to wait for the site to cool down, but things are starting to move fast and we need to get cracking with some answers.'

With a quick flicker of surprise at her directness, Ayman gave a nod. 'Right then.' He clapped his hands together and turned to Adrian. 'What information have you got?' Just as direct as Jenna, his eyebrows winged up with the question.

Adrian stepped closer. 'Gordon Lawrence is currently the subject of an investigation being conducted into a drugs ring based in London. I'm wading through a whole pile of paperwork picking up the links, but when I heard about the fire...' He shrugged and narrowed his eyes as he gazed beyond Roger at the burnt out shell of Kimble Hall.

Roger blew out a quiet breath, raised his hand to scratch the side of his nose and then shook his head. 'Well, I can't necessarily help with the drugs connection and if you're after physical evidence from within the house then you're buggered.' He squinted at the building. 'We have site mapping, but there's nothing left in there but ash. The fire crew,' he gave Charlie a nod of acknowledgement, 'have secured the building to the best of their ability and SOCO are all over it. Initial findings haven't changed from last night. Five bodies. Six members of the family missing. Voice flat and morose, Roger pointed at the house with his pen. 'That's not to say there isn't another body in there. Again, with the site mapping it seems the first floor has partially collapsed into the ground floor. And, unfortunately, that's created a forensic nightmare.'

Jenna clucked her tongue against the roof of her mouth. 'What about the bodies? How quick do you think we can get an ID on them?'

Roger's cheeks puffed out as he blew out a hefty sigh. 'There isn't a whole hell of a lot left of them. They'll probably have to rely on ID from the teeth. Unfortunately, a lot of the forensic evidence has been burnt beyond recognition or flooded by the amount of water that's had to be used to put the fire out. What we can see on initial inspection is hot spots. The fire was deliberate. Arson. We know an accelerant was used. The heat was so intense. The lads went in yesterday to recover the bodies.' He puffed out his cheeks. 'But they were so hot, when they tried to pick one of them up,' he made a scooping motion with his arms and then opened them wide, 'It melted the bag and fell through.'

Jenna chose to ignore Ryan's quickly smothered gag as her own stomach pitched. She'd already heard. It didn't make it any easier. Even the highly experienced Charlie tightened his mouth. A dead body, no matter what state it was in, never hardened you to death.

Roger ran his fingers through his short hair. 'SOCO made the decision that they'd be better left *in situ*.'

Surprise flickered through her. 'They're still in there?'

'They are. It's not unusual. Arson made it a crime scene, the bodies made it a murder scene. The firearms make it even more sinister.'

Interested, Jenna tipped her head to one side. 'They've found more?'

Roger nodded and circled his pen to point at the left side of the house. 'Three more firearms found throughout the premises. Each of them in relative proximity to the bodies.' His face tightened with grimness.

Jenna grimaced.

Mason nodded. 'Aggravated burglary gone wrong?'

Jenna shrugged. 'A lot of firearms dumped. Seems a little odd to me.'

'How about a connection to the drugs ring?' Adrian tucked his hands into his pockets. 'Maybe they sent someone to deal with him.'

'Still, why leave the firearms by the bodies?'

'Symbolic?' Ryan nudged his way into the ring of people. 'I killed this person with this gun, this one with another. It meant something.'

Jenna frowned. A good theory, but... 'That's personal.' And the ugliness of what circled in her mind clenched at her stomach.

'SOCO say the firearms were used. There are several bullets and cartridges, which again have been left in place. Our lead forensics, Jim Downey...' Roger's gaze flickered to Ryan as the connection was made. The family resemblance easy enough to spot once you knew. '...Believes there's a bullet embedded in one of the victim's skulls. He'll verify this once the body has been taken to the morgue.'

Roger tapped the pen to his lips while he thought. 'Going back to the site mapping, it appears the family could well have been in bed. And while the intensity of the fire has burnt everything beyond recognition, the fact that they were actually lying down on combustible material would have made it hotter, would have made them burn faster in those areas.'

Not wanting to flinch at the image Roger managed to conjure up in her mind, Jenna trailed her gaze across to Ryan whose pale face had turned florid. She wondered if he'd faint, or worse still throw up. He'd done it before, it all depended on what drink he'd had before they came out of the station.

Oblivious to her response, Roger continued to use his pen as a small wand, waving it periodically to indicate different parts of the fire. 'One of the bodies still has form.' He tapped the pen against the clipboard he held. 'That would be the photographs sent over last night.'

'Grim.'

Roger tilted his head to look at Mason. 'The entire situation is grim, I'm afraid.'

And sad, Jenna wanted to say, desperately sad, but she kept her words to herself.

'It appears that this particular person wasn't in bed at the time of the fire but on the landing outside one of the bedrooms.' He tracked his pen along the right side of the building. 'It could be they were on the first-floor landing, and this is just a hypothesis at the moment, but I'd say they were overwhelmed by smoke and fell on to what appears to be fibres of a woollen carpet.'

Confused, Jenna squinted at Roger, but it was Ryan who got in there with his question. 'What difference would that make?'

Roger jiggled his shoulders and indicated for Charlie to answer.

'Wool is a natural fire retardant because of its higher nitrogen and water content. It takes a lot longer to burn because it needs more oxygen in the air. Once it does burn, it doesn't drip, melt or stick to the skin.'

'But you're saying it did burn.'

'Yep.' Charlie nodded. 'But not to the extent of the victims which appeared to be lying on combustible material, i.e. their beds, which would have heated up around them. It would be like a melting pot.'

'But wool doesn't have the same effect?'

'No, it's the most flame-retardant material you can get, naturally.' Roger waved his little wand again. 'So, the body lying in this part of the building, on the woollen rug, or carpet, or runner, although not identifiable, has not been incinerated to the extent of the other bodies. It will make it easier to identify.'

Sickened by the vivid images flashing through her mind, Jenna turned away to gather herself as the rest of them fell silent.

She raked a gaze over the site. An eerie stillness settled over the area with only the sounds of muffled voices from the crew inside the building playing vaguely in the background as they made their way through.

Roger chewed his lip while he studied his notes.

She had her theory with no supporting evidence, but she had the experts to hand. 'So, who do we think set the fire? Is this someone from within the family? Gordon Lawrence perhaps? I thought he may have slaughtered his entire family and then killed himself, but we're a body short. So, did he kill them all and walk away?'

Evilness pervaded to give her a dark shiver.

She couldn't turn her mind from that one thought, even though she knew she had to have hard facts before they could draw any conclusions. She'd eke out every bit of information from the experts, but she'd hold her belief.

Roger shrugged. She suspected he wasn't the type to hazard unfounded guesses. 'Nobody, it appears, was downstairs. They were all on the first floor, by the looks of it, at the moment. So, from what Charlie says, with the intensity, the start point of this fire appears to be on the first floor. Until we can DNA the bodies, we don't know for sure who the victims are.'

Charlie nodded and turned to face the structure. 'We don't want to make any assumptions just at the moment. This is a massive, massive job. We've sectioned it into four.' He pointed up at the house with both hands spread wide, pen flicking in the air. 'There. That's where the ceiling has collapsed.' He held his left palm up and pointed to the other end of the building. 'There, they're saying that the floor hasn't given way.'

Jenna nodded her agreement.

'It's going to take time. Weeks, possibly months, on a project this enormous.' Roger skimmed his hand as he turned in a circle.

Mason stepped forward. 'And if it's arson, then we should be looking for somebody sooner rather than later.'

Cooler than she expected, Jenna quivered from the sudden chill. She tucked both hands into her jacket pockets and pushed them in deep. She stared at the tendrils of smoke coming up from the ground and gave a small shudder.

What a nightmare.

She squinted up at the building. 'You know this falls in line with what Mrs Crawford said the night of the fire. That she'd heard gunshots. Gunshots from the house.' Suspicion curdled in her stomach. 'We'll have to see what Salter and Wainwright come back with at the debrief, but I think we probably got as much as we could from Mrs Crawford the other night. She was quite a willing witness.' She turned to Adrian. 'We still don't know any more. Except we have five bodies under very suspicious circumstances. It's a mess. It's a goddamn mess.'

36

Sophie's eyes bulged with terror as she hop-stepped from one foot to the other like a first-year infant who'd left it too late to dash to the toilet.

Next to her, short, plump and middle-aged, her mother exuded a stoicism reflecting the character the girls had already portrayed of her and which Jenna could only admire.

Jenna showed no surprise to see the teenager but pushed the door of interview room three open. Rather than speak, she indicated with one hand for them to precede her so she could get them away from the overcrowded front desk. Almost a dozen people vied for attention to get their voices heard above everyone else's in their bid to explain why the pile-up in the queue to turn left into the Council car park opposite Malinsgate station couldn't possibly be their fault. A deep baritone, a high-pitched soprano, the drama of an opera. One Jenna wanted nothing to do with.

She pushed the door closed behind her, dulling the voices, but unable to block them completely.

Already settled in front of the small table, Mason came to his feet as they entered.

Jenna reached out a hand towards Sophie, noting the iciness of the young girl's fingers. 'Hi, Sophie. Good to see you.' She turned to Sophie's mum. 'DS Jenna Morgan, DC Mason Ellis.' She indicated Mason, who reached forward to take his turn with a handshake. 'Mrs Maxwell?'

'Trudy. Trudy Maxwell.' Sophie's mum exuded the understated, solid confidence of the wealthy businesswoman she undoubtedly was from her designer skirt suit, to the impeccable blonde high-lighted hair and immaculately polished nails.

'Please, take a seat.'

The chairs scraped across the floor as they settled at the small, square table while Jenna shuffled her notepad and placed a pen in front of her. She'd take notes that she considered neces-sary, but initially she needed to put the obviously terrified Sophie at ease.

Jenna leaned forward to rest her forearms on the table between them. Fingers loosely linked, she made eye contact with the young girl.

'Sophie.' She smiled at her. All teenage hysteria and excitement from their previous meeting had evaporated as Sophie reached for her mum's hand. Jenna could only admire the silent support Sophie's mother gave her, reflecting the personality the girls had hinted at previously. 'I believe you have something you'd like to talk to me about?' She injected her voice with a gentle evenness as she ran her gaze over the child in front of her, her keen eye taking in every detail. Pallid beneath the thick layers of her make-up, on-fleek eyebrows and bright pink lipstick stood out in stark contrast to the rest of her lovely face. Heavy black mascara emphasised the deep ocean blue of her eyes.

Sophie nodded, her chest expanding as she held her breath and took a moment to squeeze her mum's hand, her fingers turning white at the pressure.

'Mum says I need to tell you. It could be nothing. It could be something, but we think you need to know.'

Reluctant to rush her, Jenna kept her gaze steady on Sophie as the girl fluttered her free hand and then dipped it in her pocket to draw out her phone and place it on the table between them. She tapped one perfect acrylic nail on the screen and then touched a thumb to the ID button, so the screen lit up.

'I know they say Poppy and her family are all... dead.' She paused on a hiccup, gulping down so she could continue. 'That they died in the fire.' She blinked to wash away the fall of tears that had formed as she started to talk, her voice cracking on her next words. 'But is it possible that she's alive? I think she may be.'

The question was a plea, a desperate hope.

Surprise shockwaved through Jenna, she'd not given thought to anyone but Gordon Lawrence being alive. Without taking her gaze from Sophie, she kept her face as impassive as possible. If she over-sympathised, she could end up with drama she didn't need. She needed facts.

'What makes you think that, Sophie?' Sympathy rolled through her at the desperate desire in Sophie's eyes for it to be true. A desire that Jenna had no choice but to keep in check.

'Because I think she tried to contact me through our WhatsApp group. We have this group...' Sophie pushed herself forward to the edge of her uncomfortable chair in her enthusiasm to get her point over. 'We have several, but we have one just for us four girls. Me, Olivia, Chanel and Poppy. Because we're best friends and we're always together.' Impassioned, she rushed the words out and Jenna nodded.

'Okay. So, what happened on this WhatsApp group to make you believe Poppy is alive?'

Sophie turned the phone around so that Jenna could see the

screen. 'Last night after we'd all been chatting about Poppy and her family and how...' She hesitated and took in a swift draught of air. 'How awful it was and how we couldn't believe Poppy could possibly be dead. It was late and I didn't want to disturb Mum because...' She slanted her mum a guilty glance, '...she was supposed to have an early start this morning and I knew she'd be able to hear me, so we changed to messages from video call. After than Olivia and Chanel went to bed. I couldn't sleep and I scrolled back through the messages. I tapped on Poppy's name just...' She shrugged. 'I don't know why, just for comfort, I guess, just to see her... to look at her profile, her face. I just wanted to *see* her again...' A sob caught in her throat as she stumbled to a halt. Tears formed in her eyes, threatening to spill over the thick black layer of her mascara. Sophie raised a shaking hand to press her fingertips underneath and one large teardrop rolled down her finger onto the back of her hand.

Wordless, Mason reached for the small cube of tissues at the edge of the desk and offered them to her. Sophie took one and mumbled a thank you to Mason, who slid the box back to the edge of the desk.

'Okay, Sophie. I understand.' Jenna did understand. That need to connect, to know she could still see her best friend, her sister. To believe they were still alive. The denial that she could possibly be dead. Jenna had experienced the emotions herself, suffered the same hope and doubt and desperate desire for it not to be true. She kept her hands loose in front of her, eager to offer the young girl comfort, but aware that she needed to extract information from her before Sophie broke down altogether. Unable to ignore the slight edge of anticipation, Jenna waited for Sophie to give her eyes a delicate dab before she met her gaze. 'When you're ready, in your own time, carry on.'

Jenna placed one hand over the top of Sophie's trembling one, the wet of her tears warm in direct contrast to the iciness of Sophie's skin.

Sophie's voice shuddered out. 'When you look at someone's profile, you can see when they were on WhatsApp. I wasn't looking for that, so it took me a couple of minutes to notice.' She hitched in a shaky breath. 'The app says that Poppy last looked at WhatsApp at 2303 last night, that's when we were on. That's when we were talking to each other. She was there at the same time. Watching. Tracking our conversation before we switched to video.'

Sophie's forlorn clutch at the possibility that her friend was still alive squeezed Jenna's heart.

Without wanting to give her false hope, Jenna pulled the phone closer to her and leaned in to get a better look. She tapped on Poppy's name and a photograph of the beautiful, blonde-haired young girl appeared inside a circular frame on screen.

Jenna stared at the faded text that indicated when WhatsApp was last seen. She picked up her pen and with considered calmness wrote Sophie's name down on the notepad in front of her. She underscored it and made a note of the time registered on the WhatsApp that someone had last looked at Poppy's phone.

She slid the phone across for Mason to verify and caught the quick movement of his left eyebrow as it flicked upwards in a cool acknowledgement.

As she slid the phone back across the table, Sophie scrunched the tissue into her fist. 'I don't know if you know how WhatsApp works.'

Jenna bestowed her with a gentle smile. Sophie probably thought she was too old to understand, but she used WhatsApp all the time to keep in contact with Fliss and Adrian, Mason and Ryan. Although she tended to shy away from groups. Too much shit to wade through when she just wanted a quick answer.

She slid her attention back to Sophie.

'When somebody is typing their reply, this message up here...' Sophie tapped the screen with the very tip of her sharp acrylic nail, '...says *typing*, in italics.'

Aware of that, Jenna could only nod her head in agreement.

Sophie dabbed at her eyes. Tears almost forgotten in her desperation to get her point across. 'Well, while I was looking at her picture, the word *typing* appeared.' She stopped, her gaze sharpened on Jenna as though willing her to understand.

Jenna couldn't see the word *typing,* she'd not been privy to what Sophie may have seen the night before, either in reality or because her mind craved the comfort of believing her friend was alive. 'What did she type?'

Sophie's mouth turned downward. 'She didn't. After a few minutes, the word disappeared, and nothing came up on screen. I waited. I waited for ages. After nothing appeared, I sent her a message direct, not on the group chat.' Sophie tapped the screen. 'I didn't want the other girls to see in case they thought I was mad.'

Fear of ridicule or recrimination, Jenna wasn't sure which, reflected in Sophie's eyes. She pushed the phone towards Jenna again.

Poppy.
Are you there?
Please let me know you're alive.
I love you, babe.

Jenna stared at the screen until her eyes burnt, but if she looked up, she knew they'd all see the wash of tears in her eyes.

Sophie's messages were the last in the thread.

Jenna blew out a cooling breath and raised her head when she was ready. Not for one moment did Jenna dispute Sophie's words, but with no knowledge of the young girl's reliability she could only take the evidence in front of her. That evidence clearly showed that whether Poppy was alive or dead, someone had used her phone. A phone they believed had perished in the fire along with the occupants of Kimble Hall.

The seriousness with which Sophie had taken the matter and the sensible manner in which she conducted herself with the support of her mother gave Jenna concern. This wasn't some hysterical teenager.

Jenna placed her hand over the phone and drew it closer. 'Sophie, I'm really grateful to you for coming in. I do take this very seriously. I need to ask you if we can take your phone as evidence.' It was the only evidence of contact and although Jenna was asking out of politeness, the cold, hard truth of it was she was quite within her rights to seize the phone if Sophie refused.

Eyes rounded with shock, Sophie turned to Trudy Maxwell. 'Mum?'

For the first time, Trudy moved, her mouth springing into a wide, false smile and Jenna understood the strength of will it took for the woman not to cry. 'Of course. It's not a problem. We'll call at Tesco and buy you one of those burner phones.'

Sophie rolled her heavily laden eyes as only a teenager could. 'Mum, it's not a burner phone, we're not druggies.'

Trudy glanced at her watch and pushed away from the table. 'We'll let you follow up your investigations.' She offered her hand in a firm shake to both Jenna and Mason with Sophie following her cue. 'We appreciate your time. Thank you.'

As Sophie and Trudy made their way over the small bridge onto the car park, Jenna turned to Mason. 'Get hold of our mobile SPOC and see what they can establish. We'll need the forms filling in for RIPA.' She didn't need him circumnavigating the system of the Regulation of Investigatory Powers Act, they needed to conduct an interception of communications through the single point of contact who would follow the lead through from start to finish tracking the results and keeping on top of the case so it didn't get lost in the system.

Jenna handed the phone to Mason, they still needed to adhere to the regulations. 'Make it quick. DI Taylor can sign it off.'

'It's going to take a few hours to process.'

As they made their way back upstairs to their offices, Jenna nodded, processes and the time they took were essential, and frustratingly beyond her control. 'Sooner we can get the request in, the better.'

Mason held the door into the corridor open to let her through, then kept abreast of her as she lengthened her stride.

'You think Poppy is alive?'

Jenna stopped at the door to the main office and turned. 'I think we have one body short of a family set and we have evidence that someone, somewhere has accessed Poppy's phone. We now need to know who and where.'

37

'Sarge,' the voice on the other end of the phone was a gruff whisper. 'I'm not sure you're going to believe this, but I have someone else asking for you in connection with Poppy Lawrence, concerned parents, Mr and Mrs Abbott. They say their son is missing.'

She'd barely had time to park her bum on the seat at her desk, but at least she knew Mason was onto mobile SPOC and she could rely on him to keep that ball in the air for as long as it took.

'Pop them in interview room three, if you would.' The chairs would still be warm. 'Offer them a drink. I'll be there in a sec.'

She left her jacket on the back of her chair, scooped up the pad and pen she'd only just put down and marched through the outer office, conscious that an entire day was about to disappear from under her and the workload was piling high. She needed to prioritise and delegate, but until she knew what this was about, prioritising and delegating would have to wait.

'Ryan.' She jerked her head in the direction of the exit door and smiled as he trotted to catch up with her. As they skimmed their way down the stairs, she turned to look at him. 'We have some concerned parents. Apparently, their son is missing. I know nothing except there may be a connection with Poppy.' They paused outside the interview room and she handed him her notepad, her pen. 'You take the lead.'

His eyes shot wide. 'Me?' He'd never taken the lead in her presence. He was more than capable and had done so on many occasions, just not with her observing.

Tempted to laugh, she swung the door wide instead and introduced herself and Ryan to the anxious parents.

As Ryan fiddled with the pen top for a moment to get his equilibrium, Jenna skimmed her gaze over Mr and Mrs Abbott. Middle-class, middle-aged.

Mr Abbott wore the world-weary look of an accountant waiting for retirement. His shiny, excessively dry-cleaned suit hung limp from his shoulders as though he'd recently lost weight but not bothered to buy a new one. His tie lay flat but skewed to one side like an afterthought as he'd rushed out of the door.

Mrs Abbott's deep-set, dark brown eyes contained the sheer horror of someone who knew without a doubt the news was bad. Instinct. Premonition. Some people had it and the knowledge was already there. It was just a case of how long she could contain the truth from being confirmed. Her fingers trembled as she picked up the white plastic cup filled with water. She took a sip and placed it back down.

'Mr and Mrs Abbott, I believe you have a concern regarding your son.' Ryan scratched a note on the pad. The shortened version of the date. He raised his head and tilted it to one side with a clear invitation for them to talk.

With a quick pull of pride at her young detective's sympathetic, inviting approach, Jenna leaned back in her seat comfortable to let him continue.

'He's missing. Our son, Aiden.' Mrs Abbott's voice hitched and she sucked in a deep breath before she continued. 'He hasn't been home all weekend. And then we saw Trudy Maxwell and her daughter, umm, Sophie, outside just now and they said there'd been a fire. A fire at Poppy Lawrence's house. And Aiden is missing.'

Trying to keep up with the logic of the woman's ramblings, Jenna blinked.

As Mrs Abbott gushed, Mr Abbott reached out a hand and squeezed hers. 'Now, Sharon, don't panic. It's fine.' He turned helpless eyes on them. 'She were okay until we saw the Maxwells. We'd not heard of the fire. We've been away for a long weekend visiting 'er mother.' He gave a sideways jerk of his head to indicate his wife.

'We should never have left him.' Mrs Abbott turned her hand over in his.

'Give over, we've left him before, he's almost eighteen. There was nowt wrong with leaving him.'

'Except now he's missing.' Her voice cracked and she raised trembling fingers to her mouth.

'Not necessarily.' In a desperate bid to keep his wife's building hysteria under control, Mr Abbott appealed to Ryan. 'He's a good lad. He really is, but lately he's been a typical teenager. Bloody terrible at communicating with us. Last we heard from him was umm, Saturday night, I think?'

He looked to his wife for confirmation, and she gave a brisk nod, her jowls slack. She placed her hand over her mouth as a dull whine escaped her lips. An animal in pain.

Jenna's chest tightened and she stared down at her own hands, firmly gripping each other. She slipped them from the table and rested them in her lap.

Ryan scratched a few notes, his ears turned a burnished red and Jenna felt his compassion for the couple. 'When did you get back?'

'Late last night. We didn't want to disturb him, so we went straight to bed. Sneaked in like a pair of bloody thieves because he was supposed to be on a field trip today.'

Mrs Abbott reached for the handbag she'd placed on the table and took out a phone. She dipped her fingers back inside and came out with a small packet of pocket tissues. With controlled slowness, she unfolded one and gave her nose a loud blow. 'I got up early this morning to prepare his lunch. I always do if he's on a school trip. He had a geography field trip to Aberystwyth. And besides, I wanted to see him before he went, just to see how his weekend had been. He's a responsible boy. We trust him.'

She wiped her nose again, and then dabbed at her eyes.

'I went to check if he was up, but his bedroom was empty. His bed still made.'

'He never makes his own bloody bed, it only needs the quilt pulling straight, but he never does it. That's how she knew.' Clearly rattled, Mr Abbott squeezed his wife's hand.

Ryan let them run with their story, jotting down notes and lifting his head every so often to give them an encouraging nod. He had a good interview manner; if they wanted to pour it all out, as long as it was relevant, let them, otherwise pull them in, reel them back with relevant questions. He had no reason to yet.

'Aye.' Mr Abbott patted her hand again. 'That's when we realised, he'd not been there much, if at all.'

'All the food was still in the fridge.' A pained sob broke through as Mrs Abbott blinked away tears.

Jenna narrowed her eyes, an uncomfortable warmth building in the pit of her stomach.

''E never leaves a scrap of food in fridge by the time we come home from work, never mind a few days away.'

'We phoned the school, they said he hadn't turned up yesterday. They never told us, but they don't any more. He's considered a young adult.' She gave a little shrug of disdain. 'Hardly an adult at that age.'

'Aye, not when he's still being financed and supported by us.'

Mrs Abbott gave her husband a sharp elbow to the ribs. 'Anyway, we thought we'd come here and ask.' She drew in a long breath. 'And then we met Trudy and Sophie. We asked if Sophie had seen him. And then she told us...'

With a quick whip of interest, Jenna leaned in closer. 'Told you what?'

Mrs Abbott's mouth trembled. 'Told us that Aiden had been seeing young Poppy Lawrence. That he'd been over to their place for dinner on Saturday night because Poppy had told her mum we'd gone away, and he'd be alone.'

38

Jenna pressed her fingers deep into her eye sockets while Ryan waited patiently on the other side of her desk, notepad and pen still in his hand.

'Well, for fuck's sake! It doesn't matter which way you look at it, things just aren't adding up.' Voice muffled through her hands, she dropped them down to the desk and stared at her young DC and the older, more experienced one who'd drifted in behind him.

Ryan and Mason, her stalwarts. Her team. Silent. Sideswiped just as she was.

'We now have seven missing persons. Five bodies.'

She pushed away from her desk to pace the small office. Think. Think.

'What the hell happened in Kimble Hall on Saturday night?' She turned, looked at the pair of them.

'Could Poppy and Aiden be alive? Perhaps they were never at Kimble Hall that night?'

It was a possibility. Ryan could have hit the nail on the head.

'Two teenagers slipping off for a dirty weekend?' Mason stepped out of her way as she circled around. 'Too scared to come home when they hear of the fire.'

She rubbed the back of her neck, did another short circuit of the room and then stopped to stare out of the window.

Gut feeling. She never ignored it. Always backed it up with evidence. Proof. Her gut told her it wasn't right.

She swung around to face her two DCs. 'You were both teenage boys once.' She gave a little sneer in Ryan's direction. He was barely beyond that now. 'If your parents went away for a long weekend and you and your girlfriend wanted time alone, you wouldn't disappear off, you'd stay and have rampant sex twenty-four hours a day in the comfort of your own home.'

And that was exactly the point that didn't jibe.

Jenna strode over to her desk and thumped her forefinger on Ryan's detailed notes. 'Mr Abbott said Aiden hadn't touched the food in the fridge and he normally wouldn't leave a scrap by the time they got home from work, never mind after a whole long weekend.' Hands on hips, Jenna turned to face them again. 'Aiden and Poppy were never at Mr and Mrs Abbott's house because according to Sophie, Olivia and Chanel, Poppy's dad insisted they attend his party rather than go out with the girls. Otherwise, Poppy would have been with her girlfriends, probably with Aiden in tow, and then they would have sneaked off to his house. But they didn't.'

'So, what the bloody hell did happen?'

Jenna raised her eyebrow at Mason. 'That's exactly what we're going to find out as soon as you fast-track another request to mobile SPOC and get these phones triangulated so we can find them. Either the phones, the kids, or both.'

39

Jenna finished off the last of her limp ham salad sandwich and brushed her fingers together to get rid of any crumbs from the white bread just as Mason opened the door.

The barely contained excitement on his face gave her a quick kick of adrenaline. 'What you got?'

Mason towered over her desk, slapped down a sheet of paper and stabbed it with his forefinger. 'SPOC. They've pinpointed Poppy's phone.'

'About time.'

Jenna hit the command to lock the screen on her computer, pushed back from her desk and leapt to her feet. She swiped the jacket off the back of her chair and swept from the room with Mason in hot pursuit.

Ever the observant, enthusiastic puppy, Ryan dashed over to join them as they sailed through the main office.

'Where are we going?'

She hadn't yet had the opportunity to ask the question herself, she'd been leaving it until they were in the car, on their way.

Tempted to tell Ryan to carry on with his paperwork, Jenna

opened her mouth, but before she could reply Mason stopped her dead in her tracks. 'The Crawfords' farm.'

Jenna swung around to face him as confusion rocked her. It didn't gel with either the theory that the phone had been stolen or that Poppy was alive. It was too close to home. Which meant they were looking for a phone. A phone Poppy had most likely lost before the fire was even set.

Disappointment gave her shoulders a weary slump. Dammit, she thought they were onto something. 'Does it pinpoint where?'

Mason gave a swift nod and showed her the sheet of paper with a sketchy printed map of the area. 'Somewhere in the vicinity of here.'

'Jesus Christ, Mason.' She studied the printout of the map. 'Do you know how many outhouses that farm has?'

He snapped her a grin. 'We're about to find out.'

'What about Aiden's phone?'

With a shake of his head, Mason tucked the paperwork under his arm and swung open the door for her, while she fished the keys she'd already swiped out of her bag. 'It'll be a while longer. The request didn't go in until a couple of hours after Poppy's, but they have put a priority on it.'

'Great.'

40

Poppy's stomach cramped with hunger. The Crawfords hadn't been out for two days and all she had was a bar of chocolate and the last of her painkillers.

Her side throbbed like a bitch.

She was all out of tears and a well of anger circled in her stomach. This was shit. Shit!

She couldn't sit there any longer. She bloody well needed to move.

But where? What was she supposed to do? She'd not dared to contact the girls. She'd started to, but she'd deleted what she'd written in a blind panic. What would they think?

They'd all blame her.

Darker than anger, a resentment curdled, building to throb inside her chest.

It wasn't her fault.

She'd not raised a gun. Fired it. Daddy had done that, all by himself, and the more she'd thought it through, the more she came to the conclusion that Daddy had been about to kill her anyhow. As the fog cleared to leave her mind bright, she visualised the moment he came into the room, gun in hand.

By that time, the twins were already dead. He'd not killed them after he killed Aiden and shot her, but before. She knew for a certainty that was the way it had happened.

She snatched up her phone and jabbed her thumb against the power button. It took for bloody ever to load.

41

Gordon Lawrence surged to his feet.

He knew it.

Knew if he watched long enough, she couldn't resist using her phone again.

She was, after all, his daughter. He knew her. He'd studied her. Like a rat in a laboratory.

He poked his thick finger on the Find-a-Friend app and almost howled with frustration as the little cog whirled around while it narrowed in on Poppy's location.

'Come on. Come on.'

A soft cough had him raising his head. Phil Hutchinson stood in the doorway. 'I thought—'

'I don't care what you thought,' he interrupted. 'Fuck off and do your job.'

'But—'

'Fuck. Off!'

The man disappeared down the rathole he'd come from. Gordon couldn't be arsed with that. The vague trundle of machinery reassured Gordon that the factory was back and functioning the way it should. Not that he cared. He should be dead. He was only alive because of his daughter. Stupid little bitch. It had been his intention from the start to kill them all so they never suffered once he was gone, no longer there to protect them. But she'd made him change his mind in a blinding turnaround he regretted.

It no longer mattered. Numb, he wondered when it really ever had.

The location narrowed down, and Gordon tilted his head, a lopsided grin winged up. 'You have got to be kidding me. Those old cronies? How do you expect them to protect you?'

With studied care, Gordon made his way over to the collection of firearms, smaller than he'd had for years, but elite, rare, precious.

He made his selection and left behind the business he'd built from zero with single-minded determination and focus, pouring heart and soul into it over the years, believing it meant everything and realising it meant nothing. It no longer held any meaning. Nothing did.

He paused in the doorway of the main room where Phil Hutchinson stood over a broken down machine, his face a blotchy red under the fine sheen of sweat.

Gordon blew out a disgusted breath.

They no longer needed instruction from him.

He left it as he arrived.

With nothing.

42

'Ethel. Do you remember me? DS Jenna Morgan from the other night.'

Ethel's wizened face crinkled in a sour smile. 'I'm old, not stupid, of course I remember you.' She nodded at Mason. 'You too. DC, wasn't it? Just a constable.'

Without taking offence, Mason grinned at her. 'Yes, Mrs Crawford.'

'Ellis, if I remember right.'

Nothing wrong with the old girl's memory and a lesson learnt for Jenna.

'I haven't met this one though.' She craned her neck to look way up at Ryan.

'DC Ryan Downey, Mrs Crawford.' He smiled at her as she gawped at him with her hands on her hips.

'You'll want a nice cup of tea then if you've come to interview us.'

'Cup of tea would be lovely, Ethel.' Jenna moved deeper into the kitchen to allow the other two in. 'But we've not come to interview you.'

Stiff-legged, Mr Crawford came through a wooden door Jenna hadn't noticed previously as it blended in smoothly with the wooden panelling, giving the impression it was a cupboard.

'Afternoon, I expect you've been busy.' Mr Crawford stuck his little finger in his ear and gave it a waggle. 'You'll be wanting a cup of tea.'

Jenna smiled.

'Kettle's already on, Mr Crawford.' Ethel turned to reach fine china teacups down from the cupboard above her head. 'Take a seat. You're not on parade, you know.'

In deference to their age and slower pace, they each pulled out one of the heavy oak chairs and sat around the enormous kitchen table. Jenna reached out for the piece of paper Mason had with the triangulated point of the phone.

'Ethel, Mr Crawford. We've got some information that a phone belonging to Poppy Lawrence may be in the vicinity.'

'Oh, that poor baby. What a nasty man her father was.' Ethel poured boiling water on the loose tea leaves she'd scooped into a large teapot and then turned. 'Why would her phone be here?'

Jenna stretched her spine as she sat upright in the old chair. 'We don't know, Ethel, but we'd like to be able to check, if you don't mind.'

'We don't mind do we, Mr Crawford?'

'No. Have your cup of tea, then carry on.'

'Thank you.' Jenna suspected nothing came between Mr Crawford and his cup of tea.

As Mr Crawford settled himself at the table, Jenna pushed the paper towards him. 'You have a lot of barns, Mr Crawford.'

'We do. It used to be a real working farm at one time. Beef farming, we did most of our working lives, but mad cow disease came along and put a bit of a hole in it. Then foot and mouth. Last few years, Ethel and me, we've been getting on a little, find it's not as easy as it used to be. I dunna want to be up at the crack of dawn any more.'

She couldn't blame him.

'The farm's got a little run-down.' It was an understatement, but she wasn't there to judge.

She touched her fingertip to the paper. 'It indicates that the phone was last switched on around here.'

Mr Crawford took his time taking a pair of glasses from the pocket of his plaid shirt and positioning them just so on his nose. He studied the paper for a long moment. 'Well that's this 'ere shed.' He raised his head to look out of the window. 'Shouldn't take thee much to find owt in there. It's empty.'

'Excellent.' Desperate to move, Jenna glanced at Ethel and considered whether she needed to ask permission to leave the table.

'Off you go.' Ethel caught her gaze. 'Mr Crawford will take you and you'll be back just in time for your tea to be drinkable.'

Relieved, Jenna pushed back from the table as Mr Crawford grumbled. 'It had better be quick, I'm bloody parched.'

Ethel clipped the little teacups down in front of Mason and Ryan. 'You won't need to go. It'll be a quick job. As Mr Crawford said, it's empty.' She peered over at Jenna with a sweet smile. 'You go and find that phone now, we'll wait right here.'

43

Empty was precisely the word to describe the small, windowless brick shed, no bigger than four metres square with not a single thing in it. Nothing. Barren. Bare. Whatever naked word she could use to describe it. Jenna circled around for all of three minutes before concluding it was a no-go.

Disappointed, Jenna took a sip of her tea as they sat around the kitchen table and studied the ringed location of the area the phone had last been used.

'We had the shed cleaned out last year in case we wanted to store anything in it. Our boys came and did it. It looked so pristine, we've never brought ourselves to use it again,' Ethel explained.

'Strange.' Jenna tugged at her bottom lip as she lifted her head to gaze out of the window at the dozens of outbuildings surrounding the farmhouse. 'It's normally pretty precise.' She squinted out of the window. 'Which could mean it hasn't been lost or dropped. Maybe someone has got it.'

Ethel's small gasp had Jenna turning her head. The old lady raised a gnarled hand up and paused halfway to her lips.

Ryan's eyes sharpened. Mason tilted his head.

'What is it, Ethel?' Jenna asked gently.

'I don't know.' She gave a delicate sniff. 'It may be something, it may be nothing.'

'Okay. Any little piece of information could help.' Jenna hated to rush her, but they needed to get on.

Ethel pushed up from the table and made her way to a cupboard, which she pulled open, leaving the door wide for them to see inside. Ceiling to floor, the shelved interior was filled with enough produce to survive a pandemic.

Jenna's mouth fell open. She'd never seen a cupboard arranged with such precision. Every package and tin neatly stacked, not only in categories, but with the labels turned outwards. Her dream cupboard and one she could never aspire to.

Admiration was one thing, but she didn't grasp Ethel's point.

'I thought it was me.' Palm outwards, Ethel skimmed her hand along each row of the cupboard. 'Yesterday, I wanted to give Mr Crawford some baked beans with his full English.'

Jenna quirked a smile as she studied the neat row of baked beans. Enough to feed an army. 'I see.' But she didn't.

'I thought I was losing my marbles because there was a tin of them missing. So, I checked, and I found there was a tin of ravioli astray too and a packet of biscuits and some chocolate.'

Everything inside of Jenna stilled.

'Now, there could have been some Uncle Ben's rice gone too, I'm not sure because sometimes the grandkids help themselves.' She pursed her lips. 'Although they know the rules, they occasionally slip.' Her face wreathed with a big smile, obviously delighted with her great-grandchildren in reality. Ethel carried on, with no one willing to stop her. Mason and Ryan's stunned expressions reflected Jenna's sentiments to perfection. 'We do our shop on a Friday morning.' Jenna nodded and let the old lady run with it. 'Everything was there.'

Ryan was the first to break. 'Are you saying someone took food out of your cupboard?'

Ethel flipped the door shut and turned to face them, crossing her arms over her chest. 'I'm saying precisely that.'

44

'DI Taylor.'

'Sergeant Morgan. How are things progressing?'

Bloody awful she wanted to say as she caught the flicker of Mason's eyebrow and smiled.

She paced away down the cracked and worn path and stood at the rusted green wrought-iron gate at the Crawfords' farm. 'Not so well, sir. We've checked the area where Poppy's mobile phone registered as last used, but it literally is an empty brick building.'

'Anything there to be marked up for evidence?'

'No, sir. When I say empty, I do mean literally. Square brick building, brick floor. Used to house their goats, according to Mrs Crawford. The sons came last year, cleared it out, painted some sort of sealant over the floor and it hasn't been used since.' She glanced back at Mr and Mrs Crawford watching from their kitchen window. 'Sir, Mrs Crawford believes someone has been in the house and taken food out of the cupboard. It may be whoever has this phone is still in the vicinity. There are quite a number of outbuildings and barns to cover. Can I request Air One to come to seek a heat source, and is the dog handler available?'

'I'll check that for you, Sergeant, and get back to you. In the meanwhile, I'll deploy anyone in the vicinity that's not committed. You'll need a few extra pairs of eyes by the sound of things.'

'Yes, sir.' She scanned the farm. 'We certainly will.' She pressed her thumb to the off button.

As she turned, Ethel came down the path towards her, astute gaze pinning her. 'You don't have enough bodies.'

Jenna kept her expression as neutral as possible, but it was hard not to let the surprise show.

'You don't think that nasty Gordon Lawrence has murdered his wife and children and is hiding out in our barns, do you?'

'No, Ethel.' The thought hadn't even occurred to her. Why would Gordon Lawrence still be on the scene? If he'd murdered his family, surely he would have moved on. He'd never have stayed in the area, let alone in such close proximity.

Unless he was injured and couldn't. 'There's no reason for you to think that. It's Poppy's phone we're looking for.'

Ethel harrumphed as she placed her hands on her hips. 'Well, I hope for all our sakes, we're not under any threat. I'd hate to think Mr Crawford could get hurt.'

Jenna reached out to smooth a hand down Ethel's arm. 'Ethel, you couldn't be safer. You have us here and you're about to be surrounded by officers any minute now.'

'But that man had guns.' Jenna's heart pinched as Ethel's face crumpled with concern. She reached out and stroked the old lady's arm.

'Oh, Ethel, there's nothing for you to worry about. Gordon Lawrence most likely died in the fire. If it was him, he wouldn't have filched a few tins of food.' He'd more likely have been in the farm-house gun in hand. 'It's more likely someone stole Poppy's phone. Possibly a kid, a homeless person.' She squeezed Ethel's arm and started to walk back towards the house, doubting her own reassuring words. Shit, she needed to get on and look. 'Come on inside now, there's nothing for you to concern yourself about. We'll do everything in our power to look after you and Mr Crawford.'

She released Ethel's arm as they reached the door and turned at the sound of vehicles approaching. Two police-issue cars kicked up dirt as they rattled along the track towards the farmhouse.

Mason stepped up beside her. 'They were bloody quick.'

Jenna clipped her phone onto her utility belt and rested her fists on her hips. 'They must have been at Kimble Hall.'

'Yeah.' Mason chuckled in her ear. 'I bet there was a race on to get away from scene guard duty.'

'Yep.' Ryan nudged her shoulder as he stepped in close. 'Most boring job on the planet.'

Airwaves hissed to life. 'Sergeant Morgan.'

'DI Taylor, sir.'

'I have an update for you. The dog handler has just finished up and will be with you within the hour. Same with the Air Unit. It's down for refuelling and will also be with you within the hour.'

Impatient to make progress, Jenna stared past the oncoming vehicles. 'Sir, I'm going to initiate a ground search. Could you please make Air Unit aware so they let us know when they start their heat search?'

'I can do that, Jenna.'

The radio buzzed for a second before going silent.

'What do you want from us, Sarge?'

Jenna glanced at Ryan. 'There aren't many of us yet, but I think we need to make a start. I'm not sure I can take any more of Ethel's tea.'

'I'm beginning to slosh.'

She laughed. 'We'll split up. I'll start with the little shack on the right. Ryan, you take the asbestos shed; Mason, you take the tin barn. We'll get uniform to conduct a ground search from here outwards and then if we all converge on that big black barn in the middle, we can do that one together. Hopefully both the Air Unit and the dog handler will be here by then.'

She flexed her shoulders keen to make a start and looked around as the car doors slammed.

Her heart sank as Lee Gardner stepped from the driver's side of the second vehicle. If she could have got away with dropping her head into her hands she would have, instead she settled for the pained groan that refused to be restrained. She bloody well knew he'd be in her path again.

He jerked his head to crick his neck as his steely, arrogant gaze met hers.

45

White-hot pokers seared her skin as Poppy touched icy fingertips to the vivid red, pulsing hot flesh on her side, knowing for certain she had an infection.

She tugged the sweatshirt back into place, little whimpers coming from her lips. She grappled with the phone. Unable to grasp it properly, it slipped from her fingers and down onto the barn floor.

Poppy edged off the bales of straw, dropped to the floor and stumbled to her knees.

She needed help.

It no longer mattered if her daddy found her and killed her, if she didn't get help soon, she was going to die. Die of hunger, die of thirst, or die of a horrible infection that shuddered through her body to make her hot and cold all at the same time.

Her teeth chattered as she scrabbled around in the dusty straw layering the concrete floor.

Her fingers knocked against her iPhone and she forced them to hold on.

She could switch it on and phone Sophie. She could phone the police. She depressed the button, waiting for it to load with painful slowness. She couldn't wait, she needed help now.

Eyes blurred with pain, Poppy tucked the phone into the sweat-shirt pocket and crawled on her hands and knees towards the barn door.

She'd go to the farmhouse.

Mrs Crawford would know what to do.

46

Gordon Lawrence looked at his phone for the hundredth time in as many minutes.

Bingo!

He fucking knew she couldn't resist. A curl of pride circled in his stomach. No daughter of his could.

He'd just had to move in closer and wait. Contain the fury that had burnt bright when she wasn't in the location it had indicated. An old brick shed. Clean as a whistle. Why that was clean when every other outhouse looked as though a bomb had hit it was beyond him.

Clever little girl. She must have sneaked in there to switch her phone on just in case. Either that or the satellite wasn't as accurate as it could be, or the phone had been on such a short while, the location hadn't had time to narrow in.

He sniffed as he thought through the process. Maybe she'd needed a stronger signal.

He jumped down from the old bale of hay he'd been waiting on in the little tin roofed outhouse he'd chosen and reached for the double-barrelled shotgun he'd placed at his side. His back-up pistol was already tucked away in the waistband of his trousers.

One for her.

One for him.

Boom!

Boom!

It would all be over.

Detached, he stared at the phone.

He should have done it right in the first place, but there was a reason he hadn't killed himself then. That reason was his daughter. If he'd died, she would have been left behind and she was his, just as her mum, brother and sisters were his and he'd take them all with him. Every one of them.

Fate had given him a second chance.

He strode to the door, all the time looking at his phone.

Ironic.

If only he'd decided to wait one barn over in old man Crawford's outbuildings, he would have found her. As it was, he'd parked way down the old disused dirt track bordering the two pieces of land so he could check out his property first. Logically, a child might make their way back home but as the place was swarming with fire and police services, he'd given them a wide birth. He assumed she had too.

Puzzled by her thought processes initially, he'd made his way through the back of the Crawford's land careful not to encroach too near their house, not wanting to risk them seeing him. They may be old but neither one of them was stupid and he'd never liked the look in the old woman's eye as she studied him, judging him. As though he was beneath contempt.

Ordinarily, he'd not consider her worthy of his attention. Now, avoidance was the better option. His priority was to find Poppy before the police pieced together their puzzle, realised he was alive and came looking for him.

The police.

Why hadn't Poppy gone to the police? There was an enigma.

He cocked his head to one side. Could he hear voices?

He waited. Nothing.

He didn't want to stumble over the Crawfords and have to shoot them. The police would hear the gunshot from Kimble Hall and be all over the place like a rash.

They'd hear it when he dispatched Poppy, of course, but by the time they arrived, it would be too late. He couldn't afford for them to arrive before he located Poppy.

He paused before he stepped through the rickety old door, virtually off its hinges. The furthest little shed away from the house. He squinted, letting his eyes adjust to the brilliant sunlight.

Poppy hadn't gone to the police because she thought she'd done something wrong.

And on the rare occasion when Poppy was naughty, it was in her nature to stick her head in the sand and wait until the storm was over.

He checked his phone and headed towards the huge black Dutch barn dominating the skyline. 'Not long now, Poppy. Not long, my sweet daughter.'

He'd known the rough proximity, but not the exact location. It had just proved to be a waiting game.

The wait was over.

47

TUESDAY 21 APRIL 1600 HOURS

'Oh, forthefuckoffucksake!'

Poppy whipped her head back inside the black barn, the strangled sound of panic lodging in her throat.

Daddy!

She grabbed the wooden crossbar on the barn door, digging her nails in deep to haul back on it so it closed, leaving only a sliver of a gap.

She turned and stumbled a few paces before she sank to her knees and toppled sideways, the energy she needed failing her.

Come on! Come on! He wasn't far away, he'd be there within minutes.

She sank her cheek to the straw covered floor and drew in a breath.

Keep calm. Get up. Move.

Poppy raised her head and focused on the furthest point of the barn where she'd made her nest so no one could find her. With the knowledge she couldn't possibly make it, she blew out a breath, pushed herself to her knees and staggered to her feet.

One foot in front of the other as her eyesight wavered while the dust motes danced on the air drawing her to the side of the barn where the edge of a piece of farm machinery poked out from under a huge black tarpaulin.

Knees buckling, Poppy reached out and grasped one corner of the tarpaulin to lift it away from the machinery. Lightheaded and dizzy she lurched forward. Dropping to her knees, she crawled under the huge rotary blades of a hedge cutter and tugged the tarpaulin back into place around her, plunging herself into the dark.

With shaky fingers, Poppy took out her phone and switched it on.

Too late. She'd left it too late.

The stale mustiness of the tarpaulin coated the back of her throat as she waited for the phone to switch on and then punched the emergency button before she even entered her code.

'Emergency, which service do you require? Fire, Police or Ambulance?'

Poppy drew in a breath, pain radiating through her side, her body vibrating with little convulsions, her teeth chattering in her head. 'Police.'

The soft creak of the barn door stopped the breath in her throat.

Daddy.

Daddy had come for her.

48

Mason shot a glance over to where Lee Gardner lurked and then kicked his toe in the dirt before he gave a quick scan of the area. Looked like Gardner was up to no good as usual. Lazy git, probably looking for somewhere to sit down while everyone else did the work.

As Gardner wandered off, hands in pockets, he cast a furtive glance over his shoulder that had Mason's senses prickling with interest. He kept his gaze on Gardner until the man made his move. In the direction Jenna had taken.

They'd agreed to converge on the black barn, but this was taking the piss.

Mason sighed.

The little prick was going to have a go at her. This time, she'd probably have his warrant card from him. Hopefully, she'd give him a swift kick in the balls first.

Without a doubt, she could handle him. Mason ambled over towards the enormous black Dutch barn where Jenna had headed. She may be able to handle Gardner, but there was a possibility she'd need a witness.

Failing that, he could always give him a quick smack. Teach him not to pick on women. Because it was women Gardner appeared to have a problem with. Most of them, like Donna, he ignored. But Jenna's authority meant he couldn't ignore her.

He scanned around until Ryan emerged from the derelict old brick shed that he'd checked out. 'Nothing?'

'Nah.'

Mason jerked his head in a come-over motion. He contemplated whether it was wise to have a witness to the fact that he was about to deck Lee Gardner, but it might be just as well. For somebody to be there to say who swung the first punch. Perhaps he'd let Lee get the first one in. Mason snapped a grin – or let him think he had because there was no way Mason would let Lee land a punch, but if he took a swing, it would be self-defence.

With his boyish enthusiasm, Ryan raced across the cracked concrete of the farmyard as Mason headed towards the barn Jenna had rounded the side of, disappearing out of view as Gardner followed.

'What's going on?' Ryan bounced along with barely harnessed energy.

Mason squinted into the distance. 'Bloody Lee Gardner decided to follow the Sarge.'

'What for?'

'Dunno. Don't trust him. Let's go see. Perhaps we'll find this bloody phone while we're there too.'

'Be nice to get it before the dog handler arrives. A key find.'

'Yeah.' Mason doubted it. 'It's a bit like looking for a needle in a haystack.'

They may be able to triangulate within so many feet of the last known location. But it hadn't been in that location. So, they'd widen the search and hope whoever had the phone, whether it was Poppy or some kid who'd stolen it, found it, whatever, decided to switch it on again.

Mason squinted as Gardner put a spurt on and disappeared around the same side of the building as Jenna had. He broke into a trot with Ryan by his side. He wanted to get closer, so Gardner didn't get much of chance to face off with Jenna before they arrived.

With barely a hitch in his gangly, loose-legged stride, Ryan stayed abreast of him.

'Nice couple, the Crawfords.'

'Very nice.' Distracted, Mason slowed down again as he reached the corner of the barn.

'Helpful.'

'Yeah.'

49

With a quick check over her shoulder, Jenna hesitated as PC Lee Gardner approached from the other side of the outbuildings he was supposed to be checking out. With purpose in his stride, he made straight for her. Arrogant little bugger was going to have another go.

Well, he could try. He didn't frighten her, and she wasn't about to allow him to intimidate her either. She raised her gaze beyond him as Mason and Ryan made their way over.

They weren't far behind and Mason was astute enough to know Gardner was squaring up for another confrontation. If he was, he was about to get a rocket up his arse. He'd had all the chances she was prepared to give him and if he was gunning for her with such single-minded determination, she was about to hit him with another disciplinary.

When would the guy learn? He wasn't going to put her down. She wouldn't let him. His macho shit didn't scare her, but it was wearing to have him permanently on the offensive.

Discipline was one option. Then again, Mason might just punch him for her. She might allow him.

She grinned to herself as she turned the corner of the black

Dutch barn and came to an abrupt halt, the smile dropping from her face.

She stepped in close to inspect the broken padlock hanging loose from the huge wooden door.

Tension coiled in the pit of her stomach: iPhones didn't break into houses and steal food all on their own, nor did they break open padlocks.

She glanced behind her. The guys had her back, they were only minutes behind her. By the time she got herself ready and carried out some preliminaries, they'd be there.

She dipped her hands into her pockets to take out the pair of nitrile gloves she had stowed that had turned out to be redundant so far for the operation. She snapped them on while she studied the door, just half an inch proud of the doorjamb, and reached out to touch the loose padlock. The solid weight of it fell into her gloved hand.

With no evidence bag to put it in, Jenna flipped her gloves off her hands so they rolled inside out over the padlock and then tucked them into her pocket. Hardly classified as sterile she could only hope she didn't get hell from Jim Downey for the pocket fluff deposit that would most likely compromise the forensic evidence on the item. It wouldn't wipe off fingerprints though. There was always an upside.

She lifted the radio to her mouth and spoke just above a whisper in case there was someone there to alert. 'DI Taylor.'

'Go ahead.'

'I've found evidence of tampering with a padlock on one of the barns. I've bagged the evidence.' She crossed her fingers at the technicality of the white lie. It was pocketed, not bagged. 'PC Gardner and DCs Ellis and Downey are two minutes behind me, I'm going in to take a look.'

'Confirmed, Sergeant. Both the Air Unit and dog handler are on their way, ETA twelve minutes and twenty respectively.'

'Acknowledged.'

She left Airwaves open and dropped the radio back onto her belt.

With no handle in sight, she reached out to dig her fingers into the gap between the black-painted door and the frame. She pulled until the soft give of it persuaded the door to creak open outwards.

Jenna's throat jammed shut. Her lungs burned hot enough to ignite a flame deep inside. Ice formed around her heart, as the man whose photograph she'd had emblazoned on her mind over the past few days stepped from the murky depths of the barn with the twin eyes of a double-barrel shotgun trained on her.

Frozen in place, Jenna stared straight ahead with wary respect for the weapon and an abiding fear of the man in front of her. Gordon Lawrence, a dead man. With nothing left to live for.

Instinct told her all along he'd murdered his family. With the body count in dispute, suspicion had hinted that he was still alive. She was hardly in a place to gloat over being proved right.

Jenna raised her gaze above the shotgun to meet the eyes of a killer. One who had every intention of killing again. Golden lion's eyes ringed with chocolate brown blinked with the bleakness of an empty soul.

Conscious of the approach of her three unsuspecting officers, Jenna took a cautious step back as Gordon moved out of the barn into the sun. A slant of bright sunlight struck his face to make his eyes glow with an unnatural luminescent sheen. A cold stillness washed over her at the steely, single-minded control of the man.

Slow and cautious, Jenna raised one hand in appeal, palm outwards, as he approached. Death was written in his face. Her veins turned to ice with the knowledge she was about to die. Why would a man who'd slaughtered his entire family even consider not pulling the trigger? He had nothing more to lose.

Breath burned deep in her chest and her sister's face flashed before her eyes. Fliss! She didn't want to leave her. She never wanted to leave her on her own. She might have Mason, but he wasn't enough. Not yet. It was too early.

Jenna parted her lips. What words could possibly make any difference to the man's decision? He was a dead man anyway. Gordon Lawrence's life was over whether he killed her or not. What was one more body?

All she could hope for was to delay the inevitable.

'Gordon,' she appealed. 'There's no need for this. There are police everywhere. Do you really want another death on your hands?'

She took another step away. Away from the gun, away from the direct shot.

Emptiness deadened his eyes as they narrowed in the late afternoon light pouring golden across the fields.

His mouth tightened with nostrils pinched and white around the edges. 'It doesn't matter. Nothing. None of it matters any more. I'm not sure it ever did.'

About to answer, Jenna's heart jammed in her throat as she caught a movement inside the barn in her peripheral vision and could only hope Gordon Lawrence hadn't noticed her harsh flinch.

Seemingly oblivious, he shrugged. 'Death is only life in another realm.'

Ice ran through her veins as the figure in the barn pushed up to crawl on hands and knees towards the door. The figure raised its head and Poppy Lawrence's soul-destroyed eyes stared at her from a gaunt, pallid face.

Aware of the tremble in her fingers and the tremor in her voice,

Jenna raised her chin. If nothing else, she could give the girl a chance.

'Gordon, it doesn't have to be this way.'

'Oh it does. You see, I came for my daughter.'

The dull thwack, thwack, thwack of the approaching helicopter filled the air.

Gordon Lawrence shrugged and, with a casual disregard that sent ice coursing through her veins, he engaged the lock mechanism with a double ratcheting click.

From around the corner of the black barn, Lee Gardner stormed, his view of Gordon obscured by the barn door. Vibrating with anger he'd allowed to build in his own mind, he came straight at her at the same time Poppy Lawrence staggered to her feet and stumbled out into the daylight.

Poppy lurched to a halt just behind Gordon, her long skinny legs trembled with the effort to stay upright.

Unaware of his daughter's presence, Gordon Lawrence swung the barrel of the gun in a smooth arc to train it on PC Gardner.

Jenna's breath burned in the depths of her chest.

PC Gardner turned his head in slow motion, only just aware of another presence.

Skin florid from anger, he screwed up his face, his mouth a vicious twist.

'Put the fucking gun down now!'

Arrogance and ego burst from him in a torrent of fury and sealed his fate.

Gordon raised the gun.

Poppy rushed forward. '*Daddy!*'

50

BOOM!

Gunshot exploded, filling her head with nothing but roaring thunder.

Jenna slammed her eyes closed, instinct making her whip her head away, but not before the hot gush of what she could only imagine was blood and grey matter hit her and splattered its hot, wet slime over her skin.

The unmistakable metallic taste of blood filled her mouth as a jelly-like substance slithered down her face and clogged her nose. Her breath jammed in her throat. Her world spiralled down to slow motion as every muscle, sinew and tissue turned to water.

Boneless, Jenna flung her arms around Poppy and dropped. She knocked the child to the ground, covering the girl's smaller body with her own. Her forehead slammed into the stony ground. With only a vague perception of the pain burning through her knees as numbness engulfed her, taking her down, down into a blooming white fog of amnesia.

Eyes screwed shut, the outside world crumbled away, spiralling as white noise consumed her, fizzing through her brain to blanket every coherent thought.

With vague awareness, Jenna gave an instinctive jerk as another loud bang followed the first in quick succession. The only noise to penetrate the gushing flood of water filling her head.

Nothing compelled her to move as she slithered, stretching herself full out to protect Poppy from the next gunshot.

With distant consciousness of voices barking out commands, Jenna held on to the one link with the outside world. She kept count. One, two.

It was important she hung on to the connection. They'd want to know afterwards. They would ask her questions. The echoing thunder made her doubt what she'd heard. Two gunshots, possibly three.

She screwed her eyes even tighter shut to stop the image of PC Gardner's head exploding in a Catherine wheel of blood and bone and matter. Not yet ready to face that image.

51

Jenna tucked her face into the top of Poppy's head and breathed in the dust as it rose in a furious cloud around them. Unprepared to open her eyes, she clenched her fingers into the child's hair and pushed it back from her face not sure whether Poppy had been hit or not in the spray of shot from the gun. Frozen beneath her, Jenna could only be reassured by the vague tremor that vibrated through the child's body and the heart-rending whimpers like a beaten dog.

Rough hands slapped at her to try and get her to move, but numbness invaded every muscle so even her head was too heavy to lift.

'Fuck.' Gruff tones pushed through the fog.

'Where's she hit?' The concern in the voice nudged at her.

She was okay. She needed to let them know she was okay. She'd not been hit. She simply didn't have the wherewithal to drag herself up from the wallowing clouds that grabbed at her, trying to haul her under.

'Is she hit?'

She had no idea who was talking, their voices a muffled wash of words sliding into each other. Did they mean her, or Poppy?

'I don't know. She's in shock.'

Who was in shock? She took in a sip of air.

'Fucking A, she is.'

She let out a light snort and opened her eyes to meet Mason's. The colour had leached from his face, leaving him a pallid shade of yellow. For an instant a glassy-eyed Ryan popped his head into her vision, before he was gone.

She had to pull herself together. Nothing had happened to her. She wasn't the one who'd been shot. She was uninjured.

She filled her lungs, aware her erratic breathing needed to be slowed down. She held onto the breath until her chest burned and then let it out in a soft whoosh. Too fast. She tried again.

Breathe in. Two, three.

Out. Whoosh.

In. Bam! Bam! Two shots.

Her body spasmed.

'Fuck, Jenna. Fuck.' The urgency in Mason's voice reached her and she clawed her way back to the surface as Poppy lay still beneath her. Safe. Protected. And damned if Jenna could move off her. She clung to her. A lifeline. Aware she needed to move.

They'd need her. She was a police officer and a witness. They'd want her statement. But her body refused to obey as she clung to Poppy, her sole purpose to protect.

Shock.

They said she was in shock.

She might recognise it, but it didn't mean she could push her way through it.

She blinked her eyes open, then scrunched them up against the bright white light that tore through her system. She didn't want to see. Why did she have to see? What if Poppy's face had been blown off too?

Jenna flinched as the image of Lee's head exploded in her mind.

She loosened her grip from the girl's hair and skimmed tentative fingers over the side of her face and ear. The warmth of Poppy's skin belied the stillness of her body.

Rough hands grabbed at her again.

With a voice as rusty as a ninety-year-old COPD sufferer, Jenna croaked out the one reply that would stop Mason from trying to get her to roll off Poppy and checking her over for injuries. She'd roll when she was good and ready and when she knew with absolute certainty the child was safe. Nothing was going to harm her now.

Jenna had her.

'Fuck off!'

Muscles lax, she batted him off as he yanked her up and slammed her hard against his chest.

Her gaze clashed with his desperate one as he swept away the thick coating of pulp from her cheeks with fingers that shook. The horror slashed into his features and she fluttered her eyelids closed against the rawness of his emotions.

'You stupid fucker. I thought you were dead.'

Warm wetness dripped onto her face and she risked another peep through her eyelashes. She needed him to know she was all right. Alive at least. 'Chance would be a fine thing. Jesus, Mason. Pull yourself together.' What she intended to come out as funny whispered from between stiff lips.

Face close to hers, Mason took a swipe with the back of his hand over his cheeks to rub away the tears trickling down his bleach-white skin. 'You fucking scared the shit out of me.'

Shock still buzzed through her system like a loose electrical circuit. 'Yeah, well, it didn't do me a whole host of good either.' She scraped her hand through her thick choppy hair and whipped it away as it stuck in the thick pulp coating her head. Numb, she stared at her hand as Mason covered it and lowered it to her side.

Muscles still liquified, Jenna struggled to sit upright with jerky uncontrolled movements. She twisted around in his arms to see Ryan crouching over Poppy's inert body. Face down, her stillness gave Jenna a quiver of fear.

'Poppy.' Her voice rasped from a throat so parched, she could barely swallow.

Ryan raised his head, eyes bleak and old beyond his years.

Jenna's heart gave a painful contraction. Jesus. Poppy. 'Is she hit?'

Mouth grim, he shook his head as he placed his hand on Poppy's shoulder. 'Not that I can see.' He lowered himself down until his ear was level with her mouth. 'She's breathing.' He raised up and blew out a breath while he pressed two fingers against the artery in her neck and nodded with sober satisfaction.

'Roll her over, Ryan. Put her in the recovery position.' Mason's voice came from a distance through the screech of tinnitus rattling in Jenna's head.

She nodded her agreement and her head went on a wild revolution.

'Jenna.' Mason brought his face close to hers, his lips moving with exaggerated care. 'Jenna.' He repeated and it reverberated through her head.

Nausea clamped her stomach and she fluttered her eyes closed again. 'My ears.'

'We've paramedics on the way. They'll be here any moment.'

Not daring to nod again in case she fell off the edge of the cliff she seemed to be hanging onto, Jenna forced words out through clamped teeth. 'Okay.' She didn't want a paramedic. She wanted to push herself up off her arse and walk her way out of there. If she could only go home, she'd be fine.

She placed her hands either side of her hips and pushed up, only to have a firm hand on her shoulder hold her in place and demonstrate just how weak she still was.

'Stay where you are, Jenna. The paramedics are on their way.'

Humiliation nudged its way past the weakness as she hung her head. 'I'm okay. They need to see to Poppy first. I need to get up.'

'You'll stay exactly where you are until we get you checked over.' Mason's voice rang with the authority he used when dealing with the most hardened of criminals, persuading her not to argue. She'd no desire to anyway. Not really.

Her concern more for Poppy, she shuffled so she could keep a watch on her as Ryan unzipped his fleece and laid it over her repositioned body, his voice speaking words that made no sense in Jenna's pounding head, but the tone of reassurance washed over her.

'Is she okay?' She clenched her jaw as her teeth chattered. The bloody ground was freezing. She was freezing. She tucked herself up tight into a ball, a vague memory of the effects of shock and hypothermia stirring in the thickness of her thoughts.

Ryan glanced over, his ashen face wobbled as he nodded. 'She's awake. Responsive.' He lowered his head towards Poppy's blonde one, stretching a small smile. 'She said she's okay.' He stroked a hand over the girls' shoulder. 'Stay where you are, the paramedics will be here shortly. They need to check you over before you move, in case you've been...' His gaze flickered over to Jenna and Mason. '...For injuries.'

Aware she could barely hear Poppy's mumbled reply, Jenna shuffled her backside to get closer.

Mason's hand gave her shoulder a light squeeze. 'Stay where you are. We need to make sure you haven't been shot.'

'I wasn't hit.' She considered the amount of blood and guts still dripping from her and swiped her nose with the back of her hand. Revulsion skipped through her stomach as she stared at the mess she'd swiped away and then raised her head to meet Mason's desperate gaze. 'Not by a bullet in any event.' Her mind refused to allow her to take the pathway through what had happened.

Features hardened by a challenging job in a tough world, concern deepened the shadows in Mason's nutmeg eyes as he smoothed his thick fleece over her shoulders. The warmth from his body soaked through her flesh to set up another wracking shudder.

Her own pulse pounded inside her head to compete with the rhythmic throb of emergency service sirens.

She raised her hand again, this time to press her fingers against the entrance to her ear. When she pulled them away, her gaze skittered over the fresh mucus and blood-filled pus on her fingertips. It wasn't anyone else's. It was hers. The warmth of it seeped from inside her ear in a soft glug and dribbled down her neck. 'I think I burst my eardrum.' Her shocked voice echoed inside her head.

Mason nodded as he reached out to cup her cheek in the palm of his hand. 'That's a possibility, Jenna. That gun was fucking close to your ear.' He glanced up over the top of her head. 'The paramedics are here now, just getting clearance.'

Nothing more than a grunt came from her throat. Her eyes fluttered shut as she drew in a breath. There was something she needed to ask. Important. Her mind reached out to grasp the question.

'Have you cleared the situation?'

'Yes.'

'Is he dead?'

The long silence held a grim warning not to push the door too far open yet. She wasn't ready for it.

Mason stared over the top of her head. 'Lee Gardner.' He dipped his head to bring his face closer to hers, his eyes crinkled at the edges with his grimace. 'There's no doubt.'

Confusion stole through the thick fog in her head. She knew

Lee was dead. There was plenty evidence of that. She had half his brain splattered over her. It wasn't him she needed to know about.

She coughed to clear her throat of the dust and her tongue stuck to the roof of her mouth to give a distressed clucking noise that would normally have shamed her. Too numb, she was beyond shame.

'Gordon Lawrence. Did he get away?' She needed to know, because if he was still out there, Poppy was still in danger and her boys didn't seem to be rallying.

Mason pulled back, his gaze taking on a hawk-like stare as he gave a controlled shake of his head.

She blinked up at him. It was as she thought. There *had* been a second shot. Not an echo. She was sure.

But where from?

As Mason moved, she followed the track of his gaze and rolled onto her side to look behind her.

Ethel Crawford's frail shoulders hunched forward over the still smoking double-barrelled shotgun. With the barrel cracked open from the stock to make it safe, she cradled it in competent, unshaking hands.

With the pull of Jenna and Mason's stare on her, she did a slow head turn, her watery gaze meeting theirs.

'I said he was a nasty man.' Her fingers whitened as she tightened her hold on the gun. 'Nobody listened.' Her eyes glazed over. 'They never listen when you get old.'

Jenna's mouth fell open. 'Oh, Ethel...'

52

'Hey. What have we got here?'

Jenna whipped her head around at the soft female voice.

In the ugly green uniform of paramedics, the tall woman hitched her trousers as she squatted next to Jenna. 'Would you give her some room, please?' Her tone brooked no argument as she reached for Jenna's wrist. She pushed her weathered face close to Jenna's. 'What's your name, my love.'

Her tongue thick, Jenna swallowed. She'd not lost her mind, only her voice. 'Detective Sergeant Jenna Morgan.'

'Well, Detective Sergeant Jenna Morgan. My name's Lucy. Lucy Beck. I'm just going to check you over for injuries. Is that okay?' So close that Jenna could see every fine line and wrinkle feathering over the other woman's face as she studied her. Soft eyes of lavender blue, with the short, stubby, faded eyelashes that came to women of a certain age. Strong fingers of one hand pressed against Jenna's wrist while the woman tucked salt-and-pepper strands of hair behind her ear, only to have it whipped away by an errant wind.

As awareness returned, Jenna shuddered. Her teeth rattled

inside her head as that cool wind penetrated her clothes and chilled her to the bone in one fast rush.

'Can you tell me what happened?'

'No.' She didn't want to. Not yet. She wasn't ready.

'Okay, we're going to lift you onto the stretcher and get you inside the ambulance.'

'I can walk.'

'I don't think—'

'I'm not injured, merely in shock.' She dropped her voice an octave to make her point. 'I'll walk!'

Determination shot through to give her the energy she needed to lift her arse from the cold ground and march to the ambulance no more than thirty paces away. This time no-one attempted to stop her as she clenched her jaw and struggled up. The solid, reassuring touch of Mason's hand on her elbow gave her enough resilience to put one foot in front of the other with little more than a slight waver as she passed by PC Gardner's body. She hesitated as she reached him and forced herself to look, because if there was one thing she knew for certain, her imagination would be far worse than the reality.

She sucked in a whistling breath through her teeth as she raced her gaze over him. Half his head missing, which would explain the amount of matter sprayed over her. Other than that, nothing. Not a mark on the rest of his inert body.

She swallowed the bile that threatened to rise in the back of her throat and took a deliberate look away. She'd deal with it. She had no option. She blinked. As saliva rushed into her mouth she swallowed again. It was a vision she'd never forget.

She raised her chin and followed Lucy to the ambulance, her teeth chattering until her jaw ached.

Lucy closed the ambulance doors behind them to lock out

everyone other than Mason, who slipped inside and stood, his head bowed to avoid the roof of the ambulance.

Lucy turned and flicked a switch and heat pumped out to fill the small space.

'Hop on the bed. We need to warm you up before hypothermia sets in.'

'Hypothermia. I don't have hypothermia.' Her teeth rattled in her head.

The smile was kind, creasing deep into Lucy's cheeks. 'Slip your coat off and roll up your sleeve.' Too weary to question, Jenna did as instructed while she attempted to follow the general gist of the conversation. 'You may not have hypothermia yet, but it's surprising. How long were you on the ground? Forty minutes. Forty-five?'

Confused, Jenna squinted at the other woman. Had she been down that long? Could she have been on the floor that length of time? 'I don't know, I...' It all came back to perception distortion. It happened so quickly. It was a lifetime. Two timelines intermingling in her head.

'Twenty-eight minutes.' Mason's waterproof coat rattled as he fidgeted to find a comfortable position. He'd be cold too, he only had a shirt underneath the coat. He'd given up his fleece for her. Wrapped it around her. The memory rushed back.

Without looking at him, Lucy indicated a seat at the head of the ambulance. 'Take a pew. We'll be a while.'

He squeezed past and grunted as he perched on the small pull-down seat at Jenna's head.

Lucy bustled about, she pressed buttons, moved equipment, adjusted the height of the bed once Jenna had made herself comfortable and draped a cellular blanket over Jenna's legs. 'You're young, strong. It's quite mild and you hadn't been out there long. Just imagine...' she strapped a blood pressure cuff to Jenna's exposed arm, chattering all the time, Jenna suspected just to distract her, '...elderly people who take a fall, it doesn't take long for hypothermia to set in, even in their own homes, at this time of year. At least you were dressed appropriately for the weather conditions.'

Jenna recalled a time when she hadn't been, when Fliss had gone missing. She'd learnt her lesson well then and not been caught out since. Her mother would be proud of her. She huffed out a breath.

'It wasn't my intention to take a lie-down.'

'I'm sure.'

'My legs just gave way. Crumpled under me.'

Lucy nodded and released the cuff as she skimmed a sympathetic gaze over Jenna. 'I'm not surprised. Anyone would have hit the ground under the circumstances.'

'It wasn't intentional. Just instinctive.'

'Shock. We all react in different ways. No one person can dictate what will happen.'

The warmth in the ambulance seeped through her clothes and Jenna's clenched jaw softened as the trembling lessened. Shock, hypothermia, whatever the terminology, the numbness started to wear off and as her body relaxed and she closed her eyes, PC Gardner's head exploded all over her face once more—

Her eyes sprang open and Jenna lurched up.

A soft hand applied gentle pressure on her shoulder. 'It's okay. You're safe.'

Surprised at the motion of the ambulance, Jenna peered down the length of her legs at her stockinged feet poking out of the end of the NHS blanket. She clucked her dry tongue against the roof of her mouth.

'We're almost there. You fell asleep.' The woman's voice echoed through soft cotton clouds in Jenna's head, distant and muffled. The vague ringing overriding all other sounds.

'I'm okay. I can go now. I'll be fine.'

'No, you definitely won't be fine until you're checked over by a doctor. I think your left eardrum has ruptured. We'll get it checked out for you.'

Warm and comfortable, Jenna relaxed, closed her eyes again and let herself drift. Aware of the discomfort of a stiff face, she raised her hand to investigate. As her fingers encountered PC Gardner's drying blood and grey matter, she let out a whimper. 'Oh, God.'

This time the hand that landed on her shoulder was far more robust as Mason leaned over the top of her. 'Sorry, Jenna. Don't touch it. I know you want to get it all off you, but you're a crime scene. Forensics need everything. You don't want to contaminate the evidence.'

If anyone could elicit a smile from her, it would be Mason. Ever practical. Ever down-to-earth. There was nothing she could do to help her situation but close her eyes and wait for the whole process to be over and done with.

53

Chief Superintendent Gregg hovered over the top of her bed. Steel-grey hair swept straight back from a high forehead, his normal bright, hawklike gaze softened with sympathy to make the breath catch in her throat.

Shit. It must be serious.

Strong and professional, Jenna prided herself on her ability to keep her emotions under control, but from the attention she currently had, she had serious misgivings that she could keep them in check. Sympathy had always weakened her, and she feared the compassion that oozed in the small, overcrowded side room they'd found for her in the Princess Royal Accident and Emergency department.

She skimmed her gaze over her sister, and moved on. She was there, she was her strength.

Gregg pulled back, his slow smile spread to deepen the wrinkles in his cheeks and his eyes sharpened. 'Good to see you, Jenna.' He reached out a hand and squeezed her wrist. Possibly the only part of her that wasn't a forensic crime scene. 'If you need anything, anything at all, let me know.'

Tears clogged her throat and the smile she gave him wobbled. 'Sir.'

She allowed her gaze to wander across to DI Taylor. Another of her stalwarts. At home in the discomfort of the high-back acrylic-covered chair in the corner of the room, he peered over the top of his glasses at her. Not one to hold her hand, the raw whisky that scraped at his voice still told of his care. 'Jenna. Your statement in your own time. If you'd rather someone take it, let me know.' The pause was long. Ex-Army, Taylor kept his feelings close, but the concern in his direct gaze couldn't be masked. He cleared his throat. 'We're here for you. Anything you need.'

'Poppy.' Her voice rasped out as though she'd never used it. 'What happened to Poppy?'

Taylor stretched his arms out to rest his hands on his knees. 'She's in surgery.'

'Surgery?' The fast surge to her pulse jerked through her body. 'Was she shot? I didn't think Lawrence—'

Taylor shook his head. 'He didn't. At least not today. She was shot the other night.'

She shuffled against the air-filled pillows. 'By her own dad.' The horror of it was beyond her comprehension.

'Yep. The night of the fire. She told DC Downey her daddy shot her like the rest of the family. But the bullet lodged in her rib and she escaped.'

'Lucky.' Gregg stroked his fingers over his smooth chin with eyes bleak to decry his own word.

Poor girl. Jenna couldn't bring herself to consider anything about Poppy's situation luck. Her entire family were dead. The only one left alive was Poppy. How was she to survive?

She glanced at her own sister. She survived. One day at a time and that's all anyone could hope for Poppy.

'No next of kin have come forward.' In the silence, it remained unspoken that she would go into the system. Foster parents until she was eighteen.

No. There was nothing lucky about Poppy Lawrence's situation.

'What about Fleur, the family dog? Will she get to keep her?'

In the long silence, Taylor took out his notebook and scribbled on it. 'We'll let social services know. See what can be done.'

Jenna moved her attention onwards as Gregg slipped from the room with a quick raise of his hand.

If she could have killed Mason, she would have done. Arms folded he'd wedged himself in the corner of the room. Belligerent because he knew how she felt.

He'd not needed to contact her sister and worry her unnecessarily.

Fliss's pale face and huge eyes reflected the terror that could only be escalated by her own trauma and Jenna wouldn't have put her through it all again for the world.

'Don't blame him.' Fliss's eyebrows lowered as she held Jenna's gaze with her own. 'You wouldn't have told me.'

'I would have.'

'What? After I heard it on the news?'

Helpless, Jenna fluttered her hands in front of her face. 'I would have rather cleaned up at least before you saw me.'

'I've seen worse.' Fliss's voice hardened. 'Only last time, I was on the receiving end and the injuries were mine.'

'They were.' Jenna sat forward and wrapped her arms around drawn-up knees. 'I'm not even injured.'

'You have a ruptured eardrum.'

'That's it. A ruptured eardrum is hardly a heroic injury.' The ringing in her ears had faded, but sounds were still muffled.

Fliss leaned in to whisper in her face. 'I don't need you to be a hero. I need you to be alive.'

Breath backed up in her lungs. Alive. She was. Just. If the shot had been off by a few inches, it could have been her brains blown to smithereens.

At the sound of footsteps and soft murmured voices outside of the door, they fell silent and watched as a doctor stepped inside and took the clipboard of notes from the bottom of her bed without so much as a glance in her direction.

Aloof and detached, he pulled a pen from his top pocket, filling the silence with a rhythmic click, click, as he depressed the button. In – click, click. Out – click, click.

The jaw she'd managed to unclench started to stiffen again.

When he glanced up, his eyes widened for a split second, quickly covered by a rapid blink and a look down at his notes. His narrow chest expanded as he took in a long breath and then lowered the clipboard onto the bed beside her feet.

'I'm Doctor Saunders. And you are Jenna Morgan?'

'Yes.'

'Can you confirm your date of birth?'

She waited for eye contact as she reeled off the information. 'First of December 1990.'

He pulled at his lip as he scanned her from the top of her head to the tip of her toes and notched up her irritation. She really wanted to go home.

'Doctor Saunders. Apart from a possible burst eardrum, I have no other injuries. Can I please go home?'

With a soft grunt, he clicked the pen – click, click, then one last time – click. He tucked it back into his top pocket. 'I'll check your ears in just a moment. There's a lot of blood, all over you. Are you sure you're not injured?'

Jenna ground her teeth and swivelled her attention to DI Taylor in the vain hope he might save her.

He squeezed the top of his nose between forefinger and thumb and grimaced. There would be no help forthcoming from him. Nor

Mason, the coward. Her sister just stared straight at her, her tongue lodged against the side of her cheek.

As the doctor continued his long contemplation of her, Jenna wriggled her backside on the bed.

'I suggest you change out of those clothes, into a hospital gown.'

Fliss whipped out a small, white cotton bag from inside her oversized handbag and jiggled it in front of the doctor. 'I brought PJs and slippers.'

DI Taylor pushed up from the chair and held up a hand before she could move. 'I'm afraid she can't get changed yet. Jenna, you know the form. SOCO are on their way. They need to take photographs and bag all the evidence.' He gave the doctor a tight smile. 'I'm sure you're familiar with the process.' At the doctor's blank stare, DI Taylor continued. 'DS Morgan there...' he inclined his head in her direction, gaze stony and hard, '...is what we classify a crime scene and we need a scenes of crime officer. It can't be done by any Tom, Dick or...' A look of relief flashed over his face as the door cracked open a mere few inches and their Chief Forensics Examiner peered through over the top of his half-moon glasses. '...Jim.'

Jim Downey sent her a soft smile as his astute gaze picked up every detail. 'Jenna, I thought I'd pop in and check on you.'

Heart skipping with relief, Jenna sent him a smile of her own before a swirl of doubt circled. 'Jim, I thought you'd be at the scene.'

He tugged the door closed behind him and stepped up to the bed. 'I've been in contact with them. The scene is secure. PC Gardner is in very capable hands, so too is the suspect. Both very dead.' His sad, serious gaze met hers, misty grey swirling with concern. 'You are not. Currently, my priority is securing any forensic evidence here without visiting the scene first. We don't want any cross-contamination and as my team had already arrived at the site, I volunteered to do this side of things.'

It helped to know this wasn't strictly the case. He could have sent someone else to deal with her, but his concern was for one of his own. He'd never have left the scene to someone else if he had any doubt about the abilities of his team. The warmth of his concern spread through her chest.

Flustered, the doctor backed out of the door into the corridor. 'I'll come back... later. I'll...' he stumbled over his words, 'I'll be back.'

Jim slanted her a tight smile. 'Was it something I said?'

'No, Jim.' DI Taylor shuffled himself past the tight confines of the room to plonk his backside back down in the high-back vinyl-covered chair. 'He's still at that new stage, thinks he knows everything, cocky as hell, and knows nothing. He'll learn.'

Jenna's thoughts jangled. New and cocky. They didn't always learn. PC Gardner certainly hadn't. He'd not been gifted the time to learn.

She swallowed as the conversation around her continued, oblivious of the pain touching each of her raw nerve endings.

'Could do with improving his bedside manner I suspect.'

Jenna raised both hands to scrub them across her face.

'Uh-uh.' Jim stopped her mid move. 'Not yet you can't. Let me gather my evidence, Jenna, and then we can make you comfortable.'

She sat in silence. Comfortable would be a shower so hot it sluiced the skin from her bones.

Jim slipped his PPE on over the top of his own clothes and then snapped on two pairs of gloves. He took each item from his bag, one at a time, and placed them carefully on the side table.

He glanced up, pinning each of the onlookers with his school-teacher stare. 'This will take a while. I suggest you take a break. Come back later.'

DI Taylor and Mason both moved to the door together in a fast rush to obey.

Fliss never moved a muscle. 'I'll stay.'

Jim's lips twitched. He started with the digital camera he removed from a plain black case.

'You probably know all of this, Jenna, but I'll walk you through it as we go along.'

As he snapped the first few frames, Jenna darted him a self-deprecating grin. 'Normally I'd do my hair and face before a photo shoot.'

'Hmmm.' He came in close, angled around to the side of her, too far in his zone to take notice. 'Blood splatter, this is the most important point. It proves you were standing where you say you were at the time, and the position of PC Gardner and the perpetrator.'

She shook her head. 'Gordon Lawrence. I don't think I have any of his blood on me. The angle from the second shot fired would have been wrong.' She pictured Ethel in her mind. Totally wrong. 'I don't know for sure though. I was on the ground by then.'

Jim held still, his gaze conducting a long, slow assessment of her. 'Can you slip off the bed and stand upright for me?'

Pain burned through her knees as she straightened her legs before swinging them over the side of the bed. She let out an involuntary grunt.

Over the top of his glasses, Jim's steady gaze met hers. 'You might want to mention that to the doctor.'

A sob stuck in her throat and her voice came out a croaky whisper. 'I just want to go home, Jim.'

He reached out a hand, his long, thin fingers encircled her forearm as he gave a gentle squeeze. 'I understand, Jenna. You, personally, need this finished. You, professionally, need to ensure everything is right.'

She ducked her head and blinked away the sharp sting of tears.

'I know. I think I banged up my knees when I hit the ground. They're just bruised.'

'Anywhere else?'

'No. I landed on top of Poppy. His daughter.'

Jim nodded his acknowledgement. 'Okay. Tell the doctor. Now, turn.'

She did as instructed, her watery gaze meeting Fliss's as she turned her back on him to stare directly at her sister. She mustered up a brave smile, but the edges of it wobbled and one fat tear trembled on the edge of her eye and then rolled down her cheek. She held Fliss's stare and clenched her jaw. She'd get through it. She had no choice.

The click and whirr of the camera dragged her attention back. 'I shouldn't have anything on my back, Jim. Lee Gardner stepped in front of me.' She closed her eyes and jerked them back open again as the image of PC Gardner's head exploding filled her mind with hues of crimson.

'Have you written up your notes yet?'

'No.' She shook her head and then held still for him to take more snapshots before she continued. 'I'm ready to as soon as I get cleaned up.' She held out both hands. Dried blood coated them.

Jim tucked the camera back into his bag and took a swab from the small packet he picked up from where he'd laid it on the bed. 'I need to collect samples from you. I'll start at your back. When PC Gardner was shot, what did you do?'

'I...' She thought the events through. It was essential to the case. She had to face it. She drew in a long breath through her nostrils. Business. Professional. She could do it. She started at the end. 'PC Gardner stepped in front of me.'

'To protect you?'

'No.' She had to be honest. Heat scorched up her neck into her face. 'He was a complete arse. As he always has been. He should never have been a police officer. Never once have I been impressed with the way he handled things.' Once started, the rush of emotions poured out, desperate, angry, confused. 'He didn't step in front of me to protect me. I hate to say this, the man is dead.' She paused, the pulse thundering in her ears as the scene flashed in front of her eyes again. 'But he seemed to think he was invincible. He was arrogant in his belief that Gordon Lawrence would lay down his weapon on his say-so.' She hauled in a deep breath.

Jim carried on as though it was a casual chat, but she knew he was aware that it helped to talk about it, to get it out. 'And did you?'

'No. Not by any stretch of the imagination. The moment I saw him, I knew he was going to pull that trigger. We weren't going to talk him down. He'd already killed his own family. It was just a matter of delaying it for as long as possible so we could get armed response there.'

Jim's soft sigh whispered over the top of her ear as he continued to take his samples of blood and tissue from the back of her head.

'What happened when PC Gardner was shot?'

Thick fog whirled to mask the memory. Determined to push through it, Jenna focused. 'I dropped to the floor with Poppy.'

'You protected her.'

'It was instinct. There wasn't even a conscious thought, I just grabbed her and hit the ground. I was face down. Poppy underneath me.' She raised her hand and this time Jim allowed her to touch her face as he'd already conducted evidence-gathering in that area. She touched her fingertips across her grazed skin, drawing in a sharp breath at the sting of it. 'My forehead hit the ground. It hurts.'

'We'll call the doctor back in a moment. Get you cleaned up.'

'Yeah.'

'What happened next?'

'Gunshots.'

'How many?'

She searched her memory. 'A million.'

'Think it through, we'll need your account for continuity. Keep in mind perceptual distortion.'

Aware of that factor, Jenna reined herself in. Played the scene over in her head again, again, again.

The first shot fired by Gordon Lawrence. She fell. Another gunshot echoed. It had sounded like three, but she knew there were only two shots fired.

Gunshot ricocheted around and around. And the reality of why Jim was taking swabs from the back of her head, her neck, her shoulders pushed through. Tiny tremors shuddered from her core outwards in ever-widening ripples to wrack her body as her insides turned to water.

Jim wrapped a steadying hand around her elbow. 'Jenna?'

She shook off the invading chill and raised her head. 'Am I done? Can I shower now?'

Jim stepped back and stripped off his gloves. He slipped them into a small plastic bag leaving him with a second pair he wore underneath. 'I need your clothes.'

Her fingers twitched ready to rip the clothes from her back, she couldn't divest herself of them fast enough. It didn't matter that Jim was about to see her stark naked, it didn't matter she had to preserve all forensic evidence. She needed to be out of them immediately.

With shaking hands, Jenna stripped her jacket from her body. As she turned to place it in the forensic evidence bag, her gaze clashed with Jim's measured pewter one and every flight instinct dried up in an instant.

Tensile steel strengthened her backbone and she drew herself erect. This was her job. She'd do it.

She toed her boots from her feet and let Jim pick them up as she unbuttoned her trousers, slid the zip down and let them slither down her legs to the floor. Each item was bagged by Jim, labelled, sealed.

Jenna glanced at her white T-shirt. The front V of it was soaked in blood and, if she wasn't mistaken, matted hair with a tiny piece of skull. As she raised her head, Jim leaned in to pluck the sample from her chest with a neat pair of tweezers.

'Almost missed that little sucker. It must have been inside your jacket collar. Let me check a little closer.'

He dipped his head, so the small thinning patch on the top was visible. An hysterical giggle bubbled up her throat until she could do nothing but hold her breath. The inappropriateness of it whirled through her mind. It made no difference that she knew it was her coping mechanism at the sensory overload taking place. If she let it burst free, Jim would raise his head and bestow one of his cool, assessing stares to frighten the crap out of her. He'd not had to do that for the past several years with her, but she'd witnessed it plenty of times when he'd turned it on newbies. Even his own son.

She screwed her eyes closed and clamped down on the laughter. When she opened them again, Jim was nose to nose with her. Almost cross-eyed, Jenna focused on him.

'Are we okay?'

She gave a jerky nod. 'Fine. Just fine.'

'Excellent.' He stepped back out of her personal space and reached for two more forensics bags. 'I'll step outside now. Slip your top off and put it in this bag. Your underwear needs to go in this one. Then you can slip on a hospital gown and call me back in.'

Jenna whipped off her top and shoved it in the bag. She took the proffered hospital gown from a silent, supportive Fliss, slipped it over her head before she unclipped her bra and whipped it from underneath. As she tugged it into place, she pushed her knickers down her legs and flicked them off the end of her feet.

Pain vibrated through her knees as she straightened, and she bent low again to take a peep. No clear memory of her fall existed, but the dark red on both knees promised that there was plenty of bruising to come out over the next few days.

'Are you decent?'

Jenna shot upright and yanked the hospital gown together over her arse as Jim's voice came from the other side of the partially closed door. She slipped back onto the bed and tugged the pristine white sheet up to cover her naked legs.

As Jim came back into the room, Jenna searched his face. 'Can I have a shower?'

His lips twitched, eyes filled with affection. 'Yes, Jenna, you can have a shower.'

54

Sometimes the job was difficult, often tedious. Occasionally, she hardened her heart to the evilness and atrocities people inflicted on one another. Once in a while, however, a case wrenched her heart out and left trailing arteries in its wake so she would never forget.

DS Jenna Morgan marched side by side with DC Mason Ellis to the elegant double-frontage doors painted in muted Georgian blue grey.

Trudy Maxwell swung the doors wide and stepped back as they approached. A broad smile on her face, her eyes softened as she ran her gaze over Jenna, admiration and respect lurking in their depths. 'Do come in. I'll get you coffee in a moment, but I'm sure you're anxious to see her.'

Anxious wasn't the word.

They were there to get a statement, but Jenna's heart gave a small skip of trepidation as Trudy pushed open the doors into the huge, high-ceilinged lounge.

Jenna had carried out her duty, to protect and preserve life. But her soul knew it was more than just duty. There was a connection, a bond, a feeling of continued responsibility for the young girl whose life she'd helped save. A desire to know that not only would she be safe, but she would thrive and flourish despite the horror she'd suffered.

The floor-to-ceiling windows allowed the softening evening sun to flood through and soak the room in golden light.

Three enormous cream sofas dominated the centre of the room in a U-shape around an antique woollen rug in muted hues of blues and greys.

On the middle sofa, Sophie stretched out with her back propped against cushions wedged against the high arm of the sofa. Cradled in her arms under a thick blue throw was a pale, sleeping Poppy. Smudges like bruises feathered from beneath her lashes fading across her ashen cheeks.

Sophie raised her head, her eyes widening as her gaze fell on Jenna. Her mouth popped open to form an 'o' and she nudged her friend awake.

Slow to move, Poppy struggled up as though every muscle in her body protested.

Before she could get up, Jenna stepped into the U and stood in front of Poppy.

The wild, anguished howl wrenched at her heart and tore her soul out, jerking unexpected tears that clogged her throat and filled her eyes before she could even stop them.

Wordless, she leaned forward, blinking rapidly, but the fat tears rolled down her cheeks and continued to blur her vision as she reached out and placed a wriggling, whining, hysterical Fleur into Poppy's arms and stepped back to give them time and space.

55

Heart still stuttering, Jenna cradled the coffee Trudy placed in front of her on the vast kitchen island and sent Mason a quick sideways look. He blew his nose into a clean tissue and mustered up a wobbling smile. If she'd thought to threaten him not to say anything, she had no need. His heart was as bruised as hers.

She cleared her throat. They'd come to do a job, but the right thing was to give Poppy her time alone with Fleur.

'We need to take a statement from Poppy, I'm afraid. Do you think she's up to it?'

Trudy drew out a stool and perched on the edge of it. 'Physically, she's exhausted, but she'll recover. The operation went well. They managed to remove the bullet from her rib, leaving little damage, but she's on a hefty dose of antibiotics for the infection that set in. Emotionally, she's drained.'

'We can take it a little at a time.'

'She'll be here. We've spoken with social services. Poppy has no next of kin. Apparently, she has a godmother somewhere she doesn't even know.'

Aware of that, Jenna nodded and held her breath, willing the other woman to tell her what she wanted to hear.

Trudy raised her cup to her lips, paused. 'Because of Poppy's age, she gets a say in who she would like to stay with.' Trudy's gaze flickered to Jenna's. 'We discussed it in some depth last night. She chose us.'

Relief flooded through Jenna, and she struggled to keep from wilting onto the island as another flood of tears threatened.

Trudy's voice thickened. 'And we chose her.'

Jenna blinked and this time ignored the tear that plopped from her eye to run down her cheek to the corner of her mouth. Her breath shuddered in.

Without drinking, Trudy placed the cup back down. 'I have no doubt this won't all be smooth sailing, but Poppy and Sophie are best of friends and I couldn't imagine for one moment allowing Poppy to do anything but come to us. It will be for the best. The girls will continue with their A levels and then we'll see what paths they take. If it's university, then so be it. Poppy wants to be a vet. Sophie wants to follow in her dad's footsteps and be a barrister one day.'

Jenna poked her tongue out and tasted the salt of her tears. She raised her cup and took a sip, letting the coffee wash the taste away and out of the corner of her eye noticed Mason surreptitiously wipe his nose again.

'I think it's very noble of you, Trudy.'

'There's no nobleness involved, Sergeant. The girls have always been close from the first day they started at the high school. We were already family.'

A warmth filled her chest and spread down to her stomach.

Trudy picked up her cup and this time took a sip. 'What happened with Mrs Crawford?'

Mason gave a small cough. 'She's under arrest for murder.'

'Surely not? At her age?'

Mason spread his hands wide. 'A crime is a crime at any age.'

'Won't they see it as self-defence?'

Jenna shook her head. 'No, I'm afraid not. It wasn't self-defence. Mrs Crawford loaded a gun with the sole intention of using it.'

'Oh dear.' Devastation filled Trudy's eyes. 'She's such a lovely lady.'

'She is. But the law is the law, and this is what I'm invested in upholding. For everyone.'

Cool and thoughtful, Trudy narrowed her eyes. 'Can she plead diminished responsibility?'

Jenna's gaze met Trudy's and she gave her an acknowledging smile. 'I'd leave that to her barrister to decide.'

ACKNOWLEDGMENTS

What She Saw involved a great deal of background information and research into weaponry, fires and as usual police procedure. I'd like to thank the following for their immense support, advice and patience when I asked the most obvious questions, and pressed and prodded for more detail. Although I don't go into depth, I hope the research I carried out gives the story a genuine and authentic feel. Any mistakes are my own.

Charlie Cartwright – I also borrowed his name for one of my characters. As I told him, it was a 'solid' name.

Derek Taylor

Peter Wright

Andrew Parkes

As always to my hugely patient family who always understand when I say 'I'm on a deadline.'

Andy

Laura

Meghan

And to my sister Margaret who said, 'If you'd given it to me earlier, you wouldn't have had to write the last part again, I'd have told you it was wrong.'

MORE FROM DIANE SAXON

We hope you enjoyed reading *What She Saw*. If you did, please leave a review.

If you'd like to gift a copy, this book is also available as an ebook, digital audio download and audiobook CD.

Sign up to Diane Saxon's mailing list for news, competitions and updates on future books.

http://bit.ly/DianeSaxonNewsletter

Find Her Alive, the first crime novel from Diane Saxon is available to buy now.

ABOUT THE AUTHOR

Diane Saxon previously wrote romantic fiction for the US market but has now turned to writing psychological crime. *Find Her Alive* was her first novel in this genre and introduced series character DS Jenna Morgan. Diane is married to a retired policeman and lives in Shropshire.

Visit Diane's website: http://dianesaxon.com/

Follow Diane on social media:

facebook.com/dianesaxonauthor
twitter.com/Diane_Saxon
instagram.com/DianeSaxonAuthor
bookbub.com/authors/diane-saxon

ABOUT BOLDWOOD BOOKS

Boldwood Books is a fiction publishing company seeking out the best stories from around the world.

Find out more at www.boldwoodbooks.com

Sign up to the Book and Tonic newsletter for news, offers and competitions from Boldwood Books!

http://www.bit.ly/bookandtonic

We'd love to hear from you, follow us on social media:

facebook.com/BookandTonic

twitter.com/BoldwoodBooks

instagram.com/BookandTonic

Lightning Source UK Ltd.
Milton Keynes UK
UKHW021250030221
378172UK00012B/2860